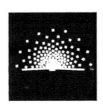

ISLAND

ISLAND

Charles Abbott

HarperCollins*Publishers*

HarperCollins books may be purchased for educational, business, or sales promotional use. For information please write: Special Markets Department, HarperCollins Publishers, Inc., 10 East 53rd Street, New York, NY 10022.

FIRST EDITION

Designed by Alma Hochhauser Orenstein

Library of Congress Cataloging-in-Publication Data

Abbott, Charles, writer.
  Island: a novel/Charles Abbott.
     p.   cm.
  ISBN 0-06-019050-7
     1. Men—United States—Fiction.   I. Title.
PS3551.B248I83   1994
813'.54—dc20
                                                                      93-25876

94 95 96 97 98 ❖/RRD 10 9 8 7 6 5 4 3 2 1

To AARON ASHER
whose editing, enthusiasm, and integrity
made this book possible.

To disguise nothing, to conceal nothing, to write about those things that are the closest to your pain, your happiness, to write about my sexual clumsiness, the agonies of Tantalus, the depths of my discouragement. . . . To write about the foolish agonies of anxiety, the refreshment of your strength when these are ended; to write about the painful search for self. . . .

—JOHN CHEEVER

In the heart of each man there is contrived by desperate devices a magical island. We place it in the past or future for safety, for we dare not locate it in the present. We call this memory or a vision to lend it validity, but it is neither, really. It is the outcome of our sadness, and of our disgust with the world that we've made.

—E. M. FORSTER

Part One

GETTING THERE

1

I HAD A WIFE NAMED JULIA AND A GIRLFRIEND NAMED Fran." He said that to himself once in a while, just to remind himself who he was. Always in the past tense. "Had," never "have," because they were both gone, washed away by his drinking. And, he had to admit, he drank a lot. Julia threw him out. He drank more, and Fran left. Her going lay on him. It bore him down. Its weight made his head hang as he walked the street.

So he drank more because, among other things, he had also lost his job, and was picked up on the sidewalk a couple of times and taken to the hospital. And the doctors there said he was killing himself and what was the matter and why didn't he put himself in the hands of a competent therapist.

Which is how he wound up with Dr. Hennerkop.

M. J. Hennerkop, Ph.D. Not a real M.D. doctor, but he called him doctor, and as he lay on the doctor's couch he wondered what kind of a name Hennerkop was—Jewish probably—and wondered if the time had come to be frank enough to admit that he was wondering about things like that and own up to the fact that he was prejudiced against Jews.

"What do your initials, M. J., stand for?"

"Why do you ask?"

"Just curious. After all, you're my doctor and I'm pouring all this crap out to you and I don't even know your first name."

"My first name is Maxwell."

Probably a jump-up from Max. And he hadn't even said what his middle name was. Avoided it. Probably Jacob. Max Jacob Hennerkop. A Jew. He was lying there being analyzed by a Jew.

* * *

Jew or not, Hennerkop did something to him. The very fact that Hennerkop was there—just sitting there to listen as he poured out things he had never mentioned to anybody else, not even faced squarely in the privacy of his own mind—did something. He quit drinking and took up crying instead. His health improved. Having no job, he sat in the park a lot and did much of his crying there. Quietly and surreptitiously, on an end bench somewhere with nobody else around. He would be sitting there, and the overwhelming loneliness would hit him, and he would crumple inside, and the inside crumpling would be matched by a crumpling around the mouth and chin, and the tears would run down his cheeks. Those days he always had a handkerchief handy, and he made it his business, while sitting crying in the park, to hold a handkerchief carelessly in his hand as if he were just about to blow his nose, in case anybody sat down near him and took a good look at him.

Self-conscious in extremis. He couldn't seem to shake that.

Those sessions. Forty dollars a throw and his bank account dwindling. And no job. And no future. And hour after hour of lying there repeating the same old crap until the mixture of boredom and anxiety made him almost want to jump out of his skin. Too many of those hours spent trying to think of something to say.

"I bought a shirt yesterday."

No answer.

"From B.H. Wragge. They're the best shirtmakers."

No answer.

"White, with a very pale blue stripe. The stripes are about a thirty-second of an inch apart."

Long silence.

"They have French cuffs—for cuff links."

"Why are you telling me this?"

Why indeed. Why, except to fill the hour he was paying for, fill those silent stretches that grew in tension the longer they lasted, that made the couch he was lying on seem like a raft on the sea. At those times Dr. Hennerkop's office walls receded rapidly and Hennerkop himself got very small. Pretty soon he would shrink to a pinpoint, and the panicky feeling would grow that Hennerkop might disappear altogether, leaving him alone.

He would talk about his shirts some more to bring Hennerkop back. Or his custom-made shoes. There was a lot to talk about there, because wearing the right things hadn't come easy. He'd had to learn what to wear—work his way up by observing how the right people dressed, then waiting until he had the money to buy the kind of clothes he felt he should have. And all that time, as he kept his eyes open and learned more, he discovered that there were inner layers, subtler gradations of good taste in clothes than he had ever realized. Finally he got there. He worked his way up from Roger Kent—which was all he could afford at first—to Brooks Brothers. And it was only when he was comfortably ensconced in Brooks Brothers that he discovered that there was a world of really subtle dressers who would no more go into Brooks Brothers than he—now—would go into Roger Kent.

He learned to spot such things. He kept his mouth shut and his eye open; you didn't make any mistakes, give anything away, if you just watched. Pretty soon he would be having lunch with one of those men who really had it, and he would slip it out casually:

"That's a nice shirt you're wearing. Where did you get it?"

"B.H. Wragge."

The important thing was not to look ignorant. Raggy? Was he kidding? The thing to do was to lift an eyebrow or nod perceptively as if he knew B.H. Raggy all along and was digesting the news that this particular shirt came from B.H. Raggy and was dispassionately comparing it with other tailor-made shirts produced by other equally in and equally obscure shirtmakers.

Back at the office, he would look up B.H. Raggy in the phone book, then just Raggy, then B.H. Raggie, etc., etc. Of course he wouldn't find him, and then would have to come the real sitting down with himself to assess his relationship with the wearer of the shirt and try to decide whether he had been kidding or not. If so, he would have to be even more careful with that man in the future and remember never to mention shirts to him again. But sooner or later he would spot that kind of shirt somewhere else in the upper levels of the advertising business. And if he got B.H. Raggy again, then he would know that the first man wasn't lying after all. Meanwhile try and figure out another way of running Raggy down.

At another lunch, with another man: "That a Raggy shirt?"

"No, it came from Sulka."

"I need to buy some shirts. I usually go to Raggy, but I hear they've moved."

"No, still across from the Harvard Club, far as I know."

There were a couple of large office buildings along there but nothing like Raggy on the street level. So he would go inside and look at the building directory. And he wouldn't find Raggy, or Raggie, and he would look under Shirts, and finally he would locate him down among the *W*'s.

That way, in due course, he learned about Stone and about Wetzel, and about Vernon & Vernon, and he gradually accumulated a wardrobe of really good suits. Things that from a distance looked something like gray flannel but up close were unmistakably something else, light soft worsteds with almost invisible little patterns or stripes in them. Of the lot, Vernon & Vernon were the best. They were the smallest, the most obscure, and the most expensive. All their materials came from England.

He learned about Whyte, the custom shoemaker; he graduated to Whyte from Peale.

The good thing about a Wragge shirt was that it had a way of identifying itself unobtrusively. Not like those blatant initials on the Countess Mara ties, which were for real slobs who had to let you know in the crudest way that they were well up there in the tie department. The thing about the Wragge shirt was that it had two buttons at the throat to make the collar sit a little better. When he was well up there himself, with a fine office and a secretary, and had reached the point where he could afford to work in his shirtsleeves—in fact, where it was almost better to be seen working in your shirtsleeves because it advertised that you no longer had to think about wearing a suit jacket—then he could also work with his tie loosened and his shirt collar unbuttoned. The two buttons would show, and anyone who was far enough up there, sophisticated enough to recognize a Wragge shirt, would see them. Nothing ever said. Just a flicker of the eye back and forth. He knew and you knew. That was enough—members of the fraternity.

Hennerkop himself wore clothes that were pure crap.

He didn't say this to Hennerkop. Instead, he said, "You must think I'm a pretty disagreeable snob, talking this way about clothes."

"Not necessarily. If you wish to talk about clothes, you will talk about clothes. Perhaps in that way you will learn something about yourself."

"All I learn about myself is—"

Hennerkop waited.

"I mean, I *talk* about clothes. I do that, yes. But—" How explain to a wearer of crap the subtle importance of clothes in helping you move in a world you wanted to move in and didn't feel comfortable in? That the clothes helped you belong. Belonging was important.

A lot about clothes. An awful lot. After a while he was left wondering if they were quite that important. And yet they *were* important. Up there they dressed right. And he had to dress right, too, to convince himself that he belonged up there with the rest of them.

"After all, there's no harm in wearing good clothes."

Silence.

"The right people wear the right clothes. Can't you understand? It's as simple as that."

"You sound angry."

"I'm angry that you don't see it. That I have to keep talking about these clothes. That you don't seem to recognize the difference between good clothes and the kind of crap that—" Oops.

"That I wear?"

"I didn't say that."

"Did you think it?"

Of course he thought it. That crappy suit and those green socks.

"It is your thought that is important. Why do you repress it?"

"Well . . . It's just that if you dressed a little better you'd look a little better." With a proper suit, Hennerkop would be able to walk into the Racquet Club without everybody looking at him. Hennerkop didn't seem to understand that at all.

"Why do you repress that thought?" he repeated.

"Nobody wants to be told he wears crappy clothes."

"Why not?"

"Well . . . " Good God, that was obvious.

"I mean, *here* why not? You talk about clothes, but my thought is that you are not really talking about clothes at all."

"What am I doing, then?"

"Exactly. What are you doing?"

Trying to get through the hour. Keep some tiny safe distance between Hennerkop and himself. Someday he might be able to say that to him. Right now he couldn't quite manage it. So at the next session he avoided clothes and talked about drinking, even though he had talked endlessly about it before.

It was a relief to tell Hennerkop something he already knew, dredging up those empty afternoons after five o'clock. When the offices let out and all the girls went whirling into the subway and he might see Fran's face here or Fran's hips there. And the day closed in and the lights went on and the bars filled up and everybody seemed paired up and laughing. And he was standing outside it all. And he had to do something, go somewhere, be *with* somebody, or he was nothing. He would stand it as long as he could, but finally it would get to be too much. He would step into a bar and order a bourbon and water and sip it slowly as he looked around, and the drink trickled through him and began to ease things a little.

The best bars curved at one end. He could sit there, leaning against the wall, looking down the bar, watching the action, not in anybody's way, gradually feeling a little better. He sipped very slowly. From long practice he knew enough to do that, because the bearable time was beginning to be right now—or just a little ahead of right now—and he wanted to stretch the goodness of right now as far as he could and savor the knowledge that just ahead of right now would be even better. Concentrate on that and obliterate what he knew came after just ahead of right now.

If he took it really slow and easy, wedged into his corner, where he couldn't be hassled by the other customers or by the bartender, the first drink would last nearly half an hour. Pretty soon, still taking it easy, he would order his second bourbon and water. And he would still be traveling through right now, and right now would be a little better, and beginning to edge into just ahead of right now, which was better yet. The important thing then was not to order his third drink too soon. The temptation was to plunge into just ahead of right now right away. Rush it. That was bad. He had to learn to control that and try to stay suspended in right now as long as he could.

Soon it would be time for the third bourbon and water, or the fourth. By now he would have begun to feel sufficiently better to think about stage two of the evening. The loneliness would still be there, the desperation, but it would be cushioned in the bourbon that took the hard corners off everything. It made the bar seem halfway decent, a place he could comfortably stay in for quite a while as the faces around him became more endurable, the men less threatening, the women softer and less unattractive.

Sometime well into the third or fourth drink—he was beginning to travel dangerously fast out of right now into the keener feeling and excitement of just ahead of right now, and that feeling was really moving in him and he was aware that he mustn't let it get too headlong but at the same time enjoying the rush of it—sometime along about there he would spot a woman in the bar who was just on the edge of passing over from unattractive to attractive. He would try to hold back on his fourth drink while he studied that possibility.

First he had to make sure she was alone. Women in bars alone fell into two categories: the pros and the drinkers. He had devoted a good deal of thought, based on experience, to which was better, or rather worse, because neither was better. Both were awful. But that awfulness had to be risked because the best part of right now or just ahead of right now was the anticipation of contact with another human being. The drinking, while it was good in itself, was also an instrument, a glove that he put on so that he could endure the touching and intimacy that he was looking for. Contact with another body, almost any body—he was down to that.

And as he came to the end of his fourth drink—or maybe the fifth because, despite all his care, things would have begun to move a little faster than he had planned, and often he would find himself in the later stages of just ahead of right now—he would have reached the delicate part of the evening. He had to be drunk enough to want somebody and still sober enough to function.

And the choice was always: pro or drinker. If he had been moving too fast, he couldn't always be sure which was which.

Each was awful in her own way. The pros were quick and methodical and cold, often so quick and cold that he extracted no warmth from them at all. Hustler was a good word. They hustled him out of his clothes, hustled him into bed, often hustled another drink into him from the bottle he kept in his closet (more about that bottle later). That last drink was often the toppler. Straight out of the bottle, it would hit him, and he would have to sit up to prevent the whirls that were a prelude to passing out or getting sick. But he couldn't sit up with a woman pressing her body against his, so more often than not he did pass out, and would wake up later to the discovery that his money and watch, and sometimes other things, were gone.

That wasn't so bad after a while, because toward the end he had nothing much left worth stealing, and he had learned the precaution of never starting an evening with more than fifty dollars in his pocket. As another precaution he had hidden his checkbook so that he could not be persuaded to begin writing drunken checks; the only way he could get more money was by going to the bank during banking hours and asking for it.

If, instead of going to his place, he had gone to one of those hotels in the West Forties, it was worse. The women who worked those hotels were really tough. They stole your clothes and your shoes, sometimes left you with nothing but your underwear in a dusty, greasy little room.

He woke up in that predicament once. Nothing but a pair of shorts, and he didn't know where he was or what time of day it was. He went to the window to see if he could discover what street was out there. Uncontrollably shaky. It took an immense effort just to get to the window. The cotton inside his head, the red-hot cotton, made it

9

hard to tell just what he was looking at. He got back into a smelly, lumpy bed and wondered what to do next.

No watch. Down in a grimy canyon with no sun to creep across the opposite wall, nothing but blank gritty windows over there. Some other hotel, probably full of other poor bastards slowly coming to, shaking, sweating it out. He was shaking and sweating himself and had no bottle to get him through that. He would have to get up, open the door, and take a look out.

An empty narrow hall with a greasy carpet and an old-fashioned elevator with openwork iron grilling at the other end. He left his door open and walked down the hall and rang the bell. Finally somebody came, a handyman in a sweatshirt who stared at him standing there shaking in his underwear.

"I've been rolled. I've got to make a phone call."

"No phones up here."

"I've got to get some clothes and get out of here."

"Pay phone down in the lobby."

Shaking. "But I can't go down like this. Could you make a call for me?"

"No change."

"I'll get you some change—a couple of bucks. Could you just borrow a dime now and make a call for me?"

"Maybe."

"Okay. Just call—" What was Belden's number? A frantic head search, but no good. It was gone. "You can look it up in the phone book. Belden and Fraser. A law firm in Wall Street."

"Can't do that."

"Look, I'm in bad shape. I'll give you five bucks to call that man and get me some clothes and some money."

"Somebody took the phone book."

Getting that far had exhausted him. The sweat was pouring out of him. Maybe if he just lay down there in the hall they'd have to come and get him, maybe call the police, call the hospital.

No. He wasn't quite there yet. "Look. I've got to get out of here. Do you have a work shirt or some pants I could borrow? Anything at all?"

"Got a ten-dollar shirt and pants I was figuring to sell."

"I'll buy them."

Boy, did they stink! But they got him to the lobby. And he sat there in a plastic chair with his head whirling, his bare feet cold on the floor, and finally Belden's number came to him, and he bummed a dime from the desk clerk.

"Mac, this is Fred. I wonder if you could do me a favor. I'm in kind of a jam." Hard to say. Oh, so hard to ask, because Mac was Julia's lawyer and had represented her in the divorce. Mac had a low opinion of him already.

He had to explain where he was. And then he had to bum a couple more dimes from the desk clerk so that he could call the super in his building and explain that he was sick in a friend's house and that the friend was coming by to pick up a change of clothes for him and to please let him in. Then he had to call Mac back and explain that and tell him please for Christ's sake hurry—because the smell of that borrowed shirt and pants was beginning to get to him and he was afraid he would be sick in the lobby. So he went upstairs again and waited. And the stink of those borrowed clothes was so bad that, even though he was now half frozen, he took them off.

Then Mac, cool and contemptuous, almost literally holding his nose.

"This is the second time, Fred. I'm not going to do it again."

"I know. The stuff crept up on me. I don't even know how I got here."

"I mean it."

Pay the desk clerk his thirty cents.

"A shitty joint you run here, mister. I got rolled upstairs." Now that he didn't need the clerk, he could afford to show some of the resentment that was building in him like a furnace. But the clerk had been through this a hundred times before. He didn't even bother to smile, just stared right through those shreds of hot cotton still in Fred's head.

Pay the man for his shirt and pants. Another flash of rage at having to lay out ten dollars for the privilege of wearing them for half an hour.

Really raging by this time. Whirl on the desk clerk again. "Asshole of a place. Roll everybody who comes in. I'll get the police. I'll—"

"Come on, Fred. Stop making a fool of yourself and get in the taxi."

Stop at the bank. Get some money. Pay off Mac, and finally get home. Even though it was a crummy little furnished one-room-with-kitchenette, it was home, and he was glad to be there. He fell into the bathtub for an hour's soak and a little snooze. When he finally felt up to getting out and making himself a cup of coffee, he dialed the time on the phone and found that it was still only one forty-five in the afternoon.

So he made the decision once again. Got to cut this out, pull himself together. He knew from the way Mac spoke that he had meant it. And if Mac was not there to bail him out, who was?

Nobody; that was the crusher. He was totally alone, and his mind flickered toward the bottle in the closet, and was already beginning to jump ahead to the afternoon and the evening and to the possibility of finding someone better than the disaster of the night before. As to what that one had been like, he had no idea. Fat, skinny, black, white, where he had picked her up, what they had said, what they had done—all a blank. He had no recollection of her whatsoever. Looking around his shambles of a room, after yet another blotted-out night, he asked himself why he got himself into these awful situations. *How could he do it?*

But he did. For months he did it, over and over again, as he felt himself go cascading down.

2

ABOUT THAT BOTTLE IN THE CLOSET. HE KEPT IT there for particularly bad mornings. Although more often than not he couldn't remember how he had got home and he was beginning to experience a sense of real terror at the way large segments of time were blanking out, still he could tell the really bad nights from the routinely bad ones by the way he felt the next morning. Sometimes he simply couldn't function at all. Obviously he had had more to drink than usual, and his whole body threatened to fly apart. Glasses jumped out of his hand, and he got himself a special heavy little shot glass that wouldn't break when it fell on the floor. Getting the top off the bottle and the glass full was a problem. Bourbon sprayed all over the place. Picking up the glass and getting it to his mouth was another problem, even though he was sitting on the bathroom floor, which was where he did this in order to be near the toilet bowl, because too often the first shot would bounce in his stomach and come winging back, and he had to be ready for that with his face over the bowl, saying to himself, *Stay down,* because retching up raw liquor was the most painful thing he had ever experienced. It obliterated nausea, a cracked head, vaulting nerves—everything—in the larger agony of broiling membranes back in his nose and deeper in his head.

"You keep a bottle in your room?"

"I just explained—"

"You do not finish it off when you are drinking?"

"No. It's not there for that."

"Your problem is not drinking."

"What the hell are you talking about? I've lost my girl, my wife, my job, my—"

"Real drinkers do not leave unfinished bottles in the closet."

"But I *drink*. I was taken to Bellevue, off the street. Why do you think I'm here talking to you? I drink every night. I can't stop."

"You will stop."

The extraordinary thing was that Hennerkop was right. He stopped in the very act of telling the whole stinking pukey story to him. He began to cry. He sobbed with sobs that tore at his guts. And Hennerkop just sat there for fifteen or twenty minutes while he cried himself out.

"Do you cry now because you get drunk and sick?"

"No. Deeper."

"What is it that makes you cry?"

"I never cry when I'm drunk or hung over. I haven't cried since I was a kid."

"Why do you cry now, then?"

"Or sick, either. I just don't cry."

"*Now* why do you cry?"

"I guess I just feel sorry for myself. Nobody ever cares for a drunk."

"But you just said you don't cry from drinking."

"Nobody cares for me."

"Drunk or sober?"

"That's right."

"Or ever did?"

More sobs. "You're right. Nobody. Never."

"Now, after crying, how do you feel?"

"I want to sit in your lap." My God!

"Yes?"

"Curl up there." A faggot, on top of everything else?

"And be comforted?"

"Yes."

"Like a mother?"

"I guess."

"Those feelings are more important than drinking or whores. We will work more on them."

But working on them was work. That first terrible burst of grief was followed by a long season of exhaustion and despair that made even keeping appointments with Hennerkop difficult, let alone dredging up anything useful during their sessions. That was when he began spending so much time in the park, sitting in the sun and doing his private crying. When he did drag himself around to Hennerkop, he cried some more. And he got mad at Hennerkop for all the crying he did. It was Hennerkop's fault: Hennerkop had dredged up those feelings; he had stopped him from drinking and got him crying—and crying was worse. He had done what Hennerkop said, but he was worse off than before, and it was Hennerkop's fault, and the bugger wasn't doing anything to help. Sometimes he sulked in Hennerkop's office. Sometimes he said nothing. At forty bucks an hour.

But when he wasn't crying he knew he was better. He wasn't sweating and terrified all the time. He wasn't feeling sick. Nobody who isn't a drinker realizes how much of a drinker's time is spent throwing up or wondering when he will throw up.

And what he had said about nobody caring wasn't quite true, either. Fran had cared.

Even so, the going was tough. He hit those dry stretches and would return to drinking as a safe topic.

"There's a big difference in bars, you know."

Silence.

"I mean, you can't go into the ones on the East Side where you might run into somebody you know."

Silence.

"And you keep out of the ones you used to go to with Fran."

Silence.

"I mean, it's too painful."

Silence.

"I mean—Why don't you say something?"

"We seem to have returned to the safe subject of your drinking. I wonder why."

"If I want to talk about drinking, I will."

"That is correct; you will."

"It's my money, my forty bucks."

"Yes."

"All right, then. Why do you try to stop me from talking about drinking?"

"I do not. I only ask you to ask yourself why it is that you wish to talk about drinking?"

So he would sail into another subject: his fantasy. There was plenty to say about it, and it went way back. It had to do with living alone on a sunny little island in a neat little gray house where nobody bothered him and nobody threatened him or told him what to do and no demands were made on him and there were no standards he had to measure up to. He just lived there in the sun.

This fantasy had its basis in reality. The summer he was sixteen, his father had been sick and nearly died. He hadn't recovered well, and the doctor had said that what he really needed, to recuperate, was a visit to the seashore. So his congregation had got together and raised the money for a month in a boardinghouse in Lincoln Harbor. His father sat with a greenish face in a rocking chair on the boardinghouse porch, staring at a hedge and a row of flowers in front of him. His mother sat alongside and after a couple of weeks would take him for little walks down the street, holding him by the arm. The sea air did him some good. By the end of the month he was able to get around fairly well, and the three of them went back to Whittington. His parents had no car, but Mrs. Fensler, who was very active in the church, came up and drove them home.

During that month he was alone. It didn't surprise him. Back in Whittington he was pretty much alone too, and the mere moving to another place hadn't held out any reasonable encouragement that his personal life would undergo a dramatic change. But there was a small hope born of the knowledge that at least he would be a stranger in Lincoln Harbor. All the things that had been holding him down in Whittington, the humiliating things, would be left back at Whittington, and the new kids at Lincoln Harbor wouldn't know about them.

That hope died. There were plenty of kids in Lincoln Harbor, but they paid no attention to him. They had their tennis rackets and their boats, and they were always whizzing around in cars, screaming at each other. They lay in clusters like daisies on the beach, their heads the dark daisy centers, their petal bodies sticking out in all directions.

Penetrate one of those closed societies? A pimply skinny shy boy who had never set foot on a tennis court and scarcely knew how to swim? He couldn't even afford the fifty cents for a bathhouse and a towel when he went to the beach. He wore his bathing trunks under his pants and then walked down to the far end and took his pants off, quickly and furtively—there was a regulation about dressing and undressing on the beach.

He practiced swimming. He waded out until the water reached his nipples. It was cold and very salty—he had never tasted salt water before—and he would splash a little on his face, then take a deep breath and plunge awkwardly in, thrashing hard.

His swimming improved, but his social life didn't. He took to spending much of his time fishing from the town wharf. That was where the commercial fishing boats came in, and he could sit there on the wharf with his feet dangling over the edge, looking straight down at one of those boats with its jumble of coiled ropes, piled nets, and other assorted junk. Men in dirty undershirts would sit in the cockpit, smoking and fiddling with this and that. Tough, interesting-looking men with brown faces, who spat into the water and scratched themselves and walked in and out of a dark cabin, who spread their clothes out in the sun to dry and seemed oblivious of the tiny smelly fish scales glued everywhere and winking in the sun. Those men were nothing like his father.

When one of them looked up at him and said: "Hey, kid, want a Coke?" he just stared back at him with his mouth open.

The man handed him a dollar. "Run up to the corner for two bottles of Bud. There's a Coke in it for you."

He got the beer. The next day the man was there again, and he asked him if he wanted another beer. The man laughed. "No, but maybe Burton does. Hey, Burton, the beer kid is here." Burton ordered a beer, and in no time he was running errands for the fishermen. One morning, instead of handing his beer down to Burton, he climbed down into the boat, the *Thelma M,* and gave it to him. He sat on a heavy splintery rail that ran around the cockpit and sipped his Coke while Burton knocked back his beer. Burton had an enormously thick neck. When other strollers came out on the town wharf and stared down at him and Burton, he pretended to ignore them, hoping that they would think he belonged aboard the *Thelma M* and that maybe he was Burton's son.

He picked a couple of fish scales from the deck and flipped them into the water, and caught Burton looking at him.

"Want to scrub down?"

He nodded, not sure what Burton meant.

"Job's worth a quarter." He handed him a broom with a square wooden end and very stiff bristles, then went back into the deckhouse to turn on something that shot a jet of water out of a hose onto the deck. "Start at the bow and work aft. Get rid of them scales."

He took off his sneakers and rolled up his pants, as he had seen the fishermen do, and went to work.

"Hey, Burton, what cooks?"

"I got me my own assistant. What's your name, kid?"

"Fred."

"Name's Fred. Works better than you."

So he scrubbed harder. And the other man laughed and offered him a cigarette. He put it behind his ear, which he had also seen the

fishermen do. Going home for lunch, he walked up the street bare-
foot, with the cigarette still behind his ear. He threw it over a fence,
rolled down his pants, and put on his sneakers a block from the
boardinghouse.

That afternoon Burton said: "Going out for a couple days. Want
to sign on?"

"Me?"

"Make coffee. Fry eggs. That kind of thing. A buck a day."

"When are you going?"

"Right now. Couple hours from now."

"I'll have to ask my mother."

He ran back to the boardinghouse, and his mother wasn't there.
Then he did something he had never done before. He wrote her a
note on the small pad she kept on her bureau and put the note in the
middle of her bed, holding it down with a round white stone he had
brought back from the beach a week before.

Dear Mother:
    I'm going out on a fishing boat for a couple of days. I have a job
    working for a fisherman and will be back in a couple of days. I took
    my sweater and my other sneakers.

                                                          Love, Fred

Then he beat it back to the town wharf and hoped that the
Thelma M would leave before she got the note. It did.

The couple of days turned out to be five. Three men on board besides
himself. They all slept in bunks in a small smelly cabin. He made coffee and eggs and opened cans of beans. He burned his hand when the
boat rolled and hot coffee spilled on it. He could scarcely sleep from
excitement and the feeling of actually being at sea with these men.
They spent their time laying out and hauling in an immense net with
corks attached to it so that it hung like a curtain in the water. When it
was hauled in, it had a cloud of glittering weaving fish in it. There had
never been anything as beautiful or as exciting as that silver waterfall
of fish pouring out of the net.

The second day it was windy and rough, and he got sick and lay
curled up all day in the cockpit. Burton said: "Come on, Fred, you ain't
earning your wages." So he got up and tried to fry some eggs, but he
got sick in the eggs and they let him alone. By the third day he was feeling all right again and was ravenously hungry. Other cascades of fish
were brought aboard the fourth day. The fifth day they went home.

Going back to Lincoln Harbor, Burton ran the *Thelma M* in close to the shore of a small island and stopped. To Fred's astonishment, the two crewmen stripped off their clothes and dove over the side. Burton threw them a big cake of coarse yellow soap, and they swam around, soaping and splashing.

"Go ahead, kid. You don't realize how bad you smell."

"Me?"

"Go ahead. Always stop here on a sunny day to fresh up. Hey, Joe, want to go berryin'?"

Joe said yes, and Burton threw a large tin can into the water.

"Good berries there. Best you'll ever see."

"Berries?"

"Raspberries. You like 'em? Swim over and get yourself a belly-ful."

He took his clothes off and stood on the gunwale of the *Thelma M,* looking down at the dark-green water, and he couldn't jump. But he felt Burton's eyes on his back, so he jumped, his arms and legs splayed out. The fear of the deep water left as he found himself swimming. It was only a few yards in to the shallows, where the two other men were already standing up and wading ashore.

He followed them in. Except for their forearms and necks, their bodies were startlingly white, with big tufts of black hair at the crotch. They were the first men he had ever seen naked. He was embarrassed to look at them, but they paid no attention to him, and he got over that. He followed them across the beach to a rough meadow with a tangle of raspberry bushes along one edge. At the far side of the meadow was a small gray house.

He wandered around among the bushes, picking berries and eating them, the sun hot on his skin. The berries were delicious and dead ripe. They were like soft furry cups, and they almost fell into his hand. His fingers got red from berry juice, and he ate more and more, working his way along the edge of the field until he came to the house. It was boarded up, but out of curiosity he went to one of the windows and tried to look through a crack in the blind. He couldn't see much, except for a fireplace with some big chairs in front of it. He walked around the house. It was compact and neat, snugged up tight. There was a rain barrel at one corner, a bug slowly swimming around in it. He took the bug out.

Standing there naked in the sun, watching the bug crawl away, he began to be washed with a sense of perfection unlike anything he had ever known. The sun and the taste of the berries and the salt on his skin and his careless nakedness and the grasses and the serene gray house . . . He shut his eyes and leaned against the rough shingles, hot on his shoulders. As he leaned there, it came to him that this was the best moment of his life.

Back at the boardinghouse, his mother was predictably upset. A long lecture followed. Terribly worried. Didn't know the name of the man he was out with. Three days overdue. Thought he was drowned. Police out looking. Dreadful way to treat an invalid father.

But the magic of that island and that house was on him. He scarcely heard her.

"On top of it all, Frederick, you smell absolutely revolting. Your sweater. It's disgusting. You'll have to take a bath right now. And remember to clean the tub. You have fish scales on you."

He lay in the tub and hated to see the fish scales go. Back in his room, he put on his other pants. His mother had already set his sweater in her basin to soak and was turning out the pockets of his dirty pants.

"What's this?"

"My pay. Burton paid me." Five fishy bills. All that was left. He never saw Burton again.

But the island stayed with him. He thought about it often as he grew up, and amused himself by pretending that he lived there. Later, when things began to get bad, it came in stronger. And when they got really bad, it was the only nice thing he had to think about, so he thought about it a great deal. He built elaborate fantasies about living there, sometimes with Fran, sometimes alone. But the perfection of the fantasies was so different from the reality of his life that he could scarcely endure it. That was one of the things that made him cry in the park. He ended up talking to Hennerkop about the island and the little gray house over and over again.

3

"BY THE WAY, ARE YOU JEWISH?"

"What makes you ask?"

"Just curious."

"Is that the only reason?"

"What else would there be?"

"There may be another reason. I ask you to consider that."

"What the hell!"

"I ask you to consider why you avoid answering certain questions."

"*Me* avoid. That's a hot one. *Me* avoid. I ask a simple question, and I get a question back."

"Is it a simple question?"

"There you go again. Of course it's a simple question. *Are you Jewish?*"

"I am of Dutch descent."

"A Dutchman."

"Yes. Are you relieved?"

"What do you mean, relieved?"

"That I am not Jewish."

"Not really. Well, maybe a little."

"Why?"

That was a complicated one. He really hadn't known any Jews when he was young. There was one boy in his class at school, Billy Solomon. The other kids called him Billy the Kike and gave him a hard time. He and Billy were at the bottom of the class, so he tried it out on him one day: Billy the Kike, and Billy hit him in the mouth. From then on, he was at the bottom and Billy was next to the bottom. But when they moved on into high school together, Billy in some mysterious way had elevated himself. He stopped being called Billy the Kike and went out with girls. Not with top girls like Joanne Fensler, but with the grungier types down in the middle or lower levels of the class. Still, Billy had somebody. He didn't.

It was not until he got to college that he began to learn that Jews were people that other people could look down on. Again, he didn't know any, but he followed the style and found that the presence of Jews in the world allowed him to lift himself up a little. Later, in business, he met Jews, was friendly with Jews, competed with Jews, actually liked some, even envied them their emotionality, their willingness to take chances with themselves. All this made him uncomfortable. It was two-faced. But his need to build himself was devouring. Like the buttons on the Wragge shirt collar, being non-Jewish was one of the innumerable bootstraps by which he could hoist himself up, a little here, a little there, and eventually be recognized as one who was up himself.

"I don't really dislike Jews."

Silence.

"I mean, they're really no different from anybody else."

Silence.

"I mean, there are a lot of them at W and W. Some of them are very nice."

Silence.

"Some of them push pretty hard."

"Do they push harder than you push?"

"That's not the point."

"Why do you mention it, then?"

"I just happened to mention it. Everybody's in there pushing. You have to do that."

"So you and Jews push the same. Is that correct?"

"That's not the point."

"What is the point?"

"Huh?"

"Why do you dislike Jews?"

"I never said I dislike them."

"*Do* you dislike them?"

"Of course not. There are good ones and bad ones."

"Why, then, do you take the trouble to explain to me that you do not dislike Jews?"

"Wait a minute. *You* asked *me*. I've got to talk about something. Everything I do talk about, you seem to be telling me it's something I shouldn't talk about."

"No. You misunderstand me. I do not ask you not to talk about something. I ask you why you choose to talk about that something. It is at that point that you change the subject and talk about something else."

"Well, you pick on me."

"Why do you think I pick on you?"

Christ almighty. He never stopped.

What Hennerkop didn't seem to understand was that it wasn't a matter of judging just Jews. He judged everybody, in terms of how dangerous they might be to him. For as long as he could remember, almost everybody was dangerous in one way or another. He learned early to be careful. He tried to anticipate what people might do to him. He was mindful of his own vulnerability, his lowliness, to use the kind of biblical word he kept encountering in prayers and sermons and hymns. Much of what he did all day long was to conceal that lowliness as well as he could. One way was to find people lowlier than himself, people with cracks or flaws who enabled him to feel better about himself.

"Not exactly better. More like safer."

Silence.

"I mean, I felt in danger all the time when I was a kid. I never knew when some other kid was going to do something terrible to me."

Silence.

"I mean, I got picked on all the time."

Silence.

"You don't know what it's like to always wear hand-me-downs from other kids in the parish. From Frenchy LaValle and his brother. Both the LaValle kids had a lot of clothes. Frenchy was in my class and Maurice was one grade ahead, and they were both big kids. When my mother gave me a new pair of pants—I don't mean new from the store but new for me to wear—it would be a pair that Frenchy had outgrown, and my mother would have shortened them. But they were big at the waist and baggy in the seat. I was a skinny kid, and I would put them on with a kind of sick feeling because I knew that when I got to school and recess let out, Frenchy would spot his pants and the trouble would start."

"What did you do?"

"What could I do? I cried. I cried a lot at recess."

"Did you tell your parents?"

"What good would that do? The minister's sissy kid bawling to his parents? What could my mother do except go to the teacher and complain, and have the teacher come out at recess and tell the other kids not to pick on nice little Frederick. As soon as she went back in, it would have been worse than before. I didn't know much, but I knew that much."

"You mentioned your mother. Why not your father?"

"He never did anything."

Elementary school was pretty awful. He tried not to go out at recess, but they made him. They found him hiding in the lavatory. Kids hung around after school, laying for him. He learned to leave by the side door on a dead run. They would chase him for a block or so and then give up. Even though he was small, he was speedy. By the fourth grade he could outrun everybody in the Whittington school except Maurice LaValle.

He would arrive home panting, still scared, trying to appear normal as he went in. His father would be in his study, supposedly composing a sermon or working on parish matters but usually asleep. His mother would be out somewhere in the neighborhood, doggedly doing one or another of the million things a minister's wife was supposed to do, walking because she had no car, enduring the condescensions of her neighbors and also their charity (his clothes, for example), because she was the wife of a failed man. A lot of the club and committee work her husband was supposed to do, she did. She taught Sunday school. He was in her class, but she had the sense never to look at him or ask him a question.

Looking back, he could see her as a tragic figure. At the time, she seemed merely formidable. She was a grim silent woman who took out her frustration on him, reminding him of his failings with a kind of exhausted sarcasm that made him feel hopelessly weak and ineffectual.

His father scarcely spoke to him. Nobody came to the rectory. Anything having to do with church affairs took place in the church basement. His house was a silent one, and he crept around, slowly learning to keep his feelings to himself. At home he spent most of his time in his room. His solace was his library card; he read a great deal.

Even the furniture at the rectory was hand-me-down from other households. He realized that when he went to birthday parties. Being the minister's son, he always got invited, but he always stood in a corner in a kind of perpetual terror, wondering when something unexpected was going to hit him. And it was all his own fault; that had been drilled into him. There were prayers at home every morning, his father, his mother, and himself kneeling in a row in the parlor: Forgive us, O Lord, our trespasses, for we are miserable sinners. He was a miserable sinner; he knew it. His mother was forever reminding him how forgetful and shiftless he was—which was true: the best way of dealing with life seemed to be to take no risks, do nothing except his homework, keep out of the way.

He envied most other people, even the milkman. He would wake up on a winter morning to the sound of the milk truck. Wrapping himself in a blanket to keep out the cold, he would creep to the end of his bed and look out. It would be pitch dark still, but the inside of the truck would be brightly lit. He would watch the milkman open a door in the back and climb in to fill his metal basket with bottles. It would look warm and cozy in there, and the milkman had a simple job that he knew how to do, and he had no troubles, and even though it was cold and he wore mittens and his feet squeaked in the snow as he walked to the Crowes' next door (one cream, eight milk) and then across to his house (two milk), the bottles clinking in his basket as he walked, the small boy couldn't help comparing the small bright coziness of that truck with the dark silence of his own home. He knew, even then, that being a milkman was better than being Frederick Fay.

The teasing stopped along about the fourth or fifth grade. But the loneliness didn't. He moved on up into high school along with Maurice and Frenchy LaValle, who had grown into immense boys who played on the football team. They were the ones who dated Joanne Fensler, the top girl in his class. He himself never spoke to Joanne, because it was her mother, Mrs. Fensler, who was so active in the church and sometimes drove his mother around on church errands. Joanne's looks and her popularity and the driving all made it impossible for him to talk to her.

But he could look at Joanne, who sat diagonally in front of him in study hall. From where he sat he could see the back of her head and most of the side of her face. She usually studied with one elbow on her desk, leaning her head on her hand. He could look under her arm at the curve of her breast, so lovingly cupped in her other hand, as only such a perfect orb should be cupped. Then that rod in his pants would spring to life. He would put his hand in his pocket to try to shove it down out of sight so that Frenchy, who sat next to him, wouldn't notice what was happening to him. But Frenchy did, and whispered to him for Christ's sake to quit flogging it during study period.

He had no defense against that, because he was a flogger; he had discovered the delights of flogging several months earlier, and he flogged it at night, thinking about Joanne Fensler's breasts as he did.

His complexion deteriorated at about the same time, which was sheer bad luck: a poor complexion was considered to be the result of excessive flogging. He would go upstairs to the bathroom and look at himself in the mirror, and the evidence would be there all over his face. He bought a special cake of soap he had seen advertised in a film magazine, but it didn't help. He knew, even as he used it, that it wouldn't, because he couldn't stop flogging.

"It did not occur to you that the other boys were masturbating?"
"No. I never talked to them. I thought they didn't."
"Your father never spoke to you?"
"No."
"How long did you feel guilty about masturbating?"
"I still do."
"About the memory of masturbation or because you still masturbate?"
"Both."

That was true. When he quit drinking and chasing women in bars, his health improved and his sexual appetite with it. But with Fran gone, he had no outlet, so what did he do? What he did was discuss with himself while waiting for the departure of Hennerkop's previous patient (a little wisp of a frightened blonde; maybe she had just got through confessing to Hennerkop that she masturbated at night because she had no man to do it for her and maybe he could be doing her a few favors, but he avoided her eye when she came out and she avoided his, and the two of them never exchanged a meaningful look or word)—discuss with himself whether he should say to Hennerkop when it was his turn to go in:

"By the way, I jerked off again last night." Fred the Flogger still.

Instead, he talked more about the island. He talked so much about it that it finally got to Hennerkop.

"You wish to talk again about that?"
"I thought I was supposed to talk about what I was thinking about."
Silence.
"I think about that island a lot."
Silence.
"It's the only decent thing I have to think about."
Silence.

"What do you want me to talk about? I've told you everything I can about Julia and Fran. I'm sick of them, sick of them both. I'm sick of telling you I felt inferior at school and college and still do. I'm sick of telling you how lonely I am."

Silence.

"What do you want me to say? What about that girl who just left. What does she talk about? If you really want to know what I've been thinking about, I've been thinking if on Monday, instead of her leaving, you left."

Silence.

"If I got her alone in here on Monday, I'd—"

Silence.

"Say something, for Christ's sake."

"You would do what?"

"Screw her. Bang her. What the hell do you think?"

Silence.

"Fuck her." Oh, Jesus. He was shouting and crying at the same time.

"This is better than islands."

"Hold her." Oh, God. Feel her body. Feel somebody's body. Even Hennerkop's. Once again he had that extraordinary impulse to cling to him.

"You feel desire for me?"

"No. *No.* I just—"

"You want contact?"

"I'm all alone."

That was a rough session. At the end he was rubber-legged from sobbing, and he asked Hennerkop if he would go across the street and have a cup of coffee with him while he pulled himself together. Hennerkop did, and as they sat facing each other over a Formica table, he really looked at Hennerkop for the first time. Out of his office he became a man, a neat man with a small neat beard and tired eyes. No longer the remote disembodied question machine, but a man who probably had troubles of his own.

"Are you married?"

"I am divorced."

This was getting dangerously intimate, but he was still floating on the euphoria of emotional exhaustion, and he asked:

"Are you ever lonely?"

"Everyone is lonely." Hennerkop's tired eyes stared deep into his, a tender look full of peril.

He decided to move Hennerkop's blond patient to the island. She cooked delicious steaks for him there. Afterward he would light a fire in the fireplace he had seen through the window that time. He would sit down on a fur rug, and she would kneel in front of him and slowly unbutton his shirt. He would unbutton her shirt (a prim silk one such as she wore for her appointments). Then he would reach around behind her and unsnap her bra, and her breasts would pop out (small ones; he knew they had to be small from the way she looked in Hennerkop's waiting room, but by God they were beautiful). On and on like that. And the next time he saw her he got an erection right there in the waiting room, but still he didn't say anything to her.

But he did manage to speak of it to Hennerkop, who said nothing.

The feeling he had about that patient was so hot that it stayed with him after his session was over. Instead of sitting in the park that day, he decided to try to walk the feeling off, up Fifth Avenue on the park side. The blonde left, and Fran took her place—very strong. He caught glimpses of her everywhere: across the street, running down the steps of the museum. . . . He walked around the reservoir and then back down Fifth and sat on the stone bench of the fountain opposite the Plaza Hotel, and he saw Fran going up the steps of the hotel and into the lobby. He almost got up to follow, but he knew she would never go into the Plaza alone—unless she had another man by this time.

That was a black thought, so he walked some more and his legs got tired and his spirits went spiraling down and the old need returned and he went over to Eighth Avenue to one of those bars for just one bourbon and water to lift him up a bit. Sometime during the evening he phoned Hennerkop to ask him for the name of his blond patient. Hennerkop refused to give it.

Later—he wasn't sure when; he was very drunk by that time—he called Hennerkop again. Hennerkop hung up on him.

"I guess I just slipped."

Silence.

"These last couple of sessions—I don't know, they've shaken me up. I was all shook up when I left here yesterday. I felt a drink would, you know, pull me together. Maybe I should make it a rule not to drink anything."

"That would be wise."

"Before, I just quit. It was so awful before, and after I got talking to you I just stopped."

"I said you would stop."

"I know. It wasn't that hard. It was just that yesterday . . . "

Silence.

"I mean, I guess I'll be hit by yesterdays again. And if I make it a rule not to drink, period . . . "

"That would be best."

"I'm sorry I called you up last night about that girl."

Nothing.

"What is her name, by the way?"

"It is not proper for me to give you her name. She is my patient."

"Then I'll just ask her myself the next time she comes out of here."

"Please do not."

"Why? Am I poison or something?"

"It would not be good for you or her."

"But—"

"Please. We do not discuss my patient further."

She got stuck there in his mind. He moved from steaks in front of the fire to walks on the island, through thigh-high waving grasses in an imagined island landscape and a plunge down into fragrant grass with that old sweet feeling of salt and sun on bare skin.

He risked a good hard look at her the next time she walked out of Hennerkop's office, and if anybody needed a friend, it was surely she. She looked like death. Death with small tits.

Hennerkop apparently did not trust him. He must have changed the blonde's appointment, because he didn't see her the next time, or any time thereafter. He charged Hennerkop with that.

"It is best not to discuss her with you."

Obsessed now, and with nothing better to do, he decided to wait her out. The next Monday, a little before nine, he was in the window of the restaurant across the street, nursing a coffee. She didn't come out at nine. In fact, she neither came nor went all day. He was there again on Tuesday.

"You some kind of detective?"

"Just a stakeout on the building opposite. Nothing for you to get excited about." Bogart—without the fedora.

She never came that week.

Naturally he said nothing of this to Hennerkop. But the tendrils of warmth that had been sprouting died away into the old suspicion and hostility. The bugger obviously didn't like him, didn't even trust him enough to give out the name of one of his patients. And when he was blindsided by another thought, he was still so angry that he didn't stop to analyze what he would do next. He would show the bugger. He went down to the public library and asked for all the daily papers of the last two weeks and began looking for certain stories: found dead in apartment, jumped or fell, young, female. He came up with three names.

Cruelly now: "That blond patient. Her name's Miriam Fein—right?"

"I told you I will not discuss my patients."

"Janice Wellgood." And by the look on Hennerkop's face, he knew. It was a look of such desolation that he could not meet it. Waves of shame poured through him as Hennerkop got up and went to the window with his back turned. He forced himself to go over, take Hennerkop's shoulder, and turn him around. There were tears in Hennerkop's eyes. With a new kind of grief roaring in him, he took the doctor in his arms.

"I'm sorry."

Nothing.

"You care for your patients."

"Yes."

"Even me?"

"Of course."

That was excruciating.

4

REMORSE, SKIN-CRAWLING REMORSE, ABOUT THE blonde effectively banished her from the island. But the island itself stayed, and grew brighter. Finally Hennerkop said:

"It would be a good idea if you went back to that place."

"What for?"

"It is serving no further use as a fantasy. It is time to get it out of your system."

That didn't suit him at all. In fact, it was a rotten idea. What was the sense in confronting, and possibly destroying, something so comforting? Go back? Oh, no. Right there in Hennerkop's office, he felt the grab of fear that he knew so well, and as it hit him he had the fleeting realization that for some months he had been feeling all sorts of other terrible emotions, but not fear.

Now, suddenly, it was back, and he skidded away from it. He had to find something else. And he hit on running. He found himself running toward running. Hennerkop knew he was a runner; he had let that slip out earlier. But he had never talked about it much, never felt the need to because it was one of the few things he had been successful at. It didn't seem to require any discussion. So, as artfully as possible, he steered the talk away from the island and toward running. Not directly—that would have been too obvious—but in a roundabout way.

"The island's a long way off, you know."

Silence.

"You need a boat to get there."

Silence.

"I mean, it would take me a couple of days to get there and hire a boat and come back."

"You have more important things to do these days?"

"I guess what I'm saying is that it scares me a little. I mean, we've talked about being scared and anxious. Scared by competition, scared by people."

"Yes."

"Well, you know, you don't *have* to be scared. Take running. I was never exactly scared when I was running. Well, nervous maybe." He had got there, he hoped smoothly.

Running, mercifully, took some explaining. Although it was competitive, although it was built around the concept of there being winners and losers, losing never got to him deep down. It hurt, make no mistake; he wanted to win—fiercely. But when he lost he was not revealed as contemptible.

When he lost he lost, and anyway he didn't lose very often. He was good at running, right from the beginning. Furthermore, it was something he did by himself, his own body responding to his orders, in a sense competing with itself as much as with others. He ran alone, inside himself, commanding himself to run even when he no longer could, punishing himself. And he could also practice by himself. A great sport for a loner. Even though he ended up in stadiums, watched sometimes by large crowds, essentially he ran alone.

Running had done a lot for him. It had lifted him up from the bottom of Whittington High and deposited him comfortably in the middle, for although he was still a very odd and spooky kid, he now had a talent that had to be respected. By graduation he had a strange niche of his own, lofty and remote, because in his senior year he came in second in the state championships, and nobody from Whittington had done anything like that before; he was a school hero.

It started when Mr. McGaw, who was his math teacher and who doubled as track coach, asked him to come out. Always obedient to authority, he showed up. It was a cold day in early April, and there was a gang of kids down at the far end of the athletic field. Some were dressed like him, in sweaters and sneakers. A couple had on track shoes, shapely light things with spikes. He looked around and was relieved to find himself surrounded by familiar faces he had run away from many times in the past. (Frenchy LaValle, who would go on to become a professional football player, was not there; he was captain of the baseball team.)

The first thing Mr. McGaw did was to line everybody up for a practice hundred-yard dash. He loped along, deciding to finish a respectable third. But halfway through, something got to him. He turned it on and ended in a dead heat with Billy Solomon. All those years when he was running home scared from school, he had been too preoccupied to notice that Billy was running too.

The next thing Mr. McGaw did was run the group four times around the football field. There it was a little harder to disappear. After the second lap there were kids strung all around the field. He hung behind the only one who seemed to be able to run at all, but that one slowed down too, and he finished easily about a dozen yards ahead of everyone else.

"You'll run the mile," said Mr. McGaw.

He was given a pair of running shorts and track shoes, and two weeks later ran in a dual meet against Milbury. He won. How he managed it was rather mysterious. There were so many conflicting things going on inside him that he couldn't concentrate on the matter of running. He felt conspicuous, slightly sick to his stomach, exposed in a strange place, lined up in a kind of daze with three other boys— one from his school, two determined and unstoppable-looking ones from the other—and he wished he were somewhere else.

But he felt light. His new track shoes were light; they fitted him perfectly. When the gun went off and he started running, he ran lightly and easily but in a daze. He could see the entire scene as he ran, trees and school buildings and knots of kids yelling from the sidelines, and two pairs of purple shorts pumping along ahead of him. Again unwilling to get conspicuously out in front, he ran behind the purple shorts. By the second time around, he could hear some of the kids yelling for him. Kids who had always yelled *at* him were now yelling *for* him; it was a fantastic feeling, and yet he was still unwilling to push out in front. By the third time around, they were screeching. Some of the daze left him, and one of the pairs of purple shorts disappeared, and he realized that he had been running much faster than he had in practice and was having trouble breathing, and he wondered if he would get to the finish line at all, let alone get by the one kid who was laboring along just ahead of him. He reached down for something—every distance runner he would talk to later put it in those same corny but accurate terms: he reached down. When he was ready to quit because his lungs were burning and his legs wouldn't work anymore, he reached down and ran by the other boy.

A week later he reached down again, but it didn't help. The other kid hung on and won. Strangely, it didn't matter that much. He had done his best, actually run a faster race than the week before. Mr. McGaw said: "Four forty-three. Tough, Fred—that should have been enough to win."

Billy Solomon, sitting next to him in the bus going home, said:

"Good race." That, coming from Billy, who hadn't even qualified in the sprints and must have been feeling low because of his failure, from the boy with whom he had not exchanged a word since the day back in grade school when Billy had hit him in the mouth, flooded him with an unfamiliar feeling. He wanted to extend a hand, acknowledge Billy's generosity, apologize for that other time. But he was far too shy. He mumbled his thanks. That summer, working the fountain at Hoffman's, he made it a point, when Billy came in, to give him an extra scoop in his malt. He wasn't sure if Billy knew this and, again, was too shy to mention it. But he did have the feeling that Billy could become a friend, his only friend in that school, in that town, in his world.

Experiences like that were so rare that he remembered Billy. Even in later life, when he ran into anti-Semitism in the business world, it was Billy who reminded him that he didn't really look down on Jews the way some people did. It was more something that was expected of him and that he was not self-assured enough to deny.

The spring of senior year was a good one. He practiced with the other members of the track team and in that way associated with them. He penetrated the school locker room, a clanging place with its steel lockers and yelling boys, a place he had been too timid to enter before. He was changing his socks there alone one afternoon when two kids came out of the shower and began talking in the next bay.

"Joanne, never." It was Frenchy.

"She would, I bet."

"I tell you, never. What she will do, she likes to have her tits tickled. What she will do, she puts her tongue in your mouth and gives you a hand job."

"She does?"

"Gives *me* a hand job. I doubt she would give one to you."

Joanne Fensler. His daydreams about her became more graphic. Still, he never spoke to her. Even after he came in second in the state championships and was a school hero he didn't. He spent that summer in Hoffman's. And the word got around that when Mr. Hoffman wasn't there he was good for an extra scoop and more malt in the malteds. The kids came in, and he achieved a relationship based on the respect he had earned as a runner and on the favors he could dispense at the fountain, and he learned to kid along—but just a little, because he was getting his first inklings of what he would learn so much of later: to move deliberately and appear calm when he wasn't, to say little when he was nervous and nothing when he was really nervous.

Be calm but friendly. And not act jerky and awkward, which was what he could not achieve when Joanne came in alone one afternoon. The place was empty. Mr. Hoffman was out in back. She sat down at the middle of the counter.

"Hi, Fred." The first words she had ever addressed to him.

"Hi."

"I'd like a vanilla malt. I hear you make those special ones."

"Vanilla malt." He clattered around, trying to assemble it. He kept his back to her. He put in three spoonfuls of malted milk powder. Finally he had to turn around and give it to her.

"Oh, that's good. Fred, you make the best."

From where he stood, the malt seemed snuggled between her breasts. Her head was bent over the glass, her mouth wrapped around the straw, her hair falling down and her eyes looking up at him.

"Enough malt?"

"Just right." The tongue that would be in Frenchy's mouth when she did her next hand job on him showed in a flicker as she licked vanilla from her lips. And there in front of him, spread out on the counter, surrounding the malt, two feet from his sweating hand, was what liked to be tickled. Why not just reach out and give one of them a stroke? He willed himself to do it, to move his arm muscle so that his hand went forward to encounter the fuzz of the sweater and the softness beneath. But he was riveted by shyness, by the glare of the sun, by the glitter of all that afternoon light bouncing from the fountain fixtures. And Joanne looked up at him again, and the malt went down in her glass, sip by sip. And Mr. Hoffman came out from in back. And that was the closest he ever came to Joanne Fensler.

"You did not tell me you ran so much or so well."

"Didn't I?"

"Is it one of those superior things you have saved?"

"I don't get you."

"Is it one of those things you keep to yourself so that you can impress me at some other time?"

"No. Oh, no." God's truth, it wasn't.

"We need not talk only about bad things."

"But they're what I worry about."

"Why did you choose to talk about running just now?"

He couldn't remember. He had gotten so engrossed by those first high school races and by the memory of Joanne Fensler.

"Perhaps I can remind you. We were talking about your island fantasies and the need to dispose of them."

"Oh, yes."

Silence.

"Honestly, I wasn't holding back on running. Believe me."

"I believe you."

"But if you want to hear about it, there's a lot of college stuff, and—"

"You wish to talk about running now?"

"Well, we might as well get through with it."

"You do not want to talk about the island now?"

"It seems to me we just had the idea that I was talking about the island too much."

"The idea is to examine why we choose to talk about things and when we choose."

"All right, you've said that before."

"Why is important. When is important. You concentrate too much on what. All the bad whats. What is not always bad. What you think is bad is sometimes not bad. What you think is good is sometimes not good."

"Like what?"

"I should not be the one to tell you, but I will give you an example. You do not make yourself good with good clothes."

Had he gotten under Hennerkop's skin at last? He had given up wearing green socks.

5

LINCOLN HARBOR HAD CHANGED. IF HE THOUGHT of a town as an organism (and that was easy if he started with the old cliché that the streets were arteries and the people walking along them corpuscles, and then went on to see the grass and bushes as skin and the houses as various things that stick out, like noses and fingers, also full of corpuscles moving around)—if he thought of a town that way, then he could think of Lincoln Harbor as having had an injection. A big shot of some kind of strong medicine, like liquid money, had been injected into it, and it was healthier than it had been twenty years before. The waterfront houses had always been elegant, with their clipped hedges and green lawns and their verandas looking over the harbor, but in the back streets there had been a general atmosphere of shabbiness. Some of this remained, but creeping money was all around, slapping on paint, shoring up sagging porches, weeding lawns. Patches of the town a couple of blocks from the water were getting fashionable. When he went looking for the boardinghouse, he didn't recognize it at first. The building was still there, but it had been transformed into a private home. The front porch with its rocking chairs was gone. There was a flagstone walk lined with box bushes. There was a fanlight over the front door, which had a large polished knocker on it. The house itself looked very smart, painted pale gray with white trim and black shutters.

He walked down Elm Street (where had the elms gone?) to the town wharf at the foot of it. That had not changed. There was even a fishing boat tied up there, and he looked for the old name on the stern. But this one was called *Buttercup*. He moseyed around and found a sign: EXCURSIONS: FISHING CHARTERS.

"There's an island out beyond Lincoln Point, a couple of miles out someplace."

"Sheep Island."

"I'd like to go there."

"Today?"

"If you're free."

"Blowing pretty fresh today."

"Too rough for you?"

The man looked him up and down. "I mean with them clothes. Get kinda wet."

He was wearing a pair of Whyte shoes and the last of his good suits. "If you have an extra slicker . . . "

Down the harbor. He had made this trip once before but had no recollection of it. He did not remember how the houses looked from the water, all that stately stability, all in a row with their carpet lawns unrolled, the rows of private docks sticking out like pickets. He had forgotten the procession of red buoys marking the channel. There was a man hammering shingles—*whack whack whack*—as they went by. Up ahead was the bluff on which the Lincoln Harbor lighthouse stood. It was an early-spring day with sparkle everywhere, and some of the old feeling returned.

Another pointed red buoy slid by, leaning slightly in the current that was carrying them down the harbor, out past the lighthouse, out to sea, faster than he wanted now. For the old feeling might be all very well with its sun and its salt, but after all it was only a dream, and you wake up from dreams.

When they came out from under the lighthouse bluff, the wind hit them. Out there the waves were steep and the boat banged into them, each time sending up a burst of spray that shot back straight into his face. The island was out there, a prickly-looking low cookie flat on the water, but he was kept so busy ducking spray that he scarcely had time to look at it. *Slam splash slam splash.* In a few minutes his face and hair were soaked and water was trickling down inside his collar. He turned his back and crouched behind the cockpit bulkhead, looking back at the Lincoln Harbor lighthouse, which got smaller as the sea got rougher.

It got smaller very slowly. Then the man throttled his engine down, and he took another look. They were coasting into the shallow bay—really just an indentation between a sandy point and a pile of rocks—where he had anchored once before and jumped into the water. *This* water. He had read somewhere that molecules of water were so tiny that if you dyed a glassful of them red and threw them into the sea, anywhere in the world, and let them circulate around for a few years, you could scoop up another glassful, anywhere in the world, and find a dozen red ones among the billions and billions of others in the glass. Which meant that, burbling around the boat right now, was water he had touched once before.

The island looked different: scrubbier, denser. The field was gone, choked with bushes, but the house was there.

The boat drifted in. Calm in the bay. Stopped.

He looked over the side. The water was at least a foot deep. He looked at the man.

"About as close in as I can get."

He rolled up his pants above the knee, took off his socks and his Whyte shoes, and slid off the bow into the water. It was numbingly cold, and he scarcely felt the stones as he waded ashore. And he wondered what the man thought as he disappeared in the bushes. It was prickly there, so he put on his shoes again, squeezing them over his wet feet.

The house was a shock. Feeling slightly disoriented anyway because things were so different from the way he had remembered, with the field gone and the bushes so high and big rocks sticking up here and there (he hadn't remembered all those rocks)—still, he was unprepared for the house. The blinds were gone, the window glass broken. He went up to the front door and tried it. It opened, and he went in.

Three rooms. A living room, bedroom, and kitchen. Also a tiny bathroom. There was nothing in them except sand, drifted leaves, and some rusty beer cans. The rain had come in season after season, and the floors were stained. All the plumbing in the kitchen and bathroom was shapeless with rust. The seat had been wrenched from the toilet. Everything but the wooden frame of the building itself seemed eaten away by the wind, the rain, and the salt.

Abandoned, useless, rotting—like him. It all suddenly hit him, and the internal crumpling started. What was the use? The wreckage of this house was a mirror of the wreckage of his own life. He couldn't stand it. He went into the bathroom and sat on the seatless toilet, where he could put his head between his hands and really let go. Oh, God, the last dream gone. What would he do?

Nothing. Nothing. He cried himself out and became aware that his feet were freezing. He dried his eyes and looked around, wondering how long he had been sitting there and if the boatman would come looking for him and find him blubbering on the toilet. And as self-consciousness took hold and he began to get control of himself again, he noticed that the bathroom window was unbroken and that no sand and rain had come in there and that it wasn't in such bad shape. He tried the bathroom door. It hung true, and the latch caught. He went out and took another look at the living room. He tried the windows. Most of them went up and down. Gradually it dawned on him that this house wasn't such a wreck after all. He went outside and looked at the roof. It seemed okay. And the dream flooded in again. Cold as he was, he went around to the back and leaned against the shingles with his eyes shut. Could he really live there? It came over him that he would like to try.

"This begins to get in the way again."
  "I can't help it. I like thinking about it. I want to live there."
  "By yourself?"
  "I'm by myself now."
  "And do nothing?"
  "I don't do anything now."
  "Would you buy this house and do those repairs? Would you rent it? What would you do?"
  "Right now I'm not sure."
  "How much would it cost?"
  "I don't know."
  "Do you know who the owner is?"
  "No."
  "Do you know if it is for sale?"
  "No."
  "I see." Hennerkop put his fingers together.

But he could find out, get rid of the sneer implied in that "I see." By phone he could do it. Go to the telephone office and get out the directory. Look in the yellow pages under Real Estate. Dial the first name: Charles Barker.
  "Sheep Island? Sure. Been for sale for years, ever since the hunting club closed down. Got a buyer?"
  "Depends on how much."
  "Lemme see." A voice bouncing with good cheer. "Thirty thousand."
  The bubble burst. "That's a lot of money."
  "Lot of island."
  "Even so. Thirty thousand."
  "*Asking* thirty. Who are you anyway? Where are you from?"
"From New York. My name's Fay."
  "Why don't you come up. Maybe we can work something out."

6

THIRTY THOUSAND. HE HAD THIRTY THOUSAND, more or less, but he had watched it shrink down from a considerably larger sum in the last year or so and it was still shrinking and he was frightened out of his wits.

He had earned nothing, literally nothing, zero dollars, since he had been thrown out of W and W. They had given him six months salary when they let him go, and that, plus what he had saved and invested, was what he had when he began to skid. He had lived on it for nearly two years. Now it was melting away, continuing to melt, because what he had previously spent on being a successful man, on clubs and clothes and entertainment, then later on booze and women, was balanced off by what he was paying for his apartment and food and for those forty-dollar sessions with Hennerkop.

He had looked so beaten down that first time, so seedy that Hennerkop charged him only twenty dollars a visit. Later, when Hennerkop realized he had all that money in the bank, he upped the fee. Since the relationship had started in suspicion, the raise almost ended it. And would have, had he not been so desperate. He had nothing else, nothing. So despite the rate hike he hung on, and the outgo at the bank continued and there was no input at all.

When he had been living with Julia, she paid the rent. He had discussed that with her, pointing out that he couldn't afford an apartment that good, couldn't even afford half a good apartment. She had said that since he was just getting started in business she would pay the rent. The temptation to live on Sutton Place was too great; he let her.

What was more, he continued to let her—rent and household bills—even when he had begun to make good money and was piling it up in the bank and opening an account with a broker and learning about General Motors and Standard Oil. Money meant respectability and safety and strength. So he piled it up and let Julia pay the bills.

"Did she mind that, paying the bills?"

"No, she was very good about it."

"Did you mind?"

"Why should I mind?"

Silence.

"I mean, it was the sensible thing to do. After she moved out of her mother's house she was going to get an apartment anyway. She could afford it. There was no sense in having a crummy one, and I couldn't afford a good one."

"I did not ask if she could afford it. I asked if you minded her paying."

"Why should I mind?"

"That does not answer my question."

"Well, why should I? If things had lasted longer and I'd gotten more prosperous, I'd have, you know, paid my way."

"But you did not."

"Only because we never got to that point. Things were getting so bad and I was drinking and she threw me out."

"And you drank out of a feeling of self-disgust and dependence on her?"

"No, *no*. It was everything. Everything got to be too much. Keeping up. Doing everything right. At the office, everywhere—I've told you about all that. And Fran. Fran was gone."

"So you were putting money in the bank to get strong, but you were coming home to a mother who paid the bills and kept you weak."

"We're talking about Julia."

"I am aware of that."

"I mean, Julia and I, we had this relationship. We made out okay for a while."

Silence.

"Pretty okay."

"But you had a love affair with another woman."

"Because of the way Julia was."

Silence.

"All right, I know what you're thinking. You're thinking Julia was never really okay. All right, she wasn't."

*   *   *

But he had married her. She was up there. Effortlessly up there, along with everybody else he wanted to be with. The depth of that feeling wasn't easy to explain. He knew he was intelligent. In some subtle way, and despite all her disparagement, his mother had got across to him that he was a superior person, that he came of "good" people. His father was a college graduate who had deliberately chosen to go into the ministry, where the rewards were not in earthly things but in service to his community and to God.

So why couldn't the three of them walk around Whittington with their heads high, poor but proud, respected by all? That was the tricky question, and the answer must have lain in the attitudes of his parents. His father wasn't proud; even he could tell that. He spent all the time he could in the little room off the dining room that he called his study. He had a desk there and a swivel chair, and he wrote sermons (or pretended to) and shuffled papers that dealt with parish matters (or pretended to), and sometimes he could hear his mother arguing with him about why he didn't do this or that. She would end up doing it herself, an overworked, apologetic, desperate woman trying to keep up appearances.

All this he took in bit by bit as he grew, getting it through his skin, because she never talked to him about his father or about herself, and his father scarcely talked to him at all. Somewhere along the line he began to realize that his mother had given up on his father. Because she was contemptuous of his father, he became contemptuous too. Because she was concentrating her hopes on him, he was afraid of her; he knew she would not forgive him for failing to live up to those hopes.

When, during his last year of high school, she began talking about college, he looked blank.

Didn't he *want* to go to college?

He wasn't exactly sure.

What did he want to do?

How could he tell her that what he really wanted was not to think about things like that? He was having enough trouble dealing with the present. And he supposed that if he really told her right out that what he wanted most was to be left alone to work at Hoffman's and . . . well, after that he couldn't think.

He couldn't tell her that, not while she was sitting there staring impatiently at him, her arm and elbow working, visible jerks of frustration at her inability to poke some action into him. The more she jerked, the more inert he became.

She got the Princeton application forms. She stood over him while he filled them out: son of the Reverend Charles Fay, Princeton '09. Honor student, number one in his class for four years. School track team. She obtained a letter from the school principal explaining that while Whittington had not previously recommended a boy for Princeton, he was making an exception in the case of Frederick C. Fay, outstanding student, athlete, etc., etc. And a letter from Mr. Fensler, president of the Merchants Bank of Whittington.

He was sent an appointment for a scholarship interview. Mrs. Fensler drove him and his mother to Princeton, he sitting in the back thinking that Mrs. Fensler's tits were nothing like Joanne's.

Princeton was stupefying. It was the most beautiful place he had ever seen, with men, *big college men,* strolling everywhere. His interview was short. Yes, he was interested in English and history, and yes, he did run track, and Mrs. Fensler drove them home. Two weeks later he came in second in the state championships, and his mother added that to his dossier. Then he took the college entrance examinations, and they were easy. A month later he learned to his dismay that he had a scholarship to Princeton.

Princeton had one big advantage: there was nobody there from Whittington. In that respect it was like the summer at Lincoln Harbor. He had shed one repulsive skin, and while he was the same person inside, he could learn to look and act differently, and nobody would know.

He had a single room in Edwards Hall, an old unpopular dorm with echoing staircases. Unlike New York luxury apartments, up was cheap, and he was on the top floor. When he arrived, the room was a bare box, and he spent his first night on the floor. The next day, with the hundred dollars his mother had given him, he went to the furniture exchange, a vast secondhand market in the gymnasium, stocked with things sold at giveaway prices the spring before by departing students. He bought a bed, a mattress, a table, a chair, and a spindly metal standing lamp. The whole lot cost forty-one dollars. Four years later, when he graduated, he sold the same stuff back to the exchange for thirty-five dollars.

He got a job with the student laundry, collecting and delivering wash in fiber laundry boxes. He did that in the evenings and soon learned his way through the complexities of the campus. Princeton was stunningly beautiful, a rich man's dream of a Gothic city but with electric lights. A maze of pointed arches, narrow mullioned windows, quadrangles, and towers—and populated by golden men who strolled their days away under enormous trees.

As at Lincoln Harbor, he was not so much scorned as ignored. He walked to his meals unnoticed through Holder Court, where clots of other freshmen were already beginning to coagulate in the fancier rooms occupied by prep school boys from Hotchkiss and Exeter. They streamed like owners, like conquerors, into the movie houses and the lunch shops and the clothing stores on Nassau Street. He did none of that. He spent virtually nothing. The cardboardlike suit he had arrived in hung in his closet, along with the khaki pants that were too shabby to wear here, except that he had to wear them until he had saved up for a couple of pairs of gray flannels—or what looked like gray flannels, picked up at the army and navy store on Witherspoon Street.

Through all the initial bewilderment of classrooms he couldn't find, of teachers he didn't know and work that piled up, and of the hundreds and hundreds of strange faces he brushed by every day; through the loneliness and the confusion and the desperate shameful poverty that had him longing for one good three-dollar silk tie from Langrock's, that forced him to sit squirming inwardly in the barber's chair as the clippers went higher and higher and he knew he would come out looking like a convict, and yet that was the price he had to pay if he was going to go another three months without having it cut again, and to stroll casually through the university store, waiting for a chance to steal a cake of soap or a package of razor blades or a toothbrush—through all that, through his laundry job and other jobs and despite the demands of running, he got through the weeks and months, and finally through four years.

He got through his courses, taking what he had to take to graduate as an English major, and the one course that gave something to him, the only one, was a course in modern American literature. That struck him in a most peculiar way. Two of the books assigned managed to link him and his hometown of Whittington with their own subjects. One was *Spoon River Anthology* by Edgar Lee Masters; the other was *Winesburg, Ohio* by Sherwood Anderson. Neither place actually bore the slightest resemblance to Whittington. Indeed, one of the books was set far enough into the past to disconnect it from the reality of the present day. And yet there was a tug of small-town life, of loneliness, of individual characters struggling in a large and essentially heartless world, that allowed him to push Whittington back across the years to a simpler time before airplanes and telephones. And the ache of unrelieved sexuality was there, the loneliness—he bore down again on that word—of both men and women. Others in the class rhapsodized over Faulkner and Hemingway, but it was those two already obscure writers who penetrated his heart and his brain.

He never saw a football game. He was always outside selling programs. He marveled at the locust swarm of polished cars that arrived to devour the fields and lawns around the stadium. He marveled at the huger swarm of people, the voltage of excitement and the jamming and pushing and laughing and the perfume and the flowers and the steamer rugs and the fur coats—a sea of careless richness flooding into the stadium. Women who stared carelessly at him while drunk men fumbled for the money for a program. Men who would occasionally give him a dollar—once five dollars—and wave off the change.

Down that narrow street between the clubs they came. From their picnic lunches on the lawns in back of the clubs. The Cadillacs were there in rows and the Lincoln Continentals, and all the girls had fur coats, and the band came thumping down the street and the river of happy people after it, and he braced himself in that river, fighting his way upstream in that mass of happy lucky people, holding out his programs and selling them one by one.

Into the stadium they would go, sucked in as if by a gigantic pump, and the roaring would begin, and on top of all the confusion of noise and rhythmic cheers slamming out through the portals there would be sudden superblasts, walls of savage sound. And he could only wonder what was going on in there and who was winning.

He rather quickly learned that there was a hierarchy in that supposedly egalitarian university. There was an aristocracy from prep schools who joined the clubs and held the class offices and set the social tone and had girls to visit over proms and weekends and who got drunk and yelled in the quadrangles at night.

The second class was second-class. It set no styles. It was too poor and too busy for that. Most of its members were from public high schools, and many of them were on scholarships and holding down jobs. If there was any doubt as to who belonged where, that doubt was resolved after the club elections in the spring of sophomore year. The student dining halls, where all the freshmen and sophomores ate, were large and crowded. But the upper-class dining hall, for the leftovers who did not join eating clubs, was small. And the crowd there was very small. You either ate in a club, and counted. Or you didn't, and didn't.

Or so it seemed at first. But during his last two years, by the time he had gotten to be "friends" with some of the other members of the track team, he discovered that it wasn't all that simple. There were good clubs and bad clubs, and it began to dawn on him that there might be more dignity in staying out of a club altogether, on principle because he didn't approve of clubs, or from poverty, than in joining one of the tail-enders, way down at the bottom of the social ladder.

He learned how to say "can't afford it" in such a way as to make it seem not only that there was some virtue in being poor and having to struggle harder than others just to stay even, but also—and this was oh so subtle—that he was just a little above all that.

"The other students felt that way about the clubs?"

"What way?"

"That they were all graded in order of social excellence?"

"Oh, sure."

"That was known?"

"Everybody knew. You just took it for granted. And from my friends on the track team. From Bob Dixon and the Ransome twins. They were in good clubs."

"They were your friends?"

"Bob Dixon."

"But you have told me you did not have friends."

"He was my *track* friend. We both ran."

"You did not otherwise associate with him?"

"Bob was in the Ivy Club."

"Aside from running, you did not associate with him?"

"How could I? They were all in clubs. They went down to Prospect Street every day and had their meals and their fun with their close friends. In track I was Bob's friend. I was a better miler; he respected me. I was a better friend than some of the ones in the bum clubs."

"He talked about those other clubs?"

"No, no. That would have been much too crude. He didn't have to. Ivy was the best club."

"Why was it the best?"

"It just was. It had the best people. It had the best reputation. The best people were in the best clubs, like anywhere."

"What was it that made them the best people?"

"Cap and Gown was the next-best club."

"Because it had the next-best people?"

"You don't seem to understand—"

"I understand only that you seem to be giving a circular argument. A club is the best because it has the best men in it. Those men are best because they are in the best club."

Bob Dixon was in the Ivy Club. If he had known about such things when he went out for track in the spring of his freshman year, he could have predicted that Bob would be in the Ivy Club. From the beginning Bob was up there, and he did it so effortlessly that the wonder was how Bob did it, to the point where he found himself secretly trying out small mannerisms of Bob's. They both ran the mile, and in freshman year he ran second to Bob. But in sophomore year he was beating him regularly and coming up on the varsity miler. He was getting good coaching, and for the first time in his life he was concentrating hard at improving himself at something.

He found his best stride. He worked at gradually speeding it up. Even though he would reach down, he was now running in a league where everybody reached down as a matter of course. He learned that he did not have the kind of killing sprint left at the end that some first-rate milers had and that no matter how far down he reached, they would blow right by him at the finish. He learned that the best milers, Glenn Cunningham, Jack Lovelock, and a Princetonian named Bill Bonthron, had all practiced assiduously, running as much as ten or twenty miles a day.

When he went home that first summer he ran his ten miles a day. He had to open up Hoffman's at eight in the morning, so he ran in the evening, on an abandoned railroad right-of-way that wound out of town through swamps and stands of trees. It was very peaceful running there, with the sun slanting lower and the water gleaming in the marshes. He floated along on strong legs, imagining that he was Jack Lovelock or Bill Bonthron, world famous, but with the outer appearance and manners of Bob Dixon.

Running, he also thought of Spoon River and Winesburg, Ohio. The abandoned railway reminded him of those books, and of the passage of time and the changes that took place in all communities and all lives. There was a melancholy in that, a sweet sadness, an identification with lonely lovers doomed to die unfulfilled, of wasted and forgotten ambitions, of souls remembered and understood only in literature. He put up a heron or a pair of ducks sometimes as he ran, and they, too, reminded him of a natural wilderness that had spread across the country in the past, of forests gone, of continental silences no modern man would ever know. He took those thoughts with him while running, and they made the running itself a kind of sacrament to the past.

Back at college, all through the fall and winter of his sophomore year, he ran. That was his secret, one of many that he kept about himself. He practiced harder than anyone else, without letting on, and when track started again in the spring, he ran away from Bob Dixon and eventually from everybody else at Princeton and became a well-known miler himself.

Not in the world class. In those days the world record was some-where around 4:05. Running was not as scientific as it later became. The body was not studied chemically, and terms like oxygen debt were not known. The four-minute mile was still an impossibility. Any-one who, like him, could consistently run at 4:20 or less could be counted on to win most of his races.

He won most of them. He tried to run the opposition into the ground by reeling off successive sixty-three-second quarters. If they tried to stay with him, they would have nothing left at the end. If they didn't try, he would get so far ahead that when he ran out of gas him-self he would probably still win. The problem was to see how close he could stay to sixty-three seconds in the last quarter mile, the real crusher, when reaching down was all that kept him going. He never quite made it. That would have been a 4:12 mile, and the best mile he ever ran was 4:14.

That was in the spring of his senior year, in a dual meet with Yale. A few days later came graduation and an influx of alumni for two days of carousing and singing and parading in funny costumes. Certain seniors were chosen to work in the tent headquarters of the various alumni classes. Because of his running he was one of those chosen, assigned to the Class of 1921 tent. He stood there, serving beer all night long to a crowd of fat drunken men wearing orange-and-black clown suits. At one moment in the evening there was a lot of yelling for *Quiet,* and the head of the reunion committee got up on a bench and said that he wanted everybody to know that the beer they had been drinking was being served by Fred Fay, the fastest miler Prince-ton had had since the great Bill Bonthron. Everybody cheered and said have another beer with me, Fred. And he choked down some beer even though they had said no drinking when they gave him the job. It made him feel good, and he never forgot the strangely exciting smell of damp canvas and trampled grass and spilled beer. He drank some more and felt better and better, and the beer began to go down like cool honey, and soon everything was pure gold—until he had to go out behind the tent and toss all that beer up again.

But earlier in the evening a man had talked to him about running. He had run the mile himself long before, and it was good to be talk-ing about it with a great runner, and what was he going to do after graduation?

He explained that he was hoping for a job with the Bankers Trust Company, which the college placement agency was trying to line up for him.

"Come see me," the man had said, and handed him a card.

He found it in his pocket the next day: FENN R. WILKING.

An engraved card. No clue to what Mr. Wilking did. Just that unusual name. No address. Not even a telephone number. The ink used in the engraving was gray, not black. There was something very careful, very understated about that card.

What city? It had to be New York or Philadelphia, so he went up to Nassau Street and looked up the name in the New York telephone book. There it was: Wilking, Fenn R., 383 Madison Avenue. With an appointment scheduled at the Bankers Trust Company in New York, he decided to call on Mr. Wilking also. His office was on the top floor of a tall building. Here, up was better. He stepped out into a paneled foyer with a thick carpet and a beautiful girl sitting at a desk made of glass and chrome pipe. On the desk was a small sign of etched glass lighted from within: WILKING AND WRIGHT, RECEPTION. But still he had no idea what business they were in.

Mr. Wilking's card got him in. In his own surroundings he was no longer a fat man in a clown suit. He was immaculately dressed, mysteriously slimmer, with a gray tie and a gray silk handkerchief rising unobtrusively from his breast pocket. Gray, he would learn, was Mr. Wilking's personal color. There were pale-gray curtains on the windows of his office, which was not really an office but a stunningly furnished living room, with comfortable chairs and a low lacquered coffee table.

That was all he remembered of the office, because he was trying so hard to attend to Mr. Wilking. He was a daunting figure, and it was not easy to see why. He was scrupulously polite, talked briefly and intelligently about track—a relief, because it showed that Mr. Wilking had not forgotten who he was. He need not have worried; Mr. Wilking seemed to know everything about everything, and he got that across without saying much. He stood with his back turned a good deal of the time, looking through his tall windows out over the city. He seemed, in fact, to be talking to himself, rehearsing the script of a play that dealt with the future of "our organization." There was a long moment in which Mr. Wilking said nothing, apparently deliberately, to intimidate. There was also the scary feeling that somehow their roles were fluid, interchangeable, and that Mr. Wilking was really addressing a long-gone but still vividly remembered version of himself: the young Wilking waiting impatiently to unfold his private vision of glory.

And yet he was not impatient, astonishingly not, seeing that he was talking to a college boy looking for a job. He exhibited a calculated courteousness, mixed with an intensity of observation that played on his interviewee like a cold light.

How could a man be so polite and yet so chilling? He ended the interview by taking a slim black leather case with gold corners from his pocket, extracting another of those cards engraved in gray, and writing on it with a slim gold pencil: *Mr Harr pls employ Mr Fay.*

He found Mr. Harris. He filled out some forms. He was told that he would be paid sixty-five dollars a week and that he would start in media research. The offer from the bank had been forty dollars, so he said okay. He discovered that Wilking and Wright—known in the trade as W and W—was an advertising agency, one of the younger ones but with a big reputation. He learned that having been hired personally by Mr. Wilking made him one of Mr. Wilking's personal people, as were others in the company. Mr. Wilking liked to have his own personal people.

He watched everything and everybody. He slowly learned how it was that Mr. Wilking was so intimidating. His courtesy was fabricated. Everything he did seemed to have been thought out in advance, every gesture, every bit of the decor that surrounded him, all of it orchestrated to produce the image of a flawless man—all so skillfully constructed that he had no idea of what Mr. Wilking was really like.

It did not occur to him that there might be flaws. The finished product was too good, and anyway he seldom got a glimpse of Mr. Wilking. What he did see was so polished, so minutely conceived, so successful, so *rich* (a limousine and a chauffeur picked him up every afternoon), so—oh, God—so enviable, that it was clear that that was the way to be.

Particularly for him it seemed the way to be. His need for self-concealment sent him unconsciously in that direction. What he did consciously was to begin constructing, matchstick by matchstick, an image of himself. It seemed to pay off. So even after he discovered that Mr. Wilking was a phony, he kept on with his own image-building. The only trouble was that it was a dreadful strain.

"You did not get satisfaction from your work?"

"It was too much of a strain. The whole thing was phony. You were selling phony products to phony people."

Silence.

"I mean, the people you were selling to. The clients."

"Not the public?"

"I'm not talking about the public. I'm talking about clients, about somebody who has a detergent he wants to market. Or a hair spray. The products are all alike. They know that. They know their stuff is no different from any other. That's why they come to us, trying to convince themselves that maybe *we* are different."

51

"You are different?"

"Yes. That's the point. If you're not different, if you're not better—I mean, if you don't *look* better, if you don't give better presentations—they give the account to somebody else."

"How does one give a better presentation?"

"That's the point. You really don't. You just have to seem better. You present it better. You know, get different artists, different packaging, some new marketing angle. You just do it smoother. You entertain. You buy them drinks and meals. You take them to your club."

Silence.

"You know, a couple of tickets to a fight at a hundred bucks a piece. That impresses them."

Silence.

"At the end you run Wilking out in front. He impresses them."

Silence.

"Now maybe you can get it through your skull why I wear Wragge shirts and joined the Racquet Club."

"You are angry?"

"I already told you all this."

"It is good to consider why one is angry. Whether you are angry with me or angry with having to wear those shirts and join that club."

"I don't *have* to wear them."

"Then perhaps you are angry with me."

"Why should I be angry at you?"

"That is the question I am asking."

"You don't understand. You do those things to get ahead. You *choose* to do them."

"You do not have to do them?"

"Of course not."

"But if you do not do them you do not get ahead?"

"Oh, for Christ's sake."

Silence.

"Okay, I guess I'm angry."

"With me or with shirts?"

He really didn't know.

7

BUT HE THOUGHT ABOUT IT. FOR THE FIRST TIME he began to wonder if Hennerkop's questions were as stupid as they sounded, and he wondered more and more about the Wragge shirt. He had said he didn't have to wear it, but was that true? There were so many things he had a desperate desire for, such a hunger for, that it was like having to do them.

Like living with Bob Dixon.

Of all the men he encountered at Princeton, he admired and envied Bob the most. He was totally up there and did it totally without effort. For him the problem of being up didn't seem to exist. He was naturally friendly and immensely popular. He was a good runner and won as easily and gracefully in freshman year as he accepted defeat later on. Of all the members of the track team, Bob was the only one he could presume to call himself friendly with—and the friendliness was mostly one-way; Bob was friendlier with him than he was with Bob.

One day just before graduation, when Bob asked him what he was going to do, he said he would be working in New York. Bob said: "Let's get together." He thought nothing of it and said: "Let's."

But then Bob said: "I mean it. Where are you going to live?"

"I don't know; find a place." His plan was to live in the YMCA for a while.

"Look—live with me."

"With you?" Had he said that?

"In September. Look, I have this house, and a bunch of us are going to be living there."

Live with Bob Dixon? "But won't that be . . . expensive?"

"It'll be cheap. Less than doing it on your own. I'll give you a room on the top floor. Fifty bucks. The more there are for meals, the cheaper it'll be."

"How will I get hold of you?"

"You can't. Not in the summer; I'll be in Europe. But after Labor Day, call. I'm in the phone book. Eighty-one East Seventy-first."

"You're sure you—"

"Sure, sure. We've got, I don't know, seven, eight rooms. Call in September."

He spent the summer in the YMCA and walked to and from work. One evening when it wasn't too hot he strolled up Park Avenue and looked at 81 East 71st Street. It was a gray stone house with a wide bay window on the second floor. One of a row of houses that stared unseeingly on the street, shades down in all the windows. Houses firmly rooted in the city's rock, anchored there by generations of wealth and security, its inhabitants off in Southampton or Newport or, like Bob, Europe.

He sweated through the summer and learned a little about media research, wondering all the while if Bob had really meant it. After Labor Day he walked up to Seventy-first Street again, and the house was still curtained. On an impulse he rang the bell.

An elderly man in shirtsleeves answered it, looking him up and down.

"Bob Dixon. Is he . . . ? Is this . . . ?"

"Mr. Dixon is not at home, sir."

"He asked me to call him."

"Mr. Dixon is in Europe, sir."

"When will he be back?"

"Can't say, sir."

He left a message with the man, giving the W and W phone number. A week passed, and two more, and he was ready to give up on Bob. But one evening he walked along Seventy-first Street again, and this time the shades were up and there were lights inside. He rang the bell and the same man answered it, this time neatly dressed in a black suit.

"I was here before. Bob Dixon . . . "

"Who is calling, sir?"

"Fred Fay."

He was left standing in the doorway, but in a moment Bob ran down the stairs.

"Where the hell have you been?"

And he was in.

*   *   *

But was he? The five who were already there were friends, not track friends but social friends. They had clubs, games, tastes, girls, parties, travel, drinking—and a past—in common. Bob and the Ransome twins had gone to the same day school in New York, the same prep school in New Hampshire, had joined the same club at college. John Burchard and Walker Virdonette were college additions, but they, too, were in the Ivy Club. They all played bridge and backgammon together. They played squash together. They invited their friends in for meals. They lived in comfortable rooms on the third and fourth floors of Bob's house.

He lived in a slot of a servant's room on the fifth floor. Up there alone with Fletcher, the one who opened the door. Fletcher and Margaret, man and wife. Margaret did the cooking and some dusting. Fletcher did everything else. They had worked for Bob's parents before their deaths—romantically in an automobile accident in Italy—leaving Bob an orphan with a fortune and a large house at the age of sixteen. Fletcher and Margaret had stayed on at the request of Bob's uncle/guardian. They had taken care of Bob and his house for six years. They did not like sharing the top floor with anyone.

So it was Princeton all over again. He was in, but he wasn't in.

His housemates were amiable enough, with the exception of John Burchard, who was mean, but he was not comfortable with any of them the way they were with each other. The threads of their lives did not intersect his, although he sat in the living room with them sometimes and ate his dinners with them. Gradually they came to regard him as a pleasant enough piece of furniture who couldn't play cards or squash and had no girls. Kept to himself. Worked hard. Didn't say much. Okay, but . . . well, you know. If Bob had been more on the ball, he might have gotten somebody slightly more congenial.

He would have settled for that if it hadn't been for John Burchard and Fletcher.

John Burchard was big and fattish and had a sharp tongue. His nickname was Red Eyes, because he often had terrible hangovers. John was disagreeable to him, and as a result he was very careful with John. But the more careful he was, the harder John was on him.

At the end of his first full month, Bob said: "Okay, boarders. Pay-up time." Dinner was ending, and Fletcher came in with some papers.

"Wallace Ransome. Let's see." Bob got out a pencil. "Wallace Ransome. Wendell Ransome. Three-ten each. No, Wally's three-twenty."

Panic. Far too high.

From Wally: "How come three-twenty?"

"You're sharing the two-hundred-dollar room. Six a day for food. You had two more guests than Wendell."

Six a day! Bob had said it would be around three. He had saved ninety dollars for food and fifty dollars for his room, and had twenty-two dollars extra.

"Red Eyes, three-thirty."

"Three-thirty? Wait a minute. Six a day? It was five last time."

"Comes out to six. Fletcher's figured it. Anyway, you shouldn't complain. You eat more than anyone else."

"Fred, two-thirty."

He felt cold.

John Burchard said: "How come he's only two-thirty when I'm three-thirty."

"Because he has a top-floor room. You've got the good third-floor room. You want to move up, you can. There's another room up there."

"Up there? Jesus, no."

Try to keep his voice steady. "I'm a little short." He put his $162 on the table. "I'll have the rest on Friday." He got paid on Friday.

"Write a check, for Christ's sake," said John, producing a check-book.

He tried to ignore him, kept his eyes on Bob. "Will Friday be okay?"

"Sure. That'll be . . . let's see. Sixty-eight by Friday."

"Why doesn't he write a check?"

He said nothing.

"Everybody else writes a check, for Christ's sake. It'll screw up the books. I thought we'd agreed—"

His hands were clammy. He kept them under the table and gripped his knees with them. He forced himself to look at John Burchard and say: "I can't write a check. I don't have a bank account." John leaned back, his point made.

Upstairs to his room, to despair, to humiliation. At $230 a month, he couldn't live there. His first step up, his first link with the right men. No matter that it was only a surface link; to the rest of the world it was a link. And he couldn't do it. And that prick Burchard. That prick.

He looked out his window at the backs of the houses opposite, thinking that he would stay until Friday, pay up, and then go back to the YMCA. As he looked, a light went on in a window across the backyards, and a girl in a black maid's dress with a white collar pulled the dress up over her head and had begun taking off her underwear before she remembered to pull down her shade.

Alone, staring out at the bright square of pulled shade, with the image of what was behind it burning his groin, he loosened his pants and tried to imagine her totally naked, tried to banish despair by concentrating on desire. It wasn't easy. In spite of the heart-thumping glimpse of armpit and white arm uplifted, he was still left with the shameful realization that he was an outsider, getting his sex by peeps and proxy, unlike the better men downstairs, who almost certainly were getting theirs directly and would continue to do so after he was gone and forgotten.

Despair won out. Instead of gritting his teeth and trying to whip up some sort of physical consolation through sheer friction, he sagged on the windowsill, looking at the pattern of chimneys and water tanks laid out against the lavender New York sky. Thrown out, thrown out. Poverty and failure, and no real life with a real girl. He would pay off Bob and go.

Instead, that week he got a thirty-dollar raise. He was able to stay.

"Your parents. Were they pleased with that?"

"My parents?"

"Yes. When you received the raise."

"They didn't know about it. They were dead."

Hennerkop looked genuinely surprised. Long, *long* silence.

He finally broke it. "They died while I was in college."

Silence.

"I mean, I hadn't gotten around to mentioning it."

Silence.

"Not together. Two years apart. My father first."

"I have been left with the impression that both your parents were living."

"I don't know how you got that idea."

"You do not mention them."

"Because they're dead. I'd have gotten around to it. I just didn't get around to it until now."

"That is true. You waited until now, and now only in response to a remark made by me. Is there any reason for your having waited until now?"

"Of course not. Why shouldn't I talk about my parents?"

"I do not know."

Shame? A sense of release at their being gone? Like a shed skin? Like leaving Whittington and going to Princeton, where nothing about his past was known? Tell that to Hennerkop? Not just yet. Although he suspected it might be true, he wasn't quite sure. Instead, talk about the deaths themselves.

His father first. There was a telegram under the door of his dormitory room, asking him to call home. He did. His father had had a stroke, his mother told him. He was paralyzed on one side and couldn't speak. Was he in any pain? No, he was resting comfortably, and the doctor considered his condition stabilized temporarily. In that case, he said, he would go ahead with his plan to travel with the track team to Ithaca that night and go home to Whittington on Sunday.

On Sunday he took the long and complicated bus trip that wriggled across New Jersey and involved three changes. He got to Whittington in the middle of the afternoon, walked up the street, and realized that he had not been home since Christmas. His mother, looking waxy, and several inches shorter, met him at the door.

"How is he?"

A whisper: ". . . Gone."

Then his mother, that enduring, striving, pressing, burden-bearing, apologetic, scrimping, poverty-stricken, loveless, disillusioned, worn-out, indestructible woman, fell on him and began to cry. Her arms were around his back and her head was on his chest. He felt her body, with which he had had no contact except for the hello peck and the goodbye peck since he could remember, pressed with indecent abandon against his. He stood there in the hall, looking over her head at the diamond-shaped panes of glass that some ecclesiastical architect had ordered for the front door, feeling acutely embarrassed for her— and, for his father, nothing.

His arms hung like ropes. He made himself raise them, touch her shoulders, pat her hair.

"When did it happen?"

"This morning at breakfast. He could eat, you know. He was beginning to be able to eat, and I'd given him his breakfast, and I went down to do the dishes. When I came back . . . "

"What do we have to do?"

"I called Mrs. Fensler. She's doing everything. I can't do anything. I just stand here in the hall. I don't know what to do."

"Where is he now?"

"Upstairs. Don't you want to see him?"

He didn't, but he went. His father was lying in the bed the two of them had shared since the day they moved into the rectory.

He was reminded that they had lives that extended back before this bed, lives that neither of them had spoken of, that started in unknown places and wound through other unknown places to this bed. He knew nothing whatsoever about his parents.

On his back. His eyes were shut. His big soft pale wandering face looked no different from the way it had looked the last time he had bothered to look at it—he couldn't remember when it had been, this year or last year. With eyes averted, his father had slipped by him for so many years, and now they were shut and he had slipped by again.

At the graveside, as he stood beside his mother in a small group of parishioners while the burial service was being read by another minister, recruited from somewhere by Mrs. Fensler, he felt exposed by his inability to feel anything. He had his head bowed and his hands clasped behind his back. He twisted his fingers together in the hope that anybody standing behind him might notice their movement and interpret it as an expression of the anguish he didn't feel.

A new rector came, a bachelor. In a daze, his mother agreed to stay on and act as his housekeeper. With what she was paid for that and with the tiny pension given the widows of Episcopalian clergymen, she would manage. And she did, for two years, until Mrs. Fensler sent him another telegram. He phoned her and learned that his mother had killed herself.

"You poor boy. What a shock. To lose them both. Such fine people."

She had cut her wrists and bled to death in the bathtub. By the time he got to Whittington, everything had been cleaned up and his mother was lying in a funeral parlor. Unlike his father, she had changed in death. Her face, never soft, now had the edges of an ax. Her cheekbones and chin were as sharply defined as mountains against the sky on a winter day. Her nose was a cleaver. She was absolutely terrifying.

Then he had to go through her things.

"Your mother was an admirable woman," said the new rector, taking him upstairs. "A devoted servant of God and her community."

"Why did she kill herself?"

"She grieved for your father. She couldn't stand a life without him."

He found this preposterous but said nothing. He shut the door of her room (the small one on the third floor that had once been his). The closet held a few clothes, the bureau some underwear and stockings and a sweater, a dark-green one that buttoned down the front and had been worn by her around the house for as long as he could

59

remember. In the top bureau drawer were a sewing basket and an old cardboard candy box with a pattern of carnations on it. Inside the box was a small china pin tray containing some hairpins and a gold chain with a heart-shaped locket attached to it. To the best of his recollection, he had never seen his mother wear this chain; in fact, he didn't remember her having worn any jewelry at all. No necklace, locket, bracelet, earring, or pin—ever. And except for this chain and locket, there was nothing left behind her for her to have worn. She didn't have jewelry. She had nothing.

With his thumbnail he pried the locket open. Inside was a tiny photograph of a man's face, round, boyish, smiling. His father, looking straight at him with hope and love as he had never seen him look in life. Staring back at this unknown father, he began to wonder if the new rector hadn't been right, after all, and if there hadn't been some dimension in his mother's life, whatever the surface appearance of it, that had been closed to him. Were his parents really the remote and shabby figures they had seemed? Or was there something wrong with his own optical equipment, some faulty circuitry between eye and heart?

In the candy box were three papers: his own birth certificate, his mother's marriage license, and her birth certificate: Louise T. Curzon, born July 7, 1891, in Cheshire, Connecticut.

Cheshire? Was that where she came from? When, how, why did she leave? Where did she meet his father? What unlikely propellant had shoved them into marriage? What did "T" stand for? Those questions circled around in the narrow bedroom, around and around, for there was no way of stopping them. He had never thought to ask, and now there was nobody to answer.

We bring nothing into this world, and we can take nothing out of it; he had heard those words less than an hour before. Still, most of us leave a little something behind for others to pick over, perhaps cry over. Except for the contents of that candy box and the skimpy wardrobe of a poor old woman, his mother had left nothing.

He put the locket and the papers in his pocket and went downstairs to tell the new rector that her clothes should be given to the rummage if there was any rummage that would take them; otherwise throw them out.

In telling this—finally—to Hennerkop, he began to feel cold inside, and the coldness grew and it frightened him inordinately. He couldn't continue, simply couldn't keep on talking. A colossal coldness at the very center of him, and a fear with it that he might be frozen forever.

He gave a kind of yelp of terror as Hennerkop's face disappeared in blackness, along with the office walls. Shaking with fright and cold, he buried his face in the pillow on his couch. Then the crying came. Not the park crying, the *real* crying.

"I never missed them. I never thought about them."

"Why do you cry, then?"

"I don't know. I don't know. I feel empty."

Silence.

"They didn't love me. I didn't love them. We didn't—"

"That is like being an orphan."

"I'm so lonely."

"Orphans are lonely."

"Are you an orphan?"

"No."

"Then what do you know about orphans?" Hurt him if he could. He was hurting.

The extra thirty dollars made all the difference. He was still a second-class citizen in his narrow room on the top floor, but he could not be dislodged for financial reasons. All he had to do now was make sure he was socially acceptable. With two exceptions, everyone seemed to like him. They were amiable at meals, but he felt that he vanished from their thoughts the moment he vanished from the room. The exceptions were John Burchard and Fletcher. Of the two, Fletcher was the larger problem. With the trained nose of the born snob, Fletcher had sniffed him out instantly as not being one of the golden boys. He was unfailingly polite, but the realization quickly came that he had made up his mind to do nothing for the interloper unless forced to.

His room was thick with dust when he moved in. Used to doing for himself, he was not bothered by that. But there were no sheets or blankets or pillow on the bed, only a dust cover over the mattress. No towels or soap in the converted closet that was his bathroom. He went downstairs.

"Bob, do sheets and towels come with the room, or do I have to get my own?"

"With it, old boy. This is a full-service hotel."

"How do I get them?"

"Ask Fletcher. Fletcher is in charge of all that."

He spoke to Fletcher.

"In just a bit, sir. Busy with the dinner right now."

After dinner on that first night, he sat around gingerly in the living room with the others for a few minutes before going upstairs. His room was as before. He went looking for Fletcher and found him in the pantry.

"Be with you in a bit, sir. The dishes."

But later Fletcher had disappeared. He asked Bob where the sheets and towels were kept.

"I'm damned if I know. Ask Fletcher."

"I can't find Fletcher."

Shooting him the perplexed look of one who has never been without servants and cannot comprehend why, with servants around, one's demands are not instantly and cheerfully met, Bob went out into the hall. *"Fletcher!"*

Fletcher's face appeared over the banister three flights up.

"Where are Mr. Fay's sheets?"

"Just getting them, sir."

Bob turned to him. "Good man, Fletcher. He runs this house like a clock. You only have to ask him."

But two weeks later his sheets had not been changed, and it became clear that the game with Fletcher was a serious one, with a serious risk: annoying Bob with details he should have managed himself. Fletcher was apparently counting on him to make such a nuisance of himself that Bob would decide he had made a mistake and begin thinking about easing him out. So right there in almost daily skirmishes with that ironically polite but obdurate old man, he began an apprenticeship in the fine art of never asking for something he hadn't carefully planned in advance. Never act on impulse. Watch others. Keep cool. Don't show anger. Learn to ask in such a way, or at a time, that you can't be turned down.

Breakfast, for example. When on his first morning Fletcher courteously asked him how he wanted his eggs, he said poached. Everybody else had ordered scrambled, and everybody got scrambled promptly. His didn't come. He looked at his watch; he had to be at work. He finally asked.

"Special order, sir. Takes a minute."

But when they did come they were delicious. Fletcher might have been mean, but he had his standards. Another lesson: wait for somebody else to order eggs and then ask for the same.

Slowly he inched his way in and up. He opened a bank account, bought a second pair of shoes and a better suit. Otherwise he spent almost nothing, terrorized by poverty, afraid to be lured into the backgammon and gin rummy games being played downstairs. He did not join in the cocktail drinking, reluctant to accept drinks that were occasionally offered him because he did not feel he could afford to contribute a bottle of his own to the community bar.

Girls came and went—and sometimes stayed, he was almost certain. He spoke to them stiffly when introduced. They frightened him in somewhat the way Joanne Fensler had: with a combination of contemptibility (his) and sexuality (theirs). He could remind himself that his contemptible past was now buried with his parents (okay, Hennerkop) and was rapidly being overgrown by a thick cover of better clothes and better friends. He could tell himself that anybody living with Bob Dixon had to be up there. But the girls he met at Bob's were up too—too far up for him to aspire to yet. Like Fletcher, they probably would be able to spot a fraud if he came too close. He kept his distance.

Weekends, the house was very quiet. Saturday and Sunday were days off for Fletcher and his wife. The others often went away. He would get up late on a Sunday morning, make himself a leisurely breakfast, and saunter through a house he could imagine as his own. He would stand in the big bay window on the second floor, the reincarnation of the robber-baron grandfather who had built this house, and, hands behind his back, stare mercilessly down into the street, waiting for somebody to look up and see the wealth and power glowering down. Nobody ever did.

He prowled the house. In the ironing room he found a couple of Bob's suits hanging there for Fletcher to press. That was one service that Fletcher performed for Bob and nobody else. He tried on a jacket. Although he was taller than Bob, they were about the same size around. Except for the sleeves, the jacket fitted perfectly. Soft and beautifully tailored, it made him feel rich, and he sauntered again to the bay window, imagining that he was also wearing a vest with a heavy gold chain looped across it. He looked for a label in the jacket collar but found none. Instead, there was one sewn on the inside of the inside pocket:

VERNON & VERNON LTD.
New York and London
Robert Dixon, Esq. Nov. 1938

All exquisitely written in India ink. He hated to take that jacket off.

On another prowl he passed John Burchard's room and couldn't resist looking at the papers on his desk. Three minutes of that, and he knew John Burchard would never intimidate him again.

What he had on John Burchard was that he was broke, hopelessly in debt to half a dozen stores. The stylish leather attaché case that he took to Wall Street every day came from Mark Cross. The bill for it was six months old. There were other unpaid bills strewn around, from Brooks Brothers, J. Press, Tripler. His checkbook was a shambles, his account apparently empty, for no check had been written in two months except for the one he had written with a flourish for Bob the last time the household accounts were totted up. Had it bounced, and was Bob covering for him? The crusher was a letter John Burchard's mother had written from Albany to explain that she could no longer keep up his two-hundred-dollar-a-month allowance but was forced to cut it to one hundred dollars.

His *allowance!* Burchard had been living off his mother all the time that he— He was already deeply in debt when he— The next monthly accounting would be a pleasure.

When it came, he took out his new checkbook and wrote a check. Then he stared across the table at John Burchard, who explained with some difficulty that a family emergency had come up and that he would be a week late with his payment. The temptation to comment on that was strong, but he said nothing. He continued to stare at John Burchard, until he caught his eye. Burchard flushed very red.

The next month Burchard's bill had doubled; he hadn't paid anything. He drank more and more heavily, and sometime during the month he vanished. Bob announced that Red Eyes had had to move to Albany to take care of his ailing mother. Still he said nothing, and the waters closed over Red Eyes, and he took that lesson to heart.

8

HE LIVED AT BOB DIXON'S FOR TWO YEARS, AND then came Pearl Harbor and a scramble by all fashionable young men to get commissions in the navy, go to Quonset, Rhode Island, and become naval intelligence officers. He was tempted to join the rush, mostly because his work at W and W was beginning to scare him a little. He had been moved out of media and put directly on accounts, working for one of the assistants to Mr. Wright. It was Mr. Wright who scared him. Unlike Mr. Wilking, he was no phony. He loved the advertising business, and whether or not he actually believed in the social benefits that advertising men liked to say flowed from it, he loved it as a technician. Everything about the organization of sales campaigns—the art, the layouts, the copy, the concept—fascinated him. He was like a surgeon who took no particular interest in his patients as people but was passionately concerned about the outcome of his operations. How he ever came to team up with that archphony Wilking, Fred had no idea. Perhaps it was nothing more than the application, on a grand scale, of his love affair with advertising: it needed a Wilking at the very top. At any rate, Mr. Wright was a ferocious worker, and he expected ferocity and devotion and flair from those who worked for him. That was not Fred's cool style. The little frills he had begun building around himself crumbled under Mr. Wright's ruthless eye. He decided that he had better join the navy, especially if he was going to be drafted pretty soon anyway.

He applied and was turned down. Too late; the rush was on, and his application would be buried at the bottom of a deep pile. He could wait, the recruiting officer said. Maybe in six months.

"I'll be drafted by then."

The recruiting officer shrugged.

In a panic, he ran around to the air force. A week later he was commissioned a second lieutenant and assigned to an air base in Sioux Falls, South Dakota. Bob and the Ransome twins were all set for the navy. There was a ceremonial dinner in the big dark dining room. Fletcher produced a monogrammed white tablecloth, a monster that covered the entire table and hung down a foot or two on every side. It was soft and rich and springy to the touch. When he surreptitiously put his hand under it, he found that Fletcher had laid it on top of a pad like a blanket to give it that softness. Fletcher also got out some special plates and some cut-glass goblets and several bottles of champagne.

After the first tart prickly taste, all was golden. Many toasts. Handclasps. See you in Berlin, General. In Tokyo, Admiral. By the end of the evening he had gotten drunk for the second time in his life.

"Leave your stuff here," said Bob the next day. "We'll leave it all here and meet again when it's all over." He looked like a young god in his uniform. He certainly seemed to do so to Julia Fanshawe, a tall thin girl who came in often to play bridge and was there that evening for a last game. Julia was a very good bridge player and played in tournaments with Bob. That night, as he watched from the doorway, she seemed fidgety and drawn. The bridge game broke up, and when Bob took Julia home he went upstairs to the top floor and fell into bed, his head spinning from champagne. He woke early the next morning with a headache, said goodbye to Bob, and left in response to what would become a familiar driving force in his life over the next three years: a flimsy mimeographed sheet directing him to appear at 0800 hours at this assembly point or that air base for movement to some other place. He was flown to Sioux Falls (his first time in an airplane) and settled down to what appeared to be an endless life as housekeeper to several hundred aircraft mechanics. As a squadron officer, he paid them, inspected their barracks, gave them lectures on venereal disease, disciplined them, drilled them, fed them, marched them off to work on airplane engines under the supervision of mechanically trained sergeants, marched them back, and then moved them on, only to receive another batch and start all over again.

Winter came, and Sioux Falls grew desolate. First dust. And then snow. And always wind, except for the rare still somber day when the coal smoke from all the barracks rose straight up in the air like darker stains on a lead sky. The smell of that coal smoke got deep in his lungs, and the memory of it stayed with him for years. A whiff of it would send him back to Sioux Falls.

An officer and a gentleman—by Act of Congress. He kept a certain distance from the other lieutenants, who were not gentlemen, by his narrow definition, but pharmacists from La Crosse or accountants from Memphis or garage men from Hartford. He was excruciatingly bored. He found some solace in his assumed superiority and some in running. Down those ruler-straight dusty roads back of the base. Later on packed snow that squeaked as he ran, fighting the wind, running every chance he got, his face and fingers freezing even though he ran in mittens and a wool cap. Then back to looking for dust under beds in barracks.

Despite the boredom, there was a degree of comfort in this life. All was ordered. There was a rule for everything. Everyone had his niche. A first lieutenant was better than a second lieutenant, a major better than a captain. No problem of being up or not up; the answer to that was on your shoulder. Even so—the boredom. It got to him more and more. He kept his eye on the bulletin board at base headquarters, where notices were posted, potential passports to special training in other places. In desperation he began signing up for things, as a cartographer, glider pilot, intelligence officer. The last worked. Suddenly he was picked up and shipped off to Harrisburg, Pennsylvania, for training in combat intelligence. An intensive series of courses there: aircraft recognition, photo interpretation, target analysis, source evaluation, briefing, debriefing. This was serious stuff. The tempo of his life accelerated. He began to feel there really was a war on. He knew it when he graduated from the school and was flown in a bomber to England, to a B-24 base near Bedford, somewhere north of London.

At Bedford, under the direction of a melancholy major named McNally, he unlearned most of what he had learned at Harrisburg, relearned it McNally's way, and settled into his small role in the gigantic air war that was building against Germany. He learned not to fraternize with the pilots or their crews except when briefing or debriefing them. An intelligence officer had to have credibility. He had to make fliers feel that he knew what he was talking about: targets, recognition points, where flak could be expected and what kind, where and how enemy fighters might appear. Credibility and authority could be preserved best by distance. Furthermore, for his own sanity, it didn't do to get too close to the men who flew the missions: they kept getting killed.

Slowly he achieved credibility. His own aloofness helped, and it also helped conceal that often he knew fatally little about what he was supposed to know a lot about.

"You may encounter light flak approaching Hannover from the east," he would say.

How did he know? Only from what the exhausted fliers themselves told him in the debriefing sessions held after every mission. He had to try to put it together piece by piece, mission after mission, and trade his information with other intelligence officers on other bases—and learn who was accurate and reliable and who was not. Too often he learned nothing.

That is what he did in the war. Sit around and wait for bombers to return. Have hot coffee and cocoa and cigarettes ready. His forms and clipboards ready. And wait. Wait for weary frightened men. He did this for two and a half years. During that time he was promoted to captain and watched the entire flying personnel of his group change at least once, from group commander on down, killed or missing in action, relieved from duty because of emotional strain, rotated home after completing a specified number of missions. He and McNally and the administrative people were the stationary boulders around which this stream of men flowed.

He would wake to the growl of bombers assembling, and he would get out of bed. If it wasn't too foggy, he could see from the window of his hut the lines of planes assembling, the high double tails sticking up in the mist, the low fat bomb-stuffed bellies, growling one after another to the far end of the runway. Then the roar, and another roar, and another, and they would vanish in the overcast. And he knew that they were slowly laboring upward, spiraling to a rendezvous point somewhere thousands of feet up in the icy sunshine, where they would meet other planes gathering, hundreds of them, which would form into a long parade of combat boxes, tight mutually defensive formations, and begin the flight east. At the height of the air effort against Germany, those immense formations were strung across the sky for two hundred miles.

Into this river of moving aircraft enemy fighters would dart, popping up through the clouds to pick and peck, diving through the formations, disappearing to gnat size, turning, climbing, and diving again. The gunners would brace themselves and squirt off jarring rounds at them. And the flak would appear, sudden chrysanthemum bursts of gray and white, and the whole procession would majestically wheel to the right for a minute in the hope of leaving those deadly bursts to one side, then wheel back before the gunners on the ground could adjust to the movement, or climb a few hundred feet— although climbing at over twenty thousand feet was hard for a B-24 loaded with fuel and bombs and weighed down with all the extra defensive equipment that had been added and added by modification orders from Washington until the pilots claimed the aircraft could scarcely fly at all.

Slow-motion, ponderous, elephantine evasive action. He could see it clearly although he had never been up there himself. He could visualize the hit, and the smoking engine, and the feathered propeller, and the frantic activity inside, and the loss of speed and the plane sagging back out of the formation, and the alert gathering of the gnats, and another hit and a lot of smoke, and the quickening spiral down. Sometimes a few chutes. More often not. Sometimes an explosion, and what had been an intact airplane one instant would become a scattering of bits of metal in the sky, and the splinters of bone and the smears of blood that had been men would not be seen at all.

During the worst days, damage was expected on every mission. There would be a fire truck and an ambulance on the runway. The mission would be due back around five, and he would be ready by four-thirty. It would already be dark in the English winter, and a heavy winter mist would have crept out of the ground. He would wait—the entire base would wait—and finally hear the faint thrumming of the first plane. If its wheels and flaps were down and it came in straight and slow, everything was okay. But sometimes they came in fast with no flaps and no brakes and they went whizzing by and demolished themselves on the rough land at the far end of the runway, and the fire truck and the ambulance would go screaming after them. Sometimes they came in with no wheels at all and would land on their bellies with a long angry squawk of metal and showers of sparks, and sometimes end up okay and sometimes not.

He briefed and he debriefed. Month after month. The strain of that work grew, and there was nothing to relieve it. He became listless, numb, and even lonelier than he could remember having been at college. McNally was the only man he saw anything of, but he, too, was feeling the strain and getting alarmingly cranky at odd moments. At others he seemed hungry for company. Once, during a week of particularly bad weather, when there was no air activity at all, he suggested a joint trip to London.

"What will we do?"

"Drink. Screw."

"Screw who?"

McNally looked at him. "How the hell do I know? You look around. You screw somebody. You come back. You've been to London. You know the drill."

"Not yet."

McNally looked at him again, harder. "Fay, don't you tease me. I'm tired and horny. I'm going to London to sleep and drink and screw. That's what you go to London for. Everybody screws there. It's one big screwing factory. I do it. The dogfaces do it. They pick up theirs in the street and get a dose. How many in our group do you think have been redlined this year because they caught a dose?"

"I don't know."

"Close to twenty. We won't run that risk. As officers and gentlemen, we'll hit the Savoy and a couple of other places. See what we can see."

They saw what they could see at the Savoy and a couple of other places. And at the fourth or fifth place, two American WACs came in and McNally instantly said to one of them: "Hello, Mabel."

"My name's not Mabel."

"Don't kid me. You're Mabel. We met a couple of weeks ago."

"Honest, it's not." An overplump WAC with a round pasty face. "My name's Alice."

"Okay, Alice. I'm Jim and this is Fred. What's your friend's name?"

"Faye."

"Okay, what'll you drink, Scotch? Four Scotches. Here, there's room at the bar."

Which was debatable; the place was already jammed. But by some good-natured pushing, the girls were moved up to the bar, he giving up his place to Alice. He opened his mouth to say to the other girl: What a coincidence, my name is Fay too, but McNally had managed to get his back between them, and he was left with Alice.

If there was a rule about girls cruising in pairs, it would have to be that one was usually pretty good and the other was a dog. Alice was the dog. At first he stood directly behind her, squashed against her by the press of bodies crowding the bar. It was like being in the New York subway during the rush hour, jammed against a stranger, against hip or belly depending on which way you were facing, looking away as if to disavow that accidental intimacy. In a minute or two Alice got herself half turned around so that he was jammed against her hip. The place was roaring with noise and friendly bodies.

"What a coincidence—my name is Fay too."

"Huh?"

"I said, what a coincidence. Your friend's name is Faye. My last name is Fay. Kind of a coincidence."

"That's right—Faye."

"Where are you from?"

"Huh?"

"I said, Where are you from?"

"Jersey."

"What a coincidence. I'm from Jersey too."

"What part?"

"Whittington."

"Where's that? Could I have another drink?" She had finished her first by swallowing it down in three or four large gulps.

"Another Scotch. The northwest. How about you?"

"Huh?"

"I said, What part of Jersey do you come from?"

"Paterson."

The drink came. She was now facing him. He reached over her shoulder, picked it off the bar, and handed it to her. She drained about half of it and held it in her two hands against her chest, which was bursting upward in her uniform. His drink was cupped in his two hands, which were also sort of resting on her chest. Their upper parts were separated by their hands and their drinks, but down below they were approaching a subway togetherness.

"How long since you made captain?"

"What?"

"I figure you just made captain. Your bars are so shiny."

"That's right. Two months ago."

"Here's to you. I like captains." She downed the rest of her drink, and he got her a third. Their faces were so close together that he couldn't focus clearly on her except by drawing his neck back like a stork's. She had nice brown eyes but a big pudding face, and there was a dew of perspiration across her forehead. She hoisted her third drink, took a good pull, then the glass slid from her hand and a good deal of its contents ran down inside her uniform.

"Ooooh."

He reached over her shoulder again to put his own glass on the bar and tried to get his hand down to his pocket for a handkerchief.

"That was cold."

He located his handkerchief. Simultaneously she located his hand and guided it upward. "Here's the wettest." In the cleft between. With her other hand she had unbuttoned the top buttons of her WAC uniform, and she pushed his hand and handkerchief in. Right there in the bar! He looked wildly around, his hand imprisoned. Nobody was paying the slightest attention. McNally and Faye were deeply occupied with each other. Meanwhile Alice guided his hand with little dab-

71

bing motions across her left breast and held it there. He could feel a nipple under the nylon, dimpling his palm.

Desperately: "Have another—for the one you dropped."

"Unh unh. We already had a couple before we came." She put an arm around his neck. "You're okay, Captain. I like captains." She pulled his face down to hers and splashed a long sopping kiss diagonally from his nose across the far corner of his mouth. He kept his lips shut, but she had a hard questing tongue and managed to get it in against his teeth. Her eyes were closed. She seemed totally oblivious of her surroundings and worked his mouth over with evident pleasure. Now she had both arms around his neck. His hand was still clutching her breast but seemed reluctant to let go.

"Captain, you're a nice captain. What did you say your name was?"

"Fred."

"Captain Fred, from Whatzzit, New Jersey."

"Whittington."

"Whippington. I'll have that other drink now. It's so hot in here."

It came.

"Let's not spill any this time, Captain Fred."

"No."

"You got my—uh, you know—my fluffies kind of wet that last time. So you drink half and I'll drink half." He took a good pull, and she drained off the rest as if it had been water and again dropped her glass. And she kissed him again a couple of times and he opened his mouth and let her tongue in, relishing the intimate sensation of her tongue roaming about in his mouth, suggesting things to him that no tongue had said before. This was the first woman he had ever kissed. Drunk as he was, he enjoyed it, and he decided to notch up the enjoyment another click with another drink apiece.

The room got noisier and hotter, and they stood locked together, moving gently like seaweed in the tidal surge along the bar, crunching bits of the dropped glasses as they shifted their feet to keep their balance. Self-consciousness, whether driven by drink or by desire, receded. This big soft body occupied him now. He had her backed firmly against the bar, and he pressed hard against her. He got his knee between her legs, which parted cordially, and he worked himself against that broad soft midsection.

"Mmmmmm."

He shut his eyes—to blot out the surging, shouting, drinking, kissing, goosing crowd around him, and also to banish Alice's face, which was getting increasingly sweaty and not something to dwell on. But he wanted to drive ahead anyway, press into her. He got his hands behind her wide buttocks and pulled her tighter against himself. And he wanted to do other things, but this was hardly the place, so he said into her ear:

"Where do you live, Alice?"

She looked at him glassily, perspiration running, her brown eyes out of focus, dark crescents showing under the armpits of her uniform as she kept her hands laced behind his neck.

"Let's go somewhere," he said.

"Okay, Captain Whipperwhipper."

"Your place."

"Okay, Whipperwhipper. My place. My place is your place."

He pried her loose to pay for the drinks, and her knees seemed to sag. She looked pretty disheveled. The buttons of her uniform were unfastened, and there was a monumental bosom back in there.

"Better button yourself up."

She looked down at herself. "I'm unbuttoned."

"Right. Cold outside. Button up."

"Whappersnapper, you button me up. You unbuttoned me down."

He did. She surveyed his work with interest. "You're a good buttoner upper, Whapper. Button now. Then unbutton. Right, Whapper?"

"At your place. Let's go."

"Where's my cap."

He steered her toward the door.

"My cap."

It was hanging on a peg. She leaned against the wall while she adjusted it slowly and carefully, tucking in strands of sweaty hair. He opened the door, and she went out of that steam-bath pandemonium into the chilling London blackout night and fell flat on her face in the street.

He tried to pick her up. She was enormously heavy.

"Having trouble, mate?"

"Yes; just give me a hand." Together he and the obliging stranger got her into a sitting position on the sidewalk. He examined her face as well as he could. Miraculously, it seemed to have survived her fall.

"Okay now, mate?"

"I guess so. Alice, where do you live?"

"Hello, Captain Whapper"—she had the hiccups—"snapper."

"Come on, Alice. Get up."

"No, Whapper. You sit down."

"Get up, Alice." He tugged at her arm.

"Dizzy, Whapper. I don't want to get up. You sit down."

"Alice, for Christ's sake."

"Nice Whapper."

He crouched next to her and took her hand. "Alice, where do you live?"

"In a nice place."

"Where is it?"

"With a nice big bed. Cold here."

"We'll get warm there. Where is it?"

"Keith Terrace."

"Where's that?"

"Over thataway." She waved her arm.

"Alice, we can't sit here in the street all night. We'll freeze. Let's go to your place, where it's warm."

"Where we'll whapper whapper."

"Yes. Just tell me where Keith Terrace is."

"Whapper." Eyes closed.

He went back to the club. McNally and Faye had disappeared. He asked the bartender where Keith Terrace was.

"Right around here somewhere, mate. I know that name. It's not far from here. I know the name well."

"Where?"

"Just nearby, mate. Around the corner, like."

"Which corner?"

"One of those right about here." He turned to a man. "Alfred, you know Keith Terrace? The captain wants to know the location of Keith Terrace."

"I do."

"Right in this general neighborhood—right, Alfred?"

"Yus."

He got Alfred's arm and dragged him into the street. Alice was still sitting on the sidewalk. "Show me."

Alfred pointed. "Tuw dahn. Turn roight. One over."

"Alice."

No answer.

He knelt and opened the pocketbook that was still hooked over her arm. It was so dark in the street because of the blackout that he had to go back into the club to examine its contents. Inside was an ID card: Alice Ponderville, 6 Keith Terrace. He went outside. Alfred was scratching his head and looking at Alice. "She's 'ad a bit."

Sobering up now, with threads of desperation beginning to run through him: "Look. You know where Keith Terrace is. Help me get her there, and I'll give you a pound."

"Roight." Alfred straddled Alice, bent down, locked his arms around her, and, although he appeared actually to be smaller than she, suddenly straightened up with her. Each of them took an arm over a shoulder and walked her down the street. She stumbled along willingly for two blocks, then began dragging her feet.

"Come on, Alice, walk."

"Have to wee-wee."

"You can do that at home. Only a block to go."

"Have to wee-wee now."

"Walk faster."

"Going to wee-wee."

"Your trick, mate," said Alfred, letting go of Alice. "Oi'll not be sploshed."

"Okay, hold it, hold it. We're stopping." He propped her against the side of a flight of stone steps. With some difficulty she hoisted her skirt and staggered out of her underpants as if she were trampling grapes.

"Help me down."

"What?"

"Can't wee-wee standing up."

He dug into her armpits and lowered her to the edge of the bottom step. In the silent street the soft *whhssshh,* clearly audible, began. "They do piss a great lot," said Alfred. "I'll 'ave me quid now, Keith Terrace bein' just there." He paid Alfred.

"All right, Alice. Up."

"All through, Whapper."

"Good girl. Now get up." But she couldn't make it on her own, and his first attempt to follow Alfred's method landed him on top of her on the steps.

"Ow."

"Come on, Alice."

"I hit my head."

"Okay. Here, let's stand up."

"My head."

"Come on." He gave her another hoist, and off they went to No. 6. He dug in her handbag for her key, but it wouldn't fit in the keyhole.

"God damn it, how do you work this thing?"

"My panties."

Her office key? He fumbled for another. There was no other.

"Left my panties."

"I'll get your panties. How do we get in here?"

"Other door."

"What other door?"

"Down there."

She lived in a basement room with its own door under the front steps. It was as black as a closet down there, and the stone wall was like ice as he felt his way along to the door. The key fitted. "Okay, Alice. Down a step."

"Down step."

He found the light.

"Beddy."

It nearly filled the room. He aimed her toward it, and she fell on it like a demolished building. In the rear was a closet with a basin and toilet, where he relieved himself and washed his face and hands, suddenly feeling inordinately dirty.

"Alice?" He gave her a gentle shake, then a harder one. She did not respond.

He looked around the room. It had one small window up near the ceiling, and a heavy curtain, which he drew carefully. He then took off Alice's shoes and rolled her over on her back. She lay there, her mouth open. He unbuttoned her uniform again and stared at her breasts, now horizontal and flattened and flowing out in all directions from under the edges of her bra. He looked at her skirt and remembered that she had nothing on under it. And he had a profound desire to see that, and he realized that this would be the time, the safe time, the *first* time, with no possibility of rejection or resistance or even knowledge from this unconscious woman. As a starter, he slid his hand under her bra and rolled it around in the center of her breast. But the heat had been left back at the club, and there began to be something revolting about this great clammy breast in which he could almost bury his hand, and he took it away and looked at his watch. It said two-thirty, and he realized how cold and tired he was, and he had just enough energy left to drag the comforter out from under Alice and cover the two of them with it.

He jumped awake at six, wondering how he could possibly have slept through the snores erupting next to his ear. Long tearing snorts, each ending with an abrupt choking gulp. She sounded as if she were strangling. He slid out of the bed and into a street that was just beginning to turn gray. After a long time he found his way to the railway station, where he sat, huddled and shivering and hungry, waiting for a train to take him back to Bedford. His mind kept skidding away from Alice; he was too miserable himself to feel sorry for her.

"Where the hell were you?" said McNally. They had agreed, in case they got separated, to meet the following afternoon in Willow Run, the big officers mess in London, and drive back to the base in McNally's jeep.

"Things didn't work out. I came back early on the train."

"What do you mean, they didn't work out? The last time I saw you, you were giving somebody's tit a pretty good workout."

"She got drunk. She passed out."

"They'll do that on you. You shouldn't let them drink too fast. Fay, you lack experience."

"I guess so."

"Fay, listen to me. Never load liquor into a woman faster than you load it into yourself. That's just plain unintelligent."

"Good thing to remember."

"The capacity to absorb liquor is a function of the size of the body. Take your little namesake we met in that bar. Very small. I figured one for her for every two for me. We made out fine."

"Lucky you."

"Yes, a firecracker. She works in the Transport Command records section, and I've got her number. I promised her the next time we got weather I'd go down for another whack. Come along. Maybe you'll have better luck."

"Maybe."

9

UT HE DIDN'T GO BACK. WHAT HE DIDN'T CARE TO explain to McNally was his woeful inexperience with women, which, with nothing to balance it against, had made the recent encounter so shocking. It still sickened him. He kept putting it out of his mind, but it kept coming back. When he was supposed to be working, sudden images would slam into focus: massaging an ugly fat woman's breast in a public bar, watching her squat on a stone side-walk with a puddle spreading between her legs. He was frightened by the dark and driving desire that made him want to fondle such a breast, revolted by the memory of wanting to feel her up when she lay unconscious on her bed, bothered most of all by the residual prickle of heat that that memory stirred in him even now—and revolted him again. There was no composing the picture he had of great pasty Alice with the things he wanted to do to her. Sometimes he felt really dirty. Meanwhile listlessness spread over him like scum.

"Fay, you don't look good. We'll go to London."

"No, thanks."

"Fay, I've been watching you. You've got cabin fever. I'm your superior officer and responsible for your morale. You don't do your-self any good just sitting here alone. I'll even let you have Faye."

"Generous of you."

"That it is. Faye is a great morale builder. In a couple of hours she can build your morale, not to mention other parts of you, to a point you wouldn't believe."

"I'm okay."

"You're not. You do nothing."

"I run. I read."

Both were true. He had taken up running again. There was comfort in getting into a sweatsuit and running down the narrow road that led from the base through open fields to the nearby village of Under Wixton. Jog along, sweat out those poisonous juices, run, run—hot lungs, leaden legs. Run.

He would run through Under Wixton, down hedged lanes, past farms, run in the morning before the photo lab opened, past fields where the night fogs still lay in blankets three or four feet thick over the furrows. He would run through clammy patches of fog in the lanes, up to his chest. Run to the edges of hills beyond the village, then turn and run back.

Under Wixton was a tiny place. As he ran back and forth through it, he got to know it well. The pub, the butcher, the post office, the library. All in a row in the high street. Since there was nothing to read at the base except Mickey Spillane and comic books, he stopped in front of the library one morning and read the notice on the door: OPEN TUESDAY: 9:00 TO 12:00.

The next Tuesday, instead of running to Under Wixton, he drove there in McNally's jeep. The library was empty except for a woman in a tweed suit and with a long sallow face, sitting behind a desk.

"Good morning, Captain. Can I help you?"

"Just thought I'd browse around. There's not much to read at the base."

"One wouldn't know that from what one sees of you Yanks. You're the first from there ever to set foot in this place."

"We're pretty busy."

"Ah, yes. Well, browse away. We're not so much for current fiction, but we're grand on standard classics."

She was right. The library, while narrow on the street, extended back considerably, and its shelves were lined with set after set of works by Dickens, Thackeray, Scott, Trollope, and others—familiar names that had bounced off him at intervals in school and college but with whose works he was unfamiliar. The bindings of many of these books were a surprise, set after set in fine tooled leather.

"Did somebody endow this library?" he asked.

"You mean the sets. No, we get them from the county families when someone dies. For fifty years people have been sending us sets. We've a beautiful library in nineteenth-century British literature, but not much else. It's sad; people don't read those books. They sit on the shelves year after year. A pity, because they are so beautiful, a pleasure to handle. And the modern trash that would lure people in we can't afford, except for the odd smash hit."

The library, it turned out, was not a public one, like those at home, but a small private enterprise whose entire revenues came from subscriptions of two pounds a year, plus sixpence a week for any book taken out.

"I don't see how you get by on that."

"We've only the upkeep of the building, and the heat in winter one day a week." She indicated a small stove that was standing next to her desk and smelled strongly of kerosene. "The rest we do ourselves. We clean and catalogue and oil the sets, turn and turn about. And in summer we put them out on good days to dry. It gets damp in here."

He disappeared into the double line of shelves and coasted his eye along the gold-and-leather spines. Shakespeare, Austen, Bulwer-Lytton, Wilde, Disraeli. Who the hell was Bulwer-Lytton? Well, he was about twenty volumes of deep-blue morocco. He picked out one called *The Last of the Barons* and plowed through a few paragraphs of Lord This and Lord That.

"You have your work cut out if you like Bulwer." She had followed him into the stacks.

"I never heard of him. I was just looking."

"He's a stick. You'd be better off with Trollope or Jane."

"Jane who?"

"My dear boy."

He flushed. She saw it. "Jane Austen. You've not read Jane Austen?"

"Only in school. I don't remember her very well."

"Then you should remember her better. Start with *Pride and Prejudice* and then try *Emma*. You've read Trollope?"

"Not much."

"Try *The Warden*." She slid three books from the shelves. "No sense to drown you at the start. If you like these, come back for more."

He started with *Pride and Prejudice*. He set himself comfortably on his bed in the hut with a couple of Milky Way bars handy, then nearly fell asleep over the first few pages. Those long convoluted sentences with their internal clauses and their stilted diction. He had been accustomed to reading fast, skimming along, and he found that he had to slow down enough to read every word that Jane Austen wrote if he was to take her in at all. That made the difference, and her magic began to sink in. The Bennets and their problems unfolded, became real, became important. He drifted more and more willingly into their distant porcelain world and its fantastically different manners. A world

in which another terrible war was being fought but whose only surface evidence was a sprinkle of elegant young officers coming down
into the country to flirt with the local young ladies. What peacocks
those officers were. Their principal occupation seemed to be strolling.
How different from the endless olive drab of now and the greasy
mechanics' coveralls and the fleece flight jackets and the mud and the
growling bombers and the eternal grinding mechanical destructive-
ness of his life—and Alice. He sank into Jane Austen with an inward
smile of relief. He read *Emma* and *The Warden,* and he went back for
more. That time there was a different, older lady sitting at the desk.

"Ah, yes, Mrs. Few-Strang mentioned you. You're the gentleman
who runs."

He paid his one-and-six and took out three more books. Over the
weeks he drowned himself in Austen, Dickens, Thackeray, and Trollope. They kept him alive. They and running.

"How shall we lure some of your fellow officers in here?" asked the
second lady one morning.

"They don't read much. Mostly murder mysteries."

"A pity. Mrs. Few-Strang thinks we should do something for
them. The men—the men, you know—they come to the pub and they
stroll about with some of the local girls. But the officers—there's little
for them in our village, and we don't see them. A pity. It must be boring on your station."

"We keep pretty busy. Some of us go to London sometimes."

"Yes. London, I expect, is livelier." Then she said: "Captain Fay.
It *is* Captain Fay, is it not?"

"Yes."

"I am the wife of the vicar. I am Mrs. Appleton. Mrs. Few-Strang
and I feel it a shame that we are not better acquainted with you and
your fellow officers. We would like to ask a few of you to tea."

That was kind, he said, but tea was out because that was when the
flights came in, and they were very busy then.

"Oh. One evening, then. After dinner for an hour or so. Your
friends should meet a few of our local young ladies."

"Listen, Fay, if you think I'm going to spend an evening with those
old biddies, think again."

"Not old biddies. She said local young ladies."

"Local young dogs."

"Come on. You said I needed to expand my social life. They've
been nice to me. They're just trying to be polite."

"All they want is sugar. They sit around drinking tea all day long, and they run out of sugar."

"Okay, I'll bring sugar. But I'll bring you too."

"One hour. We leave in one hour."

"Okay. But it can't be just the two of us. They expect three or four."

"So get three or four and include me out."

"McNally, you're the only man on this base I talk to. I can't ask any others."

"Jesus Christ, Fay."

Four went. Two lieutenants from Supply, McNally, and himself. The local young ladies totaled two. "Lay off the blonde," muttered McNally as they went in. Mrs. Few-Strang was there. Mrs. Appleton introduced them around. The blonde was a tall, loosely built, loosely dressed, loosely screaming girl named Pamela. The lieutenants immediately attached themselves to her. McNally turned his attention to the other, short, silent, and sulky-looking. That left him with the two librarians, Mrs. Few-Strang and Mrs. Appleton, and with Mrs. Appleton's husband, the vicar.

He handed over his pound of sugar. It was most appreciated. Mr. Appleton showed his stamp collection; it was strong in Falkland Islands. Mrs. Appleton talked a great deal. Mrs. Few-Strang sat and listened. After a while there was a bustle to serve tea and watercress sandwiches. During it there was some shifting around, and McNally handed him the keys to his jeep. "I'll get home by myself."

When he was settled with his tea and sandwich and looked around for McNally, he was gone. So was the short, sulky girl. He had another cup of tea, and Mrs. Appleton talked some more, and Mrs. Few-Strang listened some more. Pamela threw up a heavy barrage of giggling and yelping with the lieutenants. He was beginning to wonder how to end it, when Mrs. Few-Strang managed it for him.

"We mustn't keep the army up too late."

He seized the chance and jumped up.

"So nice."

"Yes, thank you so much."

"You must come again. So nice."

The door shut on Mrs. Appleton and Pamela and the lieutenants, and he opened the garden gate for Mrs. Few-Strang, taking the jeep keys out of his pocket. "Can I drop you?"

"I expect it would be a bit out of your way. I'd best go home on my bike."

"No trouble. Where do you live?"

"Just up the road. About three miles."

"Three *miles!* But it's a terribly cold night."

"It is a bit."

"You can't do that tonight. Here—" He put her bike into the back of the jeep and drove off with her. A front had gone through, and the temperature had plummeted. The sky was unusually clear for England, and a bright moon hung in it. A good night for the RAF, which did its work by night, spattering bombs indiscriminately on German cities and liked moonlight nights because the rivers and canals showed up as silver streaks and the cities were easy to find although blacked out.

"By the way, I liked Jane Austen," he said.

"I know that."

"But we haven't met since that first day. Mrs. Appleton—"

"Mrs. Appleton and I take turns. I looked at your card. I know what you've been reading. Turn here."

Down a narrower lane. Although he had his blackout lights on and was going very slowly, the air flowing in and around the windshield of the open jeep was pure ice. He had no gloves. He drove with one hand on the wheel and one in his pocket.

"Slow down. Turn in here."

He had a glimpse of an ivy-covered wall as the jeep lights swept across it, then a gravel drive.

"Stop just here."

They had come through a tall wrought-iron gate standing open and were in front of a low stone building attached to the inner side of the wall. The driveway continued on by, past a row of immense pine trees that blotted out the moon, giving a startling contrast between the black ahead and the near-white in the moonlight of the stone wall and the building clinging to it. He got her bicycle out of the jeep, leaned it against the wall, and stuck out his hand.

"Captain, you're frozen. Come in for a bit and warm up."

"It's rather late."

"Nonsense. It's not yet on ten. I owe you something for that ghastly evening. A drop of whiskey. We'll talk about Jane Austen."

He turned off the jeep motor and followed her out of the hard edges of the moonlight through a black door into a blacker hall with a musty smell and a climate even colder than that outside. Mrs. Few-Strang found a match and lit a candle. She led the way through a flickering dark room with looming furniture shadows and into another. It was really appallingly cold in there. What he had heard about the English and central heating was true.

"You keep your house rather cool," he said.

"Yes. Will you just see that the window is tightly shut."

The window was a narrow one with small panes, set in a stone-and-plaster wall two feet thick. The cold in the room seemed to be coming directly from the wall. The moon just managed to cut through that deep-set window. It laid a thin slice of light diagonally on the sill and across an oak table, continuing a foot or two up the opposite wall. It was brighter than Mrs. Few-Strang's candle. He looked out at the moon, through panes of old glass that pulled it out of shape and made streaks of certain stars; and he thought again of the RAF droning high, four hundred miles away. Perhaps he would be a better intelligence officer if he flew one mission himself. The window was shut tight.

"It might be better to open it," he said.

"It will be warmer here."

He turned. She had set the candle on a table and was standing by a high mounded bed, unfastening her skirt. She had already taken off her upper things and was naked to the waist. Dumbfounded, he stared at her, at two eyes big and black in the candlelight and staring back at him, and at two nipples also big and black in that light.

With his eye on her, she stopped moving but continued to stare, holding very still. She licked her upper lip. Then she got out of her skirt, peeled down her stockings one by one, then some knee-length underwear, and climbed into the bed. The candle stub on the table was so low that, up there in the high bed, she was almost lost in shadow, but he could still just make out her eyes.

Transfixed, he stared back.

"Come here. It's warm."

He couldn't move. He began to shiver, from the cold and from a new panic.

"Get undressed, you great gowk, and come into the bed before you freeze."

He turned his back, fumbled at his tie and buttons with frozen sausage fingers. As each layer came off, the air in that glacial room sank another inch into him. He arrived at his shorts, hesitated, then took them off too. Shaking violently, he got into the bed with her.

"Lad, you're as cold as a jellied eel."

More than cold. In a state of semishock. But the bed was warm, in a peculiar pattern of warm and cold spots. She was warm too.

"I put hot-water bottles in."

He became aware of them, warm pulpy things here and there. He continued to shake, his elbows close to his chest, his fists up under his chin.

She peeled his arm away and put it over her back. "You're frozen. Come here." And she laid her body against his, and the warmth flowed from it, from her breasts and belly and the long warm thighs. And it finally came through to him, through his congealed wits and his chicken-frozen skin, with a quickening jab of heat, that he was lying in bed with a sweet-smelling naked woman, and the heat went up and up with thudding bounds. He felt as if hot water were being poured into him, more than he could hold, and that he was a stretching, filling something, a balloon filling with water and stretching to the limit. The water kept running in, dangerously fuller and fuller. And to escape the certainty of overflowing, he rolled away from her onto his back. But she ran her hand down his belly, and the balloon grew enormously full.

"That's a fine thing you have here," she whispered, taking hold of it. Immediately the balloon burst. Oh, awful.

"Lad, that wasn't nice."

It was hideous. A croak came from him. "Sorry. Mess."

"Not the mess. I've a towel for that." She wiped him off. "Not the mess. That's nothing, just one little dampish spot. It's not the mess I mind but that you didn't wait for me."

"I'm sorry. I just—"

"Couldn't wait?"

"Couldn't."

"You've been without any lady for quite a bit, then?"

"I—"

"You don't run up to London to fill up the garbage pails?"

"The—"

"I call them garbage pails. They'll take any amount of swill up into them. They're running ditches of disease."

"No."

"Thank God for that. What have you been doing with yourself, then?"

"Not much."

"You've no girl here at all?"

"Not right now."

"How long have you been here?"

"A year. Longer."

"Holy Mother. Have you a wife at home that you're being faithful to?"

"No."

"Nobody at all?"

"No."

She took hold of both his ears and leaned her body across his, her face directly over his, her black eyes as large as plates. "Lad, tell me the truth. Have you ever been with a woman before in your life?"

"No."

Saying it, hating to say it, bottomlessly ashamed to say it but unable not to, he realized with a flicker of pure astonishment as the word came out of his mouth that he didn't mind. In that warm bed, the world shrunk down to two bodies together in a bed at last, the old alertness and the caution and the need to keep his cool distance had no place. There was no room for distance between two naked bodies. That thought washed over him. Bodies were for each other, without pretense. How stunningly comfortable that was. They could not pretend or conceal. His had a will of its own. It had already betrayed him and dirtied the bed, but that hadn't turned out to be dirty after all, or at least she didn't think so, and that was all that mattered.

"Well, well."

Comfortable and comforted, the burden removed, he still was terribly unsure about how to conduct things from here on. He said nothing.

"A virgin. Fancy that. You're not lying to me?"

"No."

"Not even a kiss here and there?"

"No."

"Would you like to kiss me now?"

"I do."

"You're not in church, lad. The proper response is I would."

"I would."

She drew her head down. "You taste sweet."

"You too."

"Kiss me here."

His lips surrounded her nipple. His tongue touched its tip, and it shot up inside his mouth like a tiny volcano with its miniature flat top and wrinkled slopes. He pulled his mouth away in a long sucking kiss.

She shivered. "My God, that goes right through me. Do that again."

He did, several times. He found her other breast with his hand, and its nipple stood up. Her body stirred, and he ran his hand down her side and across her navel, encountering the tuft of hair at the bottom. He timidly skated past that and down her leg and caressed her kneecap while he gathered his courage for the return journey along the inside of her thigh. He found that the upper part of her thigh was all slippery on the inside. That excited him inordinately. He was driven to lie against her, on her. He became aware that she wanted him to by her urging hand against his back. And again that relentless filling of the balloon began, fuller and fuller. He pressed down on her, and that reckless movement sent another quart or two pouring into that already bursting balloon. She spread her legs slightly. He knew what to do. He tried to do it. But an entire skyful of water fell on him, and the balloon went to smithereens.

"Look out," he gasped. But she held him tight.

"Lad, you're impossible."

He was, he was.

"You're like a soap bubble. One touch and you burst."

A better image than his. Not a balloon but something far more quick and fragile. A bubble, swelling remorselessly under the puffing breaths of desire, born only to burst.

"You must try to be a bit slower."

"I can't help it."

"I'm that attractive to you?"

"Oh, yes."

"So are you to me. I like your hands on my body. Will you caress me again?"

He knew where she meant. But partly from a dawning sense of the pleasure in delay and partly from some instinct to excite, he lingered over her belly—a little timid still—running his hand gently back and forth, just skirting the hair. And he knew he was exciting her, because she squirmed in the bed and rose up against his hand as if to urge it along. And he realized he had a power in him to please her as he ran his finger down.

"Just there." She moved her hips down and away and then returned them.

A power. It coursed through him.

"Just there. That's it. Oh, that's gorgeous."

With each of his caresses her body jumped and she gasped.

"That's it. Just there, just a bit—There. There. Faster. Oh my God. I—I—" She took his hand and thrust it into herself, her body whipping up and down. "Like that. Oh, please." She let go and seized his head, her fingers in his hair. "Just there. *That's it.*" She pulled him over on top of her and flung herself up against him, her hips grinding against his, trying to find their way through to something somewhere beyond. Apparently they did. The grinding subsided into sudden shudders. They lay clasped together, his chest riding up and down on hers, on the long breaths. Silence for a time. Then she gently slid him off her, and they lay side by side quietly on their backs.

She said: "You don't know. You just don't know."

"Know what?"

"What you did for me."

"I only—"

"I'd about had it. You'll never know. You'll never never know." She turned away in the bed. "I don't want you to know. I'm ashamed to tell you."

"Know what?"

"You must think it pretty whorish of me," she said into the pillow, "to drag you in this way and try to devour you."

"No."

"You don't think of me as whorish? You're not disgusted with me dragging you in here, with the bed all heated up and the towel ready? What must you think of that? That's not whorish?"

"Well, you did seem ready."

"I've been ready for you for weeks. I've watched you run by in the high street. I've such a heat and fever in me that I have had to work it out somehow, and I go to the library on the off day and oil the books and polish them. I've too much of a heat in me to stay at home, so I've been going to the library, and one day you ran past the window and I waited and you ran back. I watched for you again. Every day you would run by. And the day you walked in, I thought my breath would stop."

"You didn't show it."

"I could barely breathe. I was shaking inside. I couldn't resist following you into the shelves. My legs took me. I said to myself no, but there I was. And you were holding up that great book and I got hold of myself. I had a hard time speaking."

"You spoke all right."

"Only just. I'd about got to the end. You wouldn't know about that. I'd already lost control. Last month I went to London. There's nobody here, nobody at all. To join the garbage pails, I was that far gone. And some soldiers went by near the Marble Arch, where I'd wandered wondering how one went about picking up a man. A lot of soldiers. Young boys marching off somewhere together, all in step together, with their legs all striding out together. And I watched their legs, and the heat rose up in me, and I thought of all those cocks swinging along together, and I felt dizzy there in the street. When that passed, I wished to die. I came home." She began to cry. "I was ashamed."

"Don't." He was reminded of all his own shameful thoughts.

"That's nothing to be ashamed of." He was also feeling the effects of this chronicle of heat. He turned her over and she buried her face in his neck.

"You're a man. You're not married. You can go anywhere you want and do what you want. You don't know what it's like for me. I've nobody. My horse, I can't ride him anymore. I feel him under me and the motion, and I go all hot. I took a bad fall. Now a boy rides my horse for me. It's the same even with my bike. I ride it to the village, and my legs go up and down along the seat, and the seat is right there between my legs, and I go all hot and try to press down against it, but we're not fitted—What must you think?"

He was thinking that she should do what he had been doing all his lonely sexual years. "Why don't you . . . you know . . . "

"Do myself? I've tried that. Don't think I haven't. It doesn't work. It drives me frantic. I feel like screaming. I bit a piece out of my lip. I've still the mark, just here."

"But if I can . . . "

"It's not the same. It must be someone else. A man in the bed with me. His body there. I've had no man for three years, and I've stood it for more than two. But for the last months I've been out of my mind. I think about men's bodies night and day."

"Is your husband . . . ?"

"Dead? No, but he might as well be. He's a war prisoner."

"Oh." His eyes swiveled way from the pale wafer of a face in the pillow to the broader higher slice that the setting moon was now painting on the wall.

"Don't be sorry for him. He's a bad lot. I'd about made up my mind to leave him when the war broke out, but he was too quick. He dashed off into the commandos. All very patriotic, but so childish. All in their black faces and their knives in their teeth when they should have been back here growing food. But that was too dull for him. He was like a little boy playing at kings and clansmen. The war's a game to him—at least it was until he got captured. I've no doubt he was a good commando. He's small, but he's strong and courageous and restless and very quick—and he's beautiful. But he's a sod."

"Why worry about him, then? Why do you . . . ?"

"Torture myself? It's one thing to leave your husband when he's walking about free. But it's something else again to begin tossing your garlands about when he's in a German camp." She wiped her eye on the edge of the sheet.

He said that she hadn't been exactly tossing anything. That was, unless . . .

"Never fear, you're the first. I've held off till you. And you've been so innocent and timid and virginal that I find I don't feel guilty about you after all."

"Then why are you crying?"

"I'm afraid you think me a slut." She put the sheet up to her face.

He tried to comfort her and gradually succeeded.

"Ah, you've a lovely hand for an uneducated boy. That's delicious. Oh, my gorgeous virgin lover."

That time she got hold of his free hand and nibbled at his fingers and licked the palm and moaned into it and made no effort to guide him and said nothing intelligible except afterward, when she got her breath, to tell him it was better than before. "I'd no worry this time. I knew you'd bring me. My God, I feel glorious." And it turned out that all she wanted was to catch her breath again and have him do her again. And by that time she was up, up, really soaring, and she didn't need his hand at all but rode him wildly about in the bed until she was truly done.

About that time the candle stub guttered and went out. She wrapped a blanket around herself and went for another, a tall one that stood up over the edge of the high bed. The light from the candle glinted in her black eyes, and her long pale face looked soft, turned on the pillow.

She stretched and yawned. "I feel glorious. I'll sleep. I haven't had a proper sleep for nearly three years, I've been that tense."

He looked at his watch. "You won't sleep much."

"I'll sleep half the day away if I choose. I've nothing to do tomorrow but hoe in the garden. I'm so relaxed now I can scarcely keep my eyes open."

"I'd better go."

"No. Stay. We'll cuddle and cozy for a bit, and chat. We haven't talked about Jane Austen yet. I could talk about Jane now if I weren't so sleepy. But if you'd asked me last week, I wouldn't have been able to. I'd have been too nervy. I'd not have been sure what might jump out of my mouth if I opened it. You notice I said nothing at Mrs. Appleton's this evening."

"I thought you were just quiet."

"No, my boy. I was having uncontrollable crimson thoughts and scarlet feelings over you. It was your cock I had in my mind, and I was afraid I might just mention that."

Her second use of the word jarred him. She noticed, and said immediately: "You don't like that word?"

"I've never heard a woman say it before."

"I forget you're so innocent. It shocks you?"

"I'm just not used to it."

"What would you have me call it?"

"I don't know."

"If I'm to get properly acquainted with it, I'll have to call it something."

"I guess."

"What do you call it?"

"I don't call it anything."

"Well, the proper word for it is cock. Say it."

Reluctantly: "Cock."

"Does that sound so awful?"

"No."

"It's a sweet little thing."

"I wish——"

"Next time, my lover. You won't be so timid and so headlong, and I won't be so nervy. We'll be slow and tender and full of passion. And you'll put your cock in me. Don't be startled, darling; there are no dirty words between lovers. You shall do it. You'll see, lad."

"You always call me lad."

"I do alone with you here. I'm from the West. That's what they say there. I can't say chap or mate. Imagine saying chap to you. I'd feel a fool."

"You say *gel* like everybody else around here."

"I do not say *gel*. And I don't say *gurrll* like you."

"If you were really from the West, you'd say *gal*. And wear a sombrero."

"The West of England's not the West of the States, thank you. We girls don't wear fringed leather clothes and wave our hats. See, I said *girl*. And we ride better."

"Better than Dale Evans?" he asked.

"I don't know Dale Evans."

He explained that she was a movie star, a great rider.

She compressed her lips and said contemptuously: "Those film stars can't ride. All they do is jig-jig up and down in rocking-chair saddles and wave their hats. I can ride better than any film star I have ever seen. Do you ride?"

"No."

"Then you're no judge. I ride very well. And I look very fine on a horse. With a proper black habit and stock. The first time I came here to hunt, I vanned my own horse. I wanted to impress. He's a fine strong black one. Black hunters are rare, you know, and I made a

91

smashing impression with him." She sat up in bed, full of the memory of that. "My cousins wanted to show me off. They did, all right. That's where I met my husband, here in the local hunt."

"He rode too?"

"Oh, yes, very well. But not as well as me. The first day when hounds met, there was this little man, and I caught him looking at me, and I sat very straight and proud on my horse, which was a whole hand higher than his and very strong. My cousin explained that he was on for the next MFH. And he kept looking at me with bright-blue eyes. Very bold. And I paid him no heed and he went off."

She looked like an Indian squaw now, with the blanket up over her head and held at the throat, with her long high nose and the black hair falling down. But only for an instant, because she was intent on turning herself back into a figure in an English hunting print, where streams of men and dogs poured over the countryside. Always men?

"Do women hunt much?"

"Some do. I was known for it. I was brought up on horses. Anyway, that first day was a very long run, and if you don't know anything about hunting, I should explain that it is not etiquette for visitors to press ahead of the local big artillery. So I held back as much as I could, but it wasn't much of a field. At the kill, there was only this little man and myself. I'd even been holding back on him, and he was well aware of that and furious and drove his horse, which was ready to go down at the end, while mine was still strong. Darling boy, must I go on about horses?"

"Go on." He had not the slightest interest in horses, but it was nice to lie warm and lazy and watch her in the blanket on her haunches in the candlelight. Obviously it pleased her to talk about horses.

"Well, we got down. And we were breathing hard and covered in mud. He made a grab for me, and I said no. But he wasn't accustomed to that. All the girls hereabouts had been hurling themselves on their backs for him since he was about sixteen. But up to then I'd had nothing to do with men. I wasn't having that, and I had to hit him with my crop."

"How old were you?"

"I was twenty-five."

In resurrecting that conversation, he knew what Hennerkop's reaction would be. He would put the tips of his fingers together like a little pink cathedral in front of his face and say: "A repressed woman with a strong sexual drive sublimated in horses."

Instead, he said: "You do not seem to have been much occupied with clothing and status in England."

"Not so much."

"Why was that?"

"Well, I was in a foreign country. It didn't seem to matter so much there."

"But you associated only with Americans."

"Yes, but the war was on and rank didn't matter much over there. I was on a working base, in a war. People were getting killed."

Silence.

"Nobody saluted or that crap, and you weren't neat. Anyway, I was busy and tired all the time. Every other week I had the night duty. The whole thing was unreal, sending off those bombers all the time and being so grim about destroying Germany. I was like everybody else, gritting my teeth and waiting for it to be over so I could come home. As I say—unreal."

"Your woman friend was unreal?"

"Not then. Now she is."

"You did not feel compelled to impress her?"

"No. I felt natural with her. After that first— Well, I felt shy and awkward at the beginning, but— No, no, I felt fine with her."

"She was an upper-class person."

"Yes."

"The English, I understand, are very status conscious. Why did you not feel compelled to impress her or her friends?"

"I never got the chance."

She *was* an upper-class person. Obviously, when he thought about it. She spoke in that upper-class voice, and there was all that business about horses and hunting. But lying in her bed and listening to her talk about horses, he was not thinking about the upper class but about her body and the new power it gave him, the new gift, the new realization that he could make a woman happy, send her soaring.

"The hunt went three weeks," she said. "And he was always pushing about me. There were dinner parties and then the hunt ball, and he was very forward. My cousins teased me about him and made me angry at him. But he stirred me. I was innocent of men, and he would press against me at the buffet or accidentally brush my front. When I went to the ladies', he would be waiting for me and catch at me. He was utterly shameless. The more I held him off, the more insistent he became. And after two weeks I must confess he had me all foaming inside. But I was not about to let him see that, and I told him I'd

93

have nothing to do with him unless he made a proper proposal. He was so set on having what he wanted—like a baby after a rattle—that he did. And I was mad for him by that time, so I accepted."

"And lived unhappily ever after."

"Not at first. At first it was fabulous. I loved him passionately, and he taught me not to be shy about myself. That's the one good thing I got from him. We had fantastic times together, until he began to lose interest in me and start his eternal chasing of other women. That's when the hard times began. I had my dignity, you know. I couldn't go always crawling after him, and yet I wanted him fiercely and I was disgusted by his other affairs and I hated myself for wanting him so despite being disgusted. That was degrading. And yet I couldn't keep myself from going to him sometimes. He took a regular delight in that, teasing me on, week after week, and finally obliging me. You may wonder why I tell you this. It's because I've no one else to talk to this way. It's been all bottled up. I want you to understand why I behave as I do. He made me into a sensual woman—one who needed that—and then would not be respectful of it. I've been married to a horrid man, just horrid. He would fire me all up and then take delight in making me feel a slut. That was his pleasure, if you can believe it—to make me want him. The more I wanted, the more cruelly he teased, until in the midst of wanting I came to hate the sight of him. I couldn't bear to have him touch me."

Something flickered in his mind.

She tossed back her long hair in an angry gesture of dismissal. "You'll find this hard to believe, but the memory of him still fires me, while the actuality of him turns me to ice."

Now he remembered. "Not only you," he said. "Listen to this," and quoted:

> "And then suppose:
> You are a woman well endowed,
> And the only man with whom law and morality
> Permit you to have the marital relation
> Is the very man that fills you with disgust
> Every time you think of him—while you think of it
> Every time you see him?"

"That's it exactly," she said excitedly. "Lad, that's dot on. Did you just make that up?"

"No. It's from a poem by Edgar Lee Masters."

"Don't know that chap."

"He's an American. It's from his best book, *Spoon River Anthology*."

"You have it by heart?"

"Parts of it. It was my favorite book when I was a student."

"Then I shall read it. I'll get a copy."

"I'll get you one."

"Will you, lad? I like that bit, 'a woman well endowed.' That's a polite way of describing a woman like me, who needs a cock in her from time to time. Yours now, lad, not any cock."

Still jolted by that word, he managed to say: "That doesn't make you a slut."

"Ah, well. I'm a hot woman, and I'm afraid I shall become a slut."

"You won't. You live in too cold a house."

"Yes. That's another thing about him. He has this grand property, and for years he's been letting it run down. One day he'll lose it. He's for nothing but dogs and hunting and drink and women. I tell you, he thinks he's living in the eighteenth century. He wouldn't even have electricity put in; his father did without it. I wanted a fridge, and I had to have the electricity put in with my own money."

"You have it now?"

"Yes. In all but the servants'."

"You can get those little electric heaters, you know."

"I have them."

"Well, let's turn one on."

A smile cut across her long face. "Where do you think you are, lad?"

"In bed with you."

"Ah, yes. Thank God you are. But in what bed?"

"Your bed."

"You're not in my bed. My bed is in the Park House, and this is the gatekeeper's cottage."

Silence.

"I couldn't take you there. The cook and the char, they've ears like owls. They would hear your motor crunching away on the gravel at dawn, and it would be all over the village by noon that Mrs. Few-Strang had had a visitor."

Thinking it over, he decided that Hennerkop might have been right. If it had gone on long enough to become real, for them to get to know each other, for her to find out what he was really like, for her superiority and her undoubted wealth to reveal themselves, the magical evenness with which they had started might have been lost. But at the time he was not thinking about that. They *were* even. He had discovered what he could do with her. It shot him full of a kind of glory.

Cocooned in blankets, she went down to the door with him. He explained that the next week was his turn for nights but that he would then phone her the first chance he got.

"The first chance, my lover."

"What's your name?"

"Ah, my name."

"If we're going to get properly acquainted, I'll have to call you something."

She laughed and squeezed his arm. "Aren't you the clever little parrot. My name is Violet."

"Violet?"

"Too delicate for such an abandoned woman?"

He turned it over on his tongue. "At least you're not a shrinking one."

"No, lad, you're the one that's been doing that. Just don't be a clot and call me Vi."

"I won't, but I'll call."

"I'll wait, my lover. I can wait a long time now. I'll have hot-water bottles in." She embraced him, standing on his toes to keep her bare feet from the frosty stone sill. "Now I'll pop into bed for a bit and think about you. Then I'll bike on up to the house. I'll use the grass verge to the drive, and I shan't be heard." She shut the black door, and he climbed into the cold jeep.

"Fay, I owe you an apology."

He handed McNally the jeep keys.

"For running out on you. But I got the signal, and it wasn't being beamed your way. Maybe I should have hung around and tried to aim it at you." He put the keys in his pocket. "Anyway, don't say I didn't warn you about that other one."

"Pamela."

"The screamer. I think she's crazy."

"She acts a little hysterical."

"She's a wacko. Gets her blasts from punishing men. We had this dance in the mess when we first opened up here, before you came. You know, friendly with the natives. And Pamela showed up. She looks okay, you know, and she stood out among the other local talent. So Busbee, being the ranking officer, decided to have the first dance with her, and she handed it to him right there on the dance floor.

Really laid it in there. And Busbee is giving it back to her pretty good when the music stops. And she leans on him for about one second, giggling at the top of her voice. Christ, what a screamer! And Busbee's liking it but getting a little red. And the music starts again, and he reaches for her, but she's already dancing with some other guy, I forget who, and giving it to him, really stuffing it in there. And Busbee gets mad and leaves, and that's the last interracial event we have on this base."

"What was she trying to do?"

"I don't know. But practically everybody at the party got rubbed up, including me. She acted as if she was getting herself set for one great big enormous gang bang, and when the thing ended they nearly broke the door down trying to get out after her. But nobody got anything. As far as I know, nobody's ever gotten anything except a pair of aching nuts. So when I saw her there last night I said to myself, Fay, look out, she'll murder you. Did she?"

"No."

"Well, I guess it's the lieutenants who are hanging on to theirs this morning. What did you do?"

"I drove one of the librarians home."

"Tough."

10

THE NEXT WEEK HE HAD NIGHTS AND COULDN'T call. And the following week turned out to be the Battle of the Bulge. Although the weather was hopeless, they still used bombers around the clock, used everything they had, and he was on his feet for what seemed like days at a time. He would fall asleep in the briefing room, with his head on a table. They would wake him up with coffee, and he would dazedly try to absorb the torrent of intelligence that was pouring out of the Wing. Most of it didn't make any sense. Things were changing so fast that the afternoon batch obsoleted the morning batch, and he would sleep and drink coffee and try to keep up, and try to adjust himself to the fact that his bombers, those stately high-flying agents of pinpoint destruction, were being used now in the clumsy business of trying to hinder armies and destroy tank columns. But the intelligence was fearfully slow in saying where those tank columns were.

After a while things quieted down, and he slept for a couple of days. Then he called. There was no answer. He called again the next day, and again there was no answer. He let the phone ring a long time, imagining her hoeing in her vegetable garden, straightening to ease her back and wipe her face, and then hearing the distant tinkle of the phone and go running. He gave her time for that.

He borrowed McNally's jeep, and although it was not Tuesday, he drove to Under Wixton on the chance she might be waiting for him there. The library was closed. He shaded his eyes and looked through the window. There was nobody at the desk. He tapped on the glass. Nobody came.

On Tuesday he went again. She was sitting at her desk.

He stood in the doorway, his heart swatting the breath out of him, and he knew hers must be too, inside her sweater and her tweed suit.

"I phoned," he managed to say.

"I heard your jeep stop." She stood up. Her long face looked yellow.

"I phoned twice. You didn't answer."

"They never answer. They are afraid of the telephone."

"Where were you?"

"I was in London."

"London!"

"Not that. I went to get Robert. He escaped. Don't leave the door open."

He shut it.

"His camp was bombed, and he got away. He's here now."

"Here?"

"In London. In hospital. I got word that they were bringing him there, and I went up. I've been in London much of the time."

"What's the matter with him?"

"His leg was injured. I don't know all the details. He's been very ill. He got across the lines somehow. There's been a great confusion recently, and he got over." She sat down again in her chair, shivering, hugging herself.

He moved the kerosene stove aside, got another chair from the reading table, and put it next to her desk. "Here." He unpeeled one of the hands that she was clutching herself with.

"He's mad, you know. An ordinary man couldn't have done it. He had a great wound in his leg, and yet he managed to walk up near the lines and hide in a forest. Then he walked again into some sort of battle and hid again, and the Americans found him."

She continued to shiver. He got hold of her other hand. Fired by lust, he drew her to her feet.

"Not here."

He led her back into the shelves. There they ground desperately against each other for a moment, she with the back of her head against the works of George Borrow, in brown leather. He could read the titles across her shoulder: *Lavengro, Romany Rye.* Then she tried to push him off.

"We mustn't."

He went right ahead.

"Please stop. We mustn't now."

He tried to kiss her. She turned her face away.

"Please. Someone will come." She pushed at him again.

"Nobody comes." He got hold of her breasts and buried his face in them, the cashmere soft, the tweed less so.

"Oh, please."

"Tonight," he said.

"I can't. I'm going to London this afternoon."

"Tomorrow night, then."

"No. I'm bringing him back with me."

"When, then?" He had gotten his hands up inside her sweater, one around each breast. "Stop." He heard it, a faint breath, but she made no further effort to stop him. Her head was back against George Borrow, shoving back into the shelf. Her eyes were closed. He went for her mouth again and felt her fingers in his groin.

That was the moment crazy Pamela chose to enter the library. Of all the crazy moments for a crazy woman to pick—but she picked it. The door handle clicked, and they sprang apart.

Again, thinking it over—over and over, so many times, so much later—he wondered what might have happened if it hadn't been for that interruption. He had her going. In spite of herself, she was going. She had tried feebly to stop him; he was aware of that in some level of himself but disregarded it in the larger, roaring need to push ahead. She had resisted, but she was breaking down, and he was too fiercely pursuing that breaking down to consider that her resistance might have been caused by something more than a feeling that the floor of the library was a poor place for what they both knew would happen. For years afterward he followed her down to the floor in his mind. He knew where the buttons of her skirt were. He had watched her undo them. He could smell the wax on the floor and the varnish on the shelves. But Pamela stopped all that.

"Vi?" A scream.

A pink glow was coming through the yellow in her face, giving it an odd color. She tucked in her sweater, bit her lip, and walked to the front of the library.

"Oh, there you are. I just popped in."

He could hear her pull out her chair and its small creak as she sat down.

"Do you want a book?" she said. Her voice seemed steady enough.

"I thought I'd look about a bit. I've been needing something to read."

"Do you want to join?"

"Join?"

"Since you've never been here in your life before, I don't suppose you can be expected to know that it's two pounds to join before you take out a book."

"Oh." A shriek. "Oh. Then I'd best look about a bit first. Do you charge for that?"

"No."

"Whose jeep is that outside?"

"It belongs to one of the captains from the air base."

"Where is he?"

"In the shelves, I expect."

He plucked out a volume of George Borrow and began to read it.

"Why, Captain. Ha ha ha."

"Hello." He went to the front of the library. The pink had gone from her face. She looked long and sad and exhausted. "I'll take this one," he said, and she began hunting for his card as Pamela followed him out of the shelves with another of her shrieks.

"Vi, I hear Robert's escaped."

"Yes."

"And has been recovering in hospital. How marvelous," she screamed.

"It's not marvelous."

"What on earth . . . ?"

"He could have waited for the war to end and walked home like any sensible man."

"But he's back."

"He had to be a hero and get himself wounded."

"But he's here, *now*," Pamela screamed. "He'll get better. He must, if you're bringing him home. He'll be good as new with the good air here."

"Not good. No good to himself. No good to anybody." She looked Pamela up and down with hatred. "No good even to you."

"Whatever do you mean?"

"He has only one leg now. They cut off the other one."

She handed him his book.

With another of Pamela's screams in his ear, he headed for the door and McNally's jeep. Somehow Pamela arrived there at the same time he did.

"Are you going back to the base, Captain?"

"Yes."

"Could you just drop me off. It's right on your way. Ever so kind. Ha ha ha."

He handed her into the jeep. Lost a leg? And when she asked him

101

to stop in for a cup of tea, he dazedly accepted. Only one leg? He supposed he should feel sorry for the bastard, but he was seething with lust, a brutal, truncated, consuming, mind-blotting lust. She got out a tiny low table for the tea things and a rather high chair for herself, so that when she leaned over the table to pour the tea, she also served up a good look at her breasts, dangling inside her dress like a pair of bells. He stared at them, thinking not of them but of another pair, whose tips, the only time he had seen them, looked dark in candlelight, not pink. They had been in his hands not five minutes before. He could still feel them there, and he tightened his fingers around the hard hot round teacup to feel them better. He looked at Pamela's face to see if she had noticed that movement of his fingers, that involuntary tightening, but she was looking at his pants, which were clearly betraying his feelings. Not for her, though, not for her. Her eyes were fastened on his pants, and a soft look was beginning to spread around her mouth. She gave those pink bells an almost imperceptible jiggle—or didn't she? Maybe he imagined it. Anyway, she was obviously expecting some sort of reaction, but he continued to sit and stare, feeling coarse and brutal and angry and choked with desire. She stared at his pants some more and then looked up at him, and he said as coarsely as he could: "Who's going to make the first grab?"

"I beg your pardon."

"Do I grab yours or do you grab mine?"

Up on her feet with that copyrighted shriek. "Captain!" She was getting her blast, whatever it was. He was aware of a grin of outrage and satisfaction as he left.

If he had only managed in the library. He knew he could have; she was on the way. And if she had gone once, just once, she would have gone again, he knew that. Either in the back of the library, right there on the floor, or off somewhere in McNally's jeep—the weather was getting warmer. In the woods somewhere; he would bring a blanket. Or London; he'd take her to London. Somewhere. Anywhere. Again and again. He knew.

But he hadn't, and now she wouldn't. He was back in the library for one more try.

"I can't now." The desk between them. Her long sad stony face between them.

"You said—"

"Not now. He's helpless. He won't do anything. He has a wheelchair, but he won't even turn the wheels. I have to push him about from room to room."

"He'll learn. When he gets his strength back."

"He won't. He doesn't eat. He stares at me at the table, so that I can't eat, either. He hates me. He hates himself. He's gotten very small. I think it's only hatred that keeps him alive."

"Maybe he'll die."

"If only he would. My God, what am I saying?"

"But if he does?"

"No, I can't. Please go. Don't come here."

"But if something should happen, will you call me at the base?"

She picked up a bunch of index cards and began stacking them with long shaking fingers. They exploded over the desk. She tried to gather them again.

"Or after, even. Here." He took one of the cards and wrote on it:

Frederick C. Fay
c/o Dixon
81 East 71st Street
New York, N.Y., U.S.A.

"Such a lot of numbers," she said.

"You can reach me there."

"What does C stand for?"

"Curzon."

"That's a nice name."

"You can write me there."

She got up.

"Will you write?"

"Please go. I can't stand any more of this."

So, as she herself might have put it, with the directness and freedom, the boldness, that at first had so startled him and then so enchanted him, he never did get his cock into Violet Few-Strang. The war was winding down, and there wasn't as much to do. He spent a good deal of time drinking with McNally, sitting in McNally's hut and slowly deliberately getting drunk. He thought of her all the time, of her body and her dark eyes and dark hair. He was consumed by her. He wondered about her own desires and how she was handling them, and that consumed him even more. He drank with McNally nearly every night, which fuzzed up his feelings somewhat, blunted their aim, broadened them into a wide angry generalized hunger sufficiently strong for McNally to be able to persuade him to go to London again. McNally had dug up Faye and Alice and magnanimously offered him Faye. For some perverse degrading drunken self-hating furious reason of his own, he picked Alice.

The first woman he ever made it with was Alice, although he couldn't be sure of that; he was too drunk to remember.

Hennerkop asked him if he could make any connection between the events of that time and later ones in which obsessive drinking and obsessive chasing after disgusting (his word, not Hennerkop's) women were linked.

He couldn't seem to make any. "Here it's been more loneliness. I felt I had to have somebody. I didn't choose disgusting women. They were the best I could get."

"Were you not lonely in England?"

"I've always been lonely. I keep telling you that."

"You just now indicated that you were more lonely here."

"I know more here. I know more now. Up until her, I didn't know how lonely I was."

Silence.

"After her, in England, I was more angry than lonely."

"Angry about what?"

"Everything. I was angry at that stupid woman who interrupted us that time. I was angry at that stupid husband. Sometimes I was even angry at her."

"Why were you angry?"

"That's a stupid question. Wouldn't you have been angry?"

"I was not there."

"Well, whether you were there or not . . . It would have made anyone . . . It was hopeless, can't you understand? I kept feeling angry. I was so angry I didn't care what I did, whether I got dirty or not. I wanted to get dirty. I treated Alice dirty. She disgusted me, and I didn't even try to hide it. I made her cry. She was drunk too, but not so drunk she couldn't see I was disgusted with her. I *wanted* her to see."

"Yes. You have explained very well how you expressed your anger, but you have not said why you were angry."

"That's plain enough."

Silence.

"Look. There was this woman, this fantastic woman. We wanted each other. We were hot for each other. The first—the first time in my life anything decent ever happened to me. I didn't have to worry and struggle and pretend. I didn't have to pretend anything. She was *right there*."

Silence.

"I never had a decent woman. I still haven't had one."

Silence.

"Well . . . maybe one."

The Germans surrendered, and the big question for everybody became: Will I be sent to the Pacific? He was sure he would be. He was unmarried, in good health, uninjured, and his 201 file was stuffed with commendations from his various commanding officers, each of them bent on solidifying himself when he took over, each anxious to leave a good taste when he left. The group was commended. Everybody was commended. McNally made lieutenant colonel. The pilots and crews left, the planes with them, and he waited for the order that would carry him off. But he hadn't counted on the sheer size of the American air forces in Europe. Bases all over England were being packed up. There wasn't room at home for that mass exit. When his order came, it was to a blimp base in Massachusetts, the naval air station at South Weymouth. The Pacific war being a combined naval and air one, it was decided that some orientation in combined operations was needed for intelligence officers trained only in strategic bombing in Europe. So he was parked in South Weymouth while some other people somewhere began to organize the course.

He had scarcely arrived in South Weymouth when the Japanese surrendered. He spent one sunny autumn month watching the blimps blunder up to their mooring masts. The course never started. The navy didn't want him. They sent him to Washington, and Washington discharged him.

11

H E HEADED STRAIGHT FOR SEVENTY-FIRST STREET.
"My God, *Fred!*"
This time he was more in.

He had saved most of his pay throughout the war and had nearly four thousand dollars in the bank. He moved downstairs to John Burchard's old room. He and Bob Dixon and Walker Virdonette were the only members of the old crowd left. The *old crowd!* Now the three of them had not only that in common (a couple of new men had come in to occupy the room the Ransome twins had had), but they also shared the experience of the war. Fletcher sensed the change, along with improvements in his wardrobe, and became more deferential. It occurred to him one evening that he might be able to measure all his progress by how Fletcher treated him: a piece of human litmus paper.

The Ransomes didn't come back. Wally had been killed on the carrier *Lexington,* and Wendell, his identical twin, was bewildered by that loss; it was as if one of his legs had been removed. He looked at Wendell for an instant with hatred, thinking of that other one-legged man whom he hated, but by the time he had identified the source of the hate, Wendell had become himself again, a sad man coming to collect his and Wally's things and take them away.

Bob missed the Ransomes keenly. He had been their close friend since boyhood. Except for that, everything at Seventy-first Street was better than before. Much better. He was beginning to feel in at last.

His job at W and W was waiting for him. He had his uniform pressed and had his ribbons on, and he pinned on the most tarnished pair of captain's bars he could find, to make it look as if he had been a captain for a long time and didn't really care that much about rank anyway. Then he checked in at the office and was told that Wilking was in Washington but would be back that afternoon. Better stick around and check in with him; he liked to talk to everybody personally when they came out of the service.

To his astonishment, Wilking was in uniform too. A chicken colonel. And a chestful of ribbons: European Theater, Southeast Asia, Pacific, Legion of Merit, Legion of Honor, one or two he didn't recognize. Wilking explained to him that he had not been able to sit by when there was work to be done. He had been "called to Washington," as he put it, to act as a top-level public relations adviser to various air force commands around the world. "They were not always projecting the right image." He looked very impressive, but what impressed most was the speed with which he had touched all the bases and collected all those ribbons. Now, in addition to everything else, he was a much-decorated war veteran, a confidant and adviser to generals, a middle-aged man who, despite his age, had exposed himself to danger in many combat theaters.

"I would have liked to help Chennault," Wilking said, looking out of his window. "He needed help. He wasn't getting along too well with Chiang, and he wasn't getting along at all well with Stilwell. And he wasn't getting along with Roosevelt, either, which of course made him resistant to advice from Washington." All by way of explaining why he had no Chinese decorations; he hadn't been able to make it past the crusty Chennault to China. Aside from that, it was quite a job. It was clear once again that much could be learned from Fenn R. Wilking.

He played down his own war experience. "Combat intelligence," he would say. " ETO. Eighth Bomber Command." He never actually said that he had flown missions, but left the impression that that was all in the day's work for a combat intelligence officer in the Eighth Bomber Command. The very word "combat" was a good one. It suggested that he had been right in there fighting, and that his work, intelligence, had been of a secret and daring kind.

Bob had been an admiral's aide. His good looks and his charm and his social qualifications—and his wealth—all made that inevitable. He had another asset; he was a strong bridge player. His admiral liked high-stakes bridge and liked to have as a partner an aide who played as well as he did—actually better.

"He's good?" he asked Walker Virdonette as he was standing around one evening watching one of the bridge games that had already begun again in the Seventy-first Street house.

"He's good, all right. But he's not as good as she is," pointing to Julia Fanshawe, who was coming around again for bridge and with whom Bob had begun to play in duplicate tournaments. "She's a shark."

He watched her deft fingers raking in the cards and neatly stacking them in front of her, trick after trick without even having to look to see how she placed them, because she had done it so many times before, with such confidence and skill, that she no longer had to think about it. He was reminded of other hands, so hopelessly out of control that they couldn't keep library cards from scattering over a desk. Little things like that would come and go, but they were coming less often. She was moving farther away.

Having been reminded of her by Julia Fanshawe's hands, he looked at Julia Fanshawe's face and found other things to remind him. They looked vaguely alike. Both were tall and pale and had long faces and thin noses and dark eyes. But Julia was less tall and less pale and had a less thin nose. She was a scaled-down version, better-looking but less desirable because she was lacking in intensity and stillness. Despite her cool dexterity at the bridge table, she was a fidgety woman who, when the hand was over, began picking imaginary bits of fluff from her clothes. At intervals all evening long she did that. She would bend her head down and search . . . then pick. She had small breasts. He found himself wondering if she had dark nipples.

"That may have been why I started going around with her."

Silence.

"I don't mean the nipples. That was just, you know, talk. An idle thought."

"No thought is idle."

"Well, in this case it was. It was the general resemblance that caught me. Although it may not have been that, either." How could it be? Violet seemed to be receding too fast.

What really drew him to Julia was that she was so completely up there that she didn't even seem to notice it. Like Bob, she had money, but apparently she had more of it—or at least was fastened to more of it—and had had it longer. She was related to people all over New York, some with Dutch names like Bleecker and Schermerhorn and Schuyler. Streets and squares in New York were named after her ancestors. After a few evenings with her—a couple of movies, one Princeton hockey game at the Garden (to which he took her because Walker Virdonette had played on the hockey team and had got free seats), and one dinner at her house—he began to realize that, as in clothes, there were circles within circles in New York. The people who were rushing off to the Stork Club and getting their pictures in the paper were considered trash by people like Julia, particularly by Julia's mother.

His job went okay, fairly okay. He was put to work for Bill Livingston, who worked for Mr. Klein, who worked for Mr. Wright. Bill Livingston was not easy to work for, because he was nervous and insecure and shouted a lot. The shouting was because Bill wasn't all that sure about what he was doing and needed a strong bright able young man under him to do his work and his thinking for him.

Since he was also nervous and insecure and not sure about what he was doing—or what Bill Livingston ought to be doing—he was pretty tense most of the time. The difference between Bill Livingston and himself was that Bill showed it and he didn't. At least he thought he didn't. He was working on his image, not saying much, being watchful, being cool. He had Bill Livingston fooled. It was only when Mr. Wright (whom he seldom saw but wished to see even less of) looked at him that he began to be doubtful about his image. Mr. Wright wasn't interested in images, although his life was dedicated to creating them for others. After the door was shut and the client gone and the shade pulled down and it was just the troops in their fatigues, there were no such things as images with Mr. Wright. There was only work, and results.

Otherwise things went well. They had started him at a hundred and fifty a week when he got out of the service. Soon he was raised to two hundred, then to three hundred. That was fifteen thousand dollars a year! He decided he could afford to take a few dancing lessons in case he was ever asked to any of the balls and dances that Bob and the others kept going to.

"That's it. Relax."

That's it? That was what Violet had said when— Holy Christ. His heart turned over. He wanted to run out of there.

"Relax a little. Just put your hand here. That's right. Now, one two. One two. Don't be so stiff. That's right. Never mind; everybody's foot gets stepped on. Relax a little. Guide me more, with this hand. Like this." And she masterfully steered him around the room, his snowshoe feet trying to follow.

Six lessons. She tried for twelve, but he knew now how to hold a girl. He knew how to plod around a room in time to music without walking on someone's feet. That, for him, would have to be dancing.

He decided to join the Princeton Club.

"Don't," said Bob.

"I've got a little more money now. I can afford a club."

"Don't join a crud club."

He explained that all he wanted was a nice place to take business people to lunch.

"If you're going to join a club, join a good one. There are four good clubs in New York: the Racquet, the Union, the Knickerbocker, and the Links. Oh, and the Brook, if all you want to do is eat."

The first of those was the only one he had ever heard of, and that was because Bob and Walker were both members and went there constantly to play court tennis. He decided to join. Bob put him up; Walker seconded him. Bob took him on a tour of offices in Wall Street, where he was introduced one by one to the members of the Membership Committee and at each of which there was a lot of handshaking and a minimum of polite careful conversation: oh, yes, Princeton, yes; track, of course, the mile, yes; the Eighth Bomber Command, yes.

Not long after that he got an engraved card in the mail stating that at the last meeting of the board he had been elected a member. Bob took him there for an introductory lunch.

"George, this is Mr. Fay, a new member. Treat him well."

"Yes, Mr. Dixon. Glad to meet you, Mr. Fay."

(In a few years, maybe: "George, this is Mr. Wilking, a new member. Treat him well." "Yes, Mr. Fay. Glad to meet you, Mr. Wilking." Well, why not?)

The dining room was big and airy, full of men who were up. After a delicious lunch, Bob showed him around. What a place! It had squash courts, racquets courts, court-tennis courts, a swimming pool, a gymnasium room, a steam room, a card room, a billiard room, a library, a huge lounge—and up men strolling around or sitting around or lying around, taking advantage of all the things this gentlemen's gilt-edged haven had to offer. There was a faint spicy aroma of fine cigars lingering in the lounge and in the lofty second-floor hall. There was a counter that dispensed twenty or thirty kinds of those fine cigars. There were crisp papers and magazines to be read. There were thick piles of thick towels in the third-floor dressing room and in the shower room, where members dried off and washed and changed and had cocktails after their games of squash and racquets and court tennis. The shower room was big enough to contain a long marble bench where one could sit and dry one's toes. When he got around to sitting there himself, he sometimes wondered how many thousand bare bottoms of really up men had spread themselves on that marble bench.

The shower room also contained a large old-fashioned scale, the kind that had a bar and a sliding weight. Next to it was a lectern holding an enormous alphabetized ledger where members could record their weights after exercising. They all wrote their initials, and when he got around to using the shower, he did too, finding a blank page and inscribing: "FCF 2.12.48, 151." He scarcely ever used the shower room, because he played none of the racquets games for which the club was famous, and he never got his name on the wall of the cavernous dressing room, where large wooden plaques announced in gold letters the winners of various tournaments going back for thirty or forty years. But he did get his initials in the weight book in the shower room. Bob's name had already appeared several times on the court-tennis plaques; he was very good at that game. He practiced daily and once confessed that his secret ambition was to become the world champion in that esoteric sport, played really well by not more than fifty men in the United States, England, and Australia.

"It's the sport of kings," Bob told him. "Henry the Eighth was very good at it." Bob could well afford to devote time to the game. He worked at Dixon Estates, a real estate company that managed holdings in New York belonging to his family, and his duties were light. Walker Virdonette, on the other hand, worked very hard. He was also in the real estate business, but in a different way. He devoted himself to acquiring property on behalf of groups of wealthy clients who avoided taxes by writing down the buildings and then selling them at large profits. It was never clear to him exactly how Walker did this, but he apparently was getting rich. Bob was one of his small circle of clients and presumably was getting even richer himself as a result of that connection. Walker had chosen a nice name for his company: Greenwillow Management.

The Racquet Club's colors were blue and red, and he immediately bought a club tie of diagonal blue and red stripes. What a fabulous place. What a terrific feeling to go strolling in there from Park Avenue, although there wasn't all that much for him to do once he got inside. He never felt really at home there. He never got to know more than a handful of members. Also, whatever he did there cost money. For a while he couldn't afford to do anything there except belong.

He took Julia to the movies again and she asked him to dinner again and he met her mother again, a strikingly handsome woman with bluish hair, considerably smaller than Julia but of an imposing erectness. Julia appeared to be a little intimidated by her and plucked a good many bits of fluff from herself between courses. There was no Mr. Fanshawe.

The Fanshawe house was smaller than the Dixon house but more elegant. It was of pale-red brick, with black shutters and a marble doorway. There were black window boxes with ivy in all the windows. Inside, it was more elegant too. There was no Fletcher, but there were maids, two of them. The food was better.

Julia had a black cocker spaniel named Snuggles, who seemed to like having his head scratched. Snuggles kept poking him with his nose, so he scratched him a lot.

"Snuggles, go lie down. He's a nuisance."

"I don't mind."

"Do you like dogs?" asked Mrs. Fanshawe. "Animals?"

"Yes."

"Perhaps I can interest you in some of the volunteer work being done for the ASPCA."

"Mother," said Julia.

"If you'll give me your name and address, I'll send you some of our material."

"Mother, I don't think he—"

Mrs. Fanshawe ignored her. "We need active interested younger people."

He had no interest in the ASPCA, but it did give him a chance to get out the black leather memo-card case he had recently bought and with his thin gold pencil write his address on one of the cards. His name was engraved at the top: Frederick C. Fay. In black ink, not gray. He sensed that here black was better than gray. She studied it.

"What does C stand for?" she asked.

Violet again! Out of nowhere. How could he prepare himself for things he couldn't dream were coming? Would it never stop?

"Curzon," he managed to say.

"Are you related to Floyd Curzon?"

He shook his head.

"Most of the Curzons are English. Are you related to them?"

"I don't know. It's my mother's name."

"I expect she would know," said Mrs. Fanshawe.

"Mother's very interested in genealogy," explained Julia.

"I'm surprised you haven't asked her," said Mrs. Fanshawe.

"She's dead."

"Oh, I'm so sorry."

"It's all right. She died eight years ago."

"Where did she come from?"

"Connecticut."

"Where in Connecticut?"

"Mother—"

"Cheshire."

She paid no attention. "And your father, is he living?"

"No, he's dead too. He was a clergyman."

"An Episcopalian?"

"Mother."

"She likes to place people," explained Julia. They were coming home together from the theater in Mrs. Fanshawe's limousine. They had been driven there after dinner, and the chauffeur was waiting when they came out. He felt very grand, with everybody else whistling and waving for taxis. He sank back into the deep soft seat, a glass panel between them and the chauffeur.

"She sometimes grills people. You mustn't mind."

"I don't mind."

How could he, sitting in this soft dark limousine with this elegant up girl? His parents were gone, safely buried. What would she think of them, of his mother in her old green sweater? He turned to look at her, catching just the side of her face, which seemed from that angle to be longer and thinner than it really was and, in the darkness of the car, paler. What does *C* stand for? He had another dizzying moment of feeling that he was somewhere else. He had to look away—at the back of the chauffeur's head, with its gray cap that matched the upholstery of the limousine swimming silently uptown like a big black fish. It was warm in there, and even if it hadn't been, there was a fur lap robe hanging over a braided rope in front of them, over the jump seats. The jeep had been cold and noisy, with cold hard little seats and cold air swirling in. What does *C* stand for? The differences and the distances were too great. He felt the legs of his brain being spread too wide. Forget it. Come back. He looked again for reassurance, and again saw that desolate pale slice of face. Without further thought or knowledge of what he was doing, he leaned over and tried to kiss that face.

He got her on the cheek.

She drew back and turned her face directly toward his. The illusion vanished.

She drew back, and yet she didn't. She seemed to come forward a little, but she didn't do that, either. He was left with a blurred feeling that she was waiting for him to kiss her again. Woefully unsure, he willed himself to try again, this time catching her on the mouth.

She let him.

She pursed her lips gently. He pressed against them. She pressed gently back. He put his hand on her breast, that is to say, on her mink coat where her breast was. She let him do that too, but when he tried to slide his hand inside she removed it.

On her doorstep: "Well, uh, good night. That was a good show. And thanks for the dinner too."

"Yes, it was, wasn't it."

He was shaking her hand, seeming stuck there, unable to let go. She gave his a couple of nervous squeezes.

"Well, uh . . . "

"Yes, it was, wasn't it."

She seemed to be waiting to be kissed again, so he gave her another, getting another chaste puckery one in return.

Walking home, he began to wonder if he could ever aspire to marry this girl.

She liked him, that was obvious. He saw numerous movies with her that winter, gradually became more and more attracted to her. She was friendly, although a bit cool, was good-looking and oh so elegant. Taking her home afterward, he would kiss her in the vestibule of her house. They kissed a lot, and he tried from time to time to put his hand on her, but she prevented him. She did, gradually, let him press his body discreetly against hers. It was a confused and perilous scene. Desires were crowding up in him, shoving him toward a grossness that was clearly unacceptable. He felt clumsy and shy and hot and frustrated. His hands felt big and awkward and dangerous. He had a hard time with his hands. Maybe she was shy too; he couldn't tell. He wanted to touch her but was afraid to try too hard. Still, he did try, and was rebuffed. She had a prim mouth, but it was softening. He was afraid of those evenings, but he looked forward to them as his affection and desire grew. Sometimes they would spend half an hour in the vestibule, holding hands a good deal of the time because she held his hand to prevent it from holding her in some place where she didn't want to be held.

He tried to soften her up with longer kisses and further discreet pressing.

"Please," he whispered.

She took his hand away.

He tried to put it back. "Please. Why not?"

"We're not engaged."

"Well—uh—Would . . . ?"

"Yes."

*   *   *

My God, engaged?

Tell Bob? Get married? Holy mackerel? Did she mean it? Get married to *her*? He took her to the movies again the next night, and in the vestibule he asked her: "Did you mean it?"

"Yes."

He kissed her hungrily and went for her breasts.

"Not here."

Not here? *Not here.* An overpowering whiff of recollected kerosene and varnish. *Not here.* It bellowed its way through his head. Was it never going to stop? He let go of her.

"I mean, shouldn't we tell Mother?"

12

JULIA WANTED A SMALL WEDDING, WHICH SUITED him fine. When Mrs. Fanshawe asked him for a list of names of people he wanted to invite, he came up with six: Bob Dixon, Walker Virdonette, the two new men who had moved into the house, and Mr. Wilking and Mr. Wright. He had thought hard about the last two, wondering if it wasn't sucking up too much to ask his bosses, too obvious a sucking up since he wasn't asking anybody else at the office. Not Bill Livingston, for instance, his immediate boss. He was already beginning to get the impression that Bill Livingston was a loser at W and W. Also he wasn't sure about Bill's stentorian nervous voice. But he couldn't ask just four people, so he finally decided to risk it with Mr. Wilking and Mr. Wright.

"I don't want a lot of bridesmaids," said Julia.

She asked Mary Smallwood, her best friend, to be her maid of honor. He asked Bob to be his best man.

"Is that all?" asked Mrs. Fanshawe when she saw his list of six names.

"I haven't lived here very long. I don't know very many people."

"But your relatives."

"I haven't any."

"What about your two uncles?"

"What uncles?"

Mrs. Fanshawe gave him a funny look and then said: "You don't know about your uncles?"

"How do you know about them?" asked Julia.

"Why, I looked them up. When Fred said his mother came from Cheshire. Honestly, I've never met anyone who had so little curiosity about his own family. Do you mean to say you've never heard of your uncle George Curzon or your uncle Frederick? They're in the church records in Cheshire, along with your mother and your grandparents. I suppose you're named after your uncle Frederick. You don't even know about him?"

"No."

"Perhaps you have a lot of cousins. You should look them up."

"Maybe I will." He had no intention of ever doing that.

They were married in St. James' Church on Madison Avenue. There was a reception afterward at the Colony Club. Their honeymoon was spent on a hunting plantation in Georgia belonging to Mr. Bishop, Mrs. Fanshawe's brother. Their wedding night was spent going there, in very narrow Pullman berths.

"Not here," Julia said.

The next morning they got off the train in Pineland, Georgia. A station wagon was waiting for them, and they were driven for miles through flat stands of scrub pine to Mr. Bishop's place, Oronoque. Two gigantic live oak trees shaded a rambling white wooden building with a screen porch running around it, and many rocking chairs, and six or seven black servants standing in a row on the steps. Much smiling and giggling; Julia had been there often before, and they were consumed with curiosity and delight by her new husband. He was shown their room, with a large double bed in it.

At last.

He pulled her down on the bed, where they hugged and kissed for a bit until she said that maybe they should both get into comfortable clothes and take a walk around the place. "Maybe we shouldn't shoot today after that long night on the train."

"Okay."

"I'll have to tell Irving. He'll be waiting with the dogs. Maybe we should just stroll around. It's very pretty here. Then practice this afternoon with a few clay pigeons. I haven't shot for a year."

That was fine with him. He put on his new Abercrombie & Fitch shooting boots, which laced up his leg, and they went for a walk. They stopped at the kennels and talked to Irving and looked at eight or nine pointers crowding against the wire, whining, licking, trying to get their noses through. They strolled down an avenue of live oaks hand in hand. The air was balmy and very soft, the sun hazy. Long beards of Spanish moss were dangling from the live oak branches. He was reminded of *Gone With the Wind*.

After lunch they took their guns into the gun room. His was his wedding present from Mrs. Fanshawe and had belonged to her husband before his death. He snapped open the slim brown cowhide case and looked inside. There, neatly compartmented in dark-green velvet, was the gun. In three pieces, along with a ramrod also in three pieces, together with small bottles and objects made of wire and wool, whose purpose he didn't understand. Each had its own velvet compartment.

"That was Daddy's favorite gun," said Julia. "Holland and Holland. It's a beauty."

It was stunning. Its stock was dark and shiny, inset with a small oval piece of metal with her father's initials engraved on it. The metal sides of the stock were also engraved, with curlicues and hunting dogs and flying pheasants. But he didn't know how to put it together.

"You've never shot a gun?"

"No."

She showed him how to assemble it, how to load and break it, which trigger shot which barrel. "I don't know how it will fit you. But Daddy was about your size. He liked a gun without too much drop. I do too."

Julia was a good shot and a patient and determined teacher. She made him practice bringing the gun up to his shoulder, quick and smooth, pressing it tight into his shoulder, leaning forward, swinging his body, swinging through the bird.

Standing there in the sunny gun room in the soft southern air, he swung right around and tried to embrace her, the gun standing up between them like a metal fence post. She blushed and laughed. She was really very pretty. "Not here, silly. You have to learn how to handle this gun."

They went outside together.

"Now, when I say 'Pull,' the bird will fly. Remember to bring the gun up tight, safety off, lean forward, swing through, lead it slightly, don't jerk, squeeze."

They were in a field behind the plantation house, a black man crouching in the grass next to a small machine.

"Pull."

A round object the size of a butter plate sprang from the grass and went whizzing across the sky. He pointed his gun at it and pulled the trigger. Nothing happened.

"You left the safety on. Remember to push it off just before you raise the gun. Try another."

A second clay pigeon was released. This time he got the safety off and pulled the trigger. There was a loud crash, and the gun went slamming into his shoulder, hurting it. The pigeon landed intact, some distance off.

"You must hold the gun tighter. Take up the shock with your entire body. Try one without any bird. Just shoot."

"At what?"

"At nothing. Just get the feel of swinging the gun and holding it tight and pulling the trigger."

He practiced, trying to master the complex business of releasing the safety, getting the gun to his shoulder, aiming at the streaking bird, and pulling the trigger. Bird after bird flew by untouched.

"I don't see how you hit those things."

"That's because you're poking at them. Swing the gun through them and squeeze as you swing."

She demonstrated, and the clay pigeon became a cloud of black dust hanging in the air. *Bap.* Just like that: a moving object one instant; the next, nothing. He couldn't help thinking of bombers. He tried again, and again, finally hitting a couple. His shoulder ached, and his ears were ringing. He was given instruction in how to take his gun apart and clean it lovingly with an aromatic liquid from one of the little bottles, running a round cloth cleaner up and down in each barrel ("That's called a patch," said Julia), then a light oil, then wiping it carefully all over and putting it away in its jewel case.

After dinner they worked on a jigsaw puzzle.

"They have wonderful puzzles here," said Julia. There were about fifteen of them in boxes on a shelf. She picked one, opened up a card table, and they concentrated hard on the squiggly little pieces for about an hour. The air gradually got tenser. He stopped looking at pieces and looked at Julia's body. She moved faster and more deftly. "Look, this whole edge fits here."

"How long are we going to do this?"

"You don't like puzzles?"

"When are we going to bed?"

"Well, I'm tired too."

In the bedroom he reached for her.

"Wait. Shouldn't we get washed and undressed?"

He went into the bathroom. When he came out, she was in the bed. He started to take off his things.

"Please turn the light off."

In the dark, he put on his pajamas and climbed in beside her. She let him kiss her. She let him fondle her breast. She kept his hand outside her nightgown. He grappled and fumbled at her, kissing, sometimes getting kissed in return, sometimes not. She kept taking his hands away and trying to put them around her back. To protect herself, she pressed close against him, which only aroused him more.

"What's the matter?" he asked.

"What? Nothing."

"Don't be scared."

"I'm not."

"Well, then—"

"No. Please."

"What's the matter?"

"Nothing. It's only—I'm not used—"

"You ought to enjoy—"

"I will. I'm not used—"

"Let's get used."

"All right. But not so quick. Let's get used—"

He tried to get her used to his hand on her breast. He held it there quietly for a bit, and she seemed relieved by that.

"We're married, you know."

"I know. It's just that I'm not used—"

"Don't you like to kiss me?"

"Oh, yes, I do like to kiss you. It's just—"

"Well, let's kiss a little."

"I just don't like to talk about it."

So he stopped talking (or rather whispering, for the conversation of that night was conducted in tense whispers) and kissed instead. And the hand skirmishes continued, and she won them because, for Christ's sake, you can't use force. And when the mess came, Julia had to get up and change her nightgown.

The next day they shot. Irving was waiting outside with two dogs in a wire cage in the back of the station wagon. When they came out of the bungalow, the dogs saw them and began whining and surging in their cage, and Irving fetched it a whack on the side and said shut up, and they did.

Two horses were brought around by a black groom. Irving was white. He was the dog handler and manager.

"This side," said Julia.

He watched how she mounted and did what she did. Riding was easy. You sat on the horse and it walked down dirt roads and grassy tracks, skirting cornfields and patches of pinewoods. A nice pleasant motion that worked his spine backward and forward, and he was reminded of something else but banished it. As the morning grew, the horse got hot and a strong horsey smell came from its brown hairs, dusty-shiny in the sun. That smell, and the smell of the pines, and the smell of leather and his gun, and that indescribably sweet soft southern air, like nothing he had ever smelled or felt before—that part, the riding part, was wonderful. The shooting wasn't.

After a short ride, Irving let the dogs out of their cage, and they went tearing off into a cornfield. Back and forth they ran, Irving blowing a whistle from time to time.

"All raht," he said.

"Come on," said Julia. She got off her horse and looped the reins over a pine branch. He watched and did the same. She got her gun from the station wagon, put two shells in it, and closed it with a snap. So did he.

"Raht there," said Irving. A dog was standing with one paw raised and its head intently aimed forward. It was comically like all the pictures of hunting dogs he had ever seen.

"Come on," said Julia. "Walk up."

He walked toward the dog. It didn't move. He could see nothing in the weeds. "Where are they?"

"Go ahead," said Julia. "They're right there. You have to walk up to them."

He walked to within about eight feet of the dog. It didn't move. The brown stubble in which it was standing was only a few inches high. There was nothing there. He clutched his gun and looked.

"Go on."

He took another step, and the stubble erupted with large chestnut-colored bumblebees, hurtling in all directions. He was so astonished by the noise and the suddenness that he did nothing.

"Everybody does that the first time," said Julia.

On the next point she stepped up. The birds rose again with that heart-whacking suddenness. Julia's gun rose with them. *Bap bap.* Both barrels. So quick. One bird fell. The dog, at the sound of her gun, went racing off, and in a minute or two, with some encouragement from Irving, came back with a dead quail in its mouth.

During the rest of that day, and the following days of the week at Oronoque, he shot quail, or tried to. He never saw the birds on the ground, no matter how hard he looked. He never knew which way they would go when they jumped. They worked the coveys together, walking slowly up to the pointing dog. She would get one, and he would miss. He would aim his gun at random into that swarm of bees and fire. She would get another, and he would miss again.

"You can't just shoot blindly into a crowd. You have to pick one out and follow it."

Each time he missed, he got a patient look from Irving.

He developed a murderous hatred for those whizzing little bodies.

121

"It takes practice."

He wanted to kill them all. In the end he got only three. Julia got more than twenty. And of the three he got, when he looked at their rumpled little bodies, he wasn't sure he wanted to have got those.

After a dinner of quail—he was ravenously hungry, and even two of them didn't satisfy him with their miniature drumsticks and bones of mice—they did some more work on the jigsaw puzzle. He worked on the sky and managed to fit together a fairly large piece.

"Aren't you sleepy?" he asked.

"Well, yes, all right."

"We walked a lot today."

"Yes, I'm tired too."

Inside the bedroom door, he held her, trying to urge her body against his. She had a dress that unbuttoned down the back, and he started to undo the buttons.

"I'll wash first," she said, going into the bathroom. Beginning to feel increasingly self-conscious, he hurried into his pajamas before she came out again. When she did emerge, she had a small towel in her hand. She put it under the pillow and then turned off the light.

Julia was like a mast in the bed.

He got the feeling that her teeth were clenched. He gently stroked her, hoping to rouse the nipple, but all he succeeded in rousing was himself. He kissed her ear. He kissed her cheek and mouth. Driving along now, he couldn't tell if she was responding or not. He mashed his mouth against hers. She wrenched it away. "Here," she whispered, handing him the towel.

During his honeymoon he never did manage to get his cock into Julia Fanshawe Fay. Not even close. In fact, "cock" got to be a sort of dirty word in his mind. He would not have dreamed of saying it aloud to her. He didn't refer to it at all, not as "him" or "it," not as anything. She seemed to prefer to pretend that it didn't exist. And at night, getting ready for bed, when it stuck out in his pajamas (as it invariably did), he kept his back to her, although there wasn't much point to that, because while the light was on in the bedroom she wouldn't look at him.

He slept very little, kept awake by a jabbing desire. Julia, he imagined, did not sleep, either. By the end of the week both were exhausted. On the last day he said that his shoulder hurt so much that he wondered if it would be all right if they didn't shoot. "Of course," she said, and they spent the rest of the day on the puzzle. By working hard they got it done just before supper, and they left it triumphantly on the card table for Mr. Bishop to see the next week when he came down—to see what a fine job he and Julia had done with that exceptionally large and difficult puzzle. Then they had an early supper, were driven to the station, and caught the night train back to New York.

Although he didn't like shooting and never learned to do it well, he would go back to Oronoque three times. Bob and Walker loved to shoot. And when Mr. Bishop offered the place for another week the following year, a party of six was organized to include his two friends and Julia's friend Mary Smallwood. The sixth was Walker's girl, Irene George. Every day, all went shooting except Irene, who sat on the veranda or took short walks by herself. In the evening there was bridge. Irene read a magazine. He did jigsaw puzzles.

On those later visits, he and Julia had another room, with twin beds. Irene got the room with the big bed, and although nothing was ever said, he was sure that Walker was spending his nights in it with her. Irene was a very sexy girl. The following year Walker asked a girl named Kitty, who, like Irene, neither shot nor played bridge but was also sexy and was also up. The year after, it was Irene again. He never quite figured that one out. With a girl like Irene, who would want to change? Walker never volunteered anything about either of them, and he never felt quite comfortable enough with him to ask.

After the honeymoon Julia and he never slept in the same bed together again. It was almost a relief to get back to the new apartment in Sutton Place and find the twin beds there. They were no surprise. He had been in and out of the place half a dozen times during their engagement to say yes that chintz is nice and yes that curtain is nice while Julia was having it furnished and decorated. He just never thought about the beds. After they had discussed the size of the apartment (A spare room? Yes, I agree, we may have guests), its cost, and its location, and after he had agreed that it was okay for Julia to pay for it, he was happy to have his smart-looking intelligent up fiancée handle the furnishing and the decorating and come up with (as he knew she would) a smart-looking up apartment.

It was a beautiful apartment, no question, with a wide living room window overlooking the river and banked with houseplants. Walking in and out of the building, aware of how much it cost and how exclusive it was, saying good morning and good evening to the doorman, felt even better than walking in and out of the Racquet Club.

On the surface, he and Julia were a successful happy young couple. And except for the frustrations of bed—which, for all he knew, other husbands might be enduring—things weren't bad. He was more solid and in. He was moving up. He got a driver's license so that he could drive Julia's car, although he made her nervous in traffic and she ended up doing most of the driving. She lived a busy life. She played a lot of bridge. She worked hard for the ASPCA, gradually being nudged upward there by her mother. She was the youngest member of the board of governors of the Colony Club. She played golf.

Julia was not as good at golf as she was at bridge, but still she was very good. In summer they spent weekends at her mother's house in Lattingtown. Julia belonged to the Piping Rock Club (or rather he did, because husbands had to be members of record of that club regardless of the realities). Although he played neither golf nor tennis, he was glad to be a member, because Piping—it was always Piping to its members—was the best club on the north shore of Long Island, better than the Creek. The other clubs didn't count at all. Julia played golf at Piping on summer weekends. Sometimes he walked around with her. Sometimes he sat at Mrs. Fanshawe's and read. Sometimes he talked to Mrs. Fanshawe, more often than he would have liked about genealogy and his incomprehensible lack of interest in his relatives and ancestors.

On weekdays, in good weather, Julia often drove to Long Island to play golf with Mary Smallwood or in ladies' tournaments. Gradually the apartment began to fill up with glass ashtrays from Steuben with PRC engraved on them: golf and bridge trophies. They looked very smart with their paper matchbooks in them, the ones in shiny silver paper that Julia had ordered, with her initials on them in green. Julia kept the apartment immaculate and supervised the work of the maid, Dagmar, whom she hired and whom he saw only at breakfast and dinner. Dagmar lived next to the kitchen, in a room even smaller than the one he had first occupied at Bob Dixon's. Her bathroom was smaller too; the tub was so short that it was nearly square. But Dagmar didn't complain, or if she did, Julia took care of it.

13

IS WORK CONTINUED OKAY. IN FACT, IT IMPROVED.
Julia's mother commented again on what a nice man Mr.
Wilking was and wondered when she was going to meet him
again, so Julia asked them both for dinner. He was nervous and kept
quiet, but it went off okay. Although Julia picked imaginary bits of
fluff from herself quite a lot (she always seemed to do that more when
her mother was around), she also said some nice things, and Mr.
Wilking complimented her on the dinner and was oh so suave and
charming to Mrs. Fanshawe, and the two of them did most of the
talking.

Not long after that, Bill Livingston was fired and he got Bill's job.
His salary was raised to sixteen thousand dollars a year. Since part of
the job involved entertaining low-echelon clients, he began doing that
too, taking them to the Racquet Club for lunch. Now on an expense
account, he could charge the lunches off, also the cocktails that he
and the client would have in the big club bar, helping themselves to
the peanuts and cheese and crackers that were always on hand there.
He learned that one cocktail was okay but that two made him sleepy
during the afternoon. He tried to stick to one, but often the client
was a two-cocktail man, so he would go along with him, remembering that even if he did get sleepy he had his own assistant now, a
bright tough able young man from Yale named Corky Chalmers. In
due course, he supposed, Corky would discover what a crappy name
that was for a business executive and get back to Charlie, or even
Charles.

The only trouble with getting Bill Livingston's job was that he
also got more involved with Mr. Wright, which made him very nervous. Sometimes after a morning in Mr. Wright's office—which was

utterly unlike Mr. Wilking's; it had cork walls with things stuck to them by pushpins, and there was always a great deal going on in there, with many people, and things being pinned and unpinned on the walls, and he was sometimes asked for his opinion about something, and he always felt extremely tense in there—sometimes after one of those mornings he would go around to the Racquet Club by himself and have a drink just to unwind, occasionally a second one.

He learned not to say ambiguous things like "That might fly."

He said that once, and Mr. Wright said: "Fly where?"

"I mean, it might work."

"What I want to know," said Mr. Wright, "is *will* it work? Is this better or is this?"

He chose blindly. "That one."

"Why?"

"It's stronger."

"What's stronger about it?"

In some ways Mr. Wright was not unlike Hennerkop. He was just one hell of a lot rougher.

By luck he chose right that time. Other times he chose wrong. But it became clear that choosing wrong was better than waffling around and waiting and waiting and waiting until he was able to step unobtrusively aboard the winning train. Mr. Wright saw through that and took pleasure in pinning wafflers to the wall along with the layouts. In a nutshell, he was scared pissless of Mr. Wright. He would go over the presentation material ahead of time with Corky Chalmers, getting his opinions because he often had none of his own. How could he, when he had no interest whatsoever in presentations?

"Why did you do them if they did not interest you?"

"That's a stupid question." He had reached the point of being able to say that and enjoy it.

"Why is it stupid?"

"Because that's what my job was. You do your job. Anyway, that was the track to accounts. I figured that if I could hang in presentations long enough, and if I could depend on Corky, I might get directly into accounts and maybe work myself over into being under Mr. Wilking."

"You did that, did you not?"

"Yes. Finally into accounts."

"Was it more interesting?"

"Yes. I mean . . . You don't think of it as being more interesting.

126

It was much more of a prestige job, and I got paid a great deal more. I was able to keep Corky for a while."

Silence.

"It was much tenser."

Silence.

"I mean, I depended on Corky. If the account was lost, it was on me. I couldn't blame Corky."

Silence.

"I mean, I couldn't even trust Corky. I began to suspect that he was getting tired of me getting the credit for all his ideas. I began to suspect he might be feeding me bad ideas. He wanted my job."

"If you did not trust him, why did you keep him?"

"I needed him. Can't you understand that?"

Silence.

"Hennerkop, sometimes you're a dumb shit."

Shit? Holy Christ, how did that ever slip out?

Trust him to ask. He did.

He couldn't say.

He landed in accounts sooner than he expected. After a particularly tough morning in Mr. Wright's office, he was headed up Park Avenue alone, looking forward to that drink, when a man stopped him.

"Hey, aren't you Fred Fay?" A big man in the wrong suit.

"Yes."

"I'm Ebby Vogel. I guess you don't remember me."

He didn't.

"From track. I put the shot. I was two years behind you."

Now he did, vaguely. A big kid from the Middle West somewhere. His father was in the beer business and sent a keg of beer to the track team after it won the Yale meet.

"Ebby. Sure. I just didn't recognize you in your store clothes." They shook hands. "What brings you to New York?"

"The old man sent me. He wants to open up in the East, and I'm supposed to contact some agencies."

Just like that. Smack out of the sky onto Park Avenue.

"What are you doing for lunch, Ebby?"

"I planned to go back to the hotel and eat." He waved across the street to the Waldorf-Astoria.

"Come on, I'll buy you a decent lunch. I don't see old track friends all that often."

He took Ebby to the Racquet Club. They each had two drinks

and a big lunch: oysters, the special steak. He bought him a Cubana English-market cigar.

"Boy, this is some place."

"Yes, it is. I have a lot of fun here. Bob Dixon and Walker Virdonette are both members. You remember them?"

"Sure. Dixon was the other miler. Not as good as you, though. I remember a lot of your races. You don't know it, Fred—you never paid much attention to me—but I admired you. You and Dixon. You weren't snot-heads like those other Ivy guys."

"I wasn't in Ivy."

"You weren't? I always thought . . . What club were you in?"

"I wasn't in any club. I couldn't afford it. I was on scholarship." As he talked, he remembered Ebby better and better. An earnest pink-faced kid with an innocent expression and big pink ears. He still had the ears, but his manner had become more confident and mature. At college he had seemed like a huge man-boy with those pink ears and enormous biceps for putting the shot. Ebby didn't say what club he was in, and Fred was careful not to ask.

"Funny, I always assumed you were in Ivy. You were going around with Dixon and Wally Ransome and that crowd."

"They were my friends. After college we all lived together in bachelor quarters here in New York." He watched Ebby puff on his cigar for a moment and then said: "Wally's dead, you know."

"No, I didn't know."

"Killed on the *Lexington*. One of my close friends. In fact, he was the only real friend who didn't make it through the war. Did you lose any?"

"A couple."

"Then you know how it is."

"Yeah. Very tough."

"I still see Bob and Walker, though. Even though we don't live together anymore. I moved out when I got married."

"You married? Congratulations. Got any kids?"

"Not yet."

"What do you do?"

"I'm in the advertising business."

He had eventually gotten there, as he knew he would. He watched Ebby's jaw loosen in surprise.

"You never mentioned that. All through lunch you never—"

"We don't do things that way. Anyway, if you have a list of agencies, we're probably on it."

"Who are you with?"

"W and W."

He consulted his list. "Wilking and Wright? Yeah, you're on it."

"Anyway, if we should ever get the business, I wouldn't want it to be because we were on the same track team."

"Right."

"Although it would be fun working with somebody you knew."

"Right. Right."

"Would you like to meet W and W themselves?"

"I would, yes, Fred. Particularly if it would help you."

"I see them every day. Why don't I try to set up a meeting for one of them tomorrow?"

"That would be great, Fred, great."

"Okay. I'll get a message to your hotel or call you this evening. Anything else I can do for you?"

Ebby's ears grew, if possible, even pinker. "Well, I don't know exactly how to put this, but I'm a stranger here in New York. Could you—uh—possibly fix me up for this evening?"

"I could try." He strove to keep his face a mask.

Wilking or Wright?

Even though he was terrified of Mr. Wright, he decided on him. Mr. Wilking was capable of sliding Ebby right out from under him while they were being introduced. Besides, there was the business of the girl. He couldn't see himself asking Mr. Wilking for advice about that. So he went to Mr. Wright's office and hung around until he was let in.

"You know Vogel's Western Gold beer?"

"What about it?"

"They want to open up in the East, and they're shopping around for an agency."

Mr. Wright sat up.

"The son, Eberhardt Vogel, is a friend of mine. I just had lunch with him. He'd like to meet you or Mr. Wilking."

"Bring him in. By God, if we could ever—" He shot out one of those hard Wright looks. "You know this guy?"

"Yes, he's a friend of mine. Would tomorrow afternoon . . . ?"

Mr. Wright spun around in his chair and flipped on his squawk box. "Miss Morrison, how about three tomorrow? Four? Okay—Vogel." He twirled his chair back. "Do you really know this guy?"

"We were on the track team in college. Yes, I know him pretty well."

"Do you know that we have no beer account? We've never had a beer account?"

"I didn't know about never."

"What's he like?"

"Well, he's a big shot-putter. He likes girls."

"Then you'd better fix him up with a girl." Mr. Wright picked up a pencil and examined the point. "Find him a good girl."

"I'm not sure who in the company to—"

"Not in the company. We're not running a call girl business. Get a girl from outside somewhere. Get him a really good girl. You can expense it out under Entertainment Vogel." He turned on his squawk box again. "Miss Morrison, start an expense folder. Vogel. That's right, *V-o-g-e-l.* No, no product yet." The chair swiveled back, waiting for him to go.

"There's this problem . . . I don't know any . . . "

"In that case, you'd better start scratching around among your friends. When does he want this girl for?"

"That's the problem. For tonight."

Mr. Wright looked at him the way McNally used to—as if he were a small boy who had to be taught how to tie up his shoes—then consulted his watch. "It's four o'clock." He tapped his teeth with the pencil. He said to the squawk box: "Get me Alonzo Green. . . . No, don't get me Alonzo Green."

"Maybe if I tried to get him somebody for tomorrow night . . . "

"No. If he likes girls . . . " Mr. Wright turned to him in a fury. "You don't know *anybody?*"

He shook his head. "Nobody who . . . "

Mr. Wright was a short man with a big head and a dark seamed face. He looked like an angry baffled bulldog as he dialed a number on one of three phones on his desk. Apparently that one didn't go through the W and W switchboard.

"Miss Maxwell, please. Mr. Wright."

He swiveled around in his chair again, so that he was hidden by its tall leather back. "Mindy? . . . Yes it's me. . . . Yes, I know. . . . Yes, it has been. . . . Yes, I do too. . . . Yes, very busy. . . . Have you a date for tonight you can break? . . . No, a friend. . . . No, I don't think that. . . . Honestly I don't. . . . Please understand I would never . . . I know, but I've been up to my neck. How about Thursday for us? . . . Fifty-fourth Street—you have the key? . . . About seven? We'll have a drink, maybe cook something. Yes, I am. . . . Yes, it has been. . . . Me too. . . . Don't say that; I haven't . . . No, there isn't. . . . Honest, it's just that I've been so busy. . . . Me too, very much. . . . So how about tonight? . . . No I would never think that; I just said I would never . . . Believe me, you do yourself a disservice. . . . No, I wouldn't ever . . . Vogel . . . Eberhardt Vogel . . . That's right, the same one. . . .

Yes, very important. . . . Because I want him to meet somebody special, somebody intelligent and stylish, not just anybody. . . . Asking a lot? I agree, but . . . Well, I wouldn't if . . . You know I do. . . . I do, I do; I wouldn't be calling you if . . . Okay, honey, Thursday for us. . . . I will, I will, don't worry, I will. . . . Now, for tonight, how about the '21' Club? . . . Okay, seven. . . . Eberhardt Vogel. . . . No I guess you couldn't forget it—it is a household name. . . . I'll get a table for four. . . . Because Fred Fay from this office will be going. . . . Because he's a friend of Vogel's. Better get a girl for him. . . . I don't care—anybody. . . . No, he doesn't care. He'll be leaving with her right after dinner. . . . I know it's the last minute, but he doesn't matter—anybody at all for him. . . . All right, Thursday. . . . I won't. . . . Ahead of you, you'll see."

Mr. Wright swung back into view. Fred avoided his eyes.

"I got you a good one."

He moved toward the door.

"This isn't exactly a nice business," said Mr. Wright.

"Maybe I should have—"

"Maybe you didn't hear all that."

"What? Yes. No, I didn't."

"Not just for me. I do what I do in this rotten business. But Mindy's a nice girl."

He approached that row of enameled men that was always standing at the foot of the stairs at the "21" Club. "A table for four—for Mr. Fay. I'm supposed to meet a Miss Maxwell."

"Over there."

She was sitting on a sofa in the waiting room that the "21" Club had, next to a small dark girl. She was not what he had expected at all. She reminded him of Irene or Kitty, a tall taffy-haired girl in a simple black dress. She had the same sexy flavor that they had, well concealed but definitely there. And she was also very up. Walker would have jumped at her.

He introduced himself and Ebby. She introduced the small dark girl. Fran Collins. They had cocktails and went upstairs for dinner. Mindy favored him with a couple of quick careful glances and a couple of quick careful remarks and then devoted herself to Ebby. She dazzled him. After the first few minutes, during which he sat frozen in his chair, feeling like an apprentice pimp, he could begin to relax. He said a few things to Fran Collins but with his attention riveted to Ebby, who was riveted to Mindy. At the end of dinner he paid the bill and said that as a working man he had better be getting home. He got up.

"Why don't we stay and have one brandy?" said Mindy to Ebby.

He took Fran Collins home in a taxi. "Nice of you to fill in at the last minute."

"Oh, I was glad. Mindy is such a nice person."

"What does Mindy do?"

"Mindy is in charge of public relations and promotion for the Advertising Council."

"What do you do?"

"I also work for the Advertising Council."

"Well, it was nice of you to fill in."

"Oh, I enjoyed it. Mindy is such a nice person. I never went to '21' before. I enjoyed going." She spoke carefully, as if she had encountered English for the first time as a high school student. She was careful to pronounce the last *g* in "going." Goingg.

The next day he talked to Ebby in his office while waiting to see Mr. Wright.

"That Mindy. Fred, you're a genius."

"You make out okay?"

"Well, not exactly. That's what I mean by your being a genius. I ask you to fix me up—you know, just something. Instead, you introduce me to a *nice* girl"—he was the third person in twenty-four hours to say that about her—"but wow, what a girl! We had a great time. We talked and talked. She's very intelligent. Not the kind you just make out with the first time you see her."

"I guess not."

"You know that if you know her. Where do you know her from?"

"What did she say?"

"From her job. She works in the Advertising Something. From there."

"That's right. We meet there from time to time. I always thought she was attractive."

"I'm having dinner with her again tonight. And again Friday. She's busy someplace Thursday."

W and W got the account. He helped nail it down himself with something he said while Ebby was getting the final polish from Mr. Wilking, who was being very suave and looking out his window a lot and talking about the need to find a truly strong theme for such a distinguished product.

Something jumped into his head. "I think Ebby's already supplied that."

"I did?"

"Yes. Western Gold Comes East. Remember?"

"Oh, yeah."

Western Gold did come East, with huge billings. He was put in charge of the account. Corky Chalmers did most of the work. Ebby kept coming East too, to date Mindy Maxwell.

He finally said to Ebby: "Look, if you're going to be here so much, let's at least move you to a decent hotel. The Waldorf's okay for some people, but you'll be more comfortable at the St. Regis. We know the manager there, and he'll take really good care of you."

Ebby moved into the St. Regis. Two months later, he married Mindy Maxwell. Not long after that, proposed by him and seconded by Bob Dixon, Ebby joined the Racquet Club, and he was able to say: "George, this is Mr. Vogel, a new member. Treat him well."

"Yes, Mr. Fay. Welcome, Mr. Vogel."

That slogan—Western Gold Comes East—was one of only two contributions he made to the advertising business during his entire career in it. It shot him up in W and W like a rocket. The other, in a way he could not have anticipated, undid him.

W and W had a client, Omega Pharmaceutical, whose principal business was proprietary drugs, headache remedies, cough syrup, hemorrhoid cures, and hair shampoos. By absorbing smaller companies, Omega had become a conglomerate before the term was familiar on Wall Street. Its president, Felix Adamson, was a close friend of Mr. Wilking's. Mr. Wilking ran the account personally, although he had his own Corky Chalmers to do the work: Bill Krangold. Omega was one of W and W's largest accounts.

Back then, chlorophyll was very big for a year or two. There were chlorophyll tablets and chlorophyll toothpastes designed to cure bad breath. Exactly what chlorophyll was, aside from something in the leaves of plants (and he couldn't help wondering why all the lettuce and spinach people ate didn't help with their halitosis), was never clear to him. But chlorophyll was around, and it was booming. Also booming were antihistamines, drugs that apparently could do something about the common cold.

What he did was suggest that the two be put together into one pill: The Secret Formula That Banishes Your Cold While It Sweetens Your Breath. Since Omega Pharmaceutical was Mr. Wilking's baby, he addressed a memo to him. He assembled some market background and some projections, avoiding the tough part by explaining that while he had no experience in costing out pill production, the Omega

133

people could certainly do that. He prepared a few tables with various retail prices and hypothetical profit margins and from them came up with some ballpark figures about the kind of advertising budget that could be carried by annual sales of five million, ten million, and a hundred million units. He suggested the name Histochlor and proposed that it be produced in triangular form. Bright-green little triangles that would be packaged and sold like Life Savers—there weren't any other green triangular pills or lozenges on the market.

He didn't hear back immediately from Mr. Wilking and forgot about Histochlor. Ebby Vogel began taking up more and more of his time. For all Ebby's admiration of him and his gratitude at being edged into the niceties of up life in New York—and that included introductions to Wragge and Vernon & Vernon—Ebby was no patsy, but a tough shrewd man, a rich man's son who was used to getting his own way and was already beginning to be accustomed to deference. He moved to New York and was put in charge of eastern operations for the Vogel Brewing Company. He spent far more time building and buying breweries and developing a sales organization than he did thinking about advertising, but he found time for that too. Ebby had endless energy and would usually get around to calling about advertising late in the day, once or twice a week. He was a great believer in big billboards, so Corky Chalmers was put to work making an analysis of the billboard situation. When that was safely in hand, he could say to Ebby:

"Let's meet at the Racquet Club and discuss it over a drink."

He wanted to maximize the friend side of the friend-business relationship, and the Racquet Club was the place for that. There, cushioned by the unhurried, paneled, up background, both of them mellowed by a couple of drinks, he could manage, with the help of Corky's material, to carry off the illusion that he was on top of the Western Gold campaign.

Although Corky had access to all the special departments and facilities at W and W and knew how to use them, he quickly began to scream that he was being drowned in work. He got Corky an assistant. Later, when things really began to hum, he got him another.

Ebby wanted to know about signs with moving lights to be put in the windows of bars. He wanted to know about the design of monogrammed beer steins, he wanted to know about beer coasters and their design, he wanted to know about television versus *Life* magazine, he wanted to know about *Life* magazine versus the *Saturday Evening Post,* he wanted to know about maybe a new label, he wanted to know about designing a can, about six-pack cartons, about supermarket displays. He wanted to know about supermarket displays right now, because he was working on a deal for preferential shelf placement with Allied *this week*.

Sometimes he was late for dinner, and Julia would ask why.

"Business."

"You could at least have called me. The roast is overdone. Dagmar is upset."

Sometimes he did telephone. But sometimes he was made so tense by Ebby and his demands that he would have a drink or two extra to ease that, and he would forget again. Sometimes he came home late *and* a little drunk.

"I'm not interfering with your business life. Please understand that. I would just like to know, that's all. Is it asking too much for you to telephone when you know you are going to be late?"

"Okay, okay."

"You have a watch. I gave you a watch." True, she had given him a Patek Philippe for a wedding present. "You could at least look at it."

"You can't keep sneaking looks at your watch while you're talking business."

"I'm not talking about keeping sneaking looks."

"It breaks the rhythm, the concentration."

"You could take one look. A sensible man"—she didn't start calling him "a sensible man who hasn't had too much to drink" until he had come home a great many times having had too much to drink—"who leaves his office at about six and then sits around in his club for an hour or two should know, even without looking at his watch, that it is time for him to go home."

"Okay, okay."

"Or telephone. You could excuse yourself and telephone."

"The telephones are down at the other end of the hall."

"Well, it can't be that large a club that you can't walk to the telephone, although I've never been inside it."

"Not my fault. Women aren't allowed in."

"Yes they are. Once a year, on Ladies' Day. Bob Dixon asked me once."

"All right, all right. I'll ask you."

"I'd rather you telephoned when you were going to be late for dinner."

"For Christ's sake, Julia."

"There's no need to swear at me."

Sometimes when he realized with a guilty start that he had forgotten again, he would hurriedly phone and say that he had been kept longer than usual and for Julia to go ahead and have her dinner, he would be home later. There was a small group of men who spent a great deal of time in the club bar, and he sometimes would join one of them for another drink or two and then go in and have dinner with him. If one of them had ordered a bottle of wine, and if he had a glass or two of that, he would get home quite drunk.

Julia began commenting on that. She also complained that he snored when he had had too much to drink, so he moved his things into the spare room and from then on slept there. Julia played more and more bridge. She and Mary Smallwood were now a recognized women's team and played in a lot of tournaments. Sometimes when he got home he would find a note saying she was out for dinner and bridge and for him to go ahead and have his dinner alone.

His Racquet Club bills went up and up. He stopped trying to figure out what was a legitimate business expense and what was not. He just handed the bills over to Miss Gorce (he had a secretary now, and there was very little for her to do until the emergency when he had her type up some things that Corky had to get done in a hurry for the Western Gold account, and from then on Corky kept her much busier than he did). Miss Gorce made out his expense account each month, and the Racquet Club bill went on it in full. She also kept him supplied with memo pads and sharp pencils and tried to keep the top of his desk straightened out and his in box in some kind of order.

His salary took a huge leap when the Western Gold account came in, to thirty-five thousand. He began piling up money in the bank and decided to open a brokerage account with Merrill Lynch. He asked Miss Gorce to subscribe to the *Wall Street Journal* and would spend some time over it every morning, looking to see how the stocks that Merrill Lynch had bought for him were doing, and talking to the representative who handled his account: Jerry Grogan.

Jerry Grogan called him at least once a week: "I don't know anything. Do you know anything?"

"No."

"Market's quiet. You have six points in International Nickel. Maybe you should bank that and get into something with a little more sex appeal, like Litton Industries."

"Okay."

Litton Industries turned out to have a lot of sex appeal. He got nearly twenty-six points out of it before Jerry Grogan switched him into something else. And although Litton Industries continued on up after the sale, he couldn't really complain, because the new investment was going up too. It just wasn't going up quite as fast. So after a while

Jerry Grogan switched him back into Litton Industries. Everything was going up, and the game seemed to be to find what was going up fastest. Jerry Grogan did a great deal of switching in an effort to find that, and earned large commissions in the process. Again, it was hard to complain, because his account did grow.

He asked Ebby a couple of times if he and Mindy would like to come to dinner, but each time they had something else. He didn't press it, since it always seemed to be Mindy who had the something else. Clearly she didn't want to see him again, and considering the circumstances of their first meeting, who would?

He never mentioned Mindy to Ebby, didn't ask if she had given up her job at the Advertising Council. When he went there himself for the cocktail parties and awards parties they were always giving and to which he was now regularly asked, and to which he felt he should go for exposure and to rub against men from other agencies with big accounts of their own, he did not go out of his way to look for Mindy Maxwell.

Those parties made him nervous. There was no point in talking to Corky Chalmers or Bill Krangold or other people from W and W. On the other hand, it didn't look good to be talking to nobody. He didn't yet know many people outside of W and W, and whoever he did try to talk to was usually looking over his shoulder to see who else was there. So he circulated a lot and hit the bar a few times and gradually felt more comfortable.

The Annual Awards party wasn't bad. There was a big crowd and music. After the awards were given out, there was a buffet and dancing and more drinking than usual and a much gayer atmosphere. He was watching some of the younger kids snapping each other around the dance floor, when a girl said: "Hello, Mr. Fay."

"Hi."

"Do you think this is a good party?"

"Sure."

"I was so anxious. I helped arrange it. It was my first assignment in this position, and you would never know how many things could go wrong."

"I'll bet."

"Did you like the punch?"

"I'm not drinking the punch." Nobody was.

"I was so worried about the punch. Is it too sweet, I wondered. But if you don't make it sweet it tastes too strongg."

Now he remembered—the careful way she pronounced that last *g*.

"Why don't you have a glass?" he suggested.

"I don't think I should, with the responsibility. I don't think I should drink." She pronounced it *jrink*. She handled words as carefully as she would nettles.

He got her a glass anyway, and another bourbon for himself.

"It's not too sweet," she said, sipping. "It's got 7-Up in it. For the sparkle. It's good."

They looked at each other over the tops of their glasses.

"You don't remember me, do you," she said.

"Yes I do. I took you to dinner at the '21' Club."

"I didn't think you'd remember. You spent all the time looking at Mindy."

"I was curious to see how Mindy was getting on with my friend."

"Mindy is so attractive."

"She certainly is."

"Wasn't it romantic how she and Mr. Vogel got married."

He agreed that it was.

"I could tell that they were really fallingg for each other. They were so concentratingg on each other. But frankly I didn't think it would happen so fast."

"Frankly I didn't, either."

"Would you like to dance? Part of my responsibility is to be available for dancing."

"I'm not much of a dancer. Frankly I'm a rotten dancer."

"Everybody can dance."

"Frankly, in my set, not everybody can."

She stood waiting at the edge of the dance floor, her elbows tight against her sides, her forearms sticking out like miniature wings, palms upward, fingers snapping, body jiggling impatiently to the music. She was full of dancing. There was nothing for him to do but follow. She moved confidently into his arms, and he proceeded with the plodding one-step that he had learned, attempting to hold her arm out as he had been taught (steer with it, signal your intention to change direction with a slight forward or backward motion of the extended arm). But Fran Collins was accustomed to her own kind of dancing, and it was not the kind he had been taught. She took his hand firmly and nestled it against her shoulder for a moment. There was a considerable activity of her body against his as she began executing a variety of steps and movements that at first seemed to bear no relationship to what he was doing. Knees bumped. He stopped in confusion, started again. Suddenly she removed herself and spun away, still holding tight to his hand, unreeling herself until their arms were outstretched, then reeled herself back against him again. She twitched her shoulder with a sort of shrug. Her head tossed to the music. This was dancing. It involved the entire body.

If only he could dance. Out she went again, and through her arm there came back to him, like a faint electric current, a sense of what was required of him: to be a mooring from which she could launch herself, swaying and jigging at the end of the anchor line of his arm, a compact steel-spring figure in a red satin dress, improvising her off-beat off-step arabesques that were miraculously in step and on beat when she arrived back at him. As she spun, her skirt positively snapped around her. In this kind of dancing you were not planted awkwardly postlike against your partner. The relationship was much looser. Bodies brushed, departed, tantalized each other, retaining contact through the tips of clinging fingers, returned, brushed again, and spun off again.

If only he could dance. If only he could swing his hips, tilt his chin, hold up an index finger in a graceful twirl to complement his body's twirl. If only he were less self-conscious and could surrender to the itching locked somewhere in his calves and shoulders. Surrender—that was what he had to do. He surrendered to the extent of swaying slightly, shifting his weight from one foot to the other as Fran whirled and spun and snapped in front of him and around him.

The music stopped. He got her another glass of punch.

"Maybe I shouldn't jrink this."

"Maybe you should talk the way you dance."

"What?"

"I mean, you're a terrific dancer."

"I love to dance. That's all we used to do. Dance."

"Is Mindy still working here?"

"Mindy is retired. She retired when she got married. But she came in last week. Mindy is very happy."

"I'm glad to hear that."

"Mindy has a beautiful ring."

The musicians were putting away their instruments, and the cloths were being taken from the tables, to reveal their battered cigarette-scarred surfaces. The Annual Awards party was over. He looked at his watch. Jesus, eight o'clock; he had forgotten Julia again. Call her now? No, too late now. The bourbon in him had the mellowing effect of making unpleasant things distant and unimportant. Instead, he said: "Can I drop you off home?" reaching for a last one as they closed the bar.

"I would appreciate if you would do that."

In the cab he put his arm around her and kissed her, a long amiable relaxed easy intoxicated kiss, so different from the hurried reluctant ones he shared with Julia. Time passed slowly and drunkenly in the taxi, and they went on kissing. Then and there he became a connoisseur of leisurely kissing, of the texture of lips and the tips of tongues. When they arrived at Fran's, which was a crummy little building in a crummy street in a crummy part of town—West Ninety-eighth Street—he followed her into a crummy vestibule where there were mail slots and the names of several probably crummy tenants.

"Do you live here alone?"

"I live with my father. We live on the third floor."

"Then I guess you can't ask me in."

"I don't know you well enough. This is only our second date."

Date? He had her cornered in the vestibule, up against the mail slots. "You knew me well enough to kiss me in the taxi."

"You can kiss on the second date in a taxi. Remember, on our first date we didn't kiss in the taxi."

"But I didn't try."

"On the first date you shouldn't try."

"I didn't realize how attractive you were, or I would have tried. You're such a terrific dancer. You're really very sexy when you dance."

"No I'm not. I just dance."

"No you don't. You're sexy."

"Don't talk like that."

"You're sexy right now." He tried to kiss her again, but she squirmed and wouldn't let him.

"I jrank too much punch, or I wouldn't. A married man."

"Very sexy."

"Stop saying that. It's not nice to say that. Anyway, I shouldn't be dating a married man anyhow."

"Who said I was married?"

"You did. You told me at the '21.'"

"I don't remember that."

"I asked you if you had babies. Do you remember that?"

"What did I say?"

"You said not yet. Don't you remember that?"

"That's right. So I did."

"You don't remember anything I said. You spent your whole time looking at Mindy."

14

THE TROUBLE WITH SEEING HER AGAIN WAS HOW TO go about it. He couldn't just call her up. She had said it was improper to date married men. So it would have to be casual, sort of spur-of-the-moment, to make it hard for her to say no. He decided to catch her as she left work. There was a newspaper stand in the lobby of her building, and he stationed himself there with an evening paper, looking over the top of it at the people pouring out of the elevators, having convinced himself that there was no real harm in this, that a couple of drinks and a few more kisses wouldn't hurt, and anyway she was a working girl who probably kissed a lot of men and thought little of it.

It was the recollection of those kisses that brought him here, that and the springy little body in the red silk dress. She was a good kisser, and she had kissed him enthusiastically. He hadn't been properly kissed since . . . well, since the only time in his life that he had been properly kissed. And if not by Fran, then by whom now? There wasn't anybody else, and he was really aching for a couple of kisses and for whatever side benefits might accrue, even though going out and deliberately looking for them was something he definitely should not be doing. *He should not be doing this*—a respectable up man—and yet he was doing it. The idea had him in a panic. Doing something he knew he shouldn't do, planning it, then executing it, knowing all the time, through the planning and the execution, that he shouldn't, *and doing it anyway*, meant that he was beginning to lose control of himself. That was where the panic was, because if you couldn't control yourself, wouldn't you get caught, like a flasher in the subway? As fast as that thought came up, he stuffed it back again. But the deeper in he got, the more the thought kept coming up, and the more he gritted his teeth and went ahead anyway. Something drove him. He ran.

"Is there not a parallel here with drinking?"

There was, of course, although that early in the game he couldn't know it. He hadn't begun drinking enough yet to feel guilty or driven about it. But this new feeling was the same one that he would get to know so well in drinking: a feeling of looking at himself in a mirror and seeing a reproving self there. He could not look himself in the eye, not when he had made up his mind not to listen to himself. He just had to move faster to escape his own eye. It would be different on those later mornings, of course. He would wake up colossally hung over, shaking. Then it was easy. Never again, starting right now. But when the need grew, the loneliness and the desperation, the running would start. He just had to close his mind and run.

"And with masturbation?"

That too. Although as he grew older the guilt began to fade. It was buried with his parents and with the high school kids who were also safely buried now. By being sealed off, masturbation wasn't so bad. It had become his own private property. There was no conceivable way anymore that anyone could know—unless he told somebody. And he could be pretty sure he would never do that, until Hennerkop.

"Are you suggesting that guilt is associated with being caught?"

Well, yes, in a way. Now he was getting himself into a situation where another person was involved, where public exposure was a factor, where somebody might see him and guess what was in his mind. Suppose Walker Virdonette was to walk into the lobby of this building and catch him hanging around, waiting to date a stenographer? Suppose Mr. Wilking came in? *Wilking,* Holy Christ. Standing by the newspaper counter, he had already said to himself for the eighth or ninth time: What am I doing here; let's get out of here. But he was still there when Fran came out of the elevator. He was able to turn and buy a pack of gum, timing it just right so that when he turned back she was coming abreast of him and he could say in a totally surprised and casual way:
"Why, hello, Fran."
"Mr. Fay. What are you doing here?"

"Buying a paper."

"Oh."

"Actually I was buying some gum on the chance you might pop out of the elevator and I could offer you a piece." He held out the gum. "Come to think of it, can I offer you a drink?"

"I have to go home and cook supper for my father."

"So soon?"

"He likes his supper early."

"But that other evening when I dropped you off, after the Annual Awards, didn't he get pretty hungry that night?"

"I called him previously. He didn't expect me that night."

"So why don't you call him again?"

She considered that.

"Have supper with me. Cook's night out." He considered offering her the "21" Club again, but rejected it. What if he ran into Ebby and Mindy there? "We'll find a nice quiet place."

"All right, I'll phone." She went into a booth in the lobby. He slid into the next one to make his own call.

He took her to a bar in the Shelton Hotel; nobody ever went into the Shelton Hotel.

"What'll it be?"

"Something not too strongg. I'm not used to jrinking."

That called for something sweet. Daiquiris.

"Mmm mmm good."

"You like Campbell's soup?"

"What?"

"I mean, do you like daiquiris?"

"They're so strongg."

"They just taste strongg." She didn't even blink when he said it. Dumb? Or was she just deaf to the difference? Dumb or deaf, she was sexy. Or was it the knowledge that she enjoyed kissing that made her seem sexy. Anyway, why not concentrate more on kissingg and forget the strongg jrink stuff. No need to be such a carpingg jerk all the time.

He concentrated on her. He learned that her father, Carl, worked in construction.

"What kind of construction?"

"Building construction."

"What does he do there?"

"They put up buildings."

She didn't seem to want to talk about her father, which made her even with him. She switched to her older brothers and sisters, all mar-

143

ried, all with children, then to her mother, now dead, then to a kid brother, who still lived at home. She asked about his family and learned that he had none.

"An only child? That must be lonely. I was never lonely, with all my brothers and sisters."

"I had friends. You make friends, you know, in school. Have them over. You make friends in college, in business."

"I like your friend Mr. Vogel."

"Yes, he's nice."

"He is so friendly. Will he make a good husband for Mindy?"

"I think so. Will Mindy make a good wife for him?"

"Mindy will make a wonderful wife."

"What do you know about Mindy's private life?"

"Mindy has worked hard. Mindy is a wonderful person."

He finished his daiquiri, really too sweet, and watched her finish hers, dainty sip after dainty sip. He could imagine the alcohol filtering into her cells, warming her, loosening her. When she was through, he ordered two more without consulting her, listening with only half his mind as she chatted on about the people in her office. He thought about where to have dinner—decent but obscure—and about the taxi ride afterward, and the vestibule after that. He ordered a third daiquiri for himself while she was finishing her second.

"I was in your office the day before yesterday," she said.

"Where was I?"

"I don't mean in *your* office. I mean Wilking and Wright. Mr. Krangold wanted twenty of our new round-table brochures. He wanted them right away, and the messenger was out, so I had to take them."

"Krangold's always in a hurry."

"You have such atchractive offices."

"You should see mine."

"And your receptionist. She's atchractive."

"That's Miss Whymper. Would you like to see my office. It's very atchractive too." Cut that out.

"Well . . . "

"It's only three blocks from here. It has a spectacular view at night. Or should we have one more before we go?"

"Oh, no. I'm almost jrunk from this second."

That way, by inserting the offer of the drink, it was possible to pay the bill and leave for his office without her actually having faced up to a decision whether to go or not. It had been sort of agreed without being agreed. She just took his arm and went along. The night elevator man rode them up. Lights were still on in the hall, because the cleaning women were there.

Fran stepped out rather uncertainly. "Is this . . . ?"

"This is the executive floor. Reception is a floor below."

"Oh."

He steered her down the hall to his office, noting that Miss Gorce's wastebasket, in the little cubicle that Miss Gorce occupied, was empty. He switched on the light in Miss Gorce's office and then went on into his own. His wastebasket was empty too, which meant that the cleaning women were already through there. He led Fran to the window to look out of the dark room at the city stretching to the south. It was spectacular. The Chrysler Building was off to the left, the Empire State Building straight ahead—they and a hundred others, all lit from within like glowing boxes. Only at night do the solid piled-up skyscrapers reveal themselves as shells.

"That's the Chrysler Building there."

"It's so beautiful."

"That's Wall Street way down there." Its lights winked and flickered in the distance.

"It's so beautiful. And the river."

"The Hudson."

"How do you work up here? I would be lookingg out of the window all day."

"I sit with my back to the window. Over here."

She turned. She was facing him. It was now or never. He reached for her and kissed her. She kissed him back. He cautiously moved his body against hers, with none of the drunken assurance of the previous time. She responded to that too. Soon they were standing pressed together, her arms around his neck, exchanging longer and bolder kisses. He moved his hands on her back and up into her hair. She liked being kissed. She kissed back of her own accord and held him closer. He got the feeling that she wanted to press herself hard against him. She had strong feelings. She was expressing them. She had a terrific body. It was expressive. He ran his hand down her buttock. She pressed closer. My God. Faster than he had hoped. So much so that he dared risk:

"Shouldn't we take our coats off?"

"Shouldn't we eat? Those jrinks."

"Okay, but let's have a last look at the view."

He took his coat off and helped her out of hers, resisting an impulse to grab at her as he did so. He led her back to the window. They stood there for a moment, looking out, but inexorably they turned to each other, and the kissing began again. Desire vaulted up in him. How he wanted her. She seemed to want him just as much. They clung and kissed, stopped from moment to moment to hold hands and stare at each other. In the dim light she was indescribably beautiful, flushed with amorousness. By degrees he maneuvered her, with his own improvised infinitesimal dance steps, to his sofa (all the offices on the executive floor had sofas) and tried to nudge her down into it.

"No."

"Just for a minute."

"We should keep standing up."

He sat on the edge of the sofa, perched so that he could hold her around the knees. He had an overwhelming desire to run his hands up the backs of her legs. It was as if they might go of their own accord, up the silk stockings, up between, to part them, to expose and find. Careful, careful; he didn't really *know* yet. So he held her, her knees against his knees, his nose aimed in the general direction of her navel. He tried again to gently pull her into the sofa. She dealt with that by putting her hands on the back of his head and drawing it against herself. Just below her breasts; he was aware of their separate bulges against the top of his forehead.

"Just for a minute," he whispered into her stomach.

"No. We ought to eat." She tried to pull away. "I'm dizzy."

"From two daiquiris?"

"From two daiquiris and two hundred kisses. You make me dizzy with kisses."

"You make me dizzy too. That's why I sat down."

"We should go. Please let me go."

"Just a minute more."

"Please let go. Please, Fred. Do you mind if I call you Fred?"

They ate.

In her vestibule, another long session of kissing and pressing. The mail slots got a good polishing.

"Please, I should go up."

He continued to hold her.

"My father."

"He's probably asleep now."

"He will wait up. He will worry about me."

He hung on.

"Will we see each other again?" she asked.

"Yes." He had crossed that line.

146

"When?"

"As soon as I can. Next week maybe."

"Will you call me?"

"What's your number?"

"I mean at the office. It would be better to call at the Advertising Council. Please. I should go up." But even as she was saying it she was clinging to him. He decided to risk a hand inside her coat. That brought her to her senses. She got out her key and left him. When he got back to Sutton Place, Julia's door was shut. But this time he had phoned. It would be okay at breakfast.

He looked her up in the phone book anyway. That involved a tussle with Miss Gorce.

"If you'll give me the name I'll gladly look it up for you."

"No. I just want the book. I'm checking some old numbers."

She brought the book. He laid aside the *Wall Street Journal* and looked under Collins. No Carl. No Karl, either. In fact, no Collins of any kind on West Ninety-eighth Street. Maybe she had no father. Maybe he was a useful fiction for a working girl living alone. Maybe she had no phone.

But she had phoned somebody that night. Maybe a roommate. Maybe the time would come when the roommate could be persuaded to spend an evening somewhere else.

He decided to try her at her office.

"Miss Gorce, would you please call the Advertising Council, Miss Collins."

Miss Gorce swung into action. "Miss Collins, please. Miss Collins? One moment, please. Mr. Fay calling." She buzzed him. He picked up.

"Miss Collins?"

"Hello?"

"Miss Collins, about the Shelton Hotel matter we were discussing the other afternoon. I wonder if we—" Miss Gorce had hung up; he heard the click. But his office door was open; she could still hear him talking. "That is, Miss Collins, I'll be passing by the Advertising Council later today, and I wondered if—"

"Hello?"

"Miss Collins?"

"Is that you, Fred?"

"Yes."

"Hello, Fred."

"Yes. As I was saying, perhaps we could meet. I'll be in the neighborhood of—uh—"

"Meet?"

"I was hoping we could continue our discussion."

"Today?"

"Yes."

"Where?"

"Where as before."

"You mean the lobby?"

"Yes."

There had to be a better way. The next time he would use a pay phone downstairs. But suppose somebody saw him doing that, looked right through the glass and saw him sitting in there when he should be using his own phone and his own secretary upstairs. He went to the men's room and took a quick look at Miss Gorce as he went. She was sitting straight and neat as usual, tapping away at some of the stuff Corky kept shoving at her. He got the side of her face, impervious, neutral.

Fran showed up promptly. He was able to put away his prop paper. Again he took her to the Shelton Hotel and got two daiquiris into her. He was churning with desire but could not tell if she was. She seemed very demure. She looked at the tablecloth a good deal and played with her drinks, but she finally downed them.

"Another?"

"Oh, no. Two of these on top of an empty stomach is enough to make me feel drunk."

"Then maybe we should walk them off."

An unfathomable look. But she took his arm again, and they walked to his office. He tried to go slowly despite an almost ungovernable impatience. Also with a sinking fear that made him want to trot faster, get in out of sight where they would be alone and safe. The combination of fear and desire made him breathless. He recognized the fear. He was walking in; his eyes were open; he shouldn't; he was anyway. He did his best to appear aimless and casual as he tacked toward his building.

Once inside, in the semidarkness with the door safely shut, all pretense vanished. They clutched each other. She was all he wanted, ever, anywhere. Her body. Her mouth. Her response to him.

"Oh, Fred, you make me dizzy."

"Let's sit down."

"No."

"Right here."

"We should keep standing up."

She had her back to the sofa. With a slight nudge from him, she plopped into it.

"A married man. I shouldn't."

He kissed her again. And with kisses urged her along the cushions until they were lying side by side.

"There. This is comfy."

"I shouldn't. I shouldn't." But she clung close.

A huge longing filled him, full of sweetness and desperation, fed by increasingly reckless kissing, reckless enough, he hoped, to prevent her from noticing that he had unzipped the back of her dress and had his hand in against the narrow rear band of her bra. Above and below the bra was bare skin. There was a fastener of some sort. He fumbled and fumbled and fumbled at it. He couldn't get it undone. He ran his hand up and down her back. The feel of her skin electrified. The bra got in the way of his radiant swooping hand. He tried the fasteners again, and with his thumb and forefinger he got one open.

"Don't."

He unhooked another.

"No. Stop."

The third. Oh, Jesus. All the way up and down her back with his hand.

"No." She struggled out of the sofa. She stood with one hand splayed across her breasts as if they needed protection now that they were sprung loose inside her dress. With the other hand she tried to hoist her dress back up over her bare shoulder. She was badly disheveled, so unbearably disheveled and desirable that he pulled her down on top of him.

"Stop. Stop."

But he couldn't stop until he had to. Then he tried to roll her away, but she clung to him. Now, *now*, she wanted to keep kissing. He pushed her away and sat up.

"What's the matter?"

"Your dress. I don't want to—"

"You almost tore it."

"I mean, I don't want it to—" He got up.

"Where are you going?"

"Excuse me. I'll be right back." In the lavatory he did the best he could do with himself. When he returned, his office light was on and Fran, her dress zipped up and her hair combed, was sitting primly in a chair. Prim but observant; she immediately noticed the dark stain on his trousers.

"What happened?"

"I—uh—you know." He turned his back to her and put on his topcoat.

"You mean you had an orgasm?"

He nodded, ducking that test-tube word. The light was far too bright. He snapped it off. He held her coat for her.

"I thought that people only had orgasms when they were makingg love."

"We were making love."

"No. We were just huggingg and kissingg. Makingg love is a sin."

"Well, if you're going to be technical. But the way you kiss—"

"I mean, don't you have to be makingg love to have an orgasm?"

"You excited me. You're very exciting. It's the same. I mean, it's not the same, but the result is the same."

"Makingg love with a married man is a sin."

"We weren't making love. We were just hugging and kissing."

"I shouldn't be huggingg and kissingg a married man like this."

"If you don't want to—"

"I do want to." She held tight to his arm. "That's the chrouble. I want to kiss you. And when I kiss you I want to kiss you more."

This was gunpowder talk. He grabbed her and kissed her again. She responded avidly.

"That's what excites me," he whispered.

"That's what makes you have an orgasm?" She was positively chewing on the word.

"That and—you know—hugging."

"It makes me feel excited to think of you having an orgasm."

Reckless talk. The reckless kissing and the reckless pressing and moving had begun again. "Where?" he said recklessly.

"Where what?"

"Excited where." He tried to show her with his hand.

She snatched it away.

"Anyway, there," he said. "You could have one too."

"No."

"We both could have one."

"No. I never. I never did that. I never would do that."

"Never?"

"With a married man never."

"How about an unmarried man?"

"Not with anybody. Never. I never discussed orgasms before. I never talked like this before. I never went out with anybody who had an orgasm before."

"Never?"

"I mean before with me."

"How do you know about orgasms, then. How come you talk about them?"

"I don't know about them except from my sister. Because you just said you had one. Otherwise I would never . . . And from *Ideal Marriage*, those diagrams. But mostly from my sister. She told me you have orgasms when you make love."

"You don't always have to be making love. With a sexy girl like you—"

"Don't keep saying that."

"You're sexy. How come the other men you go out with . . . ?"

"I never kissed and hugged other men this way."

"Come on."

"No, I never. It was those drinks the night of the Annual Awards. You kissed me that way in the taxi, and I gave you those kisses back. Those kisses. And when we happened to meet in the lobby I was thinking if you would want to kiss me again, and I almost didn't go with you for drinks because I was afraid you might and I would. It was a sin."

"That's no sin."

"It is a sin. I already confessed it. Particularly with a married man it is a sin."

"You talked about me in confession?"

"I just said a fellow."

"Not my name?"

"No. Anyway, what difference would it make anyhow? To you? It's my sin." She buttoned up her coat to her chin. "Now I have to confess again. It won't be so easy this time. Father Ramirez will probably tell me to stop seeing you. If I tell him you're a married man, I think he will."

"Don't tell him."

"That would not be a true confession."

"What will you do?"

"I will stop seeing you."

15

SHE STOPPED. HE PHONED AND SHE SAID SHE WAS sorry but she couldn't. He tried to argue with her. She hung up. He called again. Again she hung up. He couldn't believe it. Worse, he couldn't stand it. She had taken root in him, and now, vine-like, she spread. She invaded his fingertips. He could taste her when he ran his tongue over his lower lip. He began doing that, moistening it, feeling his tongue (her tongue) there. She spurted through him continually and uncontrollably. Other women reminded him of her. Their sexuality became more explicit. Some days he was angry. Others, he felt crushed and listless. He drank more. He began to be restless and disagreeable at home, which was bad because, until Fran, life at home hadn't been all that bad. When he was prompt or hadn't had too much to drink, Julia was amiable and dutifully affectionate, giving him a nice little kiss and nice little pats.

"Did you have a nice day? Let me tell you what I did today."

She did a lot. She had the Colony Club. She had bridge. She was rising up in the bridge world and was now on one of the committees of the Contract Bridge Association. She was interested in politics, in birth control, in abandoned children, and, of course, overpoweringly interested in stray dogs and cats. She was interested in Adlai Stevenson. The apartment was full of the latest magazines and books, and she couldn't understand why, when he read at all, he didn't read one of those instead of burying himself in one of those interminable Victorian novels.

"Why don't you want to be a little more up on things?"

"I'm up enough."

"I mean, we should discuss politics more, or the ballet, or Dwight Macdonald."

"Who's he?"

"That's exactly what I mean."

If he was sober, those conversations would ramble on amiably enough and usually trickle away to nothing. If he wasn't, she would pick at him like a dentist working on a root canal. Despite the liquor, his nerves would begin to jump, and he would decide to pour himself another.

"Do you really need that?"

"I don't need it. I want it."

"You're not very alert, you know, when you . . . You don't follow arguments all that closely. When you interrupted me to go and get that drink, I was talking about Stevenson's domestic policies and the need for a national medical and health program, and you jumped to the Korean War."

"Stevenson's too soft on the Korean War."

"He is not. What do you know about his position on Korea?"

"Eisenhower's better."

"In what way?"

"He's the one who said: 'I'm going to Korea and fix all that,' or whatever he said."

"Exactly. Eisenhower wanted to end the war in Korea, so how can you blame Stevenson for being soft on Korea?"

"He's too soft."

"Exactly what does that mean?"

"He'll give the place away. He wants to give everything away. He spends too much money. He'll run deficits."

"But he wants to *end* the war, to cut *down* on military spending."

"He wants to run deficits."

"How can you say that? What do you know about Stevenson's fiscal policies?"

"He's a spender."

"Tell me, please. Please enumerate where in your opinion Stevenson is too extravagant."

"All over the place."

"All over the place is not specific enough. Do you know anything at all about Stevenson's programs? Did you read his April speech, his August speech? Did you read Eisenhower this week? Do you realize that Eisenhower is spending more on armaments than Stevenson wants to?"

"Got to have armaments."

"But you just said that the reason you favored Eisenhower was because he was going to end the war in Korea, which would mean the possibility of a reduction in armaments. So I don't quite understand how you can now criticize one man for doing more in the direction of what you favor the other man for doing."

It was as if he were on flypaper. The more he wriggled his legs, the deeper he got stuck. When he was sober he was alert enough to avoid those entanglements. When he was drunk Julia avoided them. It was the in-between situations that were bad.

Up until Fran, there weren't too many of them. He managed. Julia was an excellent housekeeper. She gave little dinners occasionally, to which she devoted a great deal of thought, worrying about who would go with whom. These made him nervous at first, until he learned that by keeping his mouth shut and smiling a good deal and seeing that everybody had drinks and cigarettes, he could get through the evening comfortably with the help of only a couple of bourbons. Actually he drank surprisingly little at home, although the stuff was right there in the closet. On the evenings when he came straight home or after only a short stop at the Racquet Club bar, he would have one predinner drink, always bourbon. Julia would have a glass of sherry.

Bourbon was his drink.

At first it had made him shudder because it was so strong. Gradually he got over that and began to appreciate its thick rich dark taste with that tantalizing hint of sweetness that disappeared just as he was becoming aware of it. Bourbon wasn't really sweet like rum, or musty and moldy like Scotch. It didn't taste like perfumed alcohol, like gin, or like nothing, like vodka. It reminded him of a piece of fine old furniture: solid, smooth, shiny, and strong—and the same color. Bourbon fitted him, and he settled into it as he would into a comfortable chair. Even later on, when he began to hate it as much as he loved it, he stuck to it. Even when he learned that the higher alcohols, the congeners that gave it its character, were the same things that gave him those spiking headaches and made him leap and tremble and turned his stomach into a quagmire, still he drank it. Sometimes getting his nose into the first glass of the day, late in the afternoon somewhere, he had the feeling that bourbon and he had been designed for each other.

The weekly meetings began to go badly. Mr. Wright held those every Tuesday morning to check on the progress of the Western Gold campaign. Corky had all the schedules, the rates, the allocations, the charts, the designs—the new designs to replace the ones that had not been approved last week—the budget. He would have a briefing session with Corky on Monday, and the panic would begin to build. Corky and his two assistants would set everything up in the chart room, but he would have to make the presentation.

On Monday night he would sleep badly. On Tuesday morning he would pay a token visit to the chart room, Corky with the sleeves of some crummy shirt rolled up, but knowing where everything was and what everything meant. He would go back to his office and wait for eleven o'clock, and the sweat would gather in his palms. At ten-fifty he would take a good belt of bourbon to steady himself, pop a Life Saver, and head for the chart room.

Later, a belt at ten-forty and another at ten-fifty.

Mr. Wright would ask questions. Increasingly he had to turn to Corky for answers. The sessions broke at one. By then he would be exhausted. He would bolt for the Racquet Club and usually not show up at the office again until midafternoon. Corky became more and more assertive at the weekly meetings. Sometimes he argued with Mr. Wright. Once, when Ebby came, he argued with him—over billboards.

"I like billboards, remember," said Ebby.

"Okay, but we've got two problems. How to deal with the locals, Rheingold and Schaefer. And how to deal with the nationals. You're not going to settle that with billboards. They're okay for Milwaukee, where you're established."

Ebby said: "We sell a lot of beer in Milwaukee."

"Okay, okay. But now we're talking New York. If you do just what Rheingold's doing, you're just another Rheingold. But you're not. You're the premium beer from the West. Something new, something special. That's what this whole campaign is about. That's what we're hitting with those two TV demos we're going to show you in a few minutes."

"I like billboards."

"Okay. They're in there. We've got that big Douglas Leigh special with the electric border and the pouring beer for Times Square. You saw the design; Fred showed it to you."

Corky and Ebby both looked at him. He quickly said: "Yes. Remember, you liked it."

"And another, with a clock and a thermometer, for the Triborough Bridge. Just north of that turn coming off into the city."

"Is that all?"

"All for now."

Ebby turned his back on Corky and stared at the presumed head of the campaign, his face darkening.

"We can get more," Fred said quickly. "There's a lot of billboard space in the city. It's just a matter of paying the—"

"I don't recommend it," said Corky.

"Who the hell is this guy?" said Ebby.

"The account assistant," said Mr. Wright.

"What the hell has he got against billboards?"

"Nothing. He just happens to be right about them."

"Who says?"

"Our market tests and our instincts," said Mr. Wright.

Ebby stared at him.

"Don't underestimate instinct. Your father's instinct, in my opinion, was right when he decided to go national. In twenty or thirty years, all the local breweries are going to be out of business. The survivors, the big regionals and the nationals, will all be using TV. But by that time they'll be canceling each other out. Right now the door's wide open. We have the chance to be the first to put a really good beer on TV in a really big way."

Ebby swung around like a lighthouse and beamed his malevolent stare at him again. This time he said nothing.

"You'll never have that chance again," said Mr. Wright.

There was a long pause.

"Why don't we take a look at the demos," said Mr. Wright.

Ebby looked at them and grudgingly admitted that he was impressed. After Ebby was gone and the door was shut, Mr. Wright said nothing to him, but to Corky he said: "Okay, kid."

That day he had four bourbons for lunch and slept them off in a movie somewhere. He emerged at about five o'clock, feeling desperate. He couldn't go home, just couldn't.

He walked up Madison Avenue and stood in front of the knife-and-scissors store next to the entrance of Fran's building. He looked at all the scissors and at the knives arranged in a big circle around a monster Swiss Army knife with its forest of fifteen blades sprouting from it. He kept his eye on the entrance. She came out. He caught her at the corner.

"Fran?"

"Oh!"

"How are you, Fran?"

"You scared me. You made me jump. You came up too fast."

"Can't we go somewhere and talk a little?"

"What will we talk about?"

She stood there, her arms around herself, a purple plastic handbag hanging from one wrist, her neat pointed toes at right angles. She stared straight up at him, and at that moment she was dissolvingly lovely, destroyer of the sour gripe in his belly, the headache, the stink in his nostrils. A girl with fantastic eyes in a perfect oval face. Such a sweet look, gentle but warm. Somebody for cherishing and loving as well as kissing, for admiring as well as stroking and pressing. "Just . . . talk," he managed to say. "You won't speak to me on the telephone."

"You know why."

"Can't we just talk, be friends. I miss you."

"You do?"

"You don't know."

"Yes I do."

Swooning on Madison Avenue. Both of them. He had the sense to take her arm and walk her down the street. They pressed close to each other as they walked, their thighs rubbing. In the Shelton Bar he ordered two bourbons.

"I can't drink this. It's too strongg."

"I'll order more water."

He put down half of his at one gulp. It landed on top of those four others like a carload of coal going down a chute in the sidewalk—with a dark roar. They were facing each other across a little table with a big droopy cloth. Under cover of the cloth he slid down in his seat until his knees were touching hers. He was getting drunk on one drink. But those knees. She pressed back. He put his hand under the table and found hers. He put her hand on his knee and ran it up and down there. She flushed scarlet and pulled it away as the waiter arrived with the water. He put some in her glass and she agitatedly drank about half of it. He continued to press his knees against hers. They were rubbing knees as they finished their drinks, rubbing harder and closer, staring glassily at each other, knees between knees.

"Come on."

No need to say where. They fell into the sofa, straining against each other.

"Oh, Fred. I missed you too."

Kisses, kisses. He got his hand up under her dress and tried to wedge it between her legs. She held them tight together. He pressed harder, reached her panties, which were already soaked through with the dew of her own desires.

"Darlingg, stop. Oh, God."

But he kept on. The wet slipperiness of the nylon was its own invitation. He caressed her against her panties, against her, felt her shudder and squirm, felt her thighs go slack, felt her breath accelerating. On the way. He knew. And for the second time in his life he felt that power in him. Godlike. A power in him like . . . like . . . He was a huge man, a strong man who could make a woman happy, make her feel happy, feel wonderful, feel wild, love him. An unbelievable feeling. She was his. He was giving something, giving a woman something, giving *her* something. Something nobody had ever given her. Give more, get more. And he got moans and convulsive shuddering movements, and finally a small scream or two, followed by long shuddering breaths and a flood of tears.

"Oh, darlingg."

"You okay?"

"Oh, yes, darlingg. I had an orgasm."

"I know."

"How did you know that?"

"The way you acted. And your screams."

"I screamed?"

"Just a little. Not a real scream."

"I didn't know that. I didn't know what I was doing. I didn't know where I was. I was exploding. You never told me an orgasm was like that."

"You can't exactly describe it."

"Oh, darling. To give me that. I love you. Oh, I love you. Did you have an orgasm too?"

"Yes."

"Was it like mine?"

"I don't know."

"Oh, darling, that we could do that together. Oh, how I love you. Do you love me?"

He answered by giving her a long probing kiss.

"Do you?"

"That much." He pressed himself hard against her.

"How much? Say it."

"Okay."

"Well, say it, then."

"I just did."

"No you didn't. All you said was okay."

"That's what I meant. Okay, I do."

"Oh, I love you, darling. Can't you say it to me?"

"I love you." But even as he said it he was aware of a terrible weariness, a splitting head, the state of his underwear, the steamy overwhelming femaleness of Fran, and a jittery restless urge to leap up and get away, to be by himself, to have a clean bath, to sleep. His office door had no lock. The night watchman might come. He tried to slide his arm free.

"Not yet. Hold me, darling."

His legs twitched. His skin was too tight. He had to move, jump, get clear.

"It's getting late. We really ought to go."

But by the next morning he wanted her again.

They met almost every week, sometimes more often, going to the Shelton bar for a token drink, feeding on knees, on the touch of fingertips, working themselves into a fog of desire. Going up in the elevator, they clung and kissed with snaking tongues. It was almost a race down the hall to the sofa. In the mutual boil of passion, he tried to control his own while feeding hers. It was *her* climaxes that made him reel, and he tried to prolong a high of breathlessness and power and pure physical happiness by holding back himself while spurring her on. She responded as if famished. Her capacity seemed bottomless. He wondered what would happen if she just kept coming, how long she would keep that up, but he never found out. Somewhere along the line, escalating her, he escalated himself beyond control. His fall was always catastrophic. From joy to a hunted haunted need to escape—almost within seconds.

Not for her, though. "I feel wonderful. I could lie here in your arms all night."

"We really should go."

"No, darling. Let's just lie here together for a little while and talk. I feel so jrowsy and loving now. It's even better than when we were bursting with passion. Do you love me the way I love you?"

"How can I tell that?"

"I mean, do you love anybody else as much as you love me?"

"No."

"Do you love me?"

"Yes."

"Then say it."

"I love you." A liar. His love was lust. One soared and crashed with the other.

16

TIME FOR THE KICKOFF. THE FIRST MEETING OF ALL the sales reps and distributors, a couple of hundred of them in one of the private ballrooms of the Waldorf. Western Gold signs all around the walls. Draft beer on tap. Bartenders with handlebar mustaches and red-and-black-striped vests, flipping the foam from stein after stein. He had a beer just to loosen up the ashes in his throat. Then another. He already had had three bourbons to hold him steady for the keynote speech. He had it all written down. He walked to the mike on the lectern and took out his notes. Sweat was prickling his forehead and beginning to trickle down. He was supposed to start with a short review of the ad thrust and then turn the mike over to Ebby, who would come on strong with a big marketing pitch. But by the time he got his notes out of his pocket and spread on the lectern, he realized that if he opened his mouth he might throw up. He bit down on his lip, swallowing hard, trying to steady the rows of faces starting to skid past his eye as he stared out at them. Entire mouthfuls of saliva were appearing from somewhere and had to be swallowed.

He knew he couldn't open his mouth. Even if he did, he realized that he would never be able to read his notes. The faces spun faster. He gave up. With a wide helpless gesture, he swung his arm toward Ebby, who was sitting on a chair next to the lectern. He was aware of an eruption of cheers and clapping as Ebby got to his feet.

He aimed for the door, just made it to the bathroom, and heaved up all the beer and bourbon. When he was through, his entire body was drenched with sweat. He mopped his face and neck and hands with paper towels and returned to the ballroom. Ebby was still talking, and he finished a minute later to tumultuous applause. Fred had figured out a way of possibly salvaging something, so he stepped up to the microphone and waved for silence.

"I was supposed to start this," he said, "with an ad presentation. But when I stood up here and looked out at the group of men that Ebby had put together to sell his product, I realized we had the program on ass-backwards. Eberhardt Vogel *is* Western Gold, and you should be hearing it from him and not from a couple of ad men." He got that much out. The wobble in his voice apparently sounded like emotion, because there was a lot of applause, and he was able to hold up his hand again for silence and explain that of course he and Corky Chalmers (he located Corky and asked him to stand—more applause) would be available to discuss any and all aspects of the program.

"That went over big with the distributors," said Corky a little later.

"I sort of lost it up there."

"I'm not sure about Vogel, though."

"Why do we always have to meet here and have drinks?"

"You don't like it?"

"I mean, why do we have to drink? The way we feel about each other. I'm so happy just seeing you, just being with you."

"Okay, let's go. We don't need to finish these."

"I mean, why don't we just take a walk in the park sometime? Or see a movie or just talk. I like to know what you think about things. Like, who are you going to vote for for mayor?"

"I haven't given it much thought yet."

"Well, I know who I'm going to vote for. We need better lower-middle-class housing. And the subway fare. That's who I'm going to vote for."

"All right, I'll vote for him too. For the subway fare."

"Darling, you know what I mean. Let's walk up Fifth Avenue and look in the windows of the stores. Pretend we're newlyweds on a honeymoon in New York. Buying things."

She was crazy about shoes. She would spend fifteen minutes in front of a shoe store, her arm locked through his, her body pressed close against him. She looked at shoes while he looked up and down the avenue to see if anybody he knew was coming.

Julia was asked to Hobe Sound for two weeks to visit her mother. He pleaded work and stayed behind, thinking of the time he might spend with Fran, maybe have her in the apartment overnight or over a weekend.

161

"You could fly down on a Thursday or Friday," Julia said. "Come back on Tuesday. That would give you almost a week, with only two days off."

"I'd like to, but the campaign's just starting now."

"You work too hard. You're really not looking well."

"Then there's the follow-up on the distributors' meeting. That'll be on Friday." True, but he hoped to find a way of ducking that.

"I don't like those meetings. They encourage drinking and staying up late. You're sure you'll be all right while I'm gone? You won't stay up too late?"

"I'll be fine."

"Thursday is Dagmar's day off. And Sunday-night supper also." Mary Smallwood went with her for the bridge and golf.

Fran in the apartment? Safe there with Dagmar out. What would it be like with Fran in a real bed, really safe?

Mr. Wright's secretary: "He wants to see you."

Foreboding. He took a nip just as a precaution. The foreboding was appropriate. Mr. Wright was alone in his office and closed the door after him as he came in.

"We're going to make some changes in the Western Gold account."

He waited.

"Starting the first of the month, Chalmers will be in charge."

Chalmers!

"We feel things are going well enough for him to take over. Fenn has something he wants you to do."

"What is it?"

"A drug promotion. He'll talk to you about it this afternoon."

"But—"

"It will probably take all your time."

"But Vogel. I'm his contact here. I brought him in."

"I know."

"He won't like that. I see him socially. We're close friends. We might lose the account. Don't you think you should consult Vogel?"

"Vogel was the one who asked for the switch."

He drank his lunch again and was in no condition to see Wilking that afternoon. He went home and found Julia packing.

"Fred, what's the matter with you? You look awful."

"Business lunch. Had a couple too many."

"You're drunk."

"Just tired."

"That's disgraceful. That's a terrible business you're in. Those long hours and late nights. And all that drinking."

"Business lunch. Happens once in a while."

"George Claxton's in the advertising business. He never drinks at all."

"Probably doesn't get anywhere."

"He's a vice president of Batten, Burton—whatever."

"Stuffy outfit."

"You're not going to have another?"

"Relax me. Just a little one. I'm going to take a nap."

Looking out his window: "About your memorandum."

Memorandum? He fastened on the word. He was really hung and doing his best not to show it.

"Your idea of aiming it at Omega Pharmaceutical was right, but your approach was wrong. They would rather buy a going company than start one themselves. Something already established and successful, even if they have to pay more for it. That way, it won't appear as one of their own products if it should fail."

It came to him. "Histochlor?"

"The triangular-green-pill concept is a good one. I have already taken out papers to incorporate Histochlor Laboratories. If it doesn't go, we'll write it off. If it does, Omega will buy it. Meanwhile Raoul Stumpfig has resigned from Omega to become president of Histochlor. He has wide experience in promoting and marketing drugs. I would like you to take on the advertising responsibility for Histochlor."

"You mean quit here?"

"No, no. You will operate right from here. I think it will be a good opportunity for you. You should also meet Raoul. Why don't you take him to lunch?"

"Ooooh, what a gorgeous view. What gorgeous drapes. What gorgeous plants."

He stood behind her, his hands on her breasts. She leaned back against him, watching a tug in the river, the skein of lights on the Queensboro Bridge.

"Darling, I could be so happy in a place like this." She turned and clung to him. But when she kissed him she asked: "Did you have a drink?"

"Just one while I was waiting." Actually three, for nerves. "Would you like one?"

"No, I don't like drinking. Why do we have to drink when we have each other?"

"We don't."

"I wish you wouldn't."

"What would you like to do?"

"Kiss me. Hold me."

"You're sure you don't want just one little one to take away the smell of mine?"

"All right. But next time why don't we not either of us have any."

He mixed her a light bourbon and made a double for himself. He was beginning to feel pretty good, no longer jumpy at having her there with Julia's presence all around.

"Is that you?"

"Yes."

"Why are you in your underwear?"

"That's not underwear. Those are running shorts. I was on the track team at college."

"Oh. Is that your wife?"

"Yes."

"Is that her horse?"

"No. It's one of the plantation horses. Her uncle has a plantation."

She studied the picture. "I think she should wear her hair a little softer and fuller. Make her face a little softer and rounder."

"Your hair's just right."

"I washed it last night when I knew I was goingg to be with you. I wanted it to be clean and sweet-smelling for you."

He took a double handful of it and buried his face in it. "You don't dye it?"

"No, darling. Why?"

"I've never seen such black hair."

"I like yours better. That sort of reddish."

He came to the end of his double. He was beginning to feel absolutely terrific. "I'll show you another picture of me." He led her into the bedroom and showed her the one on Julia's bureau.

"A soldier?"

"That was taken in England during the war."

"You look so handsome in your uniform. Who is that short little man?"

"That's Major McNally. He introduced me to the first girl I ever kissed." He pulled her down on the bed.

164

"Is this your bed?"

"No."

"Let's get on the other one."

"The other one is Julia's."

"Who sleeps in this one?"

"Nobody. I sleep in the next room."

"I want to go there."

He took her there.

"Does she ever come here?"

"No."

She settled herself on the bed. "When you make love to her, do you do it in her bed?"

"Yes."

"Why don't you sleep in the same room with her?"

"We sleep better this way. Sometimes I snore a little."

"Darling, if I was married to you I wouldn't care if you snored. I'd sleep in the same bed with you and make love to you every night."

He took off his jacket and shoes and lay down beside her. She snuggled up next to him.

"Do you make love to her often?"

"Not very."

"How often?"

"Not at all since I met you."

"Do you love her?"

"Yes."

"How can you love her and me?"

"It's different. She's—she's not like you at all. You're special."

"You love me the most?"

"Yes." Right then he did. He surely did. He loved her profoundly.

"That's the truth, darling?"

"Oh, yes."

"Why can't we get married?" she whispered.

"Why don't you take your dress off so that it won't get wrinkled."

She got off the bed and slowly pulled her dress up over her head. There was a black silk slip under it. She kicked off her shoes and lay down beside him again. He began caressing her.

"Darling, why not?"

"Why not what?"

"Why not us get married?"

"I'm already married."

"But if you love me most, you should get a divorce and marry me."

"We couldn't live here."

"I don't care where we live. I just want to live with you."

"Oh, Fran." Love and liquor choked him. Right now he might. If only right now could endure forever. He got up and took off his trousers.

"Don't do that, darling."

"I don't want to wrinkle them."

"But we're getting all undressed."

"Only half. Besides, don't you like the feel of your legs against my legs?" He felt her legs with his, got a knee between them, a hand inside her slip.

"Darling, you mustn't—"

Got a hand in back and undid her bra. Pulled her bra. Couldn't get it off. Got a hand in front. Pulled again.

"Don't."

Shoulder straps of bra caught in shoulder straps of slip. Big and strong and hot and reckless now. Rip slip. Did so. Boy, did it ever rip, right down the middle. Flip up bra. Feast on breasts.

"Fred! *Stop!*"

No way. For all her squirming and scratching, he could not.

She cried a lot. He felt so awful that he went and sat in the living room. He could hear her in the bathroom, and later in his room, putting on her dress. She came out to go.

"I didn't know what to do with the slip. It's ruined. I left it on your bed. You'll have to throw it away."

"I'll get you another."

"I don't want another. Goodbye, Fred."

In anguish: "Fran, I'm sorry. It was the liquor. I didn't know what I was doing."

She went to the door.

"Please. Oh, Fran."

"Why don't you just not drink?"

"I won't." He hugged her. She endured that stiffly. "I won't. Let me take you home. You're in no shape to go home by yourself."

They held hands in the taxi. He told it to wait while he took her up the steps. "I'll call you Wednesday." He saw her safely inside, and the door shut. Then he studied all the names on the mailboxes.

17

RAOUL STUMPFIG WAS A SMOOTH TALKER IN A Wragge shirt, with a Tiffany tank watch on his wrist. He was obviously impressed by the Racquet Club but made no mention of it. Over a couple of drinks, they sized each other up. He came to the conclusion that Raoul Stumpfig was more his kind and that he could manage with him if he didn't say too much. Stick with questions. Ask about the manufacturing.

"In Hempstead, Omega has a wholly-owned subsidiary, Beta Drug. Beta owns another company, Long Island Products. We'll use some facilities that Long Island will lease out to us, and the connection to Omega won't show."

"Why shouldn't it show?"

"Left hand, right hand."

He didn't understand that and decided to risk looking stupid and ask.

"Basic," said Raoul Stumpfig. "If your left hand and your right hand are really the same, your left hand shouldn't be selling something to your right hand for a big markup. You're just moving money from one pocket to the other and screwing the people in the middle, the stockholders."

"Oh."

"And there's always a couple of stockholders out there with sharp pencils who would love to catch you at that. You have to make sure you keep your distance."

He remembered what Mr. Wilking had said, something quite different: that it would hurt the image of Omega Pharmaceutical if it developed Histochlor directly and Histochlor then failed.

"Not that at all," said Raoul Stumpfig. "This is a capital gains play. That's what you set up the separate company for. Your friend Wilking and my friend Adamson have done this before. They will own Histochlor. They will sell it to Omega for big bucks. No point in paying themselves bigger salaries. Uncle just takes it away from them in taxes. But the capital gain—they can keep most of that. So they incorporate Histochlor. Adamson goes in for forty-five percent. Wilking and Wright each go in for twenty-two percent. You're in for one percent. To make you folks even with Adamson."

"How about you?"

"I'm the swing man. I get ten percent. And I guarantee Adamson control."

Histochlor was floated on a million shares of common stock worth ten cents a share. He was delighted to be given the opportunity to subscribe to ten thousand shares himself, equally delighted to be financially involved with his bosses. He put up his thousand dollars and two days later received a certificate with a bright-orange ornamental border and an engraving of a nymph sitting on a globe of the world and holding three arrows in one hand and a test tube in the other. In the appropriate places were typed his name and the amount of his holding: 10,000 shares.

He had never seen a stock certificate before; all his dealings with his broker had been on paper. Now that he had a certificate in his hand, he felt more like the owner of something than he had felt with those other investments, which were mere names on monthly statements, their values fluctuating from day to day. His certificate was No. 5.

A week later he went out to Hempstead with Stumpfig to inspect the production facilities where the pills would be made, and he asked to see the stock-certificate book of the corporation. It had entries in it like stubs in a checkbook. As Stumpfig had said, there were only five stockholders: himself with his 10,000 shares, Stumpfig with 100,000 shares, Wilking and Wright with 220,000 shares each. The owner of certificate No. 1, with 450,000 shares, was something called Bahamian Floral Enterprises, with an address in Nassau. He looked at Stumpfig.

"That's Adamson."

"Floral Enterprises?"

"Just a name. He wants to keep as far away from Omega as he can."

He phoned Wednesday, sober and subdued.

"Did you drink?"

"No."

"I would like to take a walk."

So they walked up Fifth Avenue again, window-shopping. Then they walked along Central Park South. It was raw and windy, and they walked slowly, huddled together in the dark.

"I like this better when we don't drink."

At Columbus Circle she kissed him good night and scuttled into the subway. He was shivering and hit the nearest bar.

"My friend has set up May first for delivery of production and store displays."

He listened and sipped.

"I'm going to make that. I'll start shipping April first."

He sipped again.

"You were supposed to have a campaign rough for me on Friday." Stumpfig's voice was mild, but his eyes were hard. He was paying no attention to the up atmosphere of the Racquet Club bar.

"I'll have something next Friday. I'm breaking in a new man, and he's very slow."

"My friend's leaning on me. If he leans any harder on me, I'll have to lean on your friend."

"Okay."

"We've got to move to sign up space, or we won't get it."

"Okay." His sips became gulps.

The new man wasn't any Corky Chalmers. He was anxious to please, would do what he was told. Indeed, he wanted to be told, but he wasn't being told. The days passed. The tension rose.

Fred would sit in his office in a kind of paralysis, looking at rate schedules, shuffling papers, relieving himself from time to time with a nip from his bottle. When Friday came and Stumpfig called, he told Miss Gorce to say he was out but would call him back.

Fran had become the only refuge in a terrifying world. He was usually fairly well loaded by lunch and would spend the afternoon in the steam room at the Racquet Club, having a rub and a snooze so that he could be sober enough to see her that evening. But she would still smell the liquor in him.

"You drank."

"Just one. At lunch. I couldn't avoid it."

"You said you wouldn't."

"Look—one drink."

On Friday, after Stumpfig's call, with no campaign ready—

nothing—he fled to the Racquet Club bar and spent such a long and desperate late-morning and lunch hour there that he was still in bad shape when he picked up Fran at six.

"You drank."

"Just one. At lunch."

"You said that yesterday."

"I know, but I'm feeling bad. Pressure of work. Please."

Together they went to his office, where he clung to her on the sofa, not from desire but from a need to cling to the only warm and unthreatening thing he knew.

"Darling, if you didn't drink, I know you'd feel better. You'd work better. You wouldn't worry."

"Everybody drinks in the advertising business. It's a way of life."

"Maybe you should leave the advertising business."

"I won't be able to make that kind of money anywhere else."

"I don't care about money. Anyway, I got a promotion. I'm now in charge of all the catering at the Council. Aren't you proud of me?"

He lay close to her, she as still as he, turning that over. For a moment it seemed so simple and easy. Lower his sights. No strain. A quiet life.

"Darling," she whispered.

"What?"

"Why can't we get married? I have an important job now, but I would give it up for you."

He said nothing.

"Mindy did. See how happy she is."

"I never see Mindy."

"I do. Mindy is very happy. She is expecting a baby."

What had been festering in him erupted. "Collins. That's an Irish name, isn't it?"

"I guess."

"You're not Irish, are you. What are you, Italian, Spanish?"

"What do you mean, darling?"

"Your name. On the mailbox. Carlo Colinari. Is that your father?"

"Yes."

"You said his name was Carl."

"Only to make it easy to say. Anyway, what difference does it make—if we love each other?"

"Collins. Why did you do that?"

"I had to get a job. On account of prejudices. I would have told you."

"After we got married?"

"No, darling. I would do it soon. I already was thinking about it. Mindy did it."

"Did what?"

"She told Ebby." Her voice fell to a whisper. "Mindy is not Mindy. I should not tell you this, because it is her secret. Mindy is really Minda Mackstein. A Jewish girl. When she went on that trip to England for the Advertising Council, the time Mr. Wright arranged for her to go at the last minute, she had to get a passport. But she was in such a rush, getting clothes and all, she had to send me. I found out that way."

Mackstein? Minda? That totally up girl?

"She asked me not to tell anybody. To make her feel good, I told her about myself. We share a secret—except now I told you."

Minda Mackstein?

"If Mindy and Ebby, why not us?"

"I told you. I'm already married."

"I know, darling, but if you don't really love your wife . . . I don't think she really loves you, or she wouldn't want to have a separate room from you."

Christ. Oh, Christ. "I'll think about it. Honest, I will, Fran—if that's your name. What is your real name?"

"Francesca."

"Francesca Colinari. That's a prettier name than Fran Collins."

"You really think so?"

"What is it, Spanish?"

"Actually more Italian."

"What does more Italian mean?"

"Actually more Sicilian."

That last came out in the faintest whisper of all, as if Sicilian were somehow lower than Italian.

Wright again. Handling the ax for his cowardly asshole of a partner. "I'll put it to you bluntly. Fenn has a report from Raoul Stumpfig that you aren't doing anything with Histochlor."

"I've been having trouble breaking in Watson. Held up on account of that."

"Watson's no Chalmers, huh?"

"No, he isn't. If I only had—"

"You won't. You can't lean on your assistants, Fred. And you can't hide in a bottle. I'm afraid we'll have to let you go. We've given you two important jobs, and you've dropped them both."

* * *

Stunned, but not really surprised. On the one hand, relief that the pretense was over. On the other, what was he going to do? For right now, drink a *good deal* and then get home somehow. Break the news to Julia that he'd lost his job, been fired, was no good, didn't know what to do with himself.

He rolled in at 2:30 P.M. He had never done that before. Julia wasn't in the living room, but her bedroom door was shut, so he tacked down the hall and flung it open. Though the blinds were drawn, he could see that she was in bed and that there was somebody in bed with her.

"Fred! Don't come in here."

But he was already in. Whoever it was in bed with her had his head under the covers. He walked over to the bed.

"Fred, please! Get out. Get out."

He reached for the covers.

"*No!*" Clinging to them.

Drunkenly ignoring her, dully curious as to who the bastard might be, and not quite sure what he would do when he found out, he gave a great heave and stripped the bed. For the first time in his life, he got a look at his wife stark naked. Lying next to her, also stark naked, was Mary Smallwood.

Mary Smallwood?

While he was taking that in, Mary flipped over onto her belly and hid her face. He stood, probably with his mouth open, staring at them, holding the sheet and blanket in his hand, goggling at his naked wife as she slowly sat up with a hand across her mouth and took the covers from his dumbfounded fingers. She gave the blanket to Mary, who ran into the bathroom. The sheet she wrapped around herself.

"Well, well." He sat down in a chair.

"Fred, please. Please, Fred. Go."

"Think I'll stay."

"Please, Fred. This is too humiliating. Too awful. Oh, God. Mary. I can't stand it." She had the sheet up to her mouth.

"The great bridge team."

"I beg—"

"The great screwing team."

"Fred, I implore you. She can hear."

He went and banged on the bathroom door. "Mary, you better come out. Your partner's going down. In spades."

"Fred, if you have any—"

"How do you like that from off the top of my head? Going down in spades? Come on out, Mary. Pick another suit. Pick hearts. We'll all go down together in hearts." He hammered on the door again, hurting his hand. "Let's have some action."

"Fred, in common decency—"

"Kind of action I never got."

Julia's voice went up in a swoop. He turned on her, the long rage and deprivation boiling over, and began tugging at the top of the sheet. It was an old linen one—Julia slept on nothing but linen—and very soft.

"No. No. No." She hung on.

"A little action." He ripped the sheet in two. Fred the Ripper, always good for a good rip when the rips were down. Julia clung to the pieces. As he grabbed for her, she started to scream. It was then that he became aware that Mary Smallwood had emerged from the bathroom and was hitting him on the head with the brush Dagmar used for cleaning the toilet. He took a swipe at Mary and knocked her across the bed with the back of his hand.

Mary Smallwood began to scream. For a slight woman, she had a remarkably loud scream. Both of them were screaming now. Dagmar must have called the superintendent. He was still thrashing around on the bed with the two naked women when the super arrived.

No charges were pressed. He agreed to let Julia divorce him, and she went off to Reno with the understanding that he would be out of the apartment when she got back. Dagmar refused to stay there with him and quit. He was left with a refrigerator full of food, most of a case of bourbon and other assorted bottles. The food lasted longer than the bourbon. He didn't go out. He didn't wash the dishes or shave. He didn't even bother to dress. A good deal of the time he spent lying on the sofa, sipping a glass of bourbon. He spent hours in the bathtub, sipping there, running a little more hot in when the water cooled, turning the faucet with his toe because he didn't have the energy to sit up and turn it with his hand. Besides, with no food in him, he got cold when he sat up in the tub. He ran the water hotter and hotter. The skin on his feet and his fingers crinkled and turned whitish. He sipped slowly and carefully, trying to maintain a comfortable floating equilibrium in which he could exist but did not have to bother with anything, did not have to think. From time to time the water would suddenly feel too hot. Abruptly sweat would prickle in his hair and pour down his face. He could imagine it flooding out of his body and into the bathwater. Bright pink and breathless, he would get out, attempt to dry himself off, and fall into bed. But the sweat would continue to run out of him, drenching the sheets and eventually making them smell sour. Never mind. He had a bottle by the bed as well as by the bathtub. He ran out of bourbon and began working his way through the Scotch.

One morning the phone rang. He let it ring. That afternoon it rang again, over and over. He got out of the tub, wrapped a towel around himself, and answered it, surprised at how dizzy and weak he was.

"Fred, is that you?"

"Yes." He was close to blacking out. All that hot water. He fell onto the sofa.

"We had a date for last Wednesday. You didn't call. I was worried about you."

"What day is today?"

"Today is this Wednesday."

"Wednesday?"

"I called at your office. They said you weren't there. They said they were waiting for you to come and get your things. What does that mean, Fred?"

"Huh?"

"Are you leaving your office? Did you decide after all to quit?"

"Uh?" Waves of blackness.

"You don't sound right. Are you alone? Can we talk?"

"Yes."

"Where is your wife."

"Gone."

"Gone where?"

"Gone."

"Fred, you don't sound right. Maybe I should come and see you."

"Okay."

"When?"

"Okay."

When she arrived, he was able to make it to the door and let her in over a pile of the *New York Times* stacked on the doormat. She found a pair of pajamas and some clean sheets and got him into bed. She cleaned up the mess in the kitchen, boiled him a couple of eggs, and made a cup of tea. She sat on the edge of the bed while he ate the eggs. His hands were so shaky that she had to hold the teacup.

"Darling, how can you get yourself like this?"

"Things sort of piled up."

"What things?"

"My job. Julia." Suddenly he threw up the eggs. Without warning they just bounced up all over the clean pajamas that Fran had gotten out. She rolled them up and found another pair.

"Darling, haven't you been eating?"

"Not much."

"Just drinking?"

"A little."

"You promised you wouldn't."

"I know."

"Those bottles all over. There are four in the bathroom. You promised."

"I know, but—" He couldn't look at her, couldn't continue.

"You have liquor here?"

He nodded.

"Where is it?" He couldn't speak. "Never mind; I'll find it." She did, and came back in a little while. "Darling, I found a closet full of bottles. I poured them all down the sink. Now I'm going out to buy some milk and bread and soup. I'll be back in a few minutes. I have your key ring. Which is the one to the front door?" With great difficulty he identified it.

He either slept or passed out. The next thing he remembered was Fran touching his shoulder. "I have a cup of soup. Campbell's chicken noodle. Maybe if you drink it very slowly . . . ?"

She sat on the edge of his bed, holding his hand. Gradually it grew dark. He drifted off to sleep again, and when he woke it was the next morning. The dizziness and shakiness were practically gone. He was able to shave and make himself some coffee and toast. The phone rang again.

"Darling, how are you?"

"Okay."

"How okay?"

"I'm having breakfast. I'm going to clean the apartment."

"That's very good, darling. I'm at work now. I can't leave. But I'll come up and see you around six."

The cleanup was perfunctory. Everything he did made him sweat. He was overpoweringly thirsty, and during the morning drank about a quart of water. He rested up on the sofa, tried to read the paper, couldn't concentrate on it, opened another can of soup for lunch, grew increasingly restless, then panicky as the true nature of his situation came crunching down. He decided to take a short walk. Just in case he might need them sometime, he picked up a couple of bottles of bourbon on his way home. He was deep into the first one when Fran arrived.

"Oh, *Fred!*"

"Have to taper off, you know. It isn't all that easy just to—"

But she was gone.

"During our conversations you have said how lonely you have felt throughout your life, that nobody loved you."

"That's right."

"I think this girl loved you."

"She did, that's right."

Hennerkop paused, and the pink cathedral of fingers appeared in front of his nose. "I think I should ask you if you have ever considered why it was that you drank again that last day that you saw her."

"Well, I was in bad shape, you know. Everything was falling to pieces. I'd been drinking for a couple of weeks."

"But you are not a true drinker. I have already told you that. You have confirmed it yourself when so easily and quickly you stopped drinking."

"I know."

"So I repeat: Why did you drink that last day that you saw her."

"I just said—"

"Yes. And that is not a good explanation. I ask you if the real reason was that you did not want to tell her that you would not marry her."

"Now wait a minute."

"Being drunk would have been a way to avoid a painful confrontation. You want to please women. You want to make them feel happy, to be sexually aroused, but you do not really want to get close to them. You must appease them, as you never appeased your mother. Women frighten you, despite what you see as your need and desire for them. When Fran began asking you to marry her, you were placed in a dilemma. You were afraid to marry her, but you were also afraid to tell her that you would not marry her. The solution was to turn yourself into a drunkard so that she would leave you. Being an intelligent woman with a strong character, she did that—as I suspect you suspected she would. What is your reaction to these suggestions?"

"My reaction is that they are a load of crap."

Silence.

"I was drinking *before* I met Fran. I was having trouble with Julia and with my job *before* I met her. So what is your reaction to that?"

"When a person feels a strong need for something, he will use the tool that is handiest to him. Your social attitudes, and the fact that you were already using drinking to soften other problem areas in your life, made it natural that you would seize on that same tool. Let me ask you: If Fran had stayed with you that afternoon, would you have stopped drinking, as she so often asked you to do?"

"How do I know that?"

"I think not, because I think she would have continued to press you to marry her. That would be something you would have no good excuse not to do, now that you were being divorced. So permit me to ask you another question: Why did you not wish to marry Fran?"

"Well, we weren't really compatible. Except for sex, we didn't have anything in common. Our backgrounds. After the lovemaking, there wasn't anything to talk about. No discussions about anything."

"Like the discussions you had with your wife?"

"What?"

"You have given no evidence that you had discussions with anybody. I ask you to consider that."

He considered it. What a horrible chasm it opened.

"Discussions cannot be a good reason. Why did you not wish to marry her?"

"I just couldn't."

Silence.

"Can't you understand? She was a Sicilian."

Silence.

"An immigrant. Her father was a laborer. Couldn't speak English. Her kid brother was in a street gang. Jesus Christ, you can't marry into that."

He found himself sobbing again.

Hennerkop said quietly: "You can marry whomever you love. I suggest to you that you did not love her but only needed her. I suggest that you have been so frightened and defended in your life that you have never permitted yourself to love anybody."

He tried to think of somebody. Violet? Too short. Too long ago.

"Your life has been a straight line—your account of it. There are no circles in it, no returns to people who mean something to you. You meet them. You react to them in whatever way seems most appropriate to you. You separate, and they are gone. It does not seem to make any difference to you. Why did you not make more of an effort to maintain contact with that English woman? Where did that friend the major go? Why do I hear nothing more about Bob Dixon?"

* * *

Hennerkop remembered everything. And what a hellish way he had of fitting it all together. He skipped his next appointment. Couldn't face it. Instead, he went back to Lincoln Harbor, to the real estate agent, because the island had come in again, blindingly strong, as if to blot out all the things Hennerkop had said. The island seemed to be all there was left.

18

HE WAS STILL IN THE APARTMENT WHEN JULIA GOT back from Reno. He had pulled himself together—somewhat. He no longer spent hours in the bathtub. He managed to get his clothes on every day and get out and around. He collected his things from the office. He did his drinking at the Racquet Club. It was more expensive but seemed more respectable. He ate at least one meal a day. He read the sports pages and the *Wall Street Journal*. He thought vaguely about opening an office of his own: Frederick Fay and Associates. But he never got beyond the point of wondering who the associates might be. He did think of one product he might promote: tinted condoms. Six assorted colors to a box. He even thought of names for them. Summer Twilight (pale blue). Deep Night (very dark blue). Silver Dawn (a sort of gunmetal color). First Love (natural white). April (pale green). Rosy Lips (pink). Omega Pharmaceutical had a subsidiary that sold rubber goods tucked away somewhere in its corporate tangle, but he didn't have the nerve to call Raoul Stumpfig. Rosy Lips and Summer Twilight faded away.

He came home one evening and found Julia standing in the middle of the living room. In the middle of an indescribable mess of tin cans, dirty plates, milk cartons, empty bottles, underwear strewn around. He had been living largely in the living room, because that was where the TV was.

Her mouth was like a mail slot.

"You were supposed to be gone."

"I'm going. I was just starting to pack."

"This place is a pigsty."

"You can always get Mary to help you clean it up. When is she moving in?"

"I'll give you half an hour to pack your things and get out."

He stuffed as much as he could into the largest suitcase he could find.

"I'll put the rest in a trunk and store it in the basement. You can get it from there."

"Don't put yourself out."

"It will be a pleasure. I don't want to see you here again. You live like an animal."

"A normal animal."

"A pig."

"With the healthy appetites of a healthy normal pig." She made him so angry that he felt like starting the ripping and tearing again. He put down the suitcase and waited for her to say the word, the one word that would set him off. But she didn't say it. She went into the bedroom, where he knew the mess to be equally bad. He'd been sick in there and hadn't bothered to clean up. So they parted, in silence and mutual loathing.

Having spent so many hours at the bar of the Shelton Hotel, he lugged his suitcase there and checked in. He spent the next week reading the furnished-room ads in the paper and going to see the ones that sounded least dreadful. He finally found a one-roomer, plain but fairly decent, a walk-up on East Twenty-second Street. He slept there, but he lived at the Racquet Club, gradually identifying a population of drifters like himself, who seemed to have nothing to do but read the papers, drink at the bar, and doze in the library. They lived a life apart from the noisier, healthier, more active members. He and they learned to recognize one another, nodded, but kept to themselves. Once in a while, after a mutual session at the bar, he would dine with one of them, always avoiding personalities. He didn't know the names of those dinner companions and doubted if they knew his. All the up men.

Late one afternoon he was propped against the bar, comfortably loaded, when Ebby Vogel came in with two men. They ordered drinks and had been talking for only a minute when Ebby spotted him and immediately turned his back.

He sauntered down the bar. "Hello, Ebby."

"Hello." He turned his back again.

He tapped Ebby on the shoulder. "How are things at the brewery?"

"Sorry, business to discuss. Come on." Ebby led the two men to a table.

He ordered another bourbon and put it down fast. It landed like a fat coal, feeding the blaze that was already brightening in him. He walked over to the table, leaned his hands on it, his fingers splayed among the drinks, among the plates of peanuts and soda crackers. "I asked you about the brewery, Ebby," he said.

"I heard you."

"Well, how are things?"

"Okay. Look, I'm busy."

"Too busy to say hello to the old friend who got you into this club?"

"Look, beat it."

"That's very curt, Ebby, to the old friend who got you into this club." He turned to one of the other men. "Very curt. Ask him who got him into this club. Just ask him."

The man looked uncomfortable.

"Ask him where he got the suit he's wearing, that shirt. Ask him where he got his wife. Ask him who introduced him to the Yid hooker he married. Ask him—"

Ebby was on his feet. "You shut your fucking mouth."

"Ask him who she was banging the night after he met her."

Ebby lunged at him across the table, slamming it against him, tipping plates and glasses on the floor, knocking him down. As he struggled to his feet, he saw Ebby being led out of the room by his two friends.

He was shaking with rage. A drink had been spilled on him. He brushed himself off, his hands trembling. To steady himself, he went back to the bar and ordered another bourbon.

"Sorry, Mr. Fay."

"Think nothing of it. Little disagreement. Don't forget the twist."

"Sorry, sir."

"Sorry about what?"

"Can't serve you, sir."

"Can't what?"

"Can't serve you, sir."

He leaned across the bar. "Listen, you. I want a bourbon."

"Club regulations, sir."

All his rage was now directed at the bartender. "God damn it. You get me a bourbon."

"Club regulations, sir. Noisy demonstrations or altercations—"

"Get it myself." He started around to the back of the bar and was blocked by a tall dignified man he had seen many times strolling around the club but whose name he didn't know. He tried to push by him.

"Take it easy."

"Bartender won't serve me a drink. Get it myself."

"I wouldn't. He's acting under orders."

"Whose orders?"

"The board of managers. I'm here to help out."

"And just who the fuck are you?"

"I'm Bill Moore, the club manager. We have a rule here. Any fighting in the bar, no more drinks to anybody involved."

"I wasn't fighting. He pushed the table over on me. He knocked me down. Now get out of my way." He struggled to push by, but Bill Moore was large and strong, and he was very drunk and beginning to have the drunk's feeling that the whole world was against him, which saps the will. Oh, how it saps the will and makes enemies of others who are watching your rage and your humiliation and your spreading weakness. And their scorn saps you more. The will drains away like blood. He felt it going. He let Bill Moore urge him gently but firmly into the elevator, get his coat from the cloakroom on the ground floor, and usher him out into the street.

He called Fran the next day. Twice she hung up on him. The third time a strange woman answered the phone and said Fran had gone out. When he went to the Racquet Club later that afternoon, the man at the front desk handed him an envelope, which he opened at the bar while sipping his first double bourbon of the day. In it was a typed note from the club secretary, informing him that at a meeting of the board of managers it had been voted to accept his resignation effective as of the date of the letter. He read this in a haze of fury. The sanctimonious bastards. He looked around at the large comfortable room. A few members drinking and talking quietly. The up atmosphere. The plates of peanuts. The cheese and crackers. The quick discreet service from the bar. Everything as it should be—but his no longer. Oh, the bastards. He had a second double, and another. If they were going to kick him out of their fucking club, the least he could do was get fucking blind on them, not pay their fucking bill, not pay any fucking bill.

While he was still able to walk, he left. He went around the corner to a small restaurant-bar where he had been told members sometimes picked up girls. He spotted one sitting at the bar.

"Hello, Mabel," he said.

The big slide had begun.

19

I DO NOT RECOMMEND IT."

Silence. This time *his* silence. If Hennerkop didn't recommend it, let him say why. But the silence stretched, and as usual, he broke it. "Why?"

"It is not good to live alone. With you, right now, it would be dangerous."

"But I do live alone."

"Yes."

"You pointed it out yourself; I have no friends."

"That is something the reason for which we should further explore."

"Why in the name of Christ almighty can't you get a sentence out straight?"

"My sentence did not get out straight?"

It was too complicated. He'd been up there. He had the makings of a deal. He'd come back wildly excited. There was a life there he could live, something he could look forward to. And with that stinking prissy diction Hennerkop poked holes in it. He got up and left, slamming the door although the session still had twenty minutes to run.

"Stupid to do that."

Silence.

"I mean, I should at least have stayed and had it out with you."

"Not necessarily. When one is angry, one is not always in a position to choose how he will express his anger. You have been angry through much of your life but have succeeded in suppressing it completely until quite recently. What may seem to you to have been recklessly destructive behavior—the fights, the divorce, the excessive drinking, the self-degradation—may have been necessary. It is possible to interpret them as the inexperienced and clumsy efforts to express anger by one who has had no experience in expressing anger. It is not surprising that you do it badly. But it is necessary that you do it."

He found that hard to believe.

"You deny your anger because it frightens you."

"Why shouldn't it? It's destroyed everything."

"What has it destroyed?"

"Everything. What is there left?"

"There is yourself left. You are beginning for the first time in your life to get in touch with your feelings. As you express them more clearly and begin to be more comfortable within yourself, then I think it will be possible for you not to be alone."

He stared at Hennerkop's pale earnest face behind the thick glasses.

"That is why I do not recommend that you leave now. There is much yet for you to do."

Oh, no; not that. Not the same old crap. Day after day. He could talk about lonely and loveless until he was blue in the face, but the fact remained that that was what he was. "Look, you've helped me; I don't deny that. But I'm dying in this city. I don't talk to anybody but you. I don't work. I don't do anything."

"Why do you think it is that you do not do anything?"

"I just can't. There's nothing for me to do."

"New York has many job opportunities."

"Like running elevators, licking envelopes. I mean a decent job."

"An important one with dignity, like your last one?"

"Well, yes—but I wouldn't necessarily aim that high."

"But still with dignity and prestige."

"A certain amount."

"Is the prestige more important than the job itself—than whether you can handle it?"

"What?"

"Someday you will have to work. Your money will be spent. Do you want another job with prestige that you cannot do, that frightens you so that you drink and become helpless? Or will you try to find something that you can do?"

"Like running an elevator and having every asshole in the building look down on you?"

"Why would they look down on you?"

"Because that's what they do. Don't you ever ride in elevators?

184

Don't you know how people look at elevator men?"

"I only know I would respect one who did his work conscientiously."

"Conscientiously! Where have you been? Most of the elevators in the city are automatic. How can you be conscientious in an automatic elevator? Press the button a little faster? With a little better flourish of your finger? There isn't any slob in the city who can't run an elevator."

Silence.

"Not one." His voice rose. "I'll be damned if I'll run an elevator. I just couldn't do it."

"There is a contradiction here."

"What?"

"You say any man in the city can run an elevator, but you just now say that you cannot run an elevator."

"Jesus Christ, Hennerkop."

"Are you saying you are not a man?"

"Slob. I said *slob!*" He was off the couch and standing over Hennerkop. "I'm no slob," he shouted. "Pick, pick, pick." His anger had reached the point of explosion. He reached down into the chair and got hold of a handful of coat lapel and necktie, ready to mash him, smash him. But Hennerkop was wearing those heavy eyeglasses. He let go and sat down again, caressing his still-clenched fist, feeling the knuckles with the palm of his other hand, feeling them drive into Hennerkop's nose, mash his mouth. "I could hit you, you know," he said heavily, "beat you up."

"Yes." Hennerkop looked very alert.

"I could do that. I almost did."

"I am relieved that you did not. But it is good that you expressed the impulse."

"You're not mad?"

"No, I am not. I provoked you. I felt it necessary."

"You're not scared?"

"For a moment, yes."

"Anybody ever hit you?"

"Once only. A patient with much anger to release." Alert. So alert and concerned. He found himself on the floor, hugging Hennerkop's knees. What was happening to him? How had he got there? Who was he anyway?

Getting up again, wiping his eyes, looking at that concerned face, had been awkward. By a kind of common consent, the session again ended early and he left. Awkward, but he was strangely elated. He took a long walk in the park. Instead of sitting on a bench, he walked around the reservoir, noticing the joggers and feeling for the first time in several years the impulse to run himself. As he walked, the island came back, oh so strong and sweet.

He could do it. He knew he could. He walked faster, pushing back the money problem, and also pushing back the impression that the real estate man, Charlie Barker, was dubious about the whole proposition.

"Thirty thousand," Barker had said. "I checked with the owner again. That's his price."

"I can't pay thirty thousand."

"Take out a mortgage."

"Mortgage?"

"Or rent. Why don't you just rent? He might even forgive you a year's rent if you put the house in shape. What do you want it for anyway?"

"I want to live there."

"Just summers?"

"No. All the time."

Charlie Barker gave him a careful look. "Ever spend a winter up here?"

"No."

"Know much about boats?"

"Not much."

He was sitting in Charlie Barker's office, a small neat one on Elm Street. By looking out his window, he could see down the street to the parking lot and the harbor water beyond it, glistening in the sun. Charlie Barker was a short, red-faced, infectiously cheerful man with totally impossible clothes. He had a ballpoint pen in his hand, and he spent some time examining it closely.

"You're going to think this is kind of funny," he said. "I could use the commission, but I don't think you should buy that island."

"Who pays the commission?"

"The seller. But that's not the point. I make a deal, I like to see a happy deal. I don't think you know what it'll be like out there in winter. There'll be weeks when you can't get ashore. It's cold out there in winter. And by God, it's windy. You'll have to learn how to take care of yourself."

"I guess that's something I could learn."

"You married?"

"No."

"You drink much?"

"I never drink anything."

Another careful look. "We've got a big AA chapter up here. The reason I asked. A lot of reformed drinkers for this size town. They think life will be easier here. Well, they're wrong. It isn't. Not enough for them to do to blow off steam. We create drinkers up here, we don't cure them."

"I guess you could call me a reformed drinker." Might as well come clean.

"The reason I asked."

"I mean, drinking's no problem with me now."

"You know about engines? Outboards?"

"Not much."

"You know how to run a generator? How to strip it? How to clean the line? Could you fix one?"

"I guess I could learn."

"That island's not for you. Why don't you rent it for a year with an option to buy."

It was laughable in a way. Here he'd been paralyzed, rotting. And the first thing he wanted to do, the first thing all on his own, everybody tried to talk him out of it.

Hennerkop again: "I strongly do not recommend it."

"You already said that."

"Here we are beginning to make progress. Here you are surrounded by people. Here you are in touch with me."

"All those nice friendly people surrounding me."

"To isolate yourself on an island is to run away from the central problem of your life."

"The central problem of my life is that I'm dying in this city. I've got to go somewhere."

Silence.

"Can't you for Christ's sake see that?"

"No. You have told me many times that the central problem of your life is loneliness. That is another way of saying that you do not love, cannot accept love. You will not solve that problem living alone on an island."

Again, and stronger.

"My mind's made up."

"I advise you to reconsider."

"You're just saying that to hang on to a customer."

Silence.

"I didn't really mean that."

Stronger yet.

"I've *got* to go."

"I respect your determination. I think we should discuss that further."

"Discuss. Discuss. That's all we ever do. What is there to discuss? Anyway, you hold all the cards."

"What cards are those?"

"You're the one who *knows*. You're the expert, the doctor. How can I stand up against you?"

"You are standing up well."

"I'm not. If I was really standing up, I'd just walk out of here. But if you keep saying no, I can't."

"I do not say no."

"Then what have we been arguing about all this time? You keep saying *no*."

"You misunderstand me."

"You say no."

"I am advising you not to act hastily, perhaps to defer a decision. I think such a move inadvisable at this time. I do not say no."

"You don't?"

"I do not ever order you to do anything."

"Okay, I'm going."

Hennerkop cleared his throat. "I repeat, I do not order. All I can do is advise. I have given you some reasons for my advice. Other reasons I have not given in the hope that you would find them yourself. That is the best way. But if you do go, perhaps I will not see you again."

"Perhaps not." Vast relief? Some regret?

"In case we do not meet again, I should give a small talk." Hennerkop paused and looked over his fingertips at him for a long time. "This is difficult, not the best way, but I will try. I said to you not long ago that you were like an orphan. Orphans are not orphans by choice, but it is still up to them to learn not to be orphans. That you have not yet learned. You have remained an orphan because you have not been close to anyone during your life—despite efforts. In your efforts not to be an orphan, to join the world, to become close to other people, you have, through the various circumstances and influences of your life, selected some goals and models that have not worked well for you. I do not mean to say that is your fault; rather that orphans do not always have good choices or clear vision. Nor do I suggest that the goals and models you selected were poor ones, only that they were poor for you because they did not bring you closer to others. On the contrary, they proved to be such a heavy burden that you became more isolated than before."

Hennerkop paused, as if to gauge the effect of this, the longest speech he had ever heard from him.

"I'm listening," he said.

"It is important for you to find better goals and models. Finding and recognizing them is difficult anywhere. It is probably impossible for one living alone on an island. That is my reason."

"I don't see it," he said. "I don't seem to be finding any goals or models here. I'm alone here. I'll be alone there. What's the difference?"

"You must learn not to be alone. You must learn to be more honest with yourself, more respectful of yourself."

"Easy to say."

"Yes. But you must try. When you are more honest with yourself, you can be more honest with other people. Then you can begin to trust them and achieve the intimacy that now escapes you."

"A good woman would help," he said, thinking of his endless drunken efforts to find just one among the legions of awful ones, just one bit of intimacy.

Hennerkop shook his head. "You dream always of a good woman. You think she will make you happy. That you have backwards. You do not find a good woman and because of her become healthy and happy. You first become healthy and then find a good woman. That is to say, you will be able to recognize a good woman. You cannot do that now."

"What are you talking about? If a halfway decent woman came along and gave me half a glance, I'd grab her."

"Grabbing is not enough. You did once grab a good woman, but you did not recognize her."

He rejected that. In fact, it infuriated him that the ghost of Fran was being pushed into this argument. Hennerkop had never understood the difficulty with Fran, the impossibility of Fran. He told him so loudly.

"That is what I have been trying to explain to you. You did not see that good woman clearly. You still do not."

On that fundamental disagreement they parted. "I'm going," he said, and he went.

20

SWEET JESUS, HE WENT! DESPITE HENNERKOP'S heavy pressure he went. He balanced that off against what he was beginning to feel about Charlie Barker, the real estate agent. He had seen Barker again and was touched by him. After all the showmanship and strutting, the throat-cutting, the subtle measuring and assessing, that went on in New York, Barker was refreshingly direct and honest, to the point of seeming innocent, more so than any other man he had ever met. Outside of Hennerkop, of course. But Hennerkop was a special case, neither innocent nor crafty. He was omnipotent, with his power to summon up all that terror and anger. After walking out on Hennerkop, he felt moments of true panic. With one uncontrollable slash he had severed his link with the nearest thing to God he knew, his link with everybody else too. He had ended a life. Lincoln Harbor was a flight into the unknown, with only a foolish boyhood memory to sustain it, and the hope of finding a friend. Hennerkop had said: "Make friends." Well, this new man in a totally new world, with the past totally erased, might become a friend.

So he fled, and was touched again when Charlie again tried to talk him out of buying the island. "Don't do it—at least not right off the bat. I think I can get you a year's rent and an option to buy for a thousand bucks. You'll know better in a year what you want to do."

Talking and thinking about money was a practical and reassuring thing. He had to think about it. He might be committing a lot of it, tying himself in too tight, as Charlie kept saying. He had to calculate, face things. He couldn't keep his back turned on that shrinking bank account. *He had to face it,* however the shrinkage shook him, however afraid he was of what might happen when there was no more shrinkage because there was nothing left to shrink. What would he do, run an elevator?

Okay, time for an unflinching rundown on his finances.

When Histochlor went public, he was suddenly much richer. It went public at five dollars a share. Overnight his investment of one thousand dollars zoomed to fifty thousand dollars. Later, after Histochlor went over big, after those little green pills had begun to sell by the millions, the company was bought by Omega, just as Raoul Stumpfig had predicted. In anticipation of that, there was a stampede for Histochlor stock, and Jerry Grogan, his broker, called him.

"At five bucks it's a steal. They'll have this hotshot from Omega running it."

"I already have some."

"What do you mean, you have some? You can't. It's not issued yet. You'll be lucky if I can get you a hundred shares. I'll put you down for five hundred and hope for a hundred."

"I said I already had some. I went in when it was formed."

"Oh," said Jerry. "Then you know about it. You *really* know about it, right? Tell me. Is that forty percent growth right? Is that real? We can't get to talk to management; all we see is their statement."

He pretended that he was still on the inside. "I don't think I should comment on that."

"Tell me. Jesus, you really should tell me. I'm your broker, your friend. You owe me something, Fred. I'm the one who got you into Litton."

"I really shouldn't discuss it."

"Jesus, Fred. Your *friend*. At least tell me your holding."

"Only ten thousand shares."

"*Only!* That's fifty thousand bucks."

"That's right."

"That's a hell of a lot for your account. Half your dough in one speculative company. Maybe you should sell a little."

"But you just told me I ought to buy some."

"I know, but I didn't know you had so much. To be prudent, you should diversify a little. Fred, if you want to sell half, maybe five thousand shares, I think I could place them at half a point up, maybe a point. How would you like six for yours?"

"A minute ago you were trying to sell me stock at five. Now you want to buy it at six?"

"You don't understand. I wasn't *selling* you stock. I was just telling you about it. It's a hot ticket. They'll ration the stock. I don't know if I can get you any. But as your friend, I thought I should at least mention it to you on the chance I could pick up a hundred shares or so. But if you already have it, then it's a different ball game. I think you might consider selling some at six—or six and a half."

"Even if you say it's going to thirty?"

"Well, you never *know*."

"I think I'll wait."

Which of course made Jerry Grogan even more anxious to buy. Jerry offered seven, which he turned down.

It was a good thing he did, about the only good thing he did with Jerry Grogan. When Omega bought Histochlor, the value set on the stock was ten dollars a share, and he wound up with $100,000 worth of Omega stock. His pleasure in that was tempered only by the realization that Wilking and Wright had each made more than two million on the same deal.

Jerry Grogan couldn't leave him alone. That hundred thousand dollars that he didn't have his hands on was killing him.

"Fred, you've got to diversify."

"Isn't Omega a good company?"

"The best. But they're slow compared to some others. You saw what happened to Histochlor. You ought to keep that money working a little harder for you. Take computers. Take fiberglass. Take the boat business. Do you know how many people are buying boats this year? Next year? There's a sweet little outfit down in Texas selling fiberglass boats faster than they can make them."

He ended up putting some of his Omega money into something called the Redfish Boat Co. and some more into the Span-America Boat Co. in Illinois. The latter, according to Grogan, who had now left Merrill Lynch and was running his own business, was going to be a superwinner. It was the first link in a chain of fiberglass boat-building concerns that would span the continent like a grocery chain. With everybody and his brother buying boats, selling them was going to be like selling groceries. So when Span-America fell from four dollars to two (Grogan: "A temporary glitch, ignore it"), he bought some more. But soon it went to zero. So did the Redfish Boat Co., bottom up. So did several other things.

Jerry would call him at his furnished room in the early afternoon after learning that he was never in any condition to talk in the morning. Even in the afternoons he was so shaky and miserable that he couldn't think clearly about Jerry's recommendations. He was frightened by his losses and desperate to recoup. He became a sucker for any story that promised a quick profit. Also he was burning with anger at Jerry; if he lost any more money, that would prove what a prick he was.

Jerry kept calling. He kept trying to clear his head and listen. The switches became more and more frequent. Jerry's commissions piled up as the account shrank.

With his accumulated savings and investments, with his severance pay from W and W, and with his huge windfall in Omega stock, he was worth nearly $150,000 when he began to lose all control of his life. A year later, from squandering money in bars and on women, but mostly through the activities of Jerry Grogan, his Omega stock was nearly gone and his total wealth had shrunk to less than fifty thousand dollars—as best he could reconstruct it later; those days were very hazy.

When he sobered up, he closed his account with Grogan and put all his money in a savings bank. That was what he had been living on ever since, watching it slowly dwindle as he paid for his room and his food and watched those sharklike bites go to Hennerkop every month.

One of the things he cried about in Central Park those days was the loss of his fortune. Histochlor, he realized, had been one shot in a million. Nothing like it would come his way again. Why had he been so stupid and greedy? If he had only put it in the bank, he would have all of it now, and a steady income of six or seven or maybe eight thousand dollars a year. He could buy an island. With what was left over, he could live quietly and carefully forever. He would never have to do anything again.

What he didn't tell Charlie Barker was that his total resources were now down to about $35,000. Outright purchase of the island was unthinkable. It would cost something to put the house in shape and buy a boat. After those expenses he would have nothing left. So he asked about a mortgage, and that got complicated. The island had lain unsold for so long that the local bank would not accept the property itself as a significant part of the collateral. Other banks wouldn't touch it at all.

"I keep telling you to rent," said Charlie.

How could he explain his passion to own? How explain the exhaustion of all his hopes except this one, the bright vision, the charmed glimpse of a magic past that would somehow rescue him and turn him into a human being again? Had he ever been one? Whatever he was, the island would nourish. His last, his only hope.

He ended up with a deal that seemed workable, although Charlie shook his head over it. He would pay two thousand dollars a year against purchase of the island. That would eat into his capital slowly enough for him to breathe for a few years while he figured out what to do with himself. This was not a mortgage but a straight installment purchase. If he failed to keep up the payments he would lose everything.

"Everything but the house," stipulated Charlie. "They're going to have to let you keep the house out of it. It needs work, work you'll be doing yourself. So if you ever lose the whole shebang, the house will still be yours to sell separately."

A document was prepared and signed. He handed Charlie a check for two thousand dollars.

"I think you're absolutely nuts."

"Okay, I'm nuts."

"I feel kind of responsible for you. The first thing I'm going to have to do is find you a boat."

"Okay."

"And teach you how to keep from drowning yourself in the goddamned thing."

Happily nuts, though. This was the first thing he could remember having done in his entire life—forget all the bad things—that he had not been ordered to do, that had not been suggested to him or forced on him by circumstance or by the prejudices or social standards of others. *His* decision, made in defiance of everyone else instead of at their command. Nuts? Okay, nuts, but what a wonderful sweet nuts. It stayed with him when he went to pick up his trunk in the basement of the Sutton Place apartment. Spring was plunging into summer, and the trees along the parkways were a thick green as he drove to New York in the car he had borrowed from Charlie. He sang as he drove, sometimes at the top of his lungs, off and on all the way to the city. He parked the car, nerved himself to march in past the doorman, whom he recognized and who recognized him, up to the twelfth floor and rang the bell. Dagmar answered.

"Mr. Fay!"

"Is Mrs. Fay in?"

A long scared indecisive look. "I'll just go see." She shut the door on him.

The next person to open it was Julia.

"I don't want to bother you. I came to get my trunk."

"Come in."

"In?"

194

"If you want—for a minute."

Like a couple of strange cats entering a backyard, they moved together into the living room. He sat down on the edge of a chair. The place was immaculate again, the plants and flowers banked deep along the window, the silver matchbooks with the green initials in the Steuben ashtrays. This had been his home, listed in the Social Register:

Fay, Mr & Mrs Frederick Curzon (Julia Fanshawe)
Phone No P15-0321
Rc.Cly.P'40   5 Sutton Pl S

The *Rc* and the *Cly* stood for the Racquet and Colony clubs, the *P'40* for his class at Princeton. He had always been secretly proud to have been included in that directory of socially prominent New Yorkers (automatic when he married Julia), something that neither Mr. Wilking nor Mr. Wright had achieved. During those zombie days when he was wandering around alone in the Racquet Club, he would occasionally console himself by looking up his name in the fat little black book with its orange stripes on the cover, which the club kept next to the telephone books. Finding himself there, he could remind himself that he was—or had been—up. He could find some assurance that he existed. "I had a wife named Julia. . . ." Then, although no listing for her: "I had a girlfriend named Fran. . . ."

Julia looked just the same, tall, slender, very smart in a dark-blue wool dress and dark-blue alligator shoes. For a moment the gulf opened again as she sat there, so neat, so aristocratic-looking, so up. But then she plucked an imaginary bit of fluff from her dress, and he realized that she was at least as ill at ease as he was. Pluck, pluck. His long battles with Hennerkop had taught him the value of silence. He waited for her.

"I didn't expect to see you again," she finally said.

"I don't mean to—"

"No, that's all right. I just—" Some more plucking.

"What do you call yourself—your name?"

"Oh, that. Mrs. Fanshawe Fay."

"I would have guessed you'd call yourself Mrs. Julia Fay."

"Mother. She suggested it."

"How is your mother?"

"She's very well. She's going to marry Mr. Wilking."

"*What?*"

"Next week."

Marry Wilking? He might have guessed it. Wilking had the upward mobility of a sperm cell. That suave but remorseless upward wriggle. Against all odds, hit that egg. He couldn't help laughing.

"What's so funny? He's a charming man."

That was something he didn't feel up to explaining to prissy virginal Julia. Well, not exactly virginal. But, well, maybe; he didn't know how lesbians did things. He fought down the picture of the two of them naked in bed that day. "I mean, me having been married to you and now him being married to your mother. It just seems a little—"

"Mother's been lonely. She's been a widow for eight years."

"I mean, I was only— Congratulate her for me."

"I will."

"That is, if she doesn't hold—"

"Oh, no. She always liked you. Of course, she never saw you drunk."

One from her. He decided to fire one in return. "How's Mary?"

She flushed deeply. "She's all right."

"You still"—he hunted for the saving word—"play bridge?"

Still flushing: "Yes."

"Say hello to her."

"All right."

"And apologize to her for the way I acted. I'm sorry I hit her."

"That's— That is—" She found several pieces of fluff that needed attention.

"All that liquor."

Pluck.

"I don't drink anymore." She raised her eyes to his face, as if to see if she could find any believability there.

"It's true. I'm on the wagon. I haven't had a drink for more than a year. Two years. I went to an analyst. I stopped."

"Did he . . . ?"

"I guess so. I wasn't getting any better before I went to him. Actually I was getting worse."

"Well. I must say you look—"

"I feel fine."

"What are you doing? I mean, I know you left Mr. Wilking. He told Mother you had decided to do something else."

"I'm moving out of New York. That's why I came to get my trunk."

"Where to?"

He realized he didn't want anybody from his old life intruding on the dream-reality he was sailing into. "To a quiet place," he said.

"Alone?" she asked.

"Yes. I take it you're not."

She blushed again.

He couldn't resist it. "Why did you marry me?"

She plucked, couldn't answer.

"I mean, were you and Mary . . . ? Before we married?"

"Yes. That is, no, not really. It got— I mean— After we— Please—" She was looking extremely agitated.

"I'll get my stuff." He stood up.

She didn't. "I'm going to an analyst too," she said in a low voice.

"How's it going?"

"He makes me feel guilty all the time. Not that I didn't anyway." She bit her lip. "Can't you understand? It was Mother. It was Mother's idea."

"About what?"

"You. She always hated Mary."

Part Two

THERE

21

HIS ISLAND!

That was what he couldn't quite get through his skull. His. His very own—if he made the payments. A new kind of drunkenness invaded him. Not something with which to insulate, prop up, protect, blot out the past, make the present endurable. Something totally different, an excitement that kept him so charged up that he couldn't sleep at night. He was living in a boardinghouse while his house was being made habitable. New plumbing fixtures had to be put in, along with other things. He made a list of items he had to buy, a long list. Lying in bed at night—the image of the house so vivid in his head that he was actually there, standing in the living room and looking around—he thought of other jobs to be done and other things to be bought. He would turn on the light and add to the list. When he couldn't sleep he would put on his clothes and slip out into the night streets of Lincoln Harbor, walk down Elm and along Front to where the boat Charlie had helped him buy lay tied to a dock: silent in the water, a grayish shape among other shapes, motionless, the water smooth and black, the painter hanging slack in a loop, the outboard a whitish blob at the far end.

It was not a boat he would have bought. He mumbled something to Charlie about fiberglass. He asked him if he had ever heard of Redfish boats or Span-America boats. Charlie hadn't; he waved off fiberglass.

"Bust it and you can't fix it. You've got to get some kind of a kit. You want a wood boat. Fix it yourself. All they make in fiberglass is those goddamned sleds. Flip over in a sea. Too wide to row. Nobody makes a fiberglass dory. What you need is a good wood dory."

That is what he got.

"Ever row a boat?"

"No."

"You're going to learn now."

"But what about the engine we just bought?"

"Engines bust. What you're going to do, what you're going to do right now, you're going to get in this dory. You're going to put in these oarlocks. You're going to shove yourself off and row around that buoy over there and then row back. Then you're going to stow your oars. *Under* the seat. Then you're going to take out your oarlocks and stow them. Then you're going to report to me. I've got a couple of things to do in the office. It'll take you half an hour."

Getting out of the tangle of other boats tied to the dock was a problem. He stood up in the dory to pole with an oar, but it teetered so alarmingly that he sat down again and did his poling that way. The dory seemed unreasonably narrow. It had a narrow flat bottom and seemed heavy and hard to manage. It needed a coat of paint. He got free of the other boats. Putting in the oarlocks, he dropped one over the side.

Charlie walked down the dock. He hadn't left after all.

"Well, you learned two things already."

"It slipped out of my hand."

"Don't go running around in a boat until you know boats. Always have an extra pair of oarlocks and an extra oar. Also—are you listening?—always have a bailing can. Make it a big one. Always a life jacket. Always have a can of extra gas."

"Okay."

"You're not listening."

He wasn't. He was too busy trying to get back to the dock, trying to row with one oar, sending the boat in circles.

"Sit in the stern and paddle."

He did, got back.

"Now I'll tell you again. Repeat after me."

He did.

"You may think I'm being fussy, but you don't know one goddamned thing about boats. I wouldn't take a buck bet that you won't be drowned before the end of summer." He handed over three more oarlocks. "Tie them to the thwarts with marlin."

Thwarts? Marlin?

He watched Charlie out of sight before making his second attempt. He put in the oarlocks carefully. Rowing, like horseback riding, turned out to be easy if you took it easy. Dip, pull, stretch. It was a still morning with scarcely a ripple on the water except for the puddles his oars made and the wake of the dory. It slid along remarkably easily once he got it moving. This wasn't going to take any half hour. He got to the buoy in about five minutes. It came up with surprising speed, a tall pointed red object leaning in the ripple of current flowing past it. By the time he got the dory turned around, he had been swept a hundred yards beyond the buoy. He realized that the reason he had gotten there so fast was that he was riding an outgoing tide. When he got back to the dock his arms were aching and his hands were blistered. It had taken more than half an hour.

"Learned something else too, didn't you?"

"I did?"

"You snuck in out of the worst of the current and came back along the shore."

"Oh, yes, that." He didn't explain that he had been headed crooked and found himself close to the shore by accident rather than by design, and then had stayed there because he could keep himself straighter by watching the docks out of the corner of his eye and also measure progress as he got by each one, whereas out in the middle of the harbor he had seemed to be pulling his guts out and not making any progress at all.

"Hands sore?"

"A little."

"Add something else to what you never leave home without. A pair of work gloves. Unless you want to make a habit of rowing a couple of miles every day."

"How does the outboard work?"

Charlie showed him: how to fill it, start it, throttle it, stop it, how to check the gas line, where the extra shear pin was kept. That afternoon Charlie took him for his first trip to *his* island in *his* boat. A breeze had come up. Outside Lincoln Point the water was getting rough.

"Now you see why I wanted you to get a dory. These high ends cut along nice even in this chop. Even when you get sideways to the sea—" He suddenly pushed the outboard handle, and the boat swung parallel to the waves. It tilted violently, and Fred grabbed the gunwale.

"Don't worry," said Charlie. "Made for this. But in a steep sea you goddamn well better keep your nose straight into it. Here, you take her for a while."

This was easy too. But he was beginning to learn that what seemed easy at first might not always be.

"Aim at that beach," said Charlie. "Cut your engine now. Tilt it out of the water."

"Why?"

"So you won't bust it on a rock, that's why."

He learned a lot from Charlie, from what were called My Principles on How Not to Drown. Soon he was handling the dory with some confidence. In time he would be sure he would never want any other kind of boat. That alone would have made him enormously grateful to Charlie if he hadn't been enormously grateful already. Charlie had found him a plumber, who came out to the island with a secondhand kitchen sink, washbasin, toilet, and bathtub. In one day, with a helper, the plumber installed them all. He also put in a new pipe, attaching it to a pump that Charlie had located somewhere and that in turn was attached to a Charlie-located generator.

He was given instruction in generator maintenance. "Same as an outboard, really. All these little gasoline motors are the same when you look inside. Keep the line clean. Check the plug. Have an extra plug. Check the oil. Have an extra quart. Haul your gas in five-gallon cans. You don't want to go busting yourself lugging ten-gallon cans. You won't be able to carry them. Have two cans. Always an extra of everything."

The generator ran the pump. The pump pumped water from a small pond on the island into a large metal drum behind the house. There was no well on the island; nobody had ever succeeded in drilling one, which was why it had been on the market for so long.

"Pond water's perfectly good," said Charlie. "Personally I like the taste. But for some people . . . you know, minnows in it, frogs."

The plumber wanted to attach everything at once and go home. Charlie wouldn't let him. "We'll run it in first. Stick a hose on the end and put it out the window."

It was well he did. The old pipe running to the pond was full of rust, and the water that it first spat out was bright orange. In five minutes it was running clear, and Charlie said to hook everything up.

"You wouldn't want that coming into your tank, would you?" Charlie said to the plumber.

"I didn't know it was that rusty."

"Hasn't been used in over twenty years. At that rate your own pecker would get rusty."

The plumber, instead of getting mad for having been made to look foolish, grinned. Charlie made Fred grin, too, when he did something foolish, which was often. He had to be shown how to put in windowpanes, using putty and points, how to lay shingles, using a chalk line for evenness. How would he have managed without

Charlie? Charlie reminded him to get a ladder.

So many things to learn. Not drunk but intoxicated. There was a huge difference. He was out of breath with excitement now, rushing at each job as if the day wouldn't last. When he got the windows in and the roof fixed, he tackled the interior. He scrubbed down the walls and painted them white. The windows were small, but even so the light from the sky and the sea invaded his little rooms in a torrent, flooding from one white wall to another. All that flickering light, and the breeze coming in through the windows, and the bushes outside, and an occasional gull sailing by. It was as if he were out of doors, the smell of the bushes and the sea so sweet in the strong summer sun.

The floor next. Days spent arduously scraping away several layers of iron-hard paint, then sanding, and following up with two coats of varnish. He never did entirely eradicate the water stains under the window that faced east, which was where the rain had come in for so many years during storms. But in the end he had a fine pine floor, smooth and shiny. He would go outside just for the pleasure of looking in through the window, admiring the floor and thinking about the rug he would put on it someday, and the furniture.

So much to do. He was living in the house now. He had a mattress in the bedroom, a two-burner alcohol stove (via Charlie) in the kitchen, along with a refrigerator (also via Charlie) that ran on fuel instead of electricity. For illumination he had candles and one kerosene lamp that he carried from room to room. In the kitchen he had four knives, four forks, four spoons, four cups, four saucers, four plates. Four? Well, somebody might come someday. For kitchenware he had what Charlie's wife, Lorraine, had told him to buy at the hardware store.

Lorraine seemed to regard him as Charlie did, as a curious and helpless nephew unloaded on them by a defaulting relative and for whom they were responsible. Get this, get that. He got a frying pan, a large pot, a small pot, a large and a small kitchen knife, a couple of big spoons, one with slots in it, a bottle opener, a can opener, a glass pitcher, and four tin boxes labeled coffee, tea, flour, and sugar.

"You'll need some other things when you really start cooking," said Lorraine. "You know how to cook?"

"A little." He knew how to fry eggs and make hamburgers. He was standing with Lorraine in front of the hardware store, his arms full of bundles. She was a short plump woman in a pink sweater, the sleeves pushed up beyond her elbows. Short curly hair, almost frizzy. Freckles on her arms. How would Julia or Irene or Kitty take her and her hard flat voice? Those up New York women with their New York

205

accents and their hard flat stomachs? Lorraine didn't even bother to hold hers in. It pouted slightly just below the top of her skirt, which was too tight for her.

"Can you cook a chicken?"

"I've never tried."

"You come and have supper with us on Thursday. I'll broil a chicken and show you how. Come at half after five."

He tried to remember what she did with the chicken, disgusted by the pale sick skin, the pinkish meat with traces of blood. He sliced some carrots under her direction.

"You know something?" said Charlie after supper. "I did one dumb thing. How do you wash? Your body, I mean."

"I heat a pot of water on the stove. I put it in the basin. Then I stand in the tub and wash myself down."

"You do use the tub? I suddenly thought, with no hot water hooked in, why get you a tub?"

"You be sure to wash regular," said Lorraine, inspecting him carefully. "Out there by yourself you can get slack."

He always washed and shaved before going to town, which he did once or twice a week. He took his laundry to the laundromat, sitting waiting for it to be done, surrounded by strange women, most of them with their hair done up in plastic curlers and all gossiping with each other. He was the only man in the place and felt like an exotic seabird blown by a storm onto a beach of sandpipers.

He had his list. He bought groceries. He bought tools as he needed them: hammer, saw, pliers, screwdriver, a brush saw, an ax. He bought nails. He was wearing khaki work pants now and sneakers. He began to feel a little bit at home as he padded up and down Elm Street. He got to know the clerks in the supermarket—although not by name—and said "Hi" to them when he did his shopping. If he passed Charlie's office he would glance in the window. And if Charlie was there and happened to be looking out, he would wave to him. Small contacts, but contacts.

He tried to slow down, to stop driving to get everything done in one day. He had a whole life ahead of him. A whole life. Was this really what he was going to do with the rest of it? The only one he had?

What else was there?

No answer to that. Bury the question in sweat and aching arms, cutting brush, cleaning up, collecting driftwood, some of which he had to saw up in order to carry it back to his house and add to the neat stack he was accumulating.

He got poison ivy, weeping crusts on his face and arms. He lay in bed at night with his skin itching and burning, and he listened to the lap of water on the shore, getting up to bathe his face in cold water and then standing in his doorway in the cool night with shreds of mist swirling past the corner of the house. He was aware of faint sounds drifting in the mist, birdlike twitterings all around him, coming and going in whispers, rising and falling like the breathing of the sea. He half expected to see birds hovering and darting like moths in the mist, but he saw nothing. Gradually he got used to the twittering and ceased to hear it. His poison ivy dried up. He began sleeping heavily.

He explored his island. He walked right around it and discovered to his amazement that the land rising up behind his house in a mat of thicket and scrub ended abruptly in a series of low cliffs overhanging a long sea beach. Big rocks were stuffed into the cliffs, left there by the glacier that had made this island, rocks hanging out like babies about to burst from their mothers. Some had already been delivered and lay half buried in the sand below.

His own beach. It was fairly steep. The ocean surf fell on it with solid thumps. The waves crested and fell, thump after thump, running up the beach only a short way before being sucked out of existence by the coarse thirsty sand. An ocean beach of his own. Up under the cliffs, the sand was finer and whiter. He lay down there, flat on his back, the sun red against his closed eyelids. His beach. He could come here every day and lie here all day and do nothing, and nobody would say anything. A trickle of comfort dripped through him, easing the panicky urge to be up and doing every minute. He lay for an hour, two hours, dazed by the sun and the thumping of the sea, letting all that sand sift through his mind, wondering what made sand, how little pebbles got abraded by the endless thumping of the sea, abraded smaller and smaller until they were sand. Until they were nothing. Everything eventually became nothing.

He sat up. Nearby was a big rock five or six feet across. Where had it come from, riding the ice ten thousand years ago? How long would it take for the frost to split it, for the waves to suck at it, eat away at that adamantine surface, smaller and smaller until it, too, became a pebble? Spawner of a million pebbles, a billion grains of sand.

He watched the rock, solid and unshrinking, safely embedded above the curl of the surf, willing it to split, to grow smaller just to prove that time was not as endless as it suddenly seemed to be. In its solidity it added to his sense of comfort. Its life was going to be so infinitely longer than his that his suddenly didn't matter much. You come and go, and nobody will care. You will make no difference unless you do something stupid like hammer your initials into the rock, and in the long run what will that matter? People will wander this beach someday, new owners perhaps, and not even wonder who FF was. Just another Kilroy scratching the landscape.

For all the thumping of the surf, this empty outer beach was the quietest and most peaceful part of his island. He went there often that first summer, just to lie on the sand and shut his mind. The other side, with a house to be looked after, the mainland to be seen, boats going by—that could become a clutter. Here, nothing but sand and surf and an empty horizon. Himself and a couple of gulls.

He got hooked on those afternoons of nothingness. In the morning, if he didn't have to go to the mainland for supplies, he would work at some job, attack it, exhaust himself. He found the best place on the cove shore for his boat and decided to get rid of all the rocks there so that it could slide in easily without bumping its bottom on anything. He began carrying rocks off to one side, piling them up, fitting them together to make a stone jetty, a minute harbor. He rolled some of the larger rocks into a line to form a backbone around which he would stack the smaller ones. The water was warming up now. He would wade out up to his chest and test a rock. He would get a grip on it, straining with all his strength, sometimes with his chest and face under the water. Take a breath, shut your eyes, grit your teeth, give it the total surge of muscle.

His enemy—which slipped his embrace with its green hair, cut him with its barnacles. If it didn't move, he would straighten up and try another. If a rock moved at all, it was remarkable how easily it could be nudged along under the water, coaxed into place. When he had a dozen rocks lined up, he decided he needed another dozen, parallel, for stacking others on top of. Maybe a third . . . This job could become very useful. It could occupy him savagely for years, fill his mind with a rage of grunts that he could later empty by lying on the sea beach.

He bought a bureau at an auction for three dollars. He borrowed Charlie's station wagon again to haul it to the town dock. July had come, and there were vacationers standing around. He asked a couple of them to lower the bureau to him as he stood in the dory, reminded of the time he had sat in Burton's fishing boat and pretended he was Burton's son. Now he felt the same. He thanked the respectful helpers gruffly, cranked up, and started off, feeling their eyes on his back as he went down the harbor and turned out to sea.

He put the bureau against the wall in his bedroom and cleaned out the drawers, throwing away the stained shelf paper that lined them. Under the paper in one of the two small drawers at the top he found a valentine. In a border of roses was a poem:

> The sweetest rose I ever met,
> The one that I will ne'er forget,
> The one to which I'll e'er be true,
> My one and only Rose, 'tis you.

Underneath was written in pencil: "Dear Rosie, from you-know-who."

For some reason, reading this made him well up. He stood for a while looking out of his window, the sun a bright blur on the water. He wondered who Rosie was, where she was, whether you-know-who had been faithful. Was she old now, sagging and sick? Did she remember the valentine or had she thrown it carelessly in her drawer and forgotten it? It seemed important that she remember. Links were important.

He located the source of his tears. No one had ever sent him a valentine. He had never sent one. There had been nobody to send one to—except possibly Joanne Fensler, and he could not have done that. The Joannes of this world were for the Frenchys. The thought of Frenchy and his hand jobs sent him down to the cove for more work on the rocks.

That afternoon he unpacked the trunk that Julia had filled. All the Wragge shirts—he hadn't realized how many there were—but he no longer had any cuff links; they had been stolen one of those times. Underwear and pajamas from Sulka. Some cashmere socks, a present once from Julia. Lettuce-colored and lemon-colored linen slacks for those weekends on Long Island. The two photographs of himself that Fran had looked at that day. Books. His shotgun; Julia had even packed two boxes of shells. He put the gun case in the corner and his clothes in his new bureau. Rosie's valentine he burned.

22

H E HAD ANOTHER SUPPER WITH CHARLIE AND LO-
raine.

"You eating regular? You look kind of thin."

"I always was thin."

Lorraine subjected him to a long and reflective examination: his angular frame, his squarish face and blunt nose, his reddish hair. "You could stand a little fattening up. Do you come over here regular for supplies?"

"Once a week."

"I mean like Thursday?"

"Usually Thursday—to get the Thursday specials at the market."

She turned to her husband. "You bowl Wednesdays, so whyn't Fred come Thursdays for supper?"

"You do that," said Charlie.

"Not every Thursday," he said. Too tight a knot.

"Well, if it storms . . . "

"I mean, I shouldn't do that. It would be too . . . "

Lorraine leaned back in her chair and studied his arms and chest again. "You still look kind of drawn down to me. One hot meal a week. It would make you a difference."

"That's settled," said Charlie.

"I'll pay."

"You don't pay," said Charlie. "We're friends."

Something turned over in him. Tears prickled his eyes. He felt Lorraine still staring at him.

"Lonely out there, huh?"

*   *   *

So he went to the mainland on Thursday afternoons instead of mornings, which was good in a way because the laundromat was usually empty then. Also the wind was apt to go down after supper, leaving the sea flat and silvery. Sometimes it was a pinky silver from the setting sun, and he would sit facing the stern, watching his wake cut through all that pink, scattering it, feeling the cool air on his neck. It always tasted and smelled saltier in the evenings than it did in the daytime, particularly on still evenings.

A Thursday supper date with Charlie and Lorraine meant giving up an afternoon of nothingness on his beach. He hated to miss that. The next Thursday he forced himself to visit them, feeling both deprived and grateful. They were a thread; he had to have one thread.

There wasn't all that much to talk about. Charlie worried that Allstate was planning to open an office in town. He sat at their table, spooning up their food, constrained that he had nothing to say to them, feeling crowded in a room with two other people, particularly when one of them stared at him so much. Three made the room dangerously full. He got up to go, with the excuse that it was supposed to blow that night.

"Then you should sleep over," said Lorraine. "We have the spare room."

"Okay. Sometime I'd like—"

"Good comfortable bed. I know; I've slept in it myself."

"If I ever get stuck."

"Don't you go down to the Blue Lobster and sit drinking. You'll drown yourself getting home."

Charlie gave her a scowl and shook his head.

"Oh, my. I'm sorry."

"That's all right."

"I mean, I never should have said that."

"Lorraine," said Charlie.

"What's wrong? I'm only apologizing."

"What's wrong is you don't know when to shut up."

"I was only saying I was sorry. Fred, I'm sorry. It isn't like I'm a stranger to drinking. Both my uncles have drinking problems."

"Don't worry about it."

"It slipped out. You don't look like a drinker."

"I'm not. I've stopped."

"Like my uncle Cyril. Sometimes he goes six months without a drop. Uncle John was more the regular type. Which type were you?"

"Lorraine, for Christ's sake."

She went on: "You could tell from just looking at Uncle John. We'll see you next Thursday. I'll have a nice pot roast."

Next Thursday was stormy, with a lot of rain. They would understand why he didn't show up. He spent the day in bed rereading *Persuasion,* one of the books from his trunk. It was easier to read *Persuasion* than to get up and make supper. When it got dark he rolled over and went to sleep.

The storm lasted three days. He spent most of the time in bed. He read *Mansfield Park* and identified strongly with its small dark heroine, who was so good and meant so well but whom everyone abused. He ate almost nothing and dozed a good deal.

The next morning was sunny. He woke up hungry and full of vitality. He made bacon and eggs for breakfast, then had a can of peaches. Everything was crackling with energy. The sky was deep blue, without a cloud in it. Over on the mainland, individual trees, radio masts, and water towers stood out with razor sharpness against the blue, which paled only slightly at the horizon. The water between was ragged with white from a strong chilly wind. This was a day for a heavy sweater, and he put one on. It had a felt *P* on it, for varsity track. The wind whined through the cracks in his living room, and for the first time it really came home to him that it might not be possible to live here in winter unless he insulated his house. He looked at the unfinished interior walls, which he had painted so lovingly. Insulation would have to be put in and all that lovely paint covered with wallboard.

Did he really want to do that? Questions, decisions, even here. Even in the most innocent situations, where the only judge was himself, he could make mistakes. All that paint and time wasted.

All what time? He had to keep reminding himself that time was the one commodity he had to burn. So why not stop worrying about the paint and get on to the next job? He was flooded immediately with a need to get started right away. Wallboard, how much? Insulation, what kind? He went to town although it was extremely rough and the dory rolled ominously. Later the wind grew even stronger, and he was afraid to try to go home. Although it was a Tuesday, Charlie took him back to his house for supper.

"So sleep over," said Lorraine.

The next morning, after Charlie had gone to his office, Lorraine poured him another cup of coffee. Her kitchen was spotless, with red-and-white-checked curtains in the windows, all the gadgets lined up and shining on the counter. She sat with her sweater sleeves pushed up on her plump freckled arms, elbows on the table, cradling her coffee cup.

"What's it like, living in New York?"

"Well . . . "

"I mean, why did you ever come here? This dump. I mean, nothing ever happens here. You get restless."

"It's better than New York."

"I hear the single life there is pretty racy."

"For some, maybe."

"Were you single, or were you married?"

"I was married—most of the time. I got divorced."

"Charlie didn't say. I guess you didn't tell him."

"I guess I didn't."

"Your wife leave you? I mean, I don't mean to pry."

"We didn't get along. We decided to split up."

"You don't look like the play-around type."

"I'm not."

She flicked a glance at him. "Maybe she did the playing around."

He wasn't prepared for questions like these. He said: "You couldn't exactly call it playing around."

"She did, huh? Do you hold with women playing around, or is it only right for men? I don't mean your wife. You wouldn't like that, of course. How did you catch her?"

"I—uh—" This conversation was going with giddy speed and with chasm-sized leaps.

"That must have been—you know—awful. An awful moment. Was he a friend of yours?"

He choked on his coffee.

"I mean, if you suddenly found your friend—you know—with your wife. What do you do? Do you be the gentleman and say, 'I'll wait for you in the hall and then let's talk it over?' Or do you beat him up, or what?"

He thought of that wild flailing with Julia and Mary Smallwood.

"Or do you beat your wife up? Did you ever hit your wife?"

He was so taken aback that he answered: "Once."

"Right then?"

"It was more of a drinking thing. Look, I can't really talk about this. We just didn't get along. We got a divorce."

"Did you hurt her? I mean, that time you hit her. What did he do?"

"He?"

"Her friend. Who was—you know."

He pulled his flying wits together. He had spent too little time talking to people. Her questions had been coming too fast. "There wasn't any he. I just got into a drunken argument with my wife, that's all."

She poured them both a third cup. "I guess that's enough to get anyone drinking. If his wife cheats on him. Was she really good-looking?"

"She still is."

"You know what I mean. Was. Is. Did you really go for her? I mean, it would drive any man to drink if he really went for his wife and she—you know."

She stirred her coffee, staring into it. He was able to examine her face. She looked up suddenly and caught him.

"Don't get any wrong ideas," she said. "We're just talking, you know."

He got up, still trying to keep abreast of this conversation.

"Because I'm not the play-around type. I'm definitely not the play-around type."

"I'm not, either."

"Then we got that settled. So you might as well go, or Mary Rendover—she's next door and she's pretending to mop her kitchen floor but she's sneaking a few looks—Mary Rendover might start thinking things."

Walking back to his boat, he wondered if he was going to lose Charlie.

23

H
E INSULATED HIS LIVING ROOM, WALLS AND CEIL-
ing, then covered them with wallboard, painting the walls white
and the ceiling light blue like the sky. It took a man working
alone a long time to manage the ceiling. When he was finished, the
room seemed so much smaller than before that he felt stifled. For a
while he was more comfortable with all the windows open. Gradually
he got used to the smaller size. He went ahead and did the bedroom.
Later he would do the bathroom and kitchen but not right now.

His generator broke down. Remembering Charlie's instructions,
he succeeded in fixing it and felt very much in command of himself.
He cleaned up the cove beach, which was littered with plastic contain-
ers and beer cans. He also found lobster-pot buoys of different shapes
and colors. These he nailed to the end of his house, as he had seen
done on some fishermen's shacks in Lincoln Harbor. He was gradually getting control of things. He was alive.

Thursdays with Charlie and Lorraine were mixed. He felt her
looking at him all the time, with her secret thoughts, and tried not to
be alone with her. She made him nervous, but he kept going back;
they were his only company.

He subscribed to *Time* magazine. Not only would that give him
an excuse to go to the post office for mail (the only other mail he got
was the monthly statement of his savings account in the local bank),
but it would also keep him in touch with the other world. When it
started coming he found he couldn't read it. All that unceasing uproar
out there. The brassy know-it-all language. The overpowering smell
of phony success and phony energy and phony threats and phony
puffings. The armpit of striving was too strong for him. The *Time*
magazines piled up.

They would have piled up faster if it hadn't occurred to him to bring them to Charlie and Lorraine. He also brought other things—a bottle of Scotch for Charlie, a box of chocolates for Lorraine—in an attempt to balance off the food they were giving him.

"You shouldn't," said Charlie. "You don't have to buy your supper. Here you don't."

"I know."

"You're a friend here."

Hearing that word again almost broke him. He managed to say that a friend could bring a present, couldn't he.

Lorraine accepted the chocolates with a look that he couldn't meet. Instead, he watched her fingers strip the plastic wrap from the box as if she were stripping clothes from him. When she got the wrap off, she slid the palm of her hand over the box before opening it.

"Have one," she said.

"They're for you. I don't eat candy."

"Then I'll have to eat them all myself. I'll get fat. Nobody will look at me."

"I'll look at you," said Charlie.

She smoothed her sweater down and set her shoulders back a trifle. "Do I look too fat to you, Fred?"

"No."

"Maybe too thin, huh?"

"You're just right."

She ate another, staring at him as she put it in her mouth.

Was he imagining things, losing his judgment from never talking to other people? Maybe she behaved that way with all men; he wouldn't know, because he never saw her with other men. Better not go back. But he *had* to go back; he had nowhere else. Churning with anxiety and a long-banked sexual heat, he ran the throttle full up and the dory hustled along, its bottom swatting the ripples. Instead of going directly up to his house, he walked distractedly along the shore, first thinking angrily about Lorraine and then thinking about Fran, something he had managed not to do lately. Now she came with such a rush of choked feeling that his chest actually hurt. Weeping, he came around to the ocean side. It was dark, and the waves were leaving winking dots of phosphorescence stranded on the sand. He wiped his eyes with the back of his hand to see them better and discovered that they were everywhere, washing in on every wave. Each wink was a life, a being, a separate organism sending out its signal—of what? A blink of existence, a last flash before it was snuffed out? Was this their stab in the chest, their final dying utterance? Was this all they did, wash in here to die, wave after wave, endlessly, all night long, night after night, century after century? It was staggering to think of the immensity of that dying, the shortness and utter uncontrollability of those helpless little lives, lifted from the safe sea and deposited on the lethal sand. Was he any different? He had washed up here too, with a stab of pain that was longer and a dying that was longer—so much longer that during his next breath, the next step that took him imperceptibly closer to his own end, the dying here on this one beach and during this one short moment would be immeasurable. To all those dying so swiftly he was immortal, as immortal as the rock he had been looking at a few weeks before had seemed to him.

He headed back to his house. At least he could choose where he walked, whether or not to go back to Charlie and Lorraine. He could choose to forget Fran; he told himself he could do that. He could ignore Lorraine, or tell her to knock it off. But maybe he was misjudging her. Maybe he couldn't tell her.

The next time, he brought a layer cake. Lorraine poked her finger into it. Then she put her finger in her mouth as she slowly sucked off the icing.

During supper the phone rang.

"Gotta go," said Charlie, coming back into the dining room.

"Who was that?"

"Merlin Smith. His warehouse is on fire."

"You have to go?"

"I'm his agent. He says he thinks somebody set it."

"I'll go with you," he said.

"No sense in that," said Lorraine. "Stay and finish your supper."

"Yeah, stay. I might be gone two, three hours."

After Charlie left, she watched him gulp down what was left on his plate. "I think I ought to go now," he said.

"You haven't had your cake."

"Not much for sweets."

"You brought that cake special, and you're going to have a slice." She cut one and put it on a plate. "I tasted it already. You saw that, didn't you?"

He nodded.

"That's a sweet cake, a real rich sweet cake. Here."

He put a forkful into his mouth. Her presence across the table was enormous.

"Good, huh?"

He nodded again.

"You have taste, Fred. You were nice to bring that cake. How did you know chocolate was my favorite?"

"I guess it's everybody's favorite."

"Have another piece."

"I really should be going."

"Relax. What did you do when you lived in New York?"

"I was in the advertising business."

"That's a good business, from what I hear."

"It's okay."

"Charlie makes a good living. Nothing to what you probably made in New York. But he does okay. It's all in the reputation. He has a good reputation in this town. From being responsible. You could see that when he jumped up for Merlin Smith's fire. It's not everybody would do that so quick. Without even finishing his supper."

He pushed back his chair.

"Relax. Why are you so jumpy? We never get a chance to talk. Like about why you choose to live all by yourself up there. You miss your wife?"

"No."

"Was she a blonde or a brunette?"

"Brunette." As long as she kept talking about Julia it would be all right.

"You have any children?"

"No."

"Me neither. Of course you know that. They'd be here now, wouldn't they. I wish we had children. I don't think I'd be so tense if we had children. You see, Charlie won't go to the doctor. He suspects it's his fault, but he keeps putting it off. Did you and your wife ever get tested for children?"

"No."

"You just didn't have them?"

"That's right."

"I mean, did you decide? Did you talk about it or what?"

"We didn't talk about it."

"She just saw to it, huh?"

He got up.

"Fred, sit down. You make me so nervous jumping up. What are you so jumpy about?"

"I'm not jumpy."

"Then sit down and relax. I bet you're jumpy because you think Mary Rendover's sitting in her kitchen with the light off, looking over at us and thinking things. Well, I'll tell you something to relax you:

Mary Rendover's in Providence, and you don't need to be jumpy about anything. Anyway, there's nothing to be jumpy about. I already told you I'm not the play-around type."

"I can see that."

"So why don't you sit down?" she said desperately.

"Better if I didn't."

"Well, then . . . Ohhh . . . " She buried her face on the table.

He made for the door. She looked up at him with swimming eyes. "I'll tell Charlie."

"Tell . . . ?"

"That you made a pass. It's Charlie, isn't it?"

"Yes."

"What'll you do if I tell him you made a pass?"

"I guess there isn't anything I can do."

24

SO HE LOST CHARLIE. HE FELT CRUSHED. GOING TO
the market the next time, he went around the block from the
other side so that he wouldn't have to pass Charlie's office. He
bought a lot of stuff so that he wouldn't have to go ashore again for
a long time. He didn't bother with his laundry. He let it pile up in a
corner. Rage at Lorraine alternated with a sense of desolation. One
day he would work frantically at his jetty. The next he would be incapable of getting out of bed. He would lie staring at the ceiling, staring in a fury at Lorraine's streaked face, and it would gradually dissolve into Fran's, but etherealized so that its natural oval shape came
down in a perfect curve to a faultless tiny chin. She began to look
more and more like the children in paintings sold in gift shops. Her
mouth and nose shrank and became more delicate. Her eyes
expanded and deepened, huge and black and reproachful. The rest of
her body vanished.

The island drew in closer. He became conscious of small things: of
waving grass blades, of the different colors of the stones on the beach,
of the minute flies that swarmed in the cast-up seaweed, of the way
the sun fired the twigs of bushes in the late afternoon, of cobwebs in
the corners of his rooms. He shared his house with many spiders. He
let them be. He cut a path through the thicket from his house directly
to the low cliffs overhanging the sea beach. Now he could get there
faster and stay longer.

One afternoon he climbed up the cliff again to return to his house
and saw a small cabin cruiser nuzzled up against the cove beach in the
place where he had cleared out the rocks. Charlie, he thought, come
for a showdown. That bitch Lorraine. It wouldn't matter what he
said. Deny Lorraine or agree with her, he would lose Charlie. That

being so, why not agree with Lorraine and leave Charlie with something, the illusion of a good wife if not the reality.

He was still trying to find the words for the speech (or confession?) that he would make, when he noticed a man on the beach, crouched over a fire. It wasn't Charlie. That wasn't Charlie's boat, either. His was white; this one was gray. The man was fiddling with a fireplace made of stones and drinking a beer. As he watched, the man finished the beer and threw the can aside. He then pried open a can of something else and put the contents in a frying pan. That can he also threw aside.

Thoroughly annoyed by this trespass and littering, he walked down to the cove. He noticed that the fireplace had been neatly built in two parts and that there was a frying pan on each.

"Hey," he said.

The man looked up.

"Don't go throwing all those cans around. This is private property."

The man said nothing. He had hash in one pan. He began turning it over with a fork.

"Listen," he said. "I don't like strangers messing up my beach."

The man took four eggs from a cardboard carton and broke them one by one into the other frying pan, throwing the shells one way and the carton another. He turned his back.

A rage even hotter than the one that had seized him that day at the Racquet Club roared up in his throat and nearly choked him. He looked around for a handy rock to smash that head with, looked at the back of the head to see just where that smash would go. He saw a neck at least as wide as the head and a back even broader than Burton's. He abandoned the idea of the rock and went for his shotgun. With trembling fingers, he put it together and shoved two shells into it.

The fury was still boiling in him, making him shake. When he got back to the beach, he said: "Get off my property, you cocksucker."

The man stood up, then backed off warily as he walked toward him, pointing the gun at his belly.

"Get out of here."

The man stooped for an anchor that he hadn't even noticed hooked into the sand, then climbed into his boat. It was a small flat-bottomed cabin cruiser, with another anchor off the stern to keep it from swinging against the beach. He watched the man haul in that second anchor, start his engine, and back slowly away. As the boat turned he read its name on the stern: *Stinger, Lincoln Harbor.*

Still enraged, he kicked the frying pans off the fire and stamped on them. He then kicked the cans and the egg carton. This was his fucking beach, and no other fucker was going to fuck around with it. He found himself shouting those things. He kicked the frying pans again, then, his hands still shaking, picked them up. They were gummed with sand and the remains of eggs and hash. He took them up to his house and cleaned them. The shaking subsided. He realized with a kind of horrified satisfaction that if the man hadn't left when he did, he would have shot him. He could see a big bloody spouting hole opening in the middle of his body.

What then?

The *what then* occupied him for most of the night and for several nights thereafter. Hindsight made the various steps easy when he had time to think them through. First he would take off his shirt. Using it as a cloth to prevent fingerprints, he would shove the boat out of the cove and let the current carry it away. He had no idea which way it would go. That didn't make any difference. Somebody would find it somewhere—the farther away the better—and it would be assumed that the man had fallen overboard. The body would never be recovered, because he would drag it deep into the thicket back of his house and bury it. He would also bury the frying pans. He would burn the egg carton, demolish the fireplace, smooth over the sand, and there would be no sign of him at all, except maybe blood. He would have to count on the tides to carry that away, and he might have weeks of tides and rains before they came looking. If he got any blood on his clothes he would bury them too. No, better burn them, sift the ashes for zippers and buttons and scatter them like seeds.

Having gotten away with his crime and patted the earth so smoothly over it, he experienced days when he wasn't entirely sure he had not committed it. It was only when he found himself reluctant to return to Lincoln Harbor that he realized that it was fear of meeting the man that held him back. Which meant that the man hadn't been killed but was probably walking around somewhere and would do something terrible to him if they met again—unless he was carrying his gun. Which wouldn't be the case, because he couldn't go walking around the streets of Lincoln Harbor with a loaded gun in his hand. But he could carry it on the island. For days he did that, and slept with it by his bed. He imagined the man coming at night, with burly friends, and beating him to a pulp, then setting fire to his house. One night the fear was so great that he waited behind a rock on the cove beach, the gun across his lap. He woke there, stiff and soaked with dew. There was enough of Julia left in him to make him wipe the gun dry and then oil it lightly before putting it back in its case.

But he took it out again and brought it with him to the sea beach for the afternoon nothingness there. The nothingness didn't come; he could not shut his eyes and drift off. At any moment a head, or heads, might come peering over the cliff edge. He couldn't go on like that. He would have to find the man and explain somehow, say something. Take his frying pans back.

He located the *Stinger* in the town marina and learned from the gas pump boy there that it belonged to a man named Lou Mendoza.

"Where does he live?"

"Out on Gott Street. Diggin equipment in the yard. He runs a diggin business."

Gott Street slanted away from Elm past a small park with a war memorial in it. In a couple of blocks he found himself on the outskirts of town. There was no resort neatness here. The houses were newer, smaller, plainer, and more widely spaced, with little attempt at gardening. Grass and weeds grew high. As the boy had said, Mendoza had equipment in the yard, or rather in a large beaten-earth area behind the house. There were a couple of trucks and a backhoe there, gasoline drums and assorted junk lying around. The house had three steps running up to a small stoop. He mounted those and knocked on the door.

"You!" Even burlier, in an undershirt.

He started to say: "I brought back your—" when he was hit on the side of his mouth. He landed on his back in the weeds, the wind knocked clean out of him. He couldn't breathe. He opened his mouth like a fish, but nothing came in. He began to think he would never breathe again. He was wholly preoccupied with trying to get some air, any air, into his lungs. They seemed squashed beyond the possibility of ever inflating again. He felt himself near blackout, when some life-restoring wisps trickled in. Dizzy, gasping, he got to his hands and knees.

"You the cocksucker called me a cocksucker, right?"

"I only—"

"Don't nobody call me a cocksucker." He went inside, the screen door slamming after him.

He stayed on his hands and knees for a while, making sure that he could breathe properly. Now what? Risk another swat in the mouth? Might as well; he'd come this far. He picked up the frying pans and knocked on the door again, but backed down the steps.

"Look, you. I didn't make myself plain enough?"

"Your frying pans . . . " He held them up. Mendoza ignored them.

"You called me a cocksucker. I don't take that."

"I shouldn't have."

"I never sucked a cock in my life. How come you call me that?"

"I'm sorry. I was mad. You were throwing things on my beach."

"*Your* beach. Since when your beach?"

"I just got through cleaning it up, and you threw cans on it. I got mad."

"Your beach. I been using that beach I don't know how many . . . Now you come along and run me off with a gun. Call me a cocksucker."

"I shouldn't have. I'm sorry."

"I wouldn't call you a cocksucker unless I caught you sucking cock."

"You just did."

"I never."

"Just after you hit me you called me one."

"Well, dip me in shit. I was mad."

"So was I."

Lou Mendoza began to laugh. "Two cocksuckers, right? And neither one don't know for sure about the other. You feel okay? I busted you pretty good."

"You knocked the wind out of me."

"Cut you too. You're bleeding pretty good."

He felt his mouth. His hand came away reddened. There was some blood on his shirt.

"I cut your lip pretty good. I don't hit easy."

He got out his shirttail and tried to mop his mouth, which he was beginning to realize was both numb and painful—and swelling.

"That won't do no good. What you need's cold water. Come in and wash yourself off. You can't go through town looking like that."

He went inside, into a kitchen stacked with dirty pots and dishes. Lou Mendoza swept them aside, turned on the cold water in the sink, and handed him a greasy towel. "Hold your mouth under the tap."

The water stung. He watched the pink trickle in the sink grow fainter. He mopped himself off.

"Think you could drink a beer?"

He shook his head.

"Use the other side of your mouth. You ain't that bad."

He was about to say it wasn't that. Then he thought why not. Here he was with a rough man, a real man who was reaching out. The risk of a beer could be far less than the risk of lopping off that tendril, another human contact. He accepted it, and the two of them sat at the kitchen table, drinking. Lou Mendoza was no taller than he but must have weighed seventy-five pounds more. He bulged out of his undershirt. His arms were thighs. He belonged to the category of LaValles, except that he was bigger and harder than Frenchy would ever be, and here he was drinking with him on even terms. That made him feel good, particularly when Lou said: "Took something walking up them steps a second time."

He shrugged. Understatement seemed best.

"I was watching you sucking air. That ain't comfortable."

He tested his lip with his tongue.

"So you come up for another bust in the mouth."

"Hadn't said what I came to say. About the cocksucker thing."

"Forget that."

"I just got mad at you for throwing stuff around on the beach."

"I didn't help none. I done that deliberate. I was mad at you."

"At me?"

"Private property, you said. I been using that beach since a kid. Nothing's open around here anymore. All the signs. Next thing, you're going to put up a sign. I don't take to that kind."

"I'm not that kind." It was important to convince him. "It was because you threw all that stuff around. It seemed deliberate."

"I done it deliberate."

The beer encouraged him to say: "How would you like me to throw a lot of stuff in your front yard?"

"Okay, okay."

"You can come out there anytime you want. Just don't mess it up."

"Okay."

"Okay." Even.

Lou finished off his beer. He pulled hard at his to keep up. "You gotta understand," Lou said. "Outsiders coming in all the time. Taking over. Rich outsiders."

"You think I'm rich?"

"From what I hear, you bought the whole island."

"I'm paying for it on the installment plan. You're probably richer than I am. All that equipment you have out back."

"Bank owns it. Take me four, five years to pay for it. Then it'll be wore out." He got two more beers from the refrigerator. "You really would have shot me, wouldn't you."

"I guess so. I was pretty mad."

"Why I left. I figured you for crazy mad. You weren't thinking. You would have just pushed the old *Stinger* off and then buried me, right?"

"I didn't think of that until later."

"That's something you should have thought about then. If you hadn't been so crazy mad, there's something you might have noticed. Did you really think I was going to eat that whole can of hash and them four eggs? I had me a woman on that boat."

He felt his puffed mouth opening.

Lou grinned. "Supposing you had took a look in the *Stinger* before you pushed her off and found a woman in the cabin. Think you could've shot her? You'd've had to, wouldn't you?"

He couldn't answer.

"I think I done you a good turn getting out."

The appalling possibility continued to unfold. He was speechless.

"Didn't I?"

"You're kidding," he got out.

"I am not kidding. I was cooking supper for the two of us. She was dozing. Cook supper, have a few beers. You know. Going back, she said it was my fault. Told me I was rude."

"I think you're kidding."

"I swear on my big broad bare ass I'm not."

"All right, bring her again. I'll be more cordial the next time."

"I'll do just that. You home any particular time?"

"All the time."

"You like bluefish?"

"I've never tasted one."

"Now *you're* kidding. You got a grill for your fireplace?"

"No."

"Then we'll cook em on the beach. Wrap em in wet newspaper, bake em right in the coals. No better way."

He walked back to his boat in a daze. He was light-headed from the two beers and from being punched in the mouth. His lip felt about a foot thick. He was conscious of the blood on his shirt, but nobody so much as looked at him. Back home, he examined himself in the mirror and was a little let down that his lip appeared almost normal.

The next day he cleaned up his bathroom and kitchen sink, brushed the cobwebs from the corners, swept the floors, and took his laundry to the laundromat. He also got a haircut. His nothingness afternoons were interrupted by a feeling of having to be on hand.

What if they came while he was spaced out on the sea beach and they didn't find him and went away?

Five days of that. Then the *Stinger* pulled into his cove. He peeped from his window and watched three people clamber out: Lou Mendoza and two women. He forced himself to saunter down to the beach.

"I got me four nice little bluefish. Figured we'd need four to eat em. What's your name?"

"Fred."

"Fred, this is Marge."

Marge said: "This is Emily." He shook hands all around.

"Where's my old fireplace? You kick it to pieces too?"

He nodded and tried to smile.

"Fred's some kicker. He can kick a hot frying pan twenty feet."

All three of them were in rolled-up pants and bare feet, having waded ashore. The two girls sat down in the sand. He took off his sneakers and rolled up his pants to help Lou unload things: a parcel of fish, a bottle of whiskey, a plastic cooler full of ice and beer, two heads of lettuce.

"Okay, beers all around."

"How long you been living here?" asked Marge.

"Since spring."

"All alone?"

"Yes."

"You don't get lonesome?"

"Well, you know—I come to town."

"I never see you in town."

"Marge works bar at the Blue Lobster," said Lou.

"I don't get in there much."

"You don't get in there at all," said Marge.

"That's right. At all."

He concentrated on Lou's rebuilding of the fireplace, which was done with great skill. He hauled driftwood, and Lou kept piling it on to get a good bed of coals for the fish. The fire blazed up so hot that the girls had to pull back from it. He watched them unroll their pants and carefully brush the sand from their feet, working it out from between their toes before putting their sneakers back on. He felt that he was spying on them. He hadn't watched a woman do anything so intimate in a long time. Both wore blue pants, white socks, and red sneakers. Marge reminded him uncannily of Joanne Fensler, deep-bosomed, aware of herself and her movements, slow-moving, aware of men, aware of her effect on men. Emily reminded him of himself—as he might look to others. She had sandy reddish hair and seemed thin and angular. She was the kind of woman who kept her elbows close to her sides.

"Don't go throwing your beer cans around," said Lou. "Fred don't like that." He laid four small bluefish on a board, gutted them, wrapped them in bundles of newspaper that he soaked in salt water. These bundles he laid in the coals, where they began to sizzle and steam.

"What are we gonna eat off of?" asked Marge.

"I have plates," he said.

"Let's get them. Can I look at your house?"

He led the two girls up to it.

"Bring glasses too," Lou yelled.

It was not quite dark, pearly, the best time of day. The fire on the beach was a ruddy smear. Light from the western sky painted the side of his house with pearl. He opened his door and felt invaded as two strangers walked in. It was dim inside, so he lit the kerosene lamp on the table.

"This is *nice*," said Marge. Followed by Emily, she inspected all the rooms. "So neat. You ought to see Lou's house. What a mess. I'm gonna go in there sometime when I get a week off and really clean it up. You'll have to help, Em."

"What for?" said Emily. "They'll just mess it up again." This was the first time she had spoken. She had a remarkably angry voice.

"Maybe we can teach them. By a good example."

"They won't even notice." Emily stood in the doorway, looking out.

Marge said: "I think I'll get back and see how Lou's doing with the fish. Why'n't you get the plates and stuff."

He scuttled into the kitchen to collect his four plates, four knives and forks—he was going to use them after all. Emily watched from the doorway.

"You really live here all alone?"

"Yes."

"I couldn't stand it out here. What's the matter you don't live in town?"

"I like it better here."

"What do you do all day long?"

"Well, I've had a lot of work fixing the house up. It was a mess before I got it."

"So it's fixed now."

"Pretty much."

"So what do you do now?"

"I—I write."

"You what?"

"I'm a writer. That's what I do." Maybe that would impress her.

"You forgot the glasses."

He handed her the plates and went for the glasses. By the time he had picked them from the shelf, she was already out the door and headed for the beach. He blew out his lamp and followed. Lou and Marge were embracing on the sand. Emily tapped one of them on the shoulder and handed each a glass. Lou sat up, brushed himself off, and proceeded to pour healthy belts of bourbon into the glasses. His drink. The sweet woody smell was very strong.

"None for me," he said.

"Making a mistake. This is good bourbon."

"I don't drink hard stuff."

"Not never?"

"It and I don't get along."

Lou shrugged. "Too bad Davey don't see it that way—hey, Em?"

Marge gently dusted the sand from her sweater, treating her breasts and arms with great respect, while she gave him a long sweet look. He sensed that she was disappointed that he and Emily had come back so soon. He also sensed that her concern was mainly for Emily and that he had somehow disappointed her. That made him sad. He sensed that she liked and understood men, that she liked and understood *people*. He wanted her to know that he was aware of this understanding in her, and wished there were some way he could express it.

"I almost forgot the glasses," he said.

"Good thing you didn't," said Lou. "Drinking from the bottle, sometimes your throat forgets to close off."

"I always use a glass," said Marge. "I don't hold with drinking from a bottle. How come you do, Em?"

Emily was sitting with her knees up. She tossed back what was in her glass and held it out for a refill. "You don't drink at all?" she said to him.

"Only beer."

"Why not?"

"I can't handle liquor."

"That's right," said Lou. "Stick to beer if that's the way you are. Something Davey should learn. Anyway, you can get good and mellow on beer. Ten, fifteen beers, you're soaring. Pour it in one end and piss it out the other, and in between you feel real mellow."

"A dirty tongue," said Marge.

"Not surprising, considering where it's been."

That kind of talk unnerved him, but not the others. Emily seemed not to hear it. Marge merely said blandly: "Like I said, a dirty tongue. Maybe the fish is done."

Lou got a stick and began nudging the charred parcels out of the coals.

"Do you have any kind of bowl for the lettuce? Oil or vinegar?" asked Marge.

"Yes." He got up to get them.

"I'll go with you."

"I'm counting," said Lou.

Again he walked up to his house. Deep dark this time. He fumbled to get the lamp lit.

"Don't mind about Em," said Marge.

"I don't. I wasn't even expecting her."

"We brought her along to cheer her up. On the chance, you know. You never know, do you? She might have gone for you."

"Just the opposite."

"That's not you. She's been going with Davey, but he drinks and chases around and treats her terrible. He makes dates with her and then forgets them."

"Who *is* Davey?"

"Lou's brother. He lives with Lou. You were nice to ask us back here—after that other time."

"It turned out all right."

"Lou told me. You're nice." She placed a hand on his chest. All his sleeping sexuality erupted. "We'd better get back," she said.

The fish was fantastic. When the charred paper was stripped away, most of the skin went with it and there were juicy tender fillets underneath. In the light of the low fire they looked almost orange, with bits of charcoal on them that he flicked away. The fish had a slightly smoky flavor.

"Told you, didn't I. Nothing better."

He ate almost an entire fish and a heap of lettuce, washing it all down with another beer, his third. As long as he drank with people like these, plain people he liked, it would be okay. People he wasn't afraid of and didn't have to impress. He wasn't afraid of Lou; he'd been through that. He liked him. He was sitting next to him on the sand and felt comfortable there. He also liked Marge, who was sitting on the other side of Lou. A good place for her, because he desired her strongly as well as liking her. That, too, was okay, because she was the kind of woman who would understand all that and not hold it against him. Emily he didn't like, but he could ignore her. She was sitting by herself on the other side of the fire, looking sullen. She had the bourbon bottle with her.

The fire crumbled into itself. Marge put her head in Lou's lap. He put his hand on her breast, and she put her hand over it. Nobody said anything for quite a while. Marge appeared to have fallen asleep. Emily hit the bourbon bottle again. He stared into the coals, blinking occasionally because of the heat, feeling slightly woozy and extraordinarily comfortable.

"You got a nice place here," Lou finally said.

"I know."

"Wouldn't mind living here myself. How about it, Marge?" He nudged her awake.

"Huh?"

"Like to live out here?"

"With you?"

"I wasn't thinking Fred. Just me and the fog bells and the gulls."

She reached her arm up and pulled his face down to hers. This was so naked, so natural, that it nearly split him in two. He couldn't watch them. He glanced at Emily, who seemed to be having no trouble doing that. She was glaring at them as if she didn't so much dislike what they were doing as dislike them. That annoyed him. She didn't belong here; they did. Her dislike of them fanned his affection. It crested on a wave of beer, a pouring urge to let them know. A huge gush. A drowning fondness. He leaned over and put an arm around Lou's back, then bent down close to the tangle of two heads. "Come back again," he said.

"Hey, you really getting into the act," Lou said.

"Anytime. I mean it." The closeness. The smell of the wood smoke, the dying fire. A streak of light on the distant horizon.

"Okay."

"I do get lonely out here."

"I would think," said Marge.

"Better get moving. Tide's about to turn."

Three. Alive for once.

Marge sat up. Again, she brushed herself off daintily and lovingly. Anyone who was so solicitous of her own body—so publicly solicitous—would surely be solicitous of other bodies. She would understand bodies. He envied Lou.

The next morning he picked up the beer cans on the beach. He left the fireplace and the charred logs where they were. He could see the depressions in the sand where the three of them had sat—or thought he could. He didn't disturb them, either. Last night had been something he would never want to disturb. He decided to lay in a supply of beer. Not for himself—he would never drink alone—but for them, the next time they came.

25

WEEK WENT BY, THEN PART OF ANOTHER. THEN came a tearing end-of-summer storm, which battered the island. They didn't come when it had blown itself out. He had his house neat and ready. He imagined they might want to sit around the fireplace, so he bought a wicker chair. Lou could sit in the chair. Marge could sit on the floor, with her head in Lou's lap. He could sit by the wall.

Maybe they would bring someone with them again, someone better than Emily, someone who might like him, might even want to stay. He tried to imagine what that one would be like and conjured up a mixture of the best of Marge and Joanne Fensler, but always the image would dissolve into the gift-shop picture of Fran: nothing but big sorrowful eyes and a tiny chin.

He put a sign on the beach:

LOU: I'M ON THE OCEAN SIDE
MAKE YOURSELF AT HOME

so that he wouldn't miss them when he went off for the nothingness, which now tugged at him. It was all he could do to keep from devoting his mornings to nothingness too.

After the storm the weather was magnificent. Soft golden days. The leaves on the low bushes all around his house began to glow with gold. They were so beautiful that they dragged him back from the sea beach so that he could watch them shine in the late sun. It was now setting well off to the left of where it had set in June. It skidded along the horizon, a glowing tomato, outlining a low hill with a water tower on it that he had not noticed before. The tomato sun picked it out for him late one afternoon as he sat on a driftwood bench he had made, his back against the warm shingles. Above the nearby bushes, and also ignited by the sun, swarmed a late hatch of some kind of minute gnat. Separate clouds of gnats were bobbing up and down, transparent globes of shimmering revolving electrons, glowing specks zipping around each other in the slanting golden light like tiny jigging galaxies, each gnat a star held in its crazy little orbit by the attraction of all the other gnat stars, heedless of the next galaxy, only fifty feet away. Or was it fifty light-years? How could one measure for gnats, for whom all of existence was to jiggle in a two-foot cloud for a single afternoon while remorseless blue-steel swallows, coursing the bushes, burst the little galaxies as unimaginably large comets might, carelessly gobbling up their stars, their planets and moons, a hundred at a gulp. After each swallow pass, the gnats re-formed their clouds, and he wondered if they were aware of what was happening to them, if they missed the eaten, and what kind of larger, impossible-to-know agent, operating on a different time scale, might be feeding on him.

Still they didn't come. The gnats all died. The sun skidded farther to the south. He made another trip to town. Now he had more people to avoid. Charlie and Lorraine as before, and now Lou and Marge, because he didn't want it to look as if he was chasing them. They weren't really friends. He had seen Lou three times in his life, Marge once. To them he was just a casual acquaintance with whom they had spent a beery evening on a beach. Perhaps it had been nothing more than a setup to get a date for Emily, a setup that bombed. If that was so, it would be impossible to explain how much they meant to him. He couldn't chase them; they would have to come of themselves. But they didn't, and he made his furtive trip to town, loading up at the market so that he wouldn't have to go back too soon. He drove his dory in on his beach, carried up a load of groceries, and went back for a second. He then pulled the dory out to a mooring stake with a rope and pulley that he operated from the shore.

It rode there motionless on a glaze of lead-colored water. The small ripples of the evening southerly were cut off by the jetty he had built. Sometime he would start another, to protect the dory from winds that came from the north. He would have his own harbor.

And nobody to see it but himself. Nobody to come in or go out. Nobody to know what an immense amount of labor had gone into moving all those stones, the sweating and straining, the slipping and falling, the cut feet, the calculating, the skill. He took his sign down and carried the rest of the groceries up the path and put them away, then fell into his new wicker chair. The evenings were getting cool, and he shut the windows. Now he could hear nothing, not even the lap of water on the beach. He would have liked to light a fire to break the silence, to bring a crackle and some warmth into the room, but the effort was too great. He thought about what Hennerkop had said to him once: He moved in a straight line, with no loops or returns to people. It was true; he had just lost four more. *But they were not his fault.* Violet was not his fault. Julia was not his fault. Charlie and Lorraine were not. Lou and Marge were not. He wanted them. He would be glad to be with them if he could. Fran was his fault.

Beautiful chinless Fran. She was nothing but eyes now. He wrestled with his memory to exhume something of what she was really like. Think about that one slightly crooked front tooth. Remember that her breasts were too small and her legs too short. Bring her into the room with him, a real live flawed Fran—and choke with grief.

He got out his pen, the slender gold Cross pen that had somehow survived all the lurchings, the blackouts and crashes, and wrote Fran a letter. He rewrote it several times and put a copy of the final draft in his bureau drawer:

> Dear Fran:
>
> Although it's more than two years since we last saw each other, I think of you often and wonder how you are getting along. As for me, I am well. I want to apologize for the way I behaved with you, and I want you to know that if we ever meet again it will not happen again. I am through with liquor. I know you will find that hard to believe after our last meeting. But it's true. Except for an occasional beer. I haven't had a drink for nearly two years, and I never will again. If you feel like writing to let me know how you are and what you are doing, a letter addressed to general delivery, Lincoln Harbor, will reach me.

He agonized over how to sign it: Sincerely, Fred (too formal); With love, Fred (too presumptuous); Your friend, Fred (he was more than a friend—or had been—and might be less than one now); Fondly, Fred (ugh); Kindest regards, Fred (too cool); and finally he settled for just "Fred."

The next morning he took it to the post office, collected several back copies of *Time* and some "boxholder" mail advertising a square dance and a fire-damaged-furniture sale. Chugging home, he wondered how those things got to him, since he didn't have a box like all the other people, who got lots of mail and swarmed like bees at noon to twirl the little dials on the fronts of the boxes that lined one wall of the post office like cells in a honeycomb.

When he got home he saw his spare gasoline can standing where he had put it to remind him that it was empty. He should have turned around and gone back for a refill, but the effort was too great; he would do it next time.

He gave her a week to answer and then had to sit out another storm. The harder the wind blew, the lower its voice fell. It roared across the island in a deep baritone, shredding leaves and squirting water under his door. The rain came in horizontal sheets, clattering like gravel against his windows. It rained that way, choking blinding rain, all day and all through the night. Everything in the house got increasingly damp. The food-can labels on his kitchen shelf grew blisters. Green mold appeared on his gun case and on his one remaining pair of Whyte shoes. The next day it was still raining, and he began to worry about his dory, which was getting lower and lower in the water as it whipsawed on its mooring. This was by far the worst storm he had experienced. Finally he put on a slicker and his sou'wester hat and went down to the beach with a bucket. The wind was picking sand up from the beach and stinging his face with it. He started to pull the dory in, because it looked as if it was about to sink. But it grounded in about a foot of water and was immediately filled by the waves that were churning the cove. There it stuck. He waded out and pushed. He tried to shove the stern around closer to shore. He tried to bail, but water kept sloshing in as fast as he dipped it out. His sou'wester hat blew off and vanished. He ended by unscrewing the outboard motor and staggering ashore with it. He was soaked, exhausted, and so chilled that he boiled a kettle of water for a sponge-down bath and then tried to warm his living room with a fire. But the wood was wet, and the wind blew gusts of smoke down the chimney. He finally got into a damp bed, where his shivers gradually stopped, and he went to sleep.

The following day the storm had blown itself out. It was a balmy morning, almost like spring except for the orange and red of the remaining leaves on the sumacs and bay bushes. His dory was where he had left it. A sandbar was built up against it, and sand had flowed over the top and into the dory, half filling it. A pool of salt water came right up to the gunwale. When he had bailed out the water and scooped out the sand, he was able, after a great deal of digging and scraping, to get it floating. He reinstalled the outboard and went to town. There were two copies of *Time* waiting for him at the post office, also the letter he had written to Fran. It had come back rubber-stamped RETURN TO SENDER. He opened it as if it were a letter someone else had sent him, and read the message again: "Although it's more than two years since we last saw each other . . . "

Somehow he got back to his boat and home. He felt absolutely numb.

26

ED WAS NOW THE SAFE PLACE. THE SEA BEACH WAS too far away, too open, too bright. He needed a warm dark place. He drove two nails into the wall above his bedroom window and hung his slicker over them to keep out the glare. Then he curled up in bed. He spent the day there, waking and dozing, finally falling deeply into sleep. His bladder woke him sometime during the night. He didn't want to leave that warm soft safe bed, and he hung on as long as he could, but finally he let go in a delicious easing flood, his mind soft and sleepy, thinking only of how good it was to let go and not have to worry or think about anything. He remembered having read somewhere: "When you wet the bed it was warm at first, but then it got cold." Somebody famous had written something like that. He waited for it to get cold. Gradually it did. He tried to find a dry spot, and went to sleep again.

The next morning the room was a deep yellow from the sunlight beating against the slicker hung in the window. He and his bed smelled rank. He would have to get hold of himself, not to do anything like that again. He bundled up the sheet with his underwear and pants and threw them in the corner, washed himself, and then tried to wash the mattress, which he put out in the sun to dry.

Everything was an enormous effort. He went back into his bedroom and lay on the bare springs, but they hurt, so he put down a blanket and lay on that. He put another blanket over himself and went to sleep again. When he woke, his watch had stopped—he had forgotten to wind it—but by the sun he judged it to be early afternoon. He felt hungry and ate a can of beans. It was too much of an effort to heat them, so he ate them cold, spooning them out of the can, sitting on his doorstep next to his smelly mattress and staring over at the mainland, thinking of the post office full of people, remembering how he had felt as he opened his letter to Fran. It occurred to him that it might have been undelivered because she had quit the Advertising Council and left no forwarding address. The message that the postal clerk had stamped on the envelope might tell that. He rummaged around for it, halfheartedly at first, then desperately. It was nowhere. He had a dim recollection of crumpling something in the post office. The letter too?

He had been running around naked from the waist down while looking for the envelope, and felt cold. His only remaining clean pants were the linen ones from Long Island. He put on a pair of those and lit a big fire in his fireplace. He dragged his mattress inside and propped it up so that it would continue to dry in front of the fire. The effort exhausted him. He decided to have another can of beans to keep up his strength, which seemed to be leaking out of him. He was breathing it out right now. The room was full of his breath, his ex-strength. His nostrils, his ears, even the pores of his skin, were holes from which strength leaked. He ate the beans to stop that hemorrhage. He put the mattress back on the bed with the dry side up and again fell into a heavy sleep.

When the sun came up he forced himself to get out of bed. Discipline was what he needed, a schedule. Eat breakfast—he did; he was ravenously hungry and put away four eggs and two cups of coffee and a stack of toast—then wash the pants he had wet. He put them in the kitchen sink and turned on the tap to let them soak, noticing that there were only two cans of beans left and four cans of other things. He was down to four eggs. He would have to get more food. Tomorrow he would go. Meanwhile it seemed a good idea to take the remaining cans into the bedroom, where he could keep an eye on them. He carried them there, two by two, and set them on the bureau. His room was unpleasantly stuffy and smelly, so he took down the slicker and opened the window. The sun was blinding, a stunning radiance in the sky. It felt so hot, so clean—what he needed to bring him back. He went outside and sat basking in that radiance, his back against the side of the house. He woke, cold, when the sun had passed to the other side.

He remembered the pants soaking in the kitchen sink. They were wet when he felt them, but there was no water in the sink; he had forgotten to put the plug in. He turned on the tap for more water, only to discover it already was on; the tank had emptied itself while he had been sleeping in the sun outside. He had to start the generator and switch on the pump to fill it again.

Like everything else he had done in the past day or so, that effort exhausted him. He went to bed and almost instantly fell asleep. When he woke, it was suddenly, with the sense that something had wakened him. He lay in his bed in the silence, wondering what it was, then realized it was the silence itself. His generator and pump had stopped. When he lit his lamp to investigate the cause, he discovered that the generator had run out of gas; the tank was still empty.

That was serious, because he had never filled the spare gasoline can. He checked the other. It had about half a gallon in it, so he put that into the generator and started it up again. It ran for an hour. Now he had an hour's worth of water in his tank—however much that might be, he had no idea—and no gas. He would have to pull himself together, he told himself again, clean himself up and go to town tomorrow for more gas and more food.

Wide awake now although it was deep in the night, and frightened, and feeling utterly abandoned by Fran and also extremely cold, he wrapped a blanket around himself, lit a fire in his fireplace, and pulled his wicker chair up as close as he could get it. What was left? His mind flew in a wide circle, alone on an empty plain, and came up with only the distant memory of Violet and her cold house, even colder than this one, and her warm self. He concentrated on that and succeeded in bringing her back to the point where he could place himself in her warm bed in her freezing cottage. He thought again of what Hennerkop had said about straight lines and loops. Here was a loop he had never tried to follow, and now it seemed to be the last one he had.

He decided to write Violet a letter. He got his lamp and a pad of paper. The room grew even colder, and he threw on more wood, noticing that his woodpile was dangerously low. He put the pad on his knee and began to write.

He wrote slowly. His pen pushed itself along at a snail's pace, keeping step with his crawling thoughts, which formed themselves like glue, gathering slowly on his tongue before they dripped onto the paper.

Dear Violet:

Perhaps you don't remember me, the American officer who used to run through Under Wixton. At any rate, I remember you and have been wondering lately how you are and what you have been doing since the war ended. I realize that a good deal of time has passed since then and that you may not want to pick up a thread that how would he put it?

a thread that may have worn too thin and may now be entirely broken. If not, and if you feel like writing to bring me up to date on yourself, a letter to me at the above address will reach me. As for myself, I am living quietly and alone in this small New England town, with enough time on my hands to remember some of the brighter moments of my life. Hence this letter. You may also remember my quoting a bit of poetry that you found appropriate to yourself. I enclose a copy of the book from which it came.

Sincerely,

He didn't stop to think what he might do if she replied. He wrote out of an overpowering need to talk to somebody. He had let her know he was unattached, that he still thought warmly of her.

And he had left her an out: the thread that might have worn too thin. As he wrote, in the silence and the lamplight and the cold, he was brought closer and closer to Under Wixton, to the cold and can- dlelight of Violet's room. She had been the one wrapped in a blanket that time. She was the one, the only one, always had been. The one and only. That perfect time. He copied the letter carefully and put the copy in the bureau drawer on top of the one to Fran.

He found his volume of *Spoon River* and wrapped it. Now he couldn't wait for day to come, to get it and the letter in the mail. He heated a kettle of water and shaved by lamplight, then washed himself down with the remains of the hot water, the bathtub like a frozen pavement under his feet. Shivering, he put on two undershirts, then a Wragge shirt, then both his sweaters and the cleanest of the dirty khaki pants from the laundry pile in the corner. Then he again wrapped himself in a blanket and waited for day to come. To give himself strength for the trip, he heated a can of hash and ate it hud- dled in front of the fire.

When he woke, the sun was up. He hustled into his slicker, ran down to his dory, and started off, mad to get there, bailing some rain- water as he went.

All that rush. The clock in the hardware store said 7:10, and the post office was shut. He reset his watch and sat down to wait on a bench across the street, hoping that neither Charlie nor Lorraine would come along. Neither did, the post office opened, he mailed his letter and package, and got out of there. He was halfway home before he realized that he had forgotten to ask if there was any mail for him.

He was nearly home when the outboard died; he had forgotten again to get gas.

Turn around and row back? He had no gloves. He rowed the half mile to the island with bare hands, blistering them. Without gas, of course, he was also without water, except for what was left in the tank, and almost without food. He would have to pull himself together— that was becoming a daily litany—build up his strength for the next calm day, put on his gloves, and row.

He went back to bed to rest up and spent all that day and night there. The next day he ate half a can of pineapple. A day later he had his last can of hash. He stayed in bed to keep warm while the hash built up his strength. He followed the next day with his last two eggs and some toast, scraping from the bread the mold that had formed because his refrigerator no longer worked. He moved increasingly slowly to conserve energy. Bed was the best place for that, safe and warm. He settled in there, not exactly asleep, not entirely awake. The time went along. Sometimes it was day, sometimes it was dark.

One night God came. He appeared on the wall, a large eye a foot across. It had to be God's eye, because it had three pupils, each with a fleck of light in it, staring unblinkingly at him. Remembering that he hadn't said his prayers for many years, he did so then, asking for a little strength for rowing. He then dozed off, and when he woke again in the morning, God's eye turned out to be ticks of light reflected from the last three cans of food on his bureau.

Nevertheless God stayed around. He felt His presence in the power of the sun. A couple of times he heard God talking. Not God Himself; if it had been God speaking he would have understood Him. This was probably angels traveling with Him, because the sound came from the sky, a confused honking and gabbling whose meaning he couldn't make out at all as it passed overhead. Several times he heard that.

He found the unfinished can of pineapple on the floor by his bed. Being very thirsty, he ate it and drank down the juice, although both tasted awful from having sat in the open can for so long. Soon they made him sick, or was it God who did that? He felt like throwing up but couldn't. Cramps tied him up, iron bars in his intestines that drove cruelly through the curves and corners, remorselessly downward, finally dissolving into uncontrollable surges that burst out of him. He strained and strained to purge himself of the iron pineapple, then lay in it until he became so thirsty that he had to get up. His own smell revolted him. He staggered into the kitchen, drank two glasses of water, then took off all his clothes and once again tried to wash them in the sink. He made a bad job of it, and of himself. He felt light-headed. He wiped off the mattress as well as he could and turned it over again.

Pull yourself together. Pull yourself together. He rummaged through the laundry pile in the corner and put on all the cleanest clothes he could find and got back into bed. Even there he felt cold. Only the sun, God's eye, could keep him warm. From then on he lay in the sun where and when there was sun.

He had one can of beans left, and a can of cherries. He opened the beans and ate them one by one, chewing them carefully to extract the maximum nourishment from each. There were 687 beans in the can. He made the most of every one, taking the better part of a day to eat them. They returned themselves to him little by little, bean strength flowing through him. He could feel it along his muscles and in his cells. By tomorrow he would be strong, and if tomorrow was a good day he would row.

That night, after all the beans, he got very thirsty, but only half a glass of water ran from the kitchen tap; his tank had gone dry again. How could that be? He went into the bathroom and tried there. A few drops and a gurgle, then nothing. It came to him that he had used a good deal of water trying to clean himself and his clothes after the pineapple episode. He went back to bed, his mouth getting drier and drier. He had to have water. When it was light he got a bucket and started for the pond. He couldn't see it from his house, but he knew where it was, across a little low boggy bit and over a small rise, a few hundred yards away through the bushes.

He got to the boggy bit after a long struggle. The bushes came up to his chest. He discovered how weak he was when he found it was all he could do to push through them. They rose in a dense tangle, interwoven with brambles that clung and tore. They tripped him up and he kept falling, crashing into their dagger arms, pricking his hands as he tried to get up again.

At the boggy spot he immediately went in up to his thighs in mud, and realized then that there was no way he could make it across and up the other side. His legs were trembling so violently that they could scarcely hold him up. He abandoned the bucket and concentrated on getting out of the mud and back into the bushes. He was gasping and drenched with sweat, and he sat down to rest. He must have gone to sleep there, because sometime later he found himself sitting with his head on his knees, not sure where he was or how he had gotten there. The mud on his legs reminded him, and he started back.

He was able to get to his feet and mark the chimney of his house not three hundred feet away. So close—but so hard. As he pressed into the bushes, they threw him back, tripping him and holding him down when he fell. Each time, he had to rest before being able to get up. While he rested, in the difficult embrace of a bush-and-bramble hammock, his legs continued to shudder and twitch. He couldn't stop them. He talked to them individually, telling them to calm down. Sometimes they did. When they didn't, he just had to wait for them to improve. His right leg improved faster than his left. He was grateful to his right leg and told it so. He was angry at his left and wouldn't speak to it. He had several periods of sleep or unconsciousness in the bushes while waiting for his legs to improve. Finally it got dark, and he was still in the bushes.

He was there the next day, overpoweringly thirsty and so numb with cold that he found it hard to move his legs at all. The possibility that he might die there occurred to him. These were the same bushes over which he had watched those clouds of gnats jiggling in their little galaxies a long time ago. They had all died and sunk down in these same bushes in which he now was. There were perhaps half a million gnat corpses all around him. He looked dully this way and that for them, but the mat of stems and roots was too dense. Anyway, his eyes weren't working all that well. Everything was blurry except the sun. God, the sun, was as sharp and bright as a knife. He willed himself to stand up so that the heat and strength of God would flow into him.

Standing, he could see his chimney—so close. He started toward it, fell, and rested again. Later he crawled. He had several conversations with God about helping him negotiate individual branches and bramble ropes. He reminded God that His only begotten son had worn a crown of thorns and that all the scratches he was getting were proof of his identification with His only begotten son and that He should therefore help him out of the bushes.

Sometime that day he got clear. God's sun was blinding by that time. Memory and sharp vision came and went. His best recollection later was of a copper-flavored tongue that filled his mouth, and how the cherry juice tasted when at last he found the opener and managed to get the can open.

27

THE NEXT PERIOD WAS CONFUSED. IT CONSISTED mostly of shivering and thirst. He was not always sure where he was. When God finally did come, He came in the form of a towering black shadow that seemed to stretch several hundred yards into the sky. God's shadow cut him off from the sun and made him shiver even more than he had been shivering. It was revealed to him for the first time that God and the sun were not necessarily the same, for God seemed to have the ability to separate Himself from the sun and move as an independent shadow.

The shadow spoke: "He's over here." God's voice at last; he could understand it. It sounded like someone he knew. He opened his mouth to ask God to step out of the sun, but no sound came out.

God knelt down next to him, shrinking to Lou Mendoza size, and spoke again: "What's the matter, Fred? You all right?"

He looked at Lou. He couldn't speak. His throat was closed. His swollen tongue filled his mouth.

Lou's face came and went. He earnestly desired to speak to him, and to Marge, whose face appeared too. But he couldn't.

"He's alive?"

"Course he's alive. See him breathing. We've got to get him ashore."

Lou picked him up. "Phew," he said. "He's shat himself."

In the boat Marge asked: "What's wrong with him?"

"Christ only knows. I'll take him out to the house, get him cleaned up. You get the doctor."

"Wawa." He had been working on that word for quite a while and finally got it out. Marge gave him some in a paper cup. It felt its way around his tongue, partially ungluing it. Some went down his throat.

She gave him more. Swallowing was hard. The water was cold. He was cold.

At the marina, Lou asked: "Can you walk?"

"Try."

They supported him to the truck, his legs going through the motions like an injured football player's. Marge disappeared. Lou carried him into his house and ran a hot bath while he stripped him of his clothes.

"Jesus Christ, you stink, do you know that, Fred?"

He knew.

"How come three shirts? Do you know you're wearing three shirts and three undershirts? Three pair of pants?"

"Cold."

Lou lifted him into the tub. The water was hot, but he continued to shiver. He sank down so that the water would run into his mouth. He tried to swallow a little.

"Hey, not that. Let me give you a glass of clean."

"Hot."

"Okay, hot. But not that bathwater. Jesus, Fred, you just don't know how dirty you are." Lou got down on his knees and began lathering and scrubbing him. "Got to get some of that stink off of you before the doctor comes, else he might not stay. Here." He handed him the soap and washcloth. "You do your own butt."

He did what he could.

"Now I'm gonna run this water out and put in some fresh. This here's too dirty. You lay right where you are."

He hated to feel that water go, but more, even hotter, replaced it. It was just beginning to get to him when Marge returned with a doctor. He felt too sleepy and comfortable, just on the edge of being warm, to be embarrassed by the three of them looking down at him in the tub.

"We found him sitting by his house," Lou explained. "He was wearing two, three sets of everything. He couldn't talk."

"Where's his clothes now?" asked Marge.

"I thrun them out back. They stunk."

The doctor took his temperature and pulse, told him to open his mouth, examined his sausage of a tongue, listened to his heart. "Can you talk?" he asked.

"Yes," he said. It came out "yeth."

"What happened to you?"

"I jutht—" He was too tired to tell him.

The doctor straightened up and said to the others: "There doesn't seem to be anything the matter with him except exposure and severe dehydration. He has a lot of scratches on him, but they don't seem to be infected."

"What do we do with him?"

"Except that he may be mentally disturbed. He might be better off in a hospital."

"No," he said. Here was where he wanted to be.

"You understand what we're saying, Fred?" Lou raised his voice as if insane people were hard of hearing.

He nodded.

"So what do we do with him?"

"Keep putting liquids into him. Juices. Chicken broth. I'll stop by tomorrow afternoon to see how he is. Keep him in bed."

"How about getting to the crapper?"

"If he can. Although he might be better off in a hospital."

"I want to thtay here." Proud of that long sentence.

"Fred, you hear me?" Lou shouted. "You think you can? I'm gonna put you in Davey's room." He hoisted him out of the tub, set him on the toilet seat, and dried him off more or less. He then put a work shirt on him and hauled him to his feet. "Now let's see you walk into Davey's room. It's across the hall."

He made it. A small room. Marge had sheets on the bed and was putting on a blanket.

"I got to go now," she said. "Opening time."

She left. The doctor left. Lou put a pitcher of water and a glass by the bed, also an open can of tomato juice. He put a pink plastic bucket under the bed. "Just in case." Then Lou left. He lay on his back, with his eyes closed. He was able to move his tongue around in his mouth now, and he did so gratefully. From time to time he took a sip of water or tomato juice. He kept drifting off to sleep. Pure heaven. He was warm and clean. After a while the liquids began to move through him. At first he used the bucket. Later he went to the bathroom. He took the bucket with him and rinsed it out carefully.

He had time to become acquainted with Davey, but he didn't learn much. There was a photograph of a high school baseball team on the wall, but he didn't know which one was Davey. Davey didn't come into his room all that day or night. Apparently he wasn't around. His closet, except for a very old pair of Keds, was empty. So was his bureau, empty and dusty. So was the room, empty and dusty. He prowled shakily around it and looked out the window, which faced the back where the trucks were parked. Whenever he heard anybody

247

coming he got back into bed, now extremely conscious of his shirttail nakedness. When Marge walked in with a pile of his clothes he was vastly relieved to see them.

"Took them to the laundromat yesterday," she said. "Those green and yellow pants are pretty fancy. Linen. Lou wanted to throw them out, but I knew they would wash up good. Why'n't you put something on and come into the kitchen. I'm making hotcakes."

He ate the hotcakes, forcing himself to do it slowly. Still thirsty, he followed with a glass of water, but now it went down easily into a system whose gates and sluices were open and flowing. He felt weak but well. In his own clothes, rumpled but fresh and clean. It was wonderful to feel clean.

"I went and got your gun," Lou said. "Looked around. Nothing else seemed worth taking. Fred, you left an awful mess."

"You're the one to talk," said Marge.

"I put a padlock on your door and latched the windows. Won't nobody go out there till spring anyway. Brought your dory. It's in the marina now, but we'll put it in the yard over the winter."

"I guess he could stand one more hotcake," said Marge.

"So what the hell happened to you?"

He had been trying to prepare himself for that. Wondering what to say, not quite sure himself what had happened (at least, why), not sure of their role, not at all sure they would comprehend their importance to him, assuming he could articulate it. It might be simpler not to mention their part at all, but here he was, with them. "I guess I just ran down," he said.

"You done worse. You come to a dead stop."

"I got lonely."

"I would think," said Marge. "Why didn't you come to town?"

"I ran out of gas."

"You could row in."

"I ran out of food." How could he explain the running out of will? "I got sick. I got weak." He bit his lip. "Anyway, there was nobody here to come to."

"Ain't you friendly with Charlie Barker? You were always going to his place," said Lou.

That surprised him. "How did you know that?"

"People around here know everything. They know you're here now, I guess. And I guess they know Marge moved in when you did."

"You moved in?" he asked.

"Supposed to be looking out for you; that's what I said. But people suppose she's looking out for me."

"Let them suppose," she said.

"They won't be supposing Fred."

She just smiled at him.

Lou was persistent. "So what really happened?"

"Leave him alone. He's weak."

"I want to know."

"You didn't come back. I waited for you." He got it out, but it seemed woefully inadequate.

"Come back?" said Marge.

"I asked you back, remember. You never came."

"What difference . . . ? We couldn't. I mean—"

"Tell him," said Lou.

"I mean, we were split up, like, for a while."

"She means I finally thrun out my no-good brother. You see his empty room you're in? It's empty because I finally thrun him out. So what does he do? He goes in to the Blue Lobster and loads up and charges it to me. And *she* lets him."

"So he isn't speaking to me. So what am I supposed to do, sit around? So I, you know, go on a date. So what does he do? He *hits* me."

Lou helped himself to more hotcakes. "She knew better than that."

"Gave me a black eye. I was ashamed to go anywhere." She touched the place. There was still a faint smudge there.

"Just a love tap, Fred. She bruises easy. Nothing to the one I laid on you. And then she won't speak to me for a week."

"What do you expect? Hit first, think later."

Lou's grin widened. "And here are the two busted heads eating hotcakes in my kitchen. Goes to show. Bust heads, make friends. How you feeling, Fred? Maybe if you ate it real slow, you could handle another."

He shook his head. The same affection that he had felt on the beach was welling up again and would make eating anything impossible. And control of his lower lip impossible. He got up and went into Davey's room.

Why hadn't he come to them? Always waiting for the other person to make the move. Though he couldn't trust people to make good moves. They always seemed to make bad ones. Except they didn't *always*. Here they didn't. So it wasn't just them. It had to be himself. Something whizzed through his mind (from Hennerkop?), and he tried to hang on to it. If you felt good about yourself, good enough to take risks with yourself, then you might get something back. He'd risked with Lou, even though he'd been frightened of him. He had gone back with the frying pans, never mind the reason. He had risked another punch in the jaw and risked drinking with him. On the beach he had risked letting both of them know he was fond of them.

So why hadn't he come to them? *Because he couldn't believe that they might be fond of him.*

What did it take to prove that? Did they have to save his life? He really ought to go back into the kitchen and let them know how fond he was of them regardless of how they felt. Put his arms around them—and then they would really think he was crazy. He would have to learn to watch people more carefully. Not in the old way, to protect himself. He would have to learn to let people know he was fond of them without alarming them. After all, other people might be just as frightened of closeness and displays of emotion as he had been. Look more closely for that instead of always looking at himself.

Look at himself. There was no mirror in Davey's room, so he slid across the hall to the bathroom. There he looked at himself, trying to see something human that other humans might respect and love. It had to be there. At this moment he felt so generous with himself that he knew it had to be. He stared into his own eyes, trying to see through the pupils, into the black behind them, to something that was floundering back in there. Here he was, approaching forty, staring at himself in a mirror and for the first time in his life getting a glimpse of what he might be. He didn't have to throw his arms around them, but he could nourish the feeling he had for them, and he could find ways of letting them know. If he was too stupid for that, he deserved to freeze.

Lou was still eating hotcakes. He had a gargantuan appetite.

"You saved my life, you know."

"Well . . ."

"You did."

"Okay, okay."

"How did you happen to go out there?"

"Bill Nunes, the one in the post office. I was in there one day, and he said: You still fishing? And I said yes. And he said: Do you ever fish around Sheep Island? And I said yes. And then he said he was wondering about you because you had mail piling up. I got to thinking maybe you'd busted a leg or something, so I grabbed Marge and went."

"I studied nursing," she explained. "Why didn't you come to town?"

Say it. *Say it.* "Because there's nobody here." Go on. *The impor-tant thing.* "I mean, who feels about me the way you do about each other." He willed himself to look at them, first him, then her. She put a hand on Lou's with an expression that gutted him utterly. His tears: he simply could not control them.

"He's still weak," she said, getting up and putting an arm around him, her breasts broad across his shoulders.

"I told you we should have brought someone better than Emily," Lou said.

Lou's house was a bungalow, with a kitchen, living room, bathroom, and two bedrooms. It was furnished simply in imitation Colonial maple. One pattern of chintz everywhere. Apparently he had fur-nished his entire house with a single purchase of matching everything. Marge had succeeded in cleaning up the kitchen. Now she was attack-ing the living room. Lou sprawled on the sofa, watching her.

"How about Doris?" he said.

"Doris? You have to be out of your mind."

"Who, then?"

"Who, nobody. Give him a chance to get his strength back. Let him get out of the house and around town a little."

He borrowed the dry mop from Marge and cleaned out Davey's room and closet. Even that little job was tiring. He would do the bureau tomorrow. If they let him stay.

Part Three

LEAVING THERE

28

FRED, CAN YOU DRIVE A TRUCK?"

"I can drive a car."

"Same thing. I got a lot of hauling jobs stacked up. Simple jobs, but they take somebody. If it wasn't for that son-of-a-bitching brother of mine, I wouldn't be shorthanded."

He became a truckdriver, ashamed of his weakness. He took it as carefully and slowly as he could, concealing the trembling, and gradually it went away. He hauled loads of dirt, sand, cinder block, trash—whatever had to be hauled. When Lou was satisfied that he was skillful enough to negotiate the narrow back streets and driveways of Lincoln Harbor, he put him on a garbage run he had developed. By that time Fred was strong enough to lift full garbage cans. He was paid fifty dollars a week.

"I should be paying you back something for my room and board."

"Okay, ten bucks. It ain't costing me more. Marge don't mind your being here."

"You're sure?"

"You got her here, Fred. She wouldn't move in here before you came. When we wanted to be together, like, she would sneak in when she got through work. Trouble was sneaking out again. She never liked that. One thing, she don't like to get up early. Another thing, even at six there's probably somebody up someplace. I'd leave the truck right next to the kitchen door so's she could jump right in. But she always had the feeling that somebody would see her and say there goes that Marge Kenney humping that Lou Mendoza again."

"Where does she live?"

"Except that she don't say humping. That's my dirty tongue

again. Live? She was living across town in a trailer with Doris Fane. But she don't like Doris's ways. Thinking of moving anyway. You needing care, that got her here. While I was out working, she'd sit here. Says you slept most of the time. She filled your water pitcher, kept an eye on you."

He had little recollection of that service but was filled with gratitude. "I want to tell you again. You two . . . "

"Forget it."

Make sure he knew. "I don't want to forget it. I owe you a lot. If you ever . . . "

"Okay, okay. Right now just keep working. We got work stacked up to get done before frost."

Each morning he got up at six-thirty and made his own breakfast, also a sandwich and a thermos of coffee for his lunch. During breakfast he got the day's instructions from Lou. The hardest part was learning the different places he had to go. Sometimes the man he was supposed to meet wouldn't be there. He made sure he knew where Lou would be during the day so that he could check with him to find out what he might do instead.

"That's good, Fred. Davey would have just goofed off."

He would bring the truck back to Lou's house at five. Marge would have a hot supper ready, and the three of them would eat it in the kitchen. Just before six she would leave for her job at the Blue Lobster. After supper he did the dishes, while Lou sprawled on the sofa with a cigar, expansive and disposed to talk. But he was usually so tired that he couldn't listen to Lou. Most nights he was asleep by eight. He never heard Marge come in.

There was a double bed in Lou's room. Weekdays that door was shut in the morning. Consequently, except for suppers, the only time he saw Marge was on Sunday, when nobody worked and the three of them ate a large late leisurely breakfast together. Marge had a generous soft figure. She moved deliberately and with careful regard for her movements. It was as if she had learned this from watching voluptuous women in the movies. She was conscious of men's eyes on her. She caught Lou's as she went about the house. She enjoyed being watched by him, soliciting and getting occasional pats and swats as she brushed by him. Fred felt that she also welcomed his eyes on her, and he would have been made uncomfortable about that if she hadn't been so open about it. She would sway out of the kitchen and stand in the doorway, her hip cocked, frankly enjoying being admired. There was a glow of femaleness about her all the time. She seemed to be saying: "Here I am. I know I'm desirable. In fact, I'm proud of it. So look at me and enjoy yourself. Whatever you succeed in imagining about me won't be as warm as the truth." If there were women in the world who appeared to promise much, she was one.

A great asset for a barmaid, and probably cultivated on the job. But he was wrong about that. As he got to know her better and had more chances to observe her, he began to understand that this was the way she was. Her consciousness of herself as a sexual woman was as much a part of her as her deep bosom. She didn't put it on for men. Occasionally he would catch her unaware that she was being observed. She would behave in the same way, moving deliberately and easily, her buttocks slewing and settling with each step. She would pause to smooth herself down, starting under her breasts and running the palms of her hands down her sides and over her hips. Obviously she felt good to herself.

Several weeks on the job. He questioned nothing. Getting through the day and falling into bed at night was all he seemed to want. His hands got tougher and his back stronger. The weather grew colder, and he bought a padded jacket, a pair of heavy work gloves, a pair of work shoes, and whatever else he needed. He didn't need much, because Marge took his clothes as well as Lou's to the laundromat every week. He thought of going back to the island to see what he could salvage from the mess there, but kept putting it off. Eventually that became impossible, because Lou said it was time to haul his dory, which they did together. It was now sitting in Lou's backyard.

He saw Lorraine on Elm Street. They were walking toward each other, and while he was still trying to decide what to say to her, she spotted him and ducked into the hardware store. A relief. Not exactly a surprise, though.

That afternoon he was at the town dump with a load of trash, when a man said: "You driving regular for Lou?"

He nodded.

"How much he paying you?"

He wondered if that was any of his business, but he said: "Fifty a week."

"He's screwing you."

He slammed the tailgate shut, saying nothing.

"I tell you he's screwing you. You could get a hundred from Abbey."

"I get my room and board."

"You don't have to tell me. You're sleeping in my room."

So this was Davey. He was somewhere in his late twenties, a slender dark-complexioned man with thick black hair, heavy eyebrows, and a strong nose. He was extremely handsome. He wore work clothes and a padded jacket—the winter uniform of the working class in Lincoln Harbor.

"Marge sleeping over too, I hear."

"That's right." He got into his cab.

"Cooking for the both of you?"

He nodded.

"What else she doing for the both of you?"

"Nothing."

"Then you're missing an easy lay."

He started his engine.

"A good lay," Davey said. "Take it from me."

"You left your sneakers," he said, and drove off.

That night at supper he wondered as she leaned over the kitchen table. She usually wore high-necked sweaters, but the sculpturing job underneath was bold. When she sat down, her buttocks settled carefully in her chair—cheek by cheek.

"When are you gonna shave off them whiskers?" said Lou.

"Why'n't you leave them on, Fred. On you they look good."

He fingered them.

"They're so red," she said. "I never saw such a red beard. Your hair's not that red. Anyway, I like men with beards."

"Like diving into a horsehair mattress," said Lou.

He decided to keep it. It was now bushing out all over the lower half of his face, and it was indeed very red. Against this new fox-colored beard his hair looked brown. The beard also filled out his face, making it seem wider and more powerful. He no longer had the studious aloof look, whose aristocratic lines he had tried to accentuate by tipping his head ever so slightly backward to give the impression—without actually betraying it—that he was looking down his nose. The idea that he had once done that made him squirm inwardly. Now he wanted to look straight out at people. Level, eye-to-eye.

Another day he delivered a load of fill to a man who peeled a twenty-dollar bill from his roll and handed it to him.

"What's this for?"

"The job. I always pay Lou cash."

That night he handed over the money. Lou stuffed it in his pocket.

"How are you going to remember what this was for?" he asked.

"I'll cross it off." Lou leafed a couple of times through a dog-eared school notebook that he kept on a shelf. "This one ain't even down. Must have forgot it."

That was Lou's job book. Entries were made in it in pencil in a scribbled shorthand that Fred could not always decipher. When a job was finished, Lou was supposed to cross it off but didn't always remember. It now occurred to him to ask Lou when and how he sent out bills.

"Don't send many. Rather work for cash."

He wondered why.

"Fred, you ain't very smart. Nunes needs a load of cinder block, he pays cash. I need two recaps, I pay cash. Who keeps track? No taxes."

"How do you keep track of whether you get paid?"

"Get paid, I cross off the job in this here book."

That was a jolt. He had been crossing off jobs as he completed them, and didn't always know about the payment. He confessed that to Lou.

"Jesus, Fred, don't do that. Which ones?"

Luckily he was able to show him; his lines were much neater than Lou's.

"All right, Fred. But from now on I do the crossing off. That way I know a job's done and paid for."

He picked up the notebook. "What's this one way back here?"

Lou studied it. "That one? That's something left over from last year, looks like. Must have forgot to cross it off."

"What was it for?"

"For?" He studied it some more. "That was Leaks. George Leaks. I done a job for him."

"Did he pay you?"

"Must have. No, wait a minute—he was short, so I told him he could wait. *That's* why it ain't crossed off." He chewed down on his cigar with satisfaction.

"How much does he owe you?"

"How much? What the fuck you trying to do, tell me how to run my business?"

"Yes." Getting that out was positively exhilarating.

"Well, you just run the truck and the garbage, and I'll run the business."

Pause a moment, but only for a moment, and try again. "Why do you get mad when I ask you a question?"

"Because it's none of your fucking business."

"But Leaks owes you money."

"Okay, he owes."

"You don't know how much."

"Okay, *okay!*"

"This notebook is a mess."

"I don't know bookkeeping."

He felt like a teacher trying to get the attention of a large and dangerously recalcitrant schoolboy. "You should have a ledger." He said that it should contain the date of the order, the name, the price quoted, and the amount paid. He asked Lou how he figured what to charge.

"I kind of know the going price. If I know the fellow real well and know he knows prices, I quote him low. If I don't, I figure Abbey's price and I cut a little under so's to get the job."

"How can you be sure you're making money that way?"

"I make money. I live. I got a house, two trucks, and a backhoe."

"Do you really own them?"

"And the *Stinger.* Don't forget the *Stinger.*"

"Is the *Stinger* paid for?"

Lou's face got very red; he put his hands on the table and started to get up. Fred made himself stay where he was. He hoped his stare was calm and his voice would be steady. "Don't hit me again. What would that prove?"

"It might shut you up," Lou shouted. "I don't want no asshole like you telling me what to do."

He decided it might ease things a little if he tilted back in his chair and folded his arms as Lou sat down again. "I'm not telling you what to do. I'm just asking you questions. What's wrong with that if it makes the business easier for you? What I'm trying to say is that you need a bookkeeper."

"Can't afford a bookkeeper. I beat fellows like Abbey by *not* having a bookkeeper. I got no overhead."

"And no records."

"I got *this.*" Lou pounded the notebook but no longer looked as if he was going to pound him.

"That's no good. Tomorrow I'm going to buy a ledger. I'm going to try out as your bookkeeper. I don't know anything about bookkeeping either, so we start even. We'll sit down after supper, and you'll tell me what to put in it."

Lou relit his cigar.

"You can concentrate on what's really important, running the business. What's wrong with that?"

"Nothing, I guess, for a try."

"I'll even pay for the ledger."

"No need to do that."

"I also want a ten-dollar raise."

"You want a *what?*"

"I can get a hundred a week working for Abbey."

"Who the fuck told you that?"

"Your brother."

"He's lying. He's a liar. Abbey don't pay no hundred. He pays eighty."

"So maybe I'm worth sixty."

Lou's cigar was now completely shredded. He threw it away and picked bits of tobacco from his tongue, finally treating him to a crafty grin. "You know, Fred, you ain't quite the sweet little pink asshole I took you for."

29

HE BOUGHT A LEDGER. TWO DOORS DOWN WAS THE
post office. He hadn't been inside it for a couple of months.
The magazines would be piling up. He knew Lou wouldn't
look at them, but Marge might. He went in and asked for his mail.

"Sign here."

"What for?"

"You got a registered letter."

He signed and was given a letter from the Lincoln Harbor Bank
and Trust Co. Also a pile of magazines. Also a letter from Charlie
Barker. Also a letter from England.

England! He looked at the postmark. It was weeks old. It was one
of those blue flimsy airmail letters that fold to make their own
envelopes, addressed in a staggering bold script to Frederick Fay, Esq.
He put it in his back pocket, threw the other letters and the magazines on the truck seat, and made his garbage run. He would read
Violet's that night after supper, when he had composed himself and
was alone.

He ate his lunch at the dump, sitting in the cab of the truck. Why
not read the letter right now? He took it out of his pocket and stared
at its jagged black script. Its angularity and boldness were excitingly
evocative of her. He looked around him. The dump was empty except
for the rows of sea gulls that always sat there, staring at him with their
hard yellow eyes. Then a truck pulled in. Davey, of all people, materi-
alized from somewhere—did he live at the dump?—and began talking
to the driver. This was not the place for Violet. He decided to look at
his other mail.

First the letter from the bank. It was a shocker. In legal language
it advised him that his payment on the island, due October first, had

not been received by November first, and that if payment was not made by November fifteenth, the bank, on behalf of the owner, would act to reacquire title.

My God, what day was this? He had no idea. Why hadn't Charlie said something . . . realizing as the thought hit him that this was not Charlie's responsibility but his own. He ripped open Charlie's letter: "Your October payment is overdue. The bank is yelling. Where have you been? Please get in touch with me immediately."

Where had he been? That made no sense. Didn't Charlie know that he was living at Lou Mendoza's? Wait—perhaps he didn't. Perhaps Charlie thought he was sitting out on his island right now— except that Lorraine had seen him walking on Elm Street just a few days ago. So why hadn't she told Charlie? Probably kept silent out of malice. Oh, the bitch.

He looked at the bank letter again. It was signed by Hugo Westerfeld, Vice President. Best go see him and hope to straighten the matter out. But when he walked into the bank and looked at the date on the counter calendar, he learned with a drowning feeling that it was November nineteenth. The only thing to do was to brazen it out and hope.

Hugo Westerfeld was sitting in a paneled office, a borax version of the scores of offices he had known. How Fenn R. Wilking would have sneered at the imitation-leather-covered wastebasket, the two-pen set with an onyx base sitting on a mahogany-veneer desk. In box. Out box. Clipper-ship print on the wall. Everything neat and prissy. The executive's armor of infallibility, of arcane knowledge and power. So long as it took several people scurrying around to execute a deed or make a loan, businessmen could maintain their altitude. The priests of the modern world.

Brazen it out. In his padded jacket and work shoes and bulging beard, he felt a surge of resentment against priests. He sat down next to Westerfeld's desk and made himself even bigger by sticking out his clunky clay-covered boots. He handed his letter across the desk. "I got this today."

Westerfeld looked at it. "Oh, yes."

"It seems to be past due. I'd like to settle up."

"That won't be necessary."

"I mean, if there's a penalty—interest—I'll pay that too."

"It's been paid. Charlie Barker paid it. You should talk to him."

Was he in the clear? Had Lorraine kept her mouth shut after all? Charlie's office was up the street. Same veneer desk, same two-pen set. Charlie behind it, round sunny face. Try to read his expression, verify that thought about Lorraine.

"Where the hell have you been?"

"Well . . . " That was turning out to be very difficult to explain.

"We didn't see you. You just suddenly disappeared."

"I got stuck out on the island. I forgot some of the things you told me, and I couldn't get back. I got sick. Lou Mendoza came along and got me. I'm living with him right now."

Again that enormous reluctance to explain his decline and fall. It was better to join Lorraine in a conspiracy of silence about his having been living ashore for weeks now; change the subject. "You paid the installment on the island."

Charlie blew out a great puff of breath that seemed to move the short hairs on his head toward the vertical. "Somebody had to. You've got some equity in that place now. Plus a good house you did all that work on. You don't want to lose that."

"I want to thank you. I mean, you—"

"Somebody had to. People out there are like snapping turtles. Run a couple of months over—bam, you're gone."

"I understand that. But *you* paid."

"Who else have you got around here to look after you?" Charlie got up and gave him an exasperated look. "I sold you that island. I want to see you keep it. Already it's worth more than you paid for it. In less than a year. A lot more, if you ask me. Real estate's beginning to move here. Fred, I sometimes wonder can you get along by yourself."

Under the circumstances, a fair question. "I'm not sure," he said. "But I'm surer now than I was a few months ago. How much do I owe you?"

Charlie told him.

"That include interest?"

"It does. Also interest to me on the money I had to put up. Business is business, you know."

"Not entirely," he said. This red-faced man was so . . . well, so pure. He had to tell him. "It's also friendship."

"So if it's friendship, why didn't you come around all this time?"

"I will, I promise. But I want you to know—" A great rush of feeling now. Get a grip on his voice. "If there is anything I can ever do for you . . . " Anything, ever. From the depths of his heart.

"One thing you can do. Pay attention when I tell you something."

Back to the dump. As usual it was deserted except for the watchful sea gulls, who rose in a cloud to pick over every fresh load that was brought in. There was also a man's head silhouetted in the window of a little shed labeled DUMPMASTER. When the man came out, he saw it was Davey, who walked over and watched him dump his load, standing in front of the cab door as he came around from the tailgate.

"You getting in yet?" Davey asked.

"In?"

"Marge. If you're not getting in, you're wasting your time."

He walked around to climb into the truck. Davey stepped between, chest close, and said: "I'm talking to you, man."

He shouldered Davey aside to get hold of the door. Davey pushed back.

"Don't go shoving me. I'm talking to you. You're driving my truck, sleeping in my bed. I don't like either of those things."

"Talk to Lou."

"I'm talking to *you*."

"Well, fuck off," he said, at which point Davey hit him. It was nothing like the blow his brother had delivered, and he weathered it. But Davey stepped back and hit him again. Unable to defend himself, he made a clumsy lurch at Davey and managed to get his arms around his body. In a burst of fury he slammed him against the truck. Then, in response to some deep atavistic instinct, for he was totally inexperienced in fighting, he brought his knee up as hard as he could and caught Davey squarely in the groin. With a grunt, Davey fell to the ground, curled up and holding on to himself.

The fury still in him, he knelt down and grabbed Davey by the hair to pull him to a sitting position. Davey toppled over, completely helpless. He pulled him up again and punched him in the mouth. Rage had taken over. He punched Davey again—and again. Panting, he watched him topple over once more and his nose start to bleed. That anger was like a fit. It blotted out reason. And, like a fit, it passed. He got to his feet. Davey didn't move; he was making faint grunting noises. It came over him that he had had a fight, the first fight of his life. He had won it, still scarcely conscious of how and realizing that he should not have flailed away at that defenseless face. But those apparently were the punches of a lifetime that he had failed to deliver. They gave him a blazing sense of power.

Davey was still on the ground, still holding himself. Fred knelt down again. "You okay?"

"Uh—uh—"

"I said, are you okay? Can you get up?"

"Uh."

"Here." He hoisted him to a sitting position against the wheel of the truck.

Hunched over himself, Davey gave him a glassy look. It occurred to him that Davey was hurting so much down below that he didn't even know that he had been punched above. His hands were between his legs, cradling himself. It was as if his entire body were closing in on itself, sealing over a central pain so that by squeezing itself smaller the pain would be reduced.

"You want to go back to your shed? Come on, get up." He tugged, and Davey made it to his feet, still bent over, still holding himself, and allowed himself to be walked over to the shed, where he fell into a broken-out wicker chair with a cushion stuffed into it. He still couldn't straighten up, but the color was coming back into his face, and he could talk.

"Man, that was a dirty shot."

"You hit me first."

"Yeah, but—"

"You picked a fight with me. Don't do it again."

"Jeez, you near killed me. You fight dirty."

Savoring his newfound role as roughneck: "I always do."

Davey straightened up a little and gave that roughneck face a careful and respectful scrutiny. "Your lip. I got you a couple, though, didn't I?"

"I got you a couple too. Look at your own lip."

There was a small mirror on the shelf in the shed. Davey examined himself in it, drew a bandanna handkerchief out of his back pocket, and wiped his bloody nose and mouth. Then he got out a pocket comb and combed his hair carefully. He was a vain man. "Don't show, now the bleeding's stopped." He seemed anxious to obliterate the evidence that he had been beaten up, and also to find an excuse for it. He said again: "That was a lucky shot you caught me."

"Not if you practice it." The remark slid out of him so easily. Where had it come from? He reveled in it.

"You practice?"

"I told you I fight dirty. Always did."

"I still think you caught me a lucky shot. Else I'd have—"

"Try me again. I'll break your arm. I'll bite off your ear."

"You bite?"

"Ears." He leaned on Davey's rickety table and put his big red

266

bushy-bearded face close. "When they're as dirty as yours, I spit them out."

Davey backed up in his chair.

"So maybe you should mind your own business from now on." Tough, oh so tough. A fantastic feeling.

Still looking to salvage something, Davey said: "I mean, no sense in blabbing around town about this."

"If you can keep your big mouth shut, I can. But if your brother asks me who cut my lip, I'll tell him."

"And go blabbing to Marge too, I expect."

"You're the one blabbing about her. I'm telling you to stop that." He leaned closer. "I also break fingers." He stared at Davey, their noses almost touching. "I don't like you."

"Okay, okay."

"So keep out of my way and keep your big mouth shut."

"Okay."

"About all three of us."

"Okay."

They noticed it instantly. Lou said: "Somebody pop you one?"

"Sort of. I had an argument with Davey at the dump. He didn't like my living in his room and driving his truck."

"His truck! Got no business saying that. Not his room, neither. I thrun him out, the little pisser. So he knocked you around."

"Not exactly." He explained what had happened. Marge listened intently.

"By God, Fred. You getting too big for your britches. First you near kill me with a shotgun, then you kick the balls off my brother. Maybe we should chain you out back to guard the vehicles." Lou let out a roar of laughter, tipping his chair back, nearly breaking it. "Too dangerous letting you loose in a peaceful little town like this."

Both men were laughing now. "By the way, how come you keep meeting Davey at the dump?"

"He's the dumpmaster there."

"So he found himself a job. He drinking today?"

"I don't know. I think not. I'd have smelled it on his breath."

"Wait'll the end of the week; he'll drink it up. Got a thirst, that boy."

Later, when they were alone, Marge asked: "Is that all Davey said?"

"Just about."

"I mean, did he mention me at all?"

"Just a little."

She was staring at her hands, knotted on the table. "About me and him, I mean."

The risks of friendship and intimacy were terrible, and increasing by leaps and bounds. Any close exchange with her, away from Lou, was deadly. But silence was worse. Out of an inverted sense of respect for her, he had to tell her. He managed to say: "Yes."

"Ohhh." She drew it out, and her face grew pink. She lifted it for a quick glance at him. Embarrassed, beseeching, angry—all at once. "You wouldn't believe him," she said.

"I'd rather believe you."

"Well, once—when I first came here." He realized too late (shoals everywhere) that his remark had virtually compelled that confession. Intimacy is a two-way street. Honesty begets honesty. You have to risk bearing the other's burden. And when two begin sharing their burdens . . . doesn't everything change?

"Lou doesn't know," she whispered.

He could find no answer to that. She wrapped her fingers around themselves again and risked another peek at him. "I hope he never will."

His shock must have shown.

"I don't mean you," she said quickly. "I was thinking of Davey." She reached out and touched his hand. "Not you, Fred. You're— Why do I tell you this?"

Hennerkop could have answered in a flash: Because you're frightened, because you're not sure and want to know the worst, because you have nobody else to talk to, because sharing a guilty secret eases the weight. He said none of that. Instead, he said: "I wouldn't worry about Davey."

"But he told you."

"He was mad at me and Lou. Jealous, I guess. Anyway, he won't again."

"What makes you think that?"

"Because he's scared of me now. I really hurt him, more than I said. I told him not to go blabbing about the three of us, or I'd hurt him a whole lot worse."

"You said that? That doesn't sound like you."

"Well, maybe not, but he got me mad, the way he talked about you."

"What did he say?"

"He said I should make a play for you—since he had."

She bit her lip and blushed again and put her hands in her lap. "Do you think I'm attractive?"

"Very."

"Would you make a play for me?"

"No."

Her eyes brimming, she came around the table and kissed him on the cheek. "That's the only one you'll ever get."

He went to bed that night thinking bitterly about how much of his frosty life he had wasted. He forgot that he had not opened Violet Few-Strang's letter.

He found it in his pocket the next day at the dump. Again the wrong time and place. Davey was in his shed. He went over and asked him if he was okay.

"No way. I'm still aching. Why'd you have to kick so hard?"

"I didn't. That was my medium kick."

"Medium, huh?"

"I'll save my full-strength one for when I hear any more blab about your brother or Marge from your big mouth." He would nail it down, for her.

That night he opened Violet's letter. It was a long one, one airmail sheet folded inside the other.

Dear Boy:

How could I not remember one who did his virginal best to assist me at a time of crisis in my life? And would have persisted had I not prevented him? Dear boy, of course I remember you, with gratitude, and am touched that you remember me. I sometimes wonder what would have happened to us had not Pamela Gyve burst into the library at the moment she did, for I was on the verge of losing my last scruple about betraying horrible Robert. Suppose I had locked the library door and we had moved to our appointed destiny behind the shelves. What then? There fancy eludes me. I have never been able to see beyond that imagined moment. Back in the gatekeeper's bed, you say? Never, with Robert wasting away in the Park House. We could have met only under hedges or in the back of your jeep. And don't forget what a cold spring that was.

I think on the whole that Pamela served us well. We both have a bright memory and can savour that, rather than chewing over less and less satisfying trysts that might have ended in recrimination and loathing. In your innocence you might say you could never loathe

269

me. However, I might very well come to loathe you. Remember, I was once mad for Robert and came to loathe him. What is so special about you? What do I know about you except that you like to run and are full of passion. And with all that passion in you, how is it that I was the first to unlock it? What was the matter with you that you were so bottled up all your life? And you may still be, for all I know. I don't like bottled-up men. They should be as lavish and reckless with themselves as I am. And you may be stupid. I can't abide stupid men. No, lad, it's better we go on dreaming.

You ask what has happened to me. Not much good, I am afraid. Robert continued to consume himself with hatred. He simply ate himself up and died in August. His estate was in even worse repair than I had imagined, virtually bankrupt. I had to sell the Park House to meet the death duties, and kept only the gatehouse and lifetime use of the stables. This country is filling up with postwar money. People swarm like lemmings from London for the country life and the hunting. They know nothing about either, and it is selling them broken-down horses at high prices that keeps me going. The new people at the Park House are mad for hunting. I board three horses for them and train their children. This is a full-time job, as I can afford but one boy. I no longer go to the library. I have become a leathery old woman. Whatever looks I may have had are gone. My sexual fires are banked. You would no longer like me.

Now one favor. Having written you such a reckless letter, I would like one in return. Your last was a miserable effort, a masterpiece of self-concealment. Do you truly live alone in a small town and do nothing? Most American boys with an education and good looks become millionaires and marry heiresses. What's wrong with you? I require that you tell me.

Violet

P.S. Thank you for the poetry book. I think you put to memory one of the few good bits in it.

An extraordinary letter from an extraordinary woman. It deserved an honest answer—if he could bring himself to write one.

30

AFTER SOME LENGTHY SESSIONS WITH THE NEW account book, he had things sufficiently straightened out so that he could keep track of all that was coming in. For recalcitrant accounts he suggested that Lou send out some bills.

"Don't want to do that. Most of em won't pay anyway. Claim they did and I forgot. Any that do, they'll mail a check. That'll make a paper record. Tax collector'll come calling."

"You don't pay taxes?"

"Property I pay. Can't avoid that. They see me setting here in my house. It's on the tax roll."

"Maybe you should start paying some other taxes."

"Can't, Fred. Margin's too thin as it is."

"How big is your margin?"

"Varies. Like I said when you begun fussing with the books, I size up the fellow and charge him according. Now that I'm paying you sixty a week, I have to add you on top of the topsoil or whatever."

"No charge for the truck?"

"Gas and oil."

"Where do you buy it?"

"Anyplace I happen to be. Filler up, I say. I know all them boys."

Lou was looking relaxed, so he decided to risk something. "Maybe you could save some money if you got all your gas and oil at one place. You use a lot of gas."

"That's the truth."

"So why not get it cheaper?"

"Because they don't sell it cheaper, you stupid cluck. It's posted on the pump. Joe Blow don't come by and pay forty-five, and then I come by and say, Hello, Jack, how about filling me up for forty."

"Suppose he filled you up for thirty-five?"

Lou sat forward.

He took the plunge. "Texaco will sell you gas for thirty-five if you guarantee to give them all your business."

"How the hell do you know that?"

"Because I asked them. Why do you think I check all the vehicles every night before supper with a pencil and paper?"

"How should I know, Fred? You do some peculiar things."

"I'm trying to figure out how much gas we use. By my guess, it comes to between two and three hundred gallons a month. If you save ten cents a gallon, that's about three hundred dollars a year in your pocket."

"Fred, I told you I don't like you poking in this way."

"And I asked only Texaco. Try Shell. Maybe they'll go lower."

Lou ended up with Shell at thirty-three cents. "And when I get my grader and take on Benny Waters regular, I'll be saving more."

He hadn't heard about Benny and asked who he was.

"Been working hours for Abbey, but he don't like that. Come to me, I'll pay him regular."

"How much will you pay him?"

"None of your fucking business."

He decided to pass on that and move to the grader. He asked where it was coming from.

"Empire Traction. They got the one I want."

"How are you paying for it?"

"Like I always do. Equipment loan."

"Do you know the interest?"

"Yeah. I got it writ down someplace. Anyway, they'll take care of that. They'll hit me regular every quarter."

He could see his job. For the first time in his life, he could see what had to be done, a whole series of things, all to be solved in orderly steps. First he had to figure out the order of the steps, then how to accomplish them, and finally—and most difficult—persuade Lou to take them.

Now he had managed to get a good handle on the money that was coming in but had not the vaguest idea of what was going out. Nor had Lou, who was making payments on everything he owned, probably at high and varying rates of interest. Lou had never heard of amortization, never billed time for use of his equipment. When one of his trucks wore out, he would have to go into debt to pay for another. If for any reason the company selling the truck took it into its head to examine Lou's credit, it might refuse to sell. That would force him into used trucks, a costly way to go in the end because they broke down so often and had to be replaced in their turn. If he didn't buy one at all, his business would shrink. He would end up where he started, a one-truck hustler scrambling for little jobs.

Somehow or other Fred was going to have to learn more about the outgo side of the business. He was going to have to learn something about bookkeeping. Now he went to bed every night with his head full of those problems but was usually so tired that he fell asleep before he could think any of them through.

He told Charlie Barker that he wanted to learn bookkeeping.

"Better than driving a truck for the rest of your life."

He said heavily: "I don't mind driving a truck."

"No offense," said Charlie quickly, moving his pen set around on his desk. "Don't get your back up. I was wondering why, that's all."

He explained some of the problems with Lou Mendoza's business methods.

"Asking a lot of you to build up a little hauling business with you just driving one of the trucks."

"Maybe make it a bigger business. You said yourself that things are picking up here. More building, more digging, more hauling. Somebody's going to end up with a good business."

Charlie shoved his pens around some more. "Yeah, those Portuguese are working their way up all the time."

"Yeah, and that one saved my life."

"That's right. Maybe you do owe him one. Anyway, about bookkeeping, why not get a book from the library? Come to supper Friday and we'll talk about it. You haven't been over in a long time."

Not what he wanted at all, but he went. Lorraine met him at the door. "Come in. Charlie's at the office. He'll be along any minute."

That was even worse. He hesitated on the stoop. She had seemed tentative and embarrassed; his hesitation made her more so. "I don't mean it that way," she said, flushing. Then, what she had obviously been gearing up for: "I didn't tell Charlie."

By this time he was quite sure she hadn't, but to hear it from her was a great relief. "Forget it," he said. "We all have our moments."

"You?"

"Yes."

"But you're such a kind of a hermit." She lifted her head to give him a woeful hopeful smile, and he quickly said: "A hermit these days. I was talking about when I was younger and stupider and didn't know nice people like you and Charlie." As he spoke, he was also thinking about how Hennerkop would have approved of that remark. A tactful useful lie, Hennerkop would have said; civilized people can't get through life without their share of them. It was interesting that Hennerkop had begun popping up so much recently, interesting also that the need for a lie should come so close on the heels of the need for a truth with Marge just days before.

As if he had pressed a button, Lorraine said: "Those people you live with—what's her name?"

"Marge Kenney."

"Kind of common, isn't she?"

Before he could answer, Charlie came in. Lorraine continued as she served the supper: "I was asking Fred about the people he's living with, that woman."

"Don't know her," said Charlie.

"You know, the kind of blowsy one that tends bar at the Blue Lobster."

That infuriated him, but he said nothing, concentrating on his food, stealing a look at Lorraine. She was eating in dainty little bites, her eyes mostly downcast. What was going on inside her, inside that pink sweater that was just a little too tight for a figure that was just a little too generous? How could she have even . . . ? He turned to Charlie, his face so round, so rosy, so earnest, so open and friendly as he forked down his supper. How could she? He felt a renewed rush of affection and gratitude for all Charlie had done for him, and a sense of real alarm that she might still step between them.

So what was it with Lorraine that she should have flashed such a blatant message without any signal from him? He attacked his sword-fish—succulently prepared by Lorraine; no wonder she was plump— reminded of his own past behavior. He had his demons, didn't he? Probably they had been inexplicable to the world. She undoubtedly had hers, equally inexplicable. It came to him that he had never done much speculating about the hidden springs in other people. He had never had the time. He had always been too busy worrying about how to behave himself and about what other people were thinking about him. He had looked only at surfaces, at what made up people seem up, studying how to be up himself. He plunged into his dessert—ice cream and strawberries—shaken by a sudden awareness that he didn't really know much about anybody.

But that sudden awareness was a step. It took feeling better about himself to learn that. And by God, he did feel better. Another revelation: he truly did. Suddenly he longed for Hennerkop, to tell him that. Here he was, eating strawberries with a wonderful man who, by his own generous nature, had surely helped him to this insight, and with that man's not so wonderful wife.

If he was to judge himself more gently, should he not take a gentler look at that not so wonderful wife also? He risked a more compassionate look, a more penetrating one, but what he came up with was lust, plain ordinary lust. How else explain her? And the idea that he was its target sent a quiver of heat through him. Her breasts, only a moment ago rather heavy and shapeless under her pink sweater, became more interesting. Their contours improved. He could not stop looking at them—

Charlie spoke. "You sure you want to tie yourself in so tight with that fellow?"

"Why not?" he asked.

"Helping build a business you don't have a piece of? That doesn't make sense. Anyway, he's not exactly your type. Why don't you get a place of your own?"

"I like it where I am," he said.

"They're not your type," said Lorraine. "She's common. She chases men." As she said that, it became clear that it had popped out faster than she had intended. She flushed so deeply that he wondered if Charlie might have noticed. Then, like a ruffled hen that keeps clucking: "She does. She's a barmaid, you know."

"What's wrong with being a barmaid?" he asked.

"At the Blue Lobster. That's a common place."

"Ever go to the Blue Lobster?" asked Charlie.

"I don't go to bars."

"That's where she works," said Lorraine. "Flaunts herself."

"Flaunts?" He was outraged by that and determined to skewer it.

That flustered her even more. "She does. I hear she chases around a lot."

"Then you hear wrong. She goes with one man."

"That Portuguese fellow."

"That's not the place for you," said Charlie. "You ought to move out of there. I could find you a house, something you could afford."

"I can't afford any kind of a house right now. You know that. Think of what I owe on the island."

Charlie helped himself to more strawberries. "That's where you're wrong. You could afford it. That island is going up in value every day. Your purchase agreement—value right there. You don't know what's beginning to happen here. The back streets in town—dead for years—they're beginning to move. There's like a stir in them. People are beginning to buy. Before you know it, a house that you could get today for fifteen, maybe twenty thousand will be going for fifty, maybe more. There's a house on Cedar—"

"Only two blocks from here," said Lorraine.

"A steal."

"Why don't *you* buy it?" he said.

"I would, except I'm so stretched. I already own two houses on Cedar. I've been picking up everything I can. If I figure right, in ten years I'll be . . . well, I'll be okay. Better than okay." He looked around the room, at the figured wallpaper, the mahogany sideboard, the ship model on its ledge. "Or I'll be busted."

"No," said Lorraine.

"Yes. If the boom I think's going to happen doesn't, I'm out. The bank owns me. Actually I'm not so different from that Portuguese fellow."

"Except that he has Fred to help him and you don't," said Lorraine.

"And I stand maybe to clean up and he doesn't."

"You buy that house," said Lorraine.

"I'll think about it," Fred said. "Right now I ought to be getting home."

"How did you get here?" asked Charlie.

"I walked."

"All the way from Gott Street? It's raining. Coming down pretty hard. I'd better drive you home."

"Sit around a bit," said Lorraine. "Maybe it'll let up."

Charlie went to the door and looked out. The rain was coming down in sheets. "This is going to last all night."

"Sleep over," said Lorraine.

"I really ought to get back. I have a garbage run first thing in the morning."

"Not your style to be hauling garbage," said Lorraine.

Charlie picked a slicker from a hook by the kitchen door, saying as he went out: "I'll bring the car around front."

As soon as Charlie was gone, he got up and moved to the front hall, but Lorraine was there ahead of him, getting between him and the door. "I turned you on," she said in a kind of gasp.

"No," he lied.

"I did. I saw how you looked at me at supper." She stepped up to him. He resisted an enormous impulse to bury his face in her sweater. Sleeping lust erupted. She pressed herself against him and felt it instantly. "See—I knew. Why can't we . . . ?"

Standing in the dark hallway, he was beginning to find fewer and fewer reasons why they couldn't. But the lights from Charlie's car swung through the narrow windows flanking the front door, their ruby panes throwing a quick adulterous flicker over both of them. He turned up his collar and ran out into the rain.

When he got home, Lou was sitting in the kitchen with a sheet around him. Marge was cutting his hair. "You could do with one," she said. "How about I do you too?"

Still hot from Lorraine, he watched her trim around Lou's ears. There was something rawly sensual about that attention, so intimate and deliberate, as if she were stretching out a physical pleasure with those repeated little snips. Get worked up enough yourself, and you can see sexuality wherever you look.

When she had finished with Lou, she shook the sheet out the back door. "Next."

"He's one jump past shaggy," said Lou. "Give him a good one. And do something about that beard; it's like a cranberry bush."

"I'll take care of my beard," he said, as Marge wrapped the sheet around him. He was secretly proud of how it had sprung out in all directions, curly and fiery. He had the feeling that it made his face more formidable than it had been, that it emphasized his new role as roughneck.

Lou said: "Think again about them whiskers. They won't popularize you with the women."

He said nothing.

"Maybe you don't like women?"

"What makes you think that?"

"You ain't been dating lately that I can see. You ain't been sparking Marge—I guess—though she swings her butt around here pretty good. Marge, you think Fred's attractive?"

"Yes."

"Oh oh."

"And getting more so. He doesn't smoke your smelly cigars, and he keeps a clean tongue in his head."

"So long as he keeps it there—huh, Fred?" With a broad grin, he heaved himself out of his chair and went to the bathroom.

"You see how he is," said Marge. "He makes jokes, but he's a jealous man."

"Maybe I should get out of here," he said.

"Maybe." She was cutting his hair as she spoke, carefully and affectionately. He felt engulfed by her.

"You do like girls," she said.

How could she ask that? "Oh, yes. The trouble is that I only know two and they aren't available, you and Lorraine Barker."

She seized on Lorraine. "That stuck-up. She knows me. I mean, she knows who I am. But will she speak to me or even smile in the supermarket? Anyhow, she's married to another stuck-up."

"Charlie's not stuck-up."

"Don't kid yourself. He may be a friend of yours. That's because he thinks you're like him. But people like Lou and me—he thinks we're trash. The old families around town, we call them the Oldies. Cobbs, Fullers, Waites, Hicksons. Take a walk in the graveyard: you'll find them packed in there. They started this town, and they still think they own it." She snipped more vigorously.

"Look out for my ears."

"I'm looking out. You have nice ears. Some girl would like your ears. You should find a friend."

He could no longer contain it. "One like you."

"What's that?" said Lou, coming out of the bathroom.

"I was only propositioning Fred, but he turned me down for the fourth time."

The heat, the loaded conversation. She defused it with her jokes. Apparently she had decided that that was the safest way to deal with an explosive situation. He wanted her, and she realized it. He was beginning to want her desperately. Feeling that way, how could he stay in this house with her?

She worked her way in in other ways as he learned more about her. The following evening, as he was going over the day's accounts with Lou, she said, "I could do that."

"Nah," said Lou.

"I could. It's just keeping track, isn't it? I did that for my dad."

He learned that she came from Fall River, where her father had run a small family bar. As she grew up, she began helping out there, more and more as her father's feet and back began bothering him. She learned to keep inventory and pay his bills. She also got a bartender's license and tended bar there. "We knew all the customers," she said. "That was a nice place."

"Why did you leave?"

"The owner sold the building, and my dad retired. I studied nursing for a year, but I didn't like it, so I got a job doing piecework in a factory."

"Where she met Doris," said Lou. "They come here together, Marge to tend bar, Doris to tend to the men."

"Don't put it that way," said Marge.

"How else you going to put it?" He swung around in his chair. "You didn't meet Doris yet, did you, Fred? Keep your hand on your wallet when you do."

"Doris has to live," said Marge.

"There's ways and ways. Two girls from Fall River, cutting pieces of cloth. Bored to death. One answers an ad for a bartender. The other tags along."

"I just gave my initial. Didn't want them to know I was a girl. I just said M. Kenney and gave my experience. Three years at the Shamrock in Fall River."

"And got the job," said Lou. "Took one look at her and wanted to hire her, but decided to test her out first. Threw all kinds of fancy drinks at her. She handled them perfect. Been there ever since. But Doris . . . "

Doris, it seemed, liked to party. She tried waitressing but didn't always make it on time and lost a couple of jobs. She started letting men stay over at the trailer she and Marge were sharing. "I didn't like that. I mean, it was different men, not one steady boyfriend. I asked her to move out. She asked me to move out. So I decided to go. No hard feelings. I just left and came here. In a way, I have you to thank for that, Fred."

"Ever want to meet Doris," said Lou, "she works out of the Blue Lobster too, but she ain't on the payroll."

That night in bed, among his many other thoughts about Marge, he wondered if she actually could be worked into Lou's business as a bookkeeper, and if so, if he could handle that.

31

WHERE TO LIVE? WHERE TO LIVE? HE HAD BEEN putting off going back to the island. But the arrival of warm weather and a growing sense that he simply could not continue to stay at Lou's forced the island on him. He didn't want to go back. It was no longer the refuge he had dreamed about; it seemed a dangerous place now. On jobs that had taken him down to the lighthouse point, he had been able to look out to where the island lay, a dark fuzzy streak floating on the sea. From that distance discrete objects like bushes were indistinguishable. He could just make out his house, a small gray sliver, but only because he knew where it was. Others, looking out from that low headland, would suppose it uninhabited.

It turned his stomach to think of the mess it must be in. To remember the way he had dirtied it and himself was sickening. He didn't want to look at any of that. It called up a hallucinatory period that now, after months of different and healthier living, seemed to be an almost impossible chapter in his life. Those last days—or weeks— came and went in his mind like fevered flashes interrupted by periods of blankness.

Charlie galvanized him. "Time you got your boat in the water. It doesn't do any good sitting in the sun; the seams open up. Anyway, it needs a coat of paint." So that Saturday he went to work, sanding, scraping, and painting.

"The inside's the bitch," said Lou, watching. "All them ribs and corners. What you don't realize is the inside gets the wear and tear. That's where you're jumping in and out all the time, scratching it up with sand." Lou took down the outboard, which he had drained, oiled, and hung in his shed over the winter. "You planning to move back there?"

"I'm not sure."

"How you going to make your garbage run from out there? And all them other jobs we got stacked up?"

He shrugged.

"You're working for me regular, Fred. Ain't as if you could pick up and go whenever you feel like it."

"I guess."

"I depend on you."

That was the first time anybody had ever said that to him. The feelings that Lou and Marge—and Charlie—kept releasing in him welled up again. He turned away, reluctant to let Lou see that.

"You can stay on here."

"But you get mad at me whenever I try and do things with the business."

"That's just me. Don't put no store by it."

If Lou meant that, this would be a rare opportunity to bring up the subject of outgo, so he said: "There's something I want to talk about."

"Marge?"

That jolt came from nowhere.

"You got the hots for her, right?"

He was able to say only: "What makes you think that?"

"She told me."

"But how does she . . . ? I never . . . "

"Fred." A pitying smile. "Women don't have to be told them things. I know you never. She told me that too. So don't worry about it. Any fellow with any sense would get that way around her—when they're around her as much as you are. But she's my woman and she knows it, and she won't take from you. Never. Why don't you find your own woman? The town's crawling with them."

He began to recover his balance. "Maybe I *should* move out," knowing as he said it that he didn't want to. He felt more at home here than in any other place or at any other time in his life. He could look at Marge, fantasize about her, try to keep a safe distance, be fed by her. Better than nothing.

"No need for that. I know what's in your mind. Rubbing elbows with her. But that's your problem. Not hers. Not mine. What you should do is get a woman for yourself. You could even move her in here. We wouldn't mind—that is, if she fitted in easy the way you do."

They were standing by his dory, its paint now dry. Lou ran a hand along its gunwale. "You done a good job here, better'n I thought you could. You're a good trucker. You keep good books. Whatever you put your hand to you do good. So why don't you put your hand to a good woman? And I don't mean my woman."

Charlie kept the pressure on. "You can't let that place sit there all summer. People will go out there, break in."

"I'm not ready to go by myself. I had a bad time there, you know."

"Is your boat launched?"

"Yes."

"Then I'll go with you. Sunday, if this weather holds."

Which is how he returned to Sheep Island. The trouble was that Lorraine went too.

"I brought lunch," she said, handing down a basket into the dory, then lowering herself, losing her balance, clutching at him. He could not clutch back; Charlie was standing watching, not five feet away. She settled herself in the bow seat. She appeared to have lost some weight. She looked prettier than he had remembered. She said: "I want to see what it's like living out there all by yourself. I don't think it's healthy." He thought with a shudder of his stained mattress and other signs of pollution. Lou and Marge had seen it all and knew the worst. But these two—what would they think? The bright side was that Lorraine might be so disgusted that she would leave him alone.

He grounded the dory in the cove. His small stone breakwater was still intact. All three stepped ashore and began walking up to the house, up the winding path between the bushes now leafing out, fragrant in the warm sun, gulls wheeling in the blue, up to the doorstep of the gray house in which he had lived for half a year and in which he had almost perished. He unlocked the padlock that Lou had put on the door, took a deep breath, and opened it. Lorraine and Charlie followed him in. The living room was stuffy but neat. So was the kitchen. He hesitated to enter the bedroom but forced himself to do so. It, too, looked reasonably clean. His horrible mattress was not there.

"Is this where you sleep?" asked Lorraine.

"Yes."

"What do you sleep on?"

He didn't answer. He opened the window to let in some air, the window over which he had tacked a yellow slicker sometime in the distant past. It, too, was gone, reminding him that Lou and Marge had collected his things. Obviously they had cleaned up also.

"You really like it out here?" asked Lorraine. "Nobody to talk to? Nobody to do anything with?"

They ate lunch outside in the sun. Lorraine had prepared a lobster salad, iced tea, and a bowl of fruit. Sitting there, eating it, looking down over the bushes, across the glint of the water, all so quiet and remote, bathed by that matchless late-spring air, that soft spring sun, he felt the old feeling come back. Here was the peace that he had recognized so long ago and come looking for. No Lorraine could bother him here. No Marge would haunt him. He wouldn't want—wouldn't need—anybody.

"You'll have to get yourself a new generator," said Charlie. "This one's shot."

"This place needs a good dusting," said Lorraine. "I could do that. Do you always sleep on the floor? Isn't that kind of hard?"

"Before you move back here," said Charlie, "let me show you that house on Cedar that I was talking about."

"We burned it," said Lou. "Nothing else you could do with it. Want another, you'll have to buy it. Ain't about to give you the one you're sleeping on now. You figure to keep on sleeping on it for a while?"

"For a while," he said, and tried once again to fix Lou's attention on the outgo side of his business. He persuaded him to get out all the equipment loans he had, and with some difficulty worked out what had been paid on each vehicle and how much was still owed. Ditto for the house, ditto for the boat. As he suspected, the terms varied widely. Lou was paying far too much in interest. He suggested that all the debts be consolidated into one loan.

"Could I do that?"

"You could try."

"Where?"

"Right here at the Lincoln Harbor Bank."

"They won't talk to me there. I tried once when I was short. They run me out."

So he tried for Lou. He had all the figures on a sheet of paper, but when he took them to the bank they did not impress Hugo Westerveld. "I don't think we could consolidate a loan on some used trucks."

"It's not only used trucks. It's also a backhoe. Lou's a fanatic on maintenance. All those things are worth a lot more than what he owes on them. He knows his business. He's making a living right now from it, in spite of those rates he's stuck with."

"We're not in the business of repossessing trucks. We make loans on good collateral."

"But this is good collateral. Abbey would buy any of it like a shot. You could mark it up and actually make a profit."

"Not our kind of deal."

This was discouraging. Hugo Westerveld, a polite man in a gray suit, had made up his mind and was now patiently waiting for him to leave. Something else would have to be tried. It was extraordinary how the pressures of one problem could come forward to force resolution of another. Almost without thinking, he said: "If we can't talk trucks, let's talk about something else. I'm considering buying a house on Cedar Street." My God, did he mean that? Having said it, he went on. "Would you be interested in giving me a mortgage on that?"

"What house would that be?"

He told him.

Charlie had finally persuaded him to look at it. It was a small shingled Cape Cod house on a narrow lot full of weeds, with the remains of a flower garden out front behind a picket fence needing a coat of paint and with some slats missing.

"This doesn't look like much," he said.

"It sure doesn't. I agree, it looks terrible. That's why nobody's bought it. It's been empty for two years and looking worse every day. But it's a sound house. Come in and see for yourself."

Inside, it was plainness personified. The rooms were rather small, a living room on one side of the front door, a dining room on the other. There was a kitchen in an ell behind the dining room. A flight of steep stairs ran up from a narrow hall to a second story that contained two bedrooms and a bath.

"You need cheap, Fred. This is the cheapest I know—that is, the cheapest *decent* house I know in a decent neighborhood. That's what's important: location. This house is only one block back from Harbor Road. Just give it time. This is a good street already beginning to realize itself. Look—" He pointed to several houses farther along. "Neat, right?"

He had to admit that they were.

"Fix up this fence. Grow some grass. Paint all the trim white. Fix those shutters. Paint the chimney black with a white band around the top. Put a carriage lamp by the front door. Scrape the paint off the floors—there's good pine underneath, wide boards. You'll have yourself a house."

"How much is it?"

"They're asking twenty-two. I'd offer eighteen and settle for something in between."

Hugo Westerveld said: "I know that house. What would your collateral be?"

"The house itself."

"Pretty run down. We might give you half. What about the rest?"

"Sheep Island."

Hugo Westerveld perked up. "That's right, you own that."

"Not exactly." He explained that he owned the house and had a purchase agreement for the island itself. When he was asked the amount of the agreement and said that it was thirty thousand less a small equity that he had already paid in, Hugo Westerveld was clearly astonished at that figure. He took a pair of glasses out of his desk drawer and polished them carefully. Then he said: "That's an unusually low figure."

"Worth more?"

"I would say yes, but you should consult your real estate dealer."

"Charlie Barker. I guess you know him."

"We went to high school together. Played on the same football team. I've known Charlie all my life."

He cleared his throat and made his pitch. "I do business with Charlie, and I plan to do more. But I also do business with Lou Mendoza. I would like to do it all in one place. If you can't handle Lou, I'll have to look somewhere else, maybe the Newfield Bank. I understand they plan to open a branch here."

"Believe they do."

"Looking hard for business, to get established."

"Could be."

"If I went with them, I'd have to take out my savings account with you. I mean, no sense in splitting everything up."

Hugo Westerveld didn't say anything. He put his glasses back in his desk drawer.

"How do you rate Sheep Island as a piece of collateral?"

"Better than used trucks."

"They go together."

"Tell you what," said Hugo Westerveld. "I'll send a mechanic over and have him look at that equipment. Maybe we can work something out. Would you consider cosigning his note?"

Why not, he thought. He owed Lou that.

He left the bank and walked slowly home to Gott Street, wondering if he hadn't bitten off too much. As he walked, he noticed again the gradual change in the character of the houses: new miniranches, not well built, not well kept up. This was definitely not the best part of town and probably never would be. Even the stately maples and the few remaining elms that dominated Harbor Road and Cedar Street were missing here. Some people had planted small pyramidal yews by their front doors, and an occasional dogwood, now in full bloom. But the overall effect was not encouraging. Charlie was right: location was everything.

"You owe the bank eight hundred and seventy-six dollars," he said.

"Huh?"

"And next month you will owe another eight hundred and seventy-six dollars. And the next month—"

"What the hell are you talking about?"

"Your new equipment loan. It's all consolidated in one package. Forget all those other payments you've been making. I've just saved you nine thousand dollars."

Marge jumped up and gave him a large hug. He fought down the impulse to bury himself in her.

"I don't get you, Fred."

"Your new bank is the Lincoln Harbor Bank and Trust. Your new banker is Hugo Westerveld. Sign with him, and all your equipment belongs to him as soon as you stop making those payments. Your house too."

"Not my house, Fred."

"Your house. Hugo loves houses more than he loves used trucks. No house, no deal."

"I don't care for that son-of-a-bitch. Anyway, my bank's the First County Savings."

"Not anymore it isn't."

"I won't sign with that son-of-a-bitch."

"Your choice."

"I hate the fucker."

"He's saving you nine thousand dollars. And if you're too stupid to take advantage of that, you can get yourself another garbage collector."

Lou's face purpled. He crumpled the paper and threw it on the floor. "Fred—"

He picked up the paper and handed it back. No point in mentioning the cosigning of the note. Later, maybe, if he had to.

Lou took the paper. "Fred, you've got one hard ass, do you know that?"

Throughout this, Marge had not said a word. What a woman she was!

32

THE LINCOLN HARBOR COMMUNITY LIBRARY TURNED out to be a squarish gray-shingle building on New Street, one block farther from the harbor than Cedar. Muscular privet hedges grew back there, their scent overpowering. The one in front of the library needed trimming, and the building itself looked a little down-at-heel. It proclaimed its identity with a wooden quarter board, gold initials carved into a black background, over the front door. The inevitable smell of varnish and book paper that all libraries seemed to have hit him as he went in, despite a draft of summer air coming through the slanted open panes of a large window at one end of the room. There was a reading table under this window, and at the opposite end a desk with a librarian sitting at it. When she looked up, he realized that she was Emily, the sullen girl who had come with Lou and Marge to the picnic on the island the previous summer.

"Hello," he said.

She didn't respond. Her sullen look set up a picket fence around her. She was wearing a sloppy gray T-shirt and a pair of gray corduroy pants whose ends he could see under the desk. Her sneakers were stained. Her hair was pulled back tight and fastened with rubber bands, giving her face a defiant hawklike look, as her scowl gathered together a long thin nose and an even thinner compressed mouth.

Looking at that uncompromising expression, he decided not to mention the picnic and said instead: "I'm looking for something on bookkeeping and accounting."

Instead of answering, she bent over to tie her sneaker.

"Where could I find them?"

She looked up with a baleful glance. "Card file."

"Where's that?"

Baleful changed to withering. She stabbed a finger in the direction of the file. He went over and in a few minutes had two prospects. He got out a pencil stub, wrote their titles and identifying numbers on his work pad, and returned to the desk to ask where they might be found.

"The stacks."

"I mean, where in the stacks?"

Through clenched teeth she said: "The cards are numbered. The stacks are numbered." Then bent away from him to work on her other sneaker. He entered the stacks, found the books, and returned to the desk.

"I'd like to take out these two."

"Are you a member?"

"Member?" She had to know he wasn't.

"This is a private library. Members only."

Suppressing a rising irritation, he said: "How do you become a member?"

"Summer or yearly?"

"Summer," thinking that after he had mastered bookkeeping he wouldn't be coming back.

"Ten dollars."

He fished out a ten. She fumbled in her desk and produced a pink card. "What's your name?"

"Fay. Frederick Fay."

She wrote it down and handed him the card. "Summer doesn't start until the fifteenth."

This was the tenth. "I can't take out any books until then?"

"The fifteenth."

"All right, make it a yearly membership."

"Twenty dollars."

He produced another ten. With great disdain, she tore up the pink card and wrote his name on a blue one.

"I'll take these two," he said.

"Only one book at a time."

"Okay, this one."

She looked at it. "You can't take that one; it's on the high school reserve list."

"Okay, the other one."

"That's on reserve too."

"What do I have to do, read them here?"

"Up to you."

He took the books to the reading table and sat down in front of the big window, but he was up in a minute and back at the desk. He pointed to the stamped card in the back of the volume on bookkeeping. "The last time this was out of here was six years ago," he said.

"Rules."

"But surely—"

"I don't make them."

Fuming, he returned to the reading table. He sat with his back to her and facing the window, realizing almost immediately that one of the slanted open panes framed a clear reflection of Emily across the room. If he could see her so well, could she see him? Apparently not. As he watched, she bent down for something in the bottom drawer of her desk, put it to her mouth, and took a swig. One short nip, and back went the bottle into the drawer.

Unable to concentrate on bookkeeping, he watched her. He became a voyeur, a man looking through a keyhole at a woman unaware that she was being observed. She had a habit of running a hand back across her left ear to stroke the hair that was severely contained behind it. She did this over and over again, occasionally pulling the tail ends of her gathered hair forward and across her shoulder to examine them with her fingers. He tried to read but couldn't concentrate. Her reflected movements kept catching his eye. After ten or fifteen minutes she reached into her desk drawer and took another nip.

A drinker, as well as being assertively unattractive and unfriendly. With an irritation that went beyond his inability to remove the books, he gave up and went back to the desk. "Where do I put these?"

"Over there." She indicated a table with a tumbled pile of what appeared to be returned but unshelved books. This library was as disheveled and as unapproachable as its librarian.

"Where you been since you finished at the gravel pit?" said Lou as Marge dished out heaping plates of spaghetti and meatballs.

"I was at the library, trying to learn something about bookkeeping. I ran into your friend Emily there."

"I can think of better places to look for dates than the library. Anyway, *Emily* . . . ? You already struck out on her."

"You've got that backwards," said Marge. "She struck out on him. It wasn't his fault."

"Why is she so disagreeable?" he asked. "She seemed mad at me for just going in there."

"She's cranky," said Lou. "Remember what we were saying about the old families here, the Oldies? Well, she's an Oldie, a stiff-assed cranky Oldie. Cobbs. Used to own this town. Act like they still do."

He remembered the nameplate on the library desk: Emily Cobb Watson.

"That's the bug that's up Emily's butt. She's a busted-down Oldie. Lives with her mother in that run-down big house out on Harbor Road."

"I don't think that's the reason at all," said Marge. "I think it was Davey."

"No way. He never really went for her," pushing his plate forward for more spaghetti. "I always had the feeling she was slumming, doing him the big favor by going out with him."

"Backwards again," said Marge. "She was crazy about him. He was the one with the Oldie problem. He wanted to go with an Oldie girl. When he did, he found she wasn't any different from any other girl. Maybe not as good, from his point of view, because she would have taken him seriously. He didn't want that. He dropped her."

"She's a drinker," he said.

"Headed that way," said Lou. "Could be Davey taught her. They deserve each other."

The following morning he was walking down Elm, thinking that if he had been willing to wait a few days he could have saved ten dollars on his library membership. It was a late-spring day, soft and balmy, threatening to turn hot later. Summer visitors had already begun to arrive and were strolling and shopping. The sidewalks had been washed clean by a rain the night before, and the shops on both sides of the street had a squeaky-clean Norman Rockwell look, reminding him of the day, a year ago, when he had taken possession of the island and how full of hope he had been. What had been the source of that surge? Certainly the freshness and beauty of this little town had something to do with it. But the real reason, he felt sure, had been the hope that he would be entering a new life, with all the shamefulness of the past left behind like a shed snakeskin, and that he could emerge as a fresh clean person able to live a life that he could direct himself, beholden to nobody. If all his contact with other people had stimulated the wrong reactions in him, what better way to go than by cutting himself off from everybody?

That had not worked, of course. He had discovered that a deliberate self-isolation was as corrosive as an involuntary one. This morning, as he strolled down Elm, he realized that he was no longer being pulled toward self-isolation. On the contrary, he felt at home here in town now, more and more strongly drawn to the people who had held out their hands as friends and to whom he had responded—with a great inner wrench at first, but still had responded. That was the thing he was beginning to learn. *Be* a friend; don't always wait for others. To think that he did have friends here crowded his chest with a sensation that he supposed any man or woman who had ever been truly lonely would surely recognize.

He was so taken up with those thoughts that Charlie Barker, running out of his office, had to yell at him to get his attention.

"Why doesn't your pal have a telephone? I've been trying to get hold of you for two days."

"He doesn't need one," he said. Not yet anyway. But if Lou was to grow, he would need one, and a bookkeeper and a telephone answerer to handle that growing business. Could Marge do that? Would she?

"The house on Cedar," said Charlie. "There's a bid on it. Fred, you must buy that house. You'll never get a bargain like that again."

"I already have a house."

"As an investment. Anyway, you may want to move back here sometime. Look, we can't be hollering at each other in the street. Come in and let me persuade you. The lot itself—" He flung out an arm. "It's narrow but it's deep. Goes way back. Someday some rich guy is going to want to add on there, put in a studio or a guesthouse. Fred, I have to tell you again . . . "

He was persuaded. The upshot was a phone call to the owner's agent and an offer of nineteen thousand dollars, which was accepted, followed by a trip to the bank, where Charlie and Hugo Westerveld exchanged a few old-buddy whacks on the back. He found himself quickly becoming an old buddy too, a new old buddy being gentled into a circle accustomed to doing business with old buddies. In a few minutes he became the possessor of a mortgage.

"Let's eat on that," said Charlie. "My treat." But Hugo had a loan committee meeting, so Charlie said: "Make it supper, then. I'll tell Lorraine to get a steak."

Lorraine again?

In deference to his new old-buddy status, he wore a blue shirt, freshly ironed by Marge, and a tweed jacket that she and Lou had salvaged from the wreckage of his wardrobe on the island. He shook hands with Hugo, who had already arrived, and then with Lorraine. Her expression was unreadable, her hand noncommittal as it brushed his. Or was there a lingering message as she slowly withdrew it? At the table, he sat at one end, opposite Charlie. Lorraine was at his left, across from Hugo, which gave him a chance to study her without drawing her attention. Or did it? Again, hard to tell. He felt that although she was apparently focusing her attention on Hugo, she was acutely aware of him.

In profile she was a fine-looking woman, better that way than straight on, which revealed a face a little too wide for her narrow-set eyes. Her sweater, this time a heathery blue-green, fitted her better than that distracting pink one had. Either she had taken off a few pounds or she was wearing a different bra. Whichever, and unable to forget what had transpired between them on his last visit, that short pressure of her body against his in the dark front hall, he became physically aroused again, right there at the dinner table, and ashamed of himself for it. Charlie, as usual, seemed oblivious of undercurrents and devoted much of supper to discussing property values and reminiscing with Hugo about their days as youngsters, when they shared ownership of a small catboat and spent their summers crabbing and clamming.

"How's Sylvia?" asked Lorraine, breaking in. Hugo, looking uncomfortable, said she was okay. That remark ended the catboat reminiscences. Supper being over, Hugo abruptly got up and left. Fred made to follow.

"What are you always jumping up for?" said Lorraine. "Sit and have a cup of coffee."

"Why did you ask about Sylvia?" said Charlie. "That was tactless."

"What's tactless about asking somebody how his wife is?"

"Because you know how she is, and he knows you know." Charlie turned to him. "How she is is she's gone. She's left him and is in Worcester with her mother. At least that's what the gossip is. Every long nose in town is trying to find out if that's true and why she left and maybe who she left for."

"Sylvia's a cold fish," said Lorraine. "I never cared for Sylvia."

"No need to take it out on Hugo. You see how quickly he left. I repeat, that was tactless. One reason I asked him over tonight was I figured he was lonely."

"Not to talk business?" said Lorraine acidly. "All you talk about is business. You don't talk about business when you go home, do you, Fred?"

"I'll bet he does. I'll bet he talks trucking with those truckers he lives with."

"Oh, them."

"Anyway, Hugo's a banker. It's natural to talk business with him. You shouldn't knock Hugo."

"Who's knocking Hugo?"

"Don't forget what Hugo does for this town, what he's done with the boy scouts."

"I'm careful not to ask what he does with the boy scouts," said Lorraine. "That Sylvia always was a cold fish."

"Zoning board, don't forget that. Rotary. Library trustee."

He pricked up his ears at that. He described his visit to the library and the impossibility of taking out a book that had gone untouched for more than six years.

"It's a mess there," admitted Charlie. "The board doesn't pay enough attention to it. Bunch of old fogies."

"Hugo's an old fogy?"

"Don't keep picking on Hugo. Pick on the staff."

"Staff? One woman. And you know who she is—your nutty cousin Emily. Another of your precious Cobbs. Doesn't even bother to collect fines. No new books. Nobody goes there."

"Why do they have a library at all?" Fred asked.

"They ought to close it," said Lorraine. "Or at least get rid of Emily. She can't run a library. She can't run anything. She can't even run herself."

"She seemed kind of cranky when I was in there," he said.

"*Cranky!* She's hopeless. Admit it, Charlie. She's your cousin."

"Third cousin—I think. Hard to keep track of us Cobbs. There's such a flock of us descended from the founder, James."

"Here it comes," said Lorraine, rolling her eyes. "King James Cobb the First. Hang around here long enough and you'll hear enough about Cobbs to drive you back to New York."

"James Cobb," said Charlie, undeflected, "was the biggest man this town ever had."

"See what I mean?"

"He owned most of this part of town. He gave the library. That's why we have it, why Emily works there—after she had to leave college."

"Yes, yes," said Lorraine. "Cobb, Cobb, Cobb."

"What happened to Emily at college?" he asked.

"She fell in love with her English teacher," said Lorraine. "I mean, she fell all the way. She got pregnant."

"The trouble with Emily," said Charlie, "is that she's a very passionate person."

"Putting it mildly."

"I mean passionate in everything. When she was young it was horses. Then it was writing and poetry. Whatever it was, she went all out. She wrote poems for the paper here. She got a scholarship to

Vassar. She wrote more poetry and fell in love with her professor."

"Fell into bed with him."

The professor, it seemed, was notorious for romantic involvements with his students. Emily, not knowing that, took him seriously. She could have quietly gone away and got rid of the baby. But she wanted the professor to get a divorce and marry her. That was not his plan, and he refused to acknowledge paternity. He let it be known that Emily was putting out for a lot of others.

"How do you know she wasn't?" said Lorraine.

"I know Emily. She goes for one thing at a time—strong. When her professor ran out on her, she got mad and went public."

"A dumb thing to do."

"She went to the dean and tried to press charges."

"Real dumb," said Lorraine. "She got what she deserved. They refused to hear her case, and she left college."

"What happened to the baby?" he asked.

"She didn't bring it home, so I guess she got it adopted," said Lorraine. "Now she sits around and mopes in the library. I hear it's a terrible mess."

"Actually it's a sad case," said Charlie. "Emily was a bright kid. She got that scholarship. She couldn't have afforded college otherwise. Cobb may be a big name around here, but it's not big money anymore."

"Not even a big name—except to Cobbs."

He was happy to let all that flow over him, because it passed the time and made his approaching departure seem less abrupt, and because Lorraine's irritation with Cobbs took her attention away from him. As for the Cobbs themselves, he learned that the patriarch, James, had had a flock of daughters, whose descendants (Charlie among them) now thronged Lincoln Harbor under a variety of names. James had had only one son, a second James, who carried on the princely family tradition by founding the Lincoln Harbor Bank. That James had had only one child, Emily's mother, who became the town heiress when her father died and she inherited a controlling interest in the bank. An ambitious young teller, Elbert Watson, had the gumption to court and marry her, and became the bank's president. However, he turned out to be a very poor president, and the bank had a spectacular crash. He left town in disgrace and was not seen again. Others took over, and Emily's mother wound up with scarcely more than the family mansion, in which she and Emily now lived.

"I could have run that bank better than El Watson," said Charlie.

"Anybody could have. I worked there myself, in the loan office. I could see it going down, and I jumped out into real estate. I still see properties that the bank made bum loans on. He slowed this whole town down."

"Just from bad loans?"

"Lost money for a lot of people when the bank was taken over. El's trouble was he couldn't say no to a friend. He'd make real nutty loans, like the one you promoted for your pal on those trucks."

"That's not a nutty loan."

"Nutty to a careful guy like Hugo."

"But he made it."

"Because of you. He wants to keep you as a customer, get a mortgage on a good piece of real estate. Hugo thinks the way I do. He thinks there's going to be a resort boom here. What he really wants is your purchase agreement on Sheep Island if you should ever go under. He'd be happy to see you stretched thin and grab that from you. You may not realize it, Fred, but you got in just under the wire on that one. The owner literally gave it away."

Lorraine snapped: "Nobody gives anything away. I think it was a stupid idea to get yourself stuck way out there. And anybody else who did it would be stupid too." She glared at him. "What use is it to you? You don't even live there yourself now."

He ignored that and asked Charlie: "If it's so valuable, how come you tried to keep me from buying it?"

"Not because of value, Fred, not because of value. You wanted to live there. When you first came here, you had a funny look in your eye. It didn't seem to me that you were fit to live out there all by yourself. Also you were planning to hock everything you had to get the island. I have to remind you that nothing's certain in real estate. I happen to think we're in for a boom here. I can feel it coming. I've stuck my own neck way out, but who can be sure? I just thought it was too big a risk for you. That's why we worked out the purchase agreement. Thank God it's turning out okay. Better than okay. There was someone in here last week asking about it. I said to get in touch with you. Did he?"

"Why can't we talk about something besides business?" said Lorraine.

"Like what?"

"Like practically anything. Business, business, business. It's enough to drive me wild. Why don't you talk about politics, about books or people?" She was clearing away the supper things with bursts of crackling nervous energy that threatened the plates. Unable to hold still, she began polishing the already gleaming sideboard.

"Okay, honey—what people?"

"Any people." Her voice rose. "Any people at all." She turned to him. "I hear the woman you live with is sleeping with her boyfriend and her boyfriend's brother at the same time. Is that true?"

"No," he said. "Where did you get that idea?"

She favored him with a hard glance. "Sleeping with anybody else?"

"She's not that kind."

"Well, she's been living with a woman who's sleeping with the whole town."

"Not anymore. Where do you hear those things?"

"Oh, I get around," she said airily.

He wondered if Davey had been talking, despite his threats. He watched Lorraine continue to fidget about the room, in the grip of a restlessness she could barely contain. It made him extremely uncomfortable. Even Charlie, that sunny unobservant man, seemed finally to notice Lorraine's edginess. His eye followed her speculatively as she jittered in and out of the kitchen. But all he said was: "Cobbs were big here once."

And from the kitchen: "Oh, my sweet Jesus."

To break this up, he said: "If Hugo is a library trustee, do you suppose he would give me a note to Emily so that I could take out a book?"

"What?" Charlie's thoughts were elsewhere.

He repeated himself.

"Oh, sure. Just ask him."

33

HE HANDED EMILY THE NOTE.

"What's this?" she said.

He explained. She exploded.

"Who the hell does he think he is? Asking favors. What the hell does he know about this library? I haven't seen him here once since I came to work here."

This was red-hot pepper. He tried: "Maybe I could get permission from the school. Get them to take the book off—"

"Up to you," followed by the now familiar dive in the direction of her sneaker laces.

"What I mean is," he said, spacing out the words, "if I get that permission, will you pay any attention to it?"

"Listen—"

"Because you haven't been exactly cooperative up to now."

Instant fury. "Why don't you get out of here."

"You could explain things to me without my having to drag them out of you."

"Drag them out? I can't help it if you're too stupid to find your way around in a library."

"That would be hard to do here. The books I used last week aren't in the shelves."

"Maybe you don't know how to look for them."

By this time he was so angry that he said: "Maybe you're too lazy to put them away."

She shot to her feet. "You get out of here."

"No," he said. "I'm a member. I have a right to be here, and I have a right to some service. Where are those books?"

She waved wildly at the table where he had put them.

"Please find them for me." This was a crazy charade. She was even angrier than he was. She seized the books and threw them on the floor.

"There's your service."

He picked them up and went to the reading table. Watching her reflection in the slanted window, he saw her return to her desk and take a hefty swig from her bottle, then tear the paper from a stick of chewing gum and put the gum in her mouth. That quick resort to the bottle, no mere sip this time, followed by the cover-up of gum, drained his anger. This woman was desperate. Her behavior was a shocking reminder of his own, of all the times he had done just what she was doing. The man who had swigged and sweated and concealed, who had been so strung out and frightened of everybody, who had nobody to depend on or confide in, was now sitting in this library looking at a woman in the same straits.

Nobody to confide in; that was what had made things so hopeless for him. A sickening shred of that hopelessness ran through him. He recalled what Charlie had said about her, that she went all out in anything she did. Now she was going all out in fury and drinking. He got up, dragged his chair across the room, and set it next to her desk. Not knowing quite what to say, he sat down and looked into that infuriated, desperate, hostile, locked-in face. What came out of him was: "Life Savers are better."

She was so wrought up that she didn't hear him. "It's against the rule to drag furniture around in here," she said shrilly.

"Chewing gum isn't as good as Life Savers," he said.

A glazed look.

"Take it from me. I've done it often."

She still wasn't connecting.

"I mean, if you're going to drink during the day, your best bet for hiding it is Life Savers. Peppermint."

"Who's drinking?" she said belligerently.

"You are. I can smell it from here."

"Your own breath."

"No, I'm dry. I haven't had a drink in over two years."

"Then you're imagining things."

"Like the bottle in your desk?"

"Listen," she said, "I don't want to talk to you. Either you read your book or you get out of here."

"There's a bottle in that drawer."

"No."

Before she could stop him, he reached down and pulled it out. Vodka—the secret drinker's favorite. She made a grab for it. It cracked against the metal corner of her desk and broke. Vodka splashed on the desktop and puddled her corduroys. She let out a small scream—anger or anguish?—then, mindless of the wet, put her arm on the desk, hid her face in it, and began to sob.

He watched her shoulders heave, watched her put her other arm down in the vodka, wondering what to do next. He could just go, but that would be inexcusable. He couldn't leave her in this condition, particularly since he had precipitated it.

"Sit up," he said. "You're getting all wet."

She didn't move. He was reminded of days when he had cried himself out in Hennerkop's office, so emptied that he had literally ached, and he wondered for the first time how Hennerkop might have been feeling while watching him cry. But Hennerkop was a professional; it was his job to make people cry, and to know how to handle them when they did. He remembered now that Hennerkop always did nothing, just sat there waiting for him to stop.

So he did the same, and eventually she did stop. She sat up, her face drained and dazed. She looked abstractedly at the vodka stains on her sleeves, seeming almost not to know what they were or how they had gotten there. She looked at him as if she didn't know who he was. And he remembered that too, the crying that went so deep that when you stopped, you had to catch up with yourself, remember who you were, where you were, and what you had been crying about.

"I'm sorry I broke your bottle," he said.

She looked at the pieces of glass on the floor. He bent to pick them up. "I'll get you another," he said. "No. Better: I'll get you a cup of coffee. Would you like some coffee?"

She nodded.

"Do you have anything here, a hot plate? Any instant?"

"No." A croak.

"Okay, I'll take you out for a cup."

She looked at herself again. "I can't go out like this." She tried to wring some vodka from her sleeve.

"Then let me take you home so you can change."

"And close the library? Early?"

"For God's sake," he said. "Nobody's coming in here. You know that. This place is a joke."

Her face was a struggle between returning anger and the realization that he was speaking the truth. She got up, noticing for the first time the vodka on her corduroys. "Look at that."

"You can change them too." He touched her arm and aimed her toward the door.

"Wait," she said, coming more alive every moment. "The key." She retrieved it from her desk. "All this glass."

"I'll get rid of it." He watched her lock the door with shaky fingers and guided her out to the truck, which was parked outside. She huddled in the corner, didn't speak when he turned left at the foot of Elm and started out on Harbor Road. Apparently she assumed he knew where she lived, knew, as every Lincoln Harbor resident should know, where the Cobb mansion was. He drove slowly along, almost to the end.

"It's that one." She pointed. "The one with the big yard."

It was indeed a run-down house. Large and square, with tall windows and a widow's walk on the top, it had obviously been built at a time when Cobbs were kings in Lincoln Harbor. A wide veranda ran across the front and around one side. The top of the veranda railing was broad enough to sit on, and he could imagine Victorian ladies doing just that, in straw hats and carrying parasols, carefully arranged for a group portrait by the local photographer. The veranda pillars were fluted, with Doric tops, repeated in miniature by the balusters of the porch railing. From the center of the veranda a flight of steps descended, curving wider as it went down.

A grand house, a beautiful house, but in sad disrepair, muddyish where it should have been gleaming white, and all its carefully turned woodwork blurred by careless coats of paint slapped on over the decades. The side porch had a porte cochere with a gravel drive leading to a large stable in back. He drove his truck into the porte cochere and parked. Emily disappeared inside without a glance or a word for him. He turned his motor off and settled down to wait, wondering if she might decide not to come out again.

Why would she? She was shaken by alcohol, by a nasty fight, by the realization that her secret drinking habit had been discovered by a man she didn't know, a virtual stranger who had caught her in complete emotional disarray. The longer he thought about it, the more unlikely it seemed that she would reappear. He decided to give her ten minutes and then leave. But she was out in eight—wearing a print dress, sandals instead of sneakers, and a faint dash of lipstick. She had done nothing with her hair, which, still severely pulled back, continued to give her a defiant, hawklike look.

He turned the truck around and headed back toward Elm.

"Where are we going?"

"The Nook," he said. That was a quiet coffee and ice cream place behind the post office. It was expensive, frequented mostly by trendy summer people. He chose it because it would probably have very few

301

customers. Also it had booths where one could talk quietly.

"Not there," she said.

"Why not?"

"That place is too fancy. I'm not dressed right."

"You're dressed a lot better than you were this afternoon. Besides, look at me. Jeans and work boots." He got out of the truck, crossed to her side, and opened the door. Reluctantly she stepped down and followed him around the post office and into The Nook. He steered her to a corner banquette. There was nobody else there.

"Hi, Emily," said a waitress, coming up and looking at her with unconcealed surprise.

Emily held her head down and didn't answer.

"Two coffees," he said, and turned to her. She looked both angry and frightened. Searching for something to break the ice, he said: "Actually you're better dressed than most of the people who come in here."

Still looking at the table, she said: "Why are you doing this?"

Why was he? Identification with himself? Pity? Probably both, fusing in a strong feeling that she needed somebody. He said: "I intruded on you in the library. I upset you. I figured the least I could do was apologize and explain why I did what I did."

"Why did you?"

The experienced ex-drunk to the rescue. "Because I know you can't solve your problems by looking at them through the bottom of a vodka bottle. I wanted to tell you that."

"You're the expert on vodka bottles?"

"Actually bourbon bottles. But the result's the same. Things just get worse."

"What kind of things?"

"Everything. Your whole life. Particularly the things that got you started drinking in the first place."

"What kind of particular things?"

He took a long breath, wondering how to give a résumé of his sordid past. Do it at all? What did he owe this girl, other than an explanation for an impulsive act? But he had come this far; why not continue? He said: "Loneliness, for one thing. No friends."

Another long pause. Finally she lifted her face. "You have no friends?"

"Not then. No real ones. I had people I liked to think of as friends, but I wasn't close to any of them. I kept myself to myself because I didn't like myself." How easily it came out once he got started. "Particularly I didn't like the fact that I was living a phony life."

"What kind of a phony life?" As long as she could keep firing questions at him, she could avoid answering any about herself.

"I was a phony advertising executive in a set of up people in New York, but I didn't belong there. I was in a cold marriage that I refused to face until it fell apart. I had a girlfriend, a truly nice one. I treated her rottenly. To try and hold all those things together, I drank a lot. I was scared all the time. I drank to overcome that. I was angry, and I drank because of that too. When I lost my wife and my job and my girl, and even the people I thought were friends, then I really settled down to serious drinking." The story of his life in a few sentences, a life that had taken him endless hours to explain to Hennerkop.

"What do you call serious drinking?"

Okay, tell her. "When everything else is gone. When you can't face another day without a drink. When you purposely get yourself loaded up so that you can endure the lonely night ahead of you. When you don't remember the night before or what you did. When you have to have a shot in the morning to keep yourself from shaking apart. Is that enough?"

"Go on."

"When you know that first drink won't stay down, and it doesn't and you have to try again, and maybe that one doesn't stay down, either. That sort of thing. That's serious drinking."

By this time she was looking at him intently. "You did all that?"

"More. I'm ashamed to tell you some of the things I did."

"How did you stop?"

"A therapist in New York helped me. I came up here to start over. Except for a few beers, I haven't had a drink since, and never will. I don't need it. I'm making an honest living here as a garbage collector. I'm not faking anything with anybody anymore. I have some friends here, the first friends I've ever had."

She sipped her coffee, getting ready to switch the conversation to herself. "What gave you the idea I was drinking?" she asked.

"The first time we met—at that picnic—you had your nose in the bottle all evening. Then the two times I was at the library"—no point in mentioning the reflection—"I noticed it on your breath. Three out of three is a pretty good indication, particularly when two out of the three are in the middle of the afternoon." She took that without blinking, seeming a little less stressed. She ran her hand back to smooth her hair, the gesture he had seen so many times reflected in the window. He risked nailing it down. "So you do drink."

"Sometimes. Doesn't everybody?"

His turn: "Why?"

She tensed again, gulped the rest of her coffee. He got the waitress's eye and ordered two more.

"Why?" he repeated.

She looked extremely uncomfortable. "Don't Lou and Marge talk about me all the time?"

"No, they don't. They sometimes mention Lou's brother, Davey. I know you were going with him but you broke up."

"I hear you beat him up."

"Not exactly. We had a scuffle."

"I'm glad," she said savagely. "He's a stinker."

"He's a drinker, a real one."

"He walked out on me. I was ready to like him."

"You're not a real one," he said. "At least I don't think so. I think you drink because you're angry and unhappy and lonely. Loneliness—that's the killer."

She visibly shuddered when he said that. "You think you can cure loneliness by buying me a cup of coffee?"

"No. But maybe I can get you to understand that drinking will make the loneliness so much worse that finally you won't be able to do anything, won't want to live at all."

"I feel that way now," her long face stretching longer.

"Come on."

"I do. You don't know what it's like here. I have this rotten fake job. Have you any idea what it's like to sit there day after day? Nobody comes in; maybe one or two a week. You sit there and sit there, and pretty soon you begin to feel your life draining right out of you. You don't even have the energy to put things away." Another gulp of coffee. "You were right. I did give you poor service. I *wanted* to give you poor service. I hate that library, and that makes me hate everyone who comes in there. I'm sorry I was so rude to you."

"That's all right. Maybe you'll let me take out a couple of books next time."

A trace of a smile crossed her drawn face. "Six years, you said, since that book went out?"

"Why don't you quit the library?"

"I should. They pay practically nothing. But there's nothing for me to do here. I want to *do* something."

"Everybody does."

"I wanted to go to New York, to get a job in publishing. I wanted to write. . . ." She flushed. "I dropped out of college."

"You could go back. How old are you?"

"Twenty-two."

That startled him; she seemed much older. "You're just a kid," he said. "Go back to college."

"I can't. I was on a scholarship." There came another long silence while she drained her second cup of coffee. "I got involved with a man there. On the faculty. They took away my scholarship. Didn't Lou and Marge mention that?"

"No." Another useful lie that Hennerkop would have applauded. "Maybe you could transfer. Southern Mass is cheap for state residents."

"I couldn't even afford that. We're too poor."

He ordered a third round of coffee.

"So I rattle around in a big empty house. Nothing to do. Nobody to talk to."

"Your mother . . . ?"

"We don't talk. She doesn't approve of me. She didn't approve of my relationship at college. She doesn't approve of a Portuguese boy like Davey. She doesn't approve when I drink. And Davey—what a stinker he is."

"How did you meet him?" he asked. "He doesn't seem your type."

"At the Blue Lobster. He picked me up. He's very good-looking, you know." Hand back for another stroking of her hair, this time a gesture of some elegance. "That's where the boys go, so that's where the girls go when they're looking for boys. I was so bored and lonely that I decided to go there one night. The place was full of kids I knew from high school."

"Right at home."

"No, you don't understand. When I decided I wanted to go to college, I sort of isolated myself from them." She straightened up from her crouch over her coffee cup. He caught a glimpse of an intelligent proud prickly girl already at odds with her peers. "All they think of in high school is beer and dates. I wanted to study. I wanted to be a writer or an editor, to get away from here. They thought I was stuck-up. I guess I was. Anyway . . . " She looked at him dolefully. "I've got a lot of hours to kill, and now you know how I kill them."

"And yourself too."

"Why not? What's the use?"

"You mentioned your mother. Do you ever drink at home?"

"Sometimes."

"How about not doing it tonight."

"I'll think about it."

"I'll drive you home. When we get there, will you give me the bottle you keep under your mattress?"

"You seem to know a lot about where people keep bottles."

"Personal experience."

She got into the truck. "If you want to stop at the library, I'll let you take out those books."

When they got to her house he said: "The bottle." Somewhat to his astonishment, she brought it out and handed it to him, then disappeared again into that huge worn mansion. What could be done for her? His business? Not really, but somebody ought to be doing something.

34

"FRED, YOU GOT TO QUIT GOOFING OFF."

He explained that he had been at the library, getting some books on accounting. He handed them to Marge. "If you kept the books at your father's bar, you're one step ahead of me. Maybe I can learn something from you."

"Fred, we don't need a bookkeeper. We need work. We got the big truck. You should be driving it full-time. Where we going to find somebody for the little truck?"

Marge had opened one of the books. "Hey—double entry. I always wanted to know about that."

"What the hell is double entry?" growled Lou. "Sounds like some newfangled way of doing sex."

"Your mind sometimes slips lower than your tongue," said Marge. "Double entry's a way of working from both sides with the same figures."

"Like I just said."

Marge was impervious to this talk. She went on: "That way you can always strike a balance."

"Well, you two strike your balance. Meanwhile I got to find another driver."

"Want to try Davey again?"

"Jesus no. After last time?"

"He got to taking cash from jobs and putting it in his pocket," explained Marge. "Honey, with good books we'd have caught him."

"We did catch him."

"We'd have caught him sooner. Saved you that row over the gravel load."

"So read your books. Where am I gonna get a driver?"

"Somebody at the door," said Marge. She rose to answer it, but before she got there Charlie Barker burst in, his face mottled.

"Fred, I have to talk to you."

"And who might you be?" said Lou.

Charlie ignored him. "It's urgent."

"Don't even use the knocker? Don't even say hello?"

"Shush," said Marge. "What's the matter?"

Charlie ignored her, too, and beckoned Fred out to his car, where he sat, gripping the steering wheel, apparently too worked up even to talk. Charlie's hands were small, and their knuckles were white with strain. Fred was aware that his own hands had become brown and callused, larger and stronger—the difference between a desk man's and a working man's. Devoted as he was to Charlie, the man who had taught him how to do almost everything he knew up here, he couldn't resist a flicker of superiority in his strong honest hands. He waited for Charlie to speak, and finally he did.

"It's Lorraine."

With a sinking feeling, he waited.

Charlie struggled to continue. "She—"

He waited again.

"—got caught." He put his small hands up to his face. "In the Seaview Motel. They raided it. They caught her."

"Doing what?" biting down on his tongue too late. What an incredibly stupid question.

"With Hugo."

"Hugo!"

"You're in this, Fred. You have to help us out."

"I'm in it?"

"Hugo signed your name in the motel register. That puts you there."

"Now wait—"

"It does." Charlie scrubbed his short hair with one hand, still steering the stationary car with the other. "I know you weren't *there,* but you have to be, don't you see. I mean, if it's three of you there, nothing's wrong. You were just having a meeting."

"About what?"

"About anything. About your house. Yeah, you just bought a house. Hugo wrote the mortgage. Lorraine is helping you furnish it. You need a loan to do that, so it's natural for the three of you to get together to talk it over."

"In a motel?"

Charlie had no answer for that. He'd managed to tack together the framework of a cover-up with remarkable speed, but he was stuck there. "This isn't easy, you know." Easy? It must have been utterly wrenching to admit that his wife had been caught in a motel bedroom with his oldest friend.

"When did this happen?" he asked.

"This afternoon. Only a couple of hours ago."

"How did you find out?"

"When Lorraine came home. She ran upstairs and shut her door. Fritz Booker—you know Fritz, the chief—he was right behind her. Fritz was the one who made the bust. I know Fritz. Fritz knows me. He knows Lorraine. He knows Hugo. It must have shook him, busting in on two he knew."

"Why did he do it?" he asked.

"Neighbors. That place is hot beds. When you're hot to trot, that's where you go. The neighbors have been putting up such a squawk to Fritz that he had to go. Now he doesn't know what to do. He doesn't want to arrest anybody yet. Oh, Jesus."

The preposterous idea of Lorraine and Hugo together, when all the time he had been thinking that he was the one she was making a play for, went skidding through his mind.

"Let's get out of here," said Charlie. "I need a drink. Besides, Fritz may show up here any minute."

"Why would he do that?"

"Your name, Fred. On the motel register. He's going to have to ask you about that in order to nail Hugo. I think there are laws about signing false names."

Hugo had done that with *his* name? "I can clear that up pretty fast," he said.

"No, Fred. You were there."

"But I wasn't. Fritz didn't see me."

"Because"—another instant improvisation—"because you were in the bathroom when he broke in."

"Come on, Charlie. Who's going to buy that?"

"It's our best chance." By this time they had reached Charlie's house. Charlie poured himself a half tumbler of whiskey and took a good pull at it. Lorraine was presumably still upstairs, although there was no sound from up there. His eye wandered toward the ceiling, and Charlie caught it.

"She's not talking. I got this all from Fritz. I asked him to give me overnight to talk to Lorraine. He said okay. We're all due in his office tomorrow at nine."

"What about Hugo?"

"I haven't talked to Hugo. I guess he's ashamed to come around."

Somebody would have to talk to Hugo to get this ridiculous story straight, and he was beginning to realize that he would have to be the one to do it. With that thought he crossed the line, joined the conspiracy. Now he would have to know more. "How long has this been going on?" he asked.

"I don't—" Charlie's face was contorted. "This is tough to talk about."

"If you don't want to—"

"No, it's just tough. Lorraine— You know how she is, how she's been lately. Not like herself. You've seen how she—"

He nodded.

"With you. You couldn't miss it. You didn't miss that, did you?"

"I didn't miss it."

"Did you ever . . . ?"

"Never."

"Not that I'd have minded all that much. Oh, I'd have *minded*. I mean, Lorraine was— I could see it coming. She was definitely going to. And if she was, I could think of worse people than you. You're a nice fellow. You wouldn't do her any harm. And maybe if she got it out of her system—"

This was an excruciating conversation. Charlie's round face, which seemed designed for cheerfulness, was sinking in on itself. His cheeks sagged, and his mouth was trembling.

Charlie went on, wound up tight, too tight for too long, and some inner spring now sprung. It all poured out. "I mean, she got going, you know? And I wasn't helping. You'd think I'd help, wouldn't you. Well . . . I couldn't."

"Couldn't what?" Another unbelievably inappropriate question.

Charlie flushed deeply. "You know, just . . . couldn't."

"Oh." He nodded sagely and, he hoped, sympathetically.

"I got to where I couldn't. The best I could do was have somebody like you around and hope for the best. You don't think I didn't see what was happening with you and her? You don't think I'm that dumb, do you?"

"I don't think you're dumb."

"What else could I do? It was safer with you. Maybe it wouldn't happen. Maybe it would blow over."

"Maybe it will. After this, maybe it will."

"I don't think so. She and Hugo—" His face turned scarlet. "They hadn't— Jesus, Fred, they hadn't been there long enough." A gargled sob. "They hadn't even taken their clothes off. Just their shoes."

"Fritz tell you that?"

"To make me feel better. It made me feel worse. The picture, you know. Like being there."

"Maybe he was right. Maybe they weren't . . . "

"Fred . . . " As the reality of this situation was beginning to sink deeper and deeper, Charlie's face continued to crumble. His voice went up. "They were in a motel room together, under the wrong name, for Christ's sake. What do I do now, kick her out? I love her. She's a hot woman. She can't help that. She's just that way. And I can't help her— Fred, I can't. She was always wanting more, and I couldn't. Never enough. Now I can't at all."

He watched Charlie, his shameful secret out, pour himself another drink and down it in one swallow, watched him sink into a chair and stare at his shoes. He thought of all the evenings he'd been there for supper, and wondered what must have been going through Charlie's mind as he saw Lorraine slowly coming to a boil, observed the guest's clumsy efforts to fend her off. He remembered his own reaction to the realization that this woman was ready to be plucked and wanted to be plucked by him—by hungry sex-starved him—and wondered if Charlie had been aware of that too. He desperately hoped not, because now, with Hugo, it was clear that the target was not Frederick Fay but a man, any man, which Charlie proceeded to confirm.

"One night when you were here . . . after you left she said she was going for a walk. She was so hopped up I didn't know what she might do. Maybe follow you down to where you tie up your boat. But she went the other way, to the Blue Lobster. You know—any woman goes alone to a place like that, they're there for only one reason."

He remembered her previous slighting references to the Blue Lobster.

"I don't know what she expected to find there. I didn't go in. But she was out again in two minutes, walking fast. I went in and asked the girl who tends bar—you know, the one you live with. I asked her if a lady had just been in and why she left so fast. She said yes, that Lorraine had ordered a drink, and when some guy next to her at the bar tried to give her a quick feel— She didn't say *that*, but that's what she meant. She said Lorraine ran out. She asked me if I would pay for Lorraine's drink."

Anybody? Well, not quite anybody. It also explained Lorraine's animosity toward Marge. Marge had observed that degrading encounter. "Did she see you when she came out?" he asked.

"No. She took off too fast. She went straight home. When I got there, she was in bed with the light out. I didn't say anything, and neither did she. It's just something that hangs between us, and the more things we don't talk about, the heavier it gets. Jesus, your own wife going out and getting felt up in a bar? Wondering all the time who she's going to end up with? In a way I'm grateful it was Hugo, although I'd like to kill the bastard. They could have been a little smarter about where they went. Anybody goes in there, day or night, it's for one thing."

Through this outpouring of Charlie's he had been waiting for some sound from upstairs, but there was nothing. Wasn't Lorraine curious about the reaction to all this? What would she do next? Like Hugo's wife, leave?

"This is awful," said Charlie. "It's just beginning to hit me."

Still no sound from upstairs. Maybe the door was open a crack and she was listening.

"What am I going to do?"

"The first thing," he said, "we're going to have to talk to Hugo to get all our stories straight."

"I can't do that." Clearly he couldn't.

"You'll have to. And Lorraine."

"Lorraine—she shut the door on me. She won't speak to me. I tried."

"You'll have to. It's your house, your door."

"You go."

He shook his head.

"I can't, Fred. I don't know what I'll say, what I might do. I might—"

This pleasant room, so tastefully furnished by the wife upstairs, its contents so lovingly polished, its owner now completely crumpled. He had gone as far as he could. In an initial burst of appalled energy, he had managed to put together a story, an implausible one but still a story. Now it was beyond him. He could go no further. Someone else would have to pick it up. "Okay," he said. "First we'll talk to Lorraine. You'd better take me upstairs. I don't want to go there alone."

Charlie led the way, up the staircase with its gleaming mahogany rail. There was a door at the head of the stairs, presumably their bedroom. It was shut. For one who was clearly knotted in anger, Charlie was at the same time curiously timorous as he tapped on the door. His confession of his impotence seemed to have taken all the punch out of him, made him a suppliant in his own home, the sinned-against afraid to confront the sinner. A second feeble tap. There was no answer. "See."

"Here." Fred banged smartly on the door and opened it. Lorraine was on her back in bed, the covers pulled up to her chin, held there by two fists ready to ward them off.

"Don't come in here."

"We have to talk," he said, and sat down in a chair. Charlie remained in the doorway, and in so doing became an observer, not a participant.

"There's nothing to talk about," said Lorraine, "—with you."

"Yes there is," he said. "Hugo may not have told you this, but he signed my name in the motel register."

The significance of that escaped her. "That means," he went on, "that there was nothing improper about your being there. There were three of us."

"But you weren't—"

"Yes I was." He tried to gather his thoughts, staring at that squarish face on the pillow, trying to blot out her earlier behavior, her fleeting desirability, and his own erotic thoughts. She was no longer pretty; her eyes were too close together, and her fearful guilty expression was repellent. "Yes I was," he repeated. "I was in the bathroom when the chief came in. He misread the situation completely. I mean, if there *was* a situation." Babble babble. "I just mean that the fact that you and Hugo were alone together meant absolutely nothing, because the true story—I mean, the story that we'll give—is that three of us were there together to talk about getting furniture and decorations for my house."

That drew an utter blank. She stared at him without speaking, her fists still clutching the sheet.

"Honey," said Charlie in a small voice from the door. "That's the *story*. Fred is going to help us. He's going to say he was there too."

A glimmering. "But you weren't."

"Yes I was. I was in the bathroom. That's all you have to remember. We agreed to meet there because I had a truck delivery to make at the motel and I suggested we meet there. So you drove out with Hugo— Is that how you got there?"

"You were in the bathroom?"

"Honey," said Charlie, "where's your car?"

She swiveled her head to glare at her husband, standing meekly in the doorway.

He echoed Charlie: "Where's your car?"

"The A&P parking lot."

"That wasn't very smart," said Charlie. "Somebody might have seen you."

"Leave me alone," she screamed, and put her head under the covers.

"Why don't you get her car," he said to Charlie. Anything to get him out of there. Lorraine was either so angry at him or so deeply ashamed of herself—probably both—that any productive conversation would be impossible with the three of them present. When the door closed, he said: "Come out; he's gone," and her head reappeared. There was now a furtive complicity in her expression. How could he ever have felt anything for this woman whom he was beginning to dislike intensely? Feeling more like a cross-examining lawyer than a helpful friend of the family, he said: "You switched cars in the parking lot?"

A nod.

"But you might have been seen driving away together."

"I was in the back, lying down. I got in the back."

"Even so—"

"I covered myself with a spinnaker. He put a spinnaker in the back."

"When you got to the motel?"

"I stayed under the spinnaker."

"Until he registered?"

"He drove right to the door, and—"

"And what?"

"He said: 'Okay now,' so I went in."

"Then the chief arrived?"

Another nod.

"Before you'd . . . "

Tears of frustration and humiliation were appearing. She wiped them off with the edge of the sheet. "It's your fault, you know."

"No, Lorraine."

"Yes it is. All those looks of yours. The way you looked at me. I knew what you were thinking. How do you expect me to feel when you look at me that way? And when you don't do anything—anything." That last went up in a wail. "You never did anything. You just left me all—"

"That was in your mind, Lorraine."

"Not in my mind. I could tell. And that time in the hall, I could feel you."

"No, Lorraine."

"I felt—I feel—"

"No you don't."

"Yes. There's time."

He got up.

"Right now." Pleading. She sat up in bed, her breasts pouring out of her nightgown in a warm pink cascade. The worst of it was that another surge went roaring into his loins, and she saw it.

"Fred—"

"Just remember the story. I was there. On business." He clattered down the stairs, saying to Charlie—who was still there—"I'm going to Hugo's," and he did so, wondering what under heaven Lorraine—poor Lorraine; he suddenly felt a pang of sympathy for her, remembering another woman driven beyond reason by desire—would have to say to her husband when she took off her nightgown and got into some clothes and went downstairs to cook him his supper. At some point they were going to have to face each other, talk to each other. What would they find to say?

The atmosphere at Hugo's was quite different. Hugo was so mortified that he could scarcely meet his eye. The old-buddy network was tentatively invoked. "Things happen. You know how things are. You get caught off base once in a while."

"You wrote my name in the motel register."

"Heh. That's right, I did. Wasn't thinking too fast. I had to put down somebody. When you're off base you sometimes—"

"That's against the law. Besides, you used *my* name."

"I wasn't thinking."

"It's lucky for you you weren't. You supplied yourself with an alibi."

Hugo's head shot up.

All right, once again. The second time around would be easier. "I was there in the motel with you. The three of us met to discuss a loan for furnishing my house—"

"Three of us? But the chief—"

"When the chief arrived, I happened to be in the bathroom."

"You'll say that?"

"Tomorrow morning when we all meet in the chief's office. I suggested the place. You got there ahead of me, so naturally you signed my name."

"Fred, I owe you one." Hugo stuck out his hand. A couple of old-buddy whacks followed.

"Can you keep that straight?"

"Can do." The rebound was like that of a golf ball hitting a side-walk. "I owe you one, a big one."

"I'll remember."

Since Charlie had driven him to his house, he had had to walk to Hugo's and then home to Gott Street. His mind went back to the events at Charlie's and to what Charlie and Lorraine might be doing or saying at this very moment, and he wondered if the terrible stresses between them would prevent their remembering the story that had been concocted, or if they would garble it fatally the next morning at Chief Booker's. He worried also about what Hugo's face might betray when he appeared and had to confront the almost-cuckold and the straying wife. This could burst into a really dreadful scandal: the town's leading real estate man and one of its leading bankers snarling at each other over the former's wife. And the motel room—what a sordid backdrop for the unfolding of the play. It would all depend on how the actors handled their lines. And he was one of the actors now, in it up to his neck. He was so full of all that that he was unprepared for Lou and Marge when he got home.

"You know Fritz Booker?"

"I know who he is."

"Fritz is looking for you. Wants you in his office tomorrow morning. What you been up to, Fred?"

He had no ready answer to that and went into the bathroom. There he collected his wits enough to say on emerging that it was probably the picket fence in front of the house on Cedar Street; a couple of pickets were loose and might fall out to trip pedestrians. That seemed to satisfy Lou but drew an inscrutable look from Marge. She read him too easily. He had to turn his back to her.

"You know something?" she said. "Double entry's easy, once you get the hang of it." Easing whatever his trouble was, deflecting attention from it. What a woman! How he loved her. How he envied Lou. And how he hated himself for itching for an inferior woman like Lorraine.

Marge said: "We won't be needing the accounting book. You can return that."

At Chief Booker's office, Lorraine was pale, Charlie was red, Hugo was the suave banker who had dropped in to explain some trifling misunderstanding. All gave their stories, Lorraine in such monosyllables that her guilt was oozing out of her. When the chief asked him the question, the key question that all had been expecting, he said with surprising calmness that he had been in the bathroom.

"The whole time I was there?"

"Some times take longer than others."

"Anybody see you coming or going?"

"I don't know. I didn't think to look."

"How'd you get there?"

How easy to lie when you were defending others. "In my truck. I expect you saw it parked across the street."

Fritz Booker brushed that aside and asked if he wasn't surprised to find the others gone when he came out.

"I certainly was. I didn't know what had happened. I didn't find out until later that evening, when I went to the Barkers'."

"I was too," put in Hugo. "I still think you owe Lorraine an apology. You can see how shaken she is by this." All turned to stare at Lorraine, who indeed looked shaken to her roots. The chief, to his credit, or perhaps to the credit of the power of the old-buddy network, said he was sorry he had misinterpreted the situation and would like to apologize to Mrs. Barker. She mumbled her thanks, and all went their separate ways, Fred wondering again how Charlie and Lorraine would face each other across the dinner table and if Charlie and Hugo could ever be friends again.

35

HE RETURNED THE LIBRARY BOOK ON ACCOUNT-ing that Marge had said she didn't need. Emily was at her desk, and she looked dreadful. Her face was pale and puffy. Although her hair was still drawn tight in that ugly uncompromising way she had, it failed now to engender any of the hawklike aggressiveness it had previously suggested. Somehow she looked blurred.

"Here's one of the books I borrowed." She took it without speaking and tossed it on the table with the pile of other returned books. The entire library was a mess. He couldn't help comparing it to the one in Under Wixton, with its sets of beautifully bound unread classics, everything neat and lovingly cared for, the floor spotless, all bathed in the faint smell of kerosene from Violet Few-Strang's little heater, which almost took the chill out of the place. Here it was warm with the soft air of a New England seaside summer, the breeze wafting in through those slanted windows, carrying a whiff of the wild roses banked outside. And here sat a wreck of a woman. She reminded him superficially of Violet, just as Julia once had. Both were tall and thin and had prominent noses. But after that, what a difference! This woman was rotting.

She had not moved the chair he had dragged over that other day, so he sat down in it again.

"How's it going?" he asked, and got an unfocused look in return. Remembering the mixture of exhaustion and terrible restlessness that went with bad hangovers, the awful sense of hopelessness and self-disgust, the feeling of not wanting to be bothered by anybody or anything, but at the same time the desperate need for pity, for contact, for something to break through the restlessness, the isolation, the utter dreariness of everything, he said: "Any drinking?"

A long pause. Then: "Not here."

"No bottle here?"

"You want to look?"

"I'll take your word for it," he said. "How about home?"

"A little."

"How little?"

"A little to help me sleep. I can't sleep."

"You drink yourself to sleep? That can take a lot."

"Sometimes."

"Emily, that's no good. To have all that vodka sloshing around in you all night, you wake up feeling like death."

"That's right."

"Can't you cut back?"

"Why? It passes the evening."

"But the next day—"

"Today's the next day. What's so hot about today? About any day?"

"But if you felt a little better, maybe you could clean up a little in here, get things straightened out."

A spark flickered in her dull eye. "I don't want to get things straightened out. I told you, I hate this place. The worse it gets, the better I like it. I want the whole thing to—to—" There was a box of paper clips and some library cards on her desk. A wild swing of her arm sent them flying. Some mottled color was coming into her face. "There." She spotted another card and swatted it to the floor. "See how they like that."

"That's crazy," he said. "You'll have to pick them up."

"Why should I?"

"It's crazy," he repeated.

"What's crazy about messing up something you utterly utterly hate? The crazy thing would be to clean it up." She looked around the room with a savage glare, as if trying to make up her mind about what she would mess up next. A terrible hopeless anger, like the fit that had got him thrown out of the Racquet Club.

"You should get out of here," he said.

"Out? Where?"

"Anywhere. Can you drive a truck?"

"Where would I drive it?" She thrust the idea away with a rake of her hand through her hair.

"Right here. You could become a truckdriver."

As he said that, she seemed to become a little less blurred. "Drive? For somebody?"

319

He nodded.

"I don't know how."

"Can you drive a car?"

"Yes."

"Then you can drive a truck. I'm a garbage man, remember? My truck's outside. I have a run I have to make. You can drive, and I'll pick up the cans."

"But the library—"

"To hell with the library; you hate it," he reminded her. "If you stay here any longer you'll break something, burn it down."

"But—"

"Put a sign on the door. Do you have a crayon?" She fumbled in her desk for one. He retrieved one of the cards from the floor and wrote CLOSED on it in thick letters. "Scotch tape?" Keep her moving. He taped the card to the door, watched her lock it, and guided her to the driver's seat in the truck. "Standard shift," he said. "Just drive up the street."

She didn't do it very smoothly, but she managed. He told her where to stop for his first pickup. "Now you're a truckdriver."

"Working for you?"

"Working for Lou Mendoza."

She stopped the truck with a jolt.

"That's right—Davey's brother. You'll be doing the job Davey lost by drinking and stealing."

She swung around to face him with a profoundly confused expression. Clearly there was some satisfaction in taking Davey's job away from him. But there was something else. "Me? Collect garbage in this town? What'll they all think?" Then quickly: "I didn't mean—"

"Think nothing of it. It's a noble profession."

"But Davey—"

"He probably won't like it. So what; he's been fired. But you will see him when you go to the dump. He's the dumpmaster there. If he gives you any trouble, let me know."

"I'll dump garbage on him." Her lip tightened. Vindictiveness was winning out.

"Stop up there," he said. "Mullery is your first pickup."

She stopped again, this time more smoothly.

"Think you can lift that can?"

She took a deep breath. "I can try, but I'm not in the best shape this morning." With some difficulty she hoisted the can up over the dropped tailgate. He tested it; it was one of the heavier ones. She climbed back into the truck, some drops of hangover sweat beading her forehead.

"You're a garbage collector," he said. "Now all I have to do is persuade Lou that you can be his garbage collector."

"A problem because of Davey?"

"A problem because of drinking."

She whirled around. "What makes him think I do?"

"I told him."

She slammed on the brake again. "I thought you said you didn't talk to those people about me."

"Only that."

"How would you feel if somebody went around saying you were a drunk?"

"It's happened to me, and it made me feel rotten. But I didn't say you were a drunk. I only said—"

"You say too much. What business is it of yours anyway? Why don't you—" She was close to tears again. "Just— Just—" She opened the truck door. He grabbed her arm.

"You don't have to walk back to the library. I'll drive you." Squeezing her arm hard. "I'll get you another bottle of vodka and you can sit there all day, every day. Drink yourself stupid there."

She put her face in her hands.

"Or I can get you a pair of work gloves and you can haul garbage. Your choice."

She didn't answer.

"Emily, you've got to get out of that place and do something useful. This is a hard job. It will make demands on you."

She said through her fingers: "It's just that people say all those things about me. About drinking and— What else do they say about me? What do Lou and Marge say? What did they say about me when they tried to fix me up with you on that picnic?"

"They didn't say anything. I didn't even know you were coming."

"They didn't say I was a pushover?"

"No."

"A pushover for Davey? That's what they think. An easy lay."

"Emily, they don't talk about you. All I know about you is that you drink too much because your life is nothing."

"Nothing? What do you know about nothing?"

"I've been there," he said. "I drank more than you ever will, because my life was nothing too. Now it's something. I have an honest job. I earn what I make. Nothing phony about it. I'm offering you that job, a chance to do something different." He took both of her hands. He found himself staring as earnestly as he knew how, hoping to convince her—for her sake, he realized, instead of for his own. "If I can persuade Lou that you're not a real drinker, maybe—just maybe—I can get you that job."

The look she gave him was truly heartbreaking. "He won't do it."

"Possibly. But I won't even ask him unless I'm sure you want the job and will work hard at it."

"I can work."

"And no drinking."

"Okay."

"I catch you drinking, you're gone. Understand?"

She nodded.

"I'm smart at that, remember?"

With a shaky hand she put the truck in gear. "How did you know about that bottle?"

"I told you, practice. I used to keep one in my desk when I was a hotshot advertising executive who couldn't get through the day without a nip now and then. So—I speak to Lou?"

"I guess."

A proud and prickly woman, now gone very low. Could she really be depended upon to show up for work every day? How much would that depend on her "What'll they all think?" mentality? The Cobb in her was not buried all that deep. He was still worrying about how to broach the matter of hiring her, when Lou settled it for him.

"Shake my hand, Fred—I got the school contract. Digging for the new gym." He was sitting in his chair, looking even larger than usual and insufferably smug. "Only two bids, me and Abbey. When they opened them, you shoulda seen the look on the face of that fellow from Abbey. Second time in a row I underbid him. Remember that other school job? Cut him the same way, ten percent."

"Ten percent of what?"

"Of his bid, Fred. Don't pay to be too greedy, or too close, either. If I undercut only five percent they might give the job to Abbey anyway. Claim Abbey was more reliable than me, something like that. But ten percent's too big for them boys on the school board to ignore. Killed the buggers to give it to me, but what else could they do?"

Marge was in the kitchen, getting supper. A good time of day. Work was over. He felt tired but good, and cooling out from the earlier heat as the afternoon breeze puffed up the white curtains that she had hung in the windows. He decided to ask Lou how he could be sure his bid was ten percent under when bids were sealed.

"Freddie, your nose is getting too long again. Just say I have a way of figuring that out. Done it twice running. Makes it easy for me, because Abbey does all the paperwork. They're hogs over there, getting rich off the town for years. Even cutting them ten percent, I can make a good living."

"That's fine," he said, "so long as they don't catch you."

A big innocent grin. "What's to catch? I submit a bid, I get a job. A big one this time. Lot of dirt to haul. Fred, you'll have to be on the big truck steady." Then Lou handed it to him on a plate. "How we going to manage all them little jobs with the little truck?"

"Get another driver."

"Easy said."

"I have one for you. Emily Watson."

Lou reared back in his chair. "Marge," he yelled into the kitchen, "listen to this. Fred's got me a driver. Give you sixty-nine guesses who."

She came out, wiping her hands on a towel. "Davey?"

"Not Davey, for Christ's sake. We covered that. Fred's peddling his girlfriend. Thinks Emily Watson can drive one of our trucks."

Marge looked at him in genuine astonishment.

Lou said: "She talk you into that, Fred? One of them afternoons when you were in there borrowing books, with the door locked?"

Marge said: "What makes you think she can drive a truck?"

"She's already done it," he replied. "She made the garbage run with me this morning. Drove the truck. Even picked up a few cans. Heavy ones."

Lou slapped the table. "That's not like doing it every day. She wouldn't do that regular. Even if she could, she wouldn't. Picking up garbage for her own kin and all them others spread across the town?"

"I think she would."

"Besides, she's a drinking woman. You said yourself."

"She's stopped."

"As of when?"

"As of today."

Lou looked at Marge, who raised her eyebrows. "Freddie, it seems to me like you found something in her pants that's coloring your judgment of her ability to drive a truck."

He had no answer to remarks like that. He glanced at Marge. Her eyebrows went up another notch. Surely she couldn't think what Lou thought. How could she, when she knew—had to know—how he longed for *her?* He tried to send her that message by saying: "I don't go for Emily. You ought to know that," realizing too late that the message would also hit Lou with a clang.

It did. Lou said instantly: "Maybe we *should* take her on, so she can keep your damper down, keep you flying straight. No zigzag turns in this kitchen—right, Marge?"

She said coolly: "I don't think Fred has any interest in Emily."

"Just in my mind?"

"Just in Fred's taste in women."

What a sharp and daring shot! It acknowledged—saluted—his interest in her at the same time that it defused it by its openness. It flattened Lou, who, it was becoming clear, for all his lurching macho behavior, his coarse talk, his apparently secure assumption that Marge belonged to him, was himself beginning to realize that there were depths both of subtlety and of independence in her that he had not yet plumbed and might do well to avoid. Fred's adoration of her took another upward leap.

"Okay, Fred, maybe you ain't in Emily's pants, although it surprises me she ain't in yours. You walking around free and horny and six feet tall. Why wouldn't she?"

There were edges to every remark. Did Lou really think he was attractive enough to be a rival? He said as carelessly as he could manage: "I guess she doesn't go for me any more than I go for her."

"So what's about her, then? Why, of everybody in this town, do you pick that lushed-up fucked-up librarian to drive my truck?"

"She can do the job. She'll work hard at it."

"You say."

"I say. Anyway, who else have you got?"

"The truth—nobody. That's her one asset that I can see. No competition. What do you think, Marge?"

She pursed her lips, giving some long thought to the question, staring at him, not at Lou, as if weighing the possibility of future entanglement between him and Emily, and whether that might be good or bad. Then she said: "Let's try it." And he could not tell what her thinking was on either point, or indeed which was uppermost in her mind: sympathy for and interest in another woman? or in him, the benighted housemate, a spaniel who could never expect more than to have his ears scratched?

"It ain't all garbage," Lou said. "It's hauling wood and topsoil, plants, making the nursery stop. All them things. You willing to teach her?"

*   *   *

He became Emily's teacher in those things. They were ridiculously easy, requiring only some strength, which she seemed to have, and a knowledge of the town, hers being far better than his own. In only a few days she was so well broken in and so patently reliable that Lou stopped his nightly barrage of wisecracks about her, delivered after Emily had brought the small truck back, made her report on the jobs she had done, got her instructions for the next day, and walked home. All that must have worn her out at first. He remembered the exhausted heavy sleeps he had fallen into during his first month on the job and assumed that she, too, was sleeping well. He said nothing more to her about drinking, because she was prompt in the mornings and was beginning to look so much healthier that he could assume she had quit entirely. Concerned about the long walk from Gott Street to her house, coming at the end of a long day, he suggested to Lou that she be allowed to drive the small truck home.

"No way. My equipment stays in my yard. I check it out. You know that."

Marge suggested that they get her a bicycle.

"How do you know she can ride it?" Fred asked.

"Every small-town kid in New England can ride a bike." Which turned out to be correct. When he gave the bike to Emily and said: "Company property; take care of it," she swung her leg over it without a word and went zipping up the street.

Meanwhile he was kept busy hauling dirt from the school excavation to a landfill east of town. This was Lou's biggest job yet, and it went well—so well that they completed it days ahead of schedule by working nine-hour days six days a week, with half an hour off for lunch. Toward the end of the job, Lou said, "We're making a bundle on this."

"Put it in the bank and don't worry about your loan payments for a few months."

"A bundle. It chaps my ass to think what Abbey's been getting away with all these years. Putting his thumb right in the town's eye. Trouble is nobody's thought to buck him until me."

He asked why.

"Nobody in town really set up to do it. Besides, Abbey's in close with the town boards. He *advises* them, then makes his bid. They salute. Everybody's happy except the taxpayers, and they don't know where to take their gripe."

He learned that Abbey (always called that, although the founder was long gone) had been the principal contractor in Lincoln Harbor for more than sixty years; that the company owned a sandpit; that it sold sand and gravel to the town for prices rumored to be higher than those quoted to certain private individuals; that the business was now run by a grandnephew of the original Abbey. This younger man was the brother-in-law of Hugo Westerveld, having married the sister of Hugo's recently departed wife. He learned that Lou's father had worked for Abbey all his life, starting as a laborer and moving up to foreman before retiring to Florida on a tiny pension; finally that Lou himself had worked there before striking out on his own.

"Pop sweated his life away at Abbey and got what? Peanuts. I figured to do better. I hit Pop for a loan on a used truck. Remember what I said about them banks? They wouldn't give me a nickel, and I had to go to my old man, who was barely scraping by. Anyway, I got started doing little jobs Abbey couldn't be bothered with. There was a lot of us one-truckers scuffling for jobs. But most of them drank and screwed around. Sure, I drank and screwed around too. But I did my homework on maintenance. I love machinery. I respect it. I can get three or four more years out of a truck than the next fellow. Pretty soon I was able to peck away at some of the littler jobs Abbey might be interested in. I got me a backhoe. By the time you come along, I was ready to hit him head-on. Like here."

The excavation they were working on overlooked the high school athletic fields. On some days, for unknown reasons, there would be scores of sea gulls walking around there.

"They'll do that," said Lou. "Maybe it's the weather. Maybe it's some kind of bugs hatching out in the grass." They were eating huge bologna sandwiches made by Marge. Lou didn't like crusts. He would take one big chomp into the middle of the sandwich and nibble his way to the edge with surprising daintiness. Then he would walk out to the field and throw the crusts to a cloud of rising gulls. "Don't like to waste."

This from a man who was finicky about leftover food and would throw it away if Marge didn't get there first and make a hash or stew out of what was uneaten. He was a complex and contradictory man, sloppy around the house, obsessively neat with his tools, his garage, and his equipment. He was foul-mouthed but never nasty, rough but surprisingly tender. A struggler, a doer. He didn't complain about things but tried as well as he could to cope with them. A man. No wonder Marge adored Lou. No wonder he was becoming increasingly jealous of Lou.

"Now I can go right at Abbey. This job come out good, part thanks to you, Fred. You deserve a bonus."

"Me?"

"Yep. Two hundred bucks. Get yourself a better-looking pair of work gloves. With the gauntlets, like these I got."

"I—"

"Okay, Fred, don't choke up. You earned it."

How humiliating that he almost did, but how remarkable that Lou noticed it so quickly and brushed it off so easily. What an extraordinary relationship was building. In some ways Lou was a big brother, a father. In others, in the handling of any kind of paperwork, inordinately sensitive about his shortcomings there, he was a little boy. Finally he was an unconquerable sexual rival.

"The biggie, Fred, the big one's coming up. The new water line. I'm gonna bid on that. Nearly half a mile of trench."

"Half a mile?"

"A lot of trench. Anybody could do it, of course, if he had the time. But they put a completion date on. Means that Abbey's the only one in town can meet that date. Likely Abbey suggested it. Anyway, I'm gonna bid."

"What is the date?"

"August twentieth."

"You can't dig half a mile of trench by then."

"Abbey can. Or thinks he can. He's got two shovels."

"And you have one."

"Two. Subcontract one from a fellow in Newfield."

"Won't that cost a lot?"

"Yeah, it'll cut in some. But I figure to still make out okay. I'll just cut Abbey ten percent. Like on this job."

"How do you know what his bid will be?"

"Fred." Lou gave him one of his patented paternal smiles. "Don't bother your head with them questions. I'll make my bid."

36

I T WAS NOW JULY. THE TOWN WAS JAMMED WITH SUM-
mer people, and with them came a flood of work. Lou had won
the water-main contract, as he had predicted, and was busy with
that all day, digging away at one end while a subcontractor with his
own shovel, a man named Bobby Black, worked from the other end.
That left Fred to run the big truck and handle orders, some of them
left in Lou's mailbox, some on his porch (Lou would *have* to get a
telephone). Emily made the garbage run and did innumerable small
chores. She was turning out to be a prodigious worker. What Charlie
had said about her was true: she went all out at whatever she committed herself to.

Parking in town became increasingly difficult. All the little cran-
nies and alleys between stores, behind buildings, had sprouted signs
bearing the names of business people or prominent summer residents:
those places were now reserved, and the police department began to
make a good living ticketing trespassers.

Charlie had two reserved slots in the small lot behind his office,
one for himself, one for clients. His car was always in one, but the
other was often vacant. He asked Charlie one day if he might use it
from time to time, whereupon Charlie reached into his desk and produced a round yellow sticker with the name C. Barker on it. "Put this
on your windshield. Stay all day if you want."

He explained that he was too busy for that, too busy even to do
any work on the house Charlie had sold him.

"We're all busy now," said Charlie, his round face looking positively haggard.

"Any chance I could rent out that house for the rest of the summer?"

"Can't make a summer rental on an unfurnished house."

"Maybe I could get a few things. A couple of beds—except I haven't the time."

Charlie was intent on his pen set. "Lorraine could help. She's very good at those things."

"But—I don't think—"

Charlie reddened and swung around in his swivel chair so that he was facing the window. "Lorraine could do it."

"I don't think she'd want to," he said, "considering . . . "

"I need to talk to you about Lorraine," said Charlie to the window.

"About what?"

"About her. She's—" He swung back. "Not now. I have a buyer due in. Could you come over some night after supper? Tonight? Tomorrow?"

"I'm free every night. But I really don't think—"

"Make it tomorrow, then. About eight-thirty?"

Out in the lot, he pasted the yellow sticker on his windshield, wondering what new folly Lorraine might have committed. Hot thoughts of her fought in him with the certainty that he should not go back to that house. Full of lust, he drove home for a bookkeeping session with Marge, only to discover that he was far too heated to concentrate. Her presence was unnerving. They were sitting next to each other at the kitchen table, and he had an overwhelming urge to touch her, to stroke her arm, so soft and round, her hair, her breasts. Fearful that his hands might fly out of control, he put them in his pockets, only to feel her thigh against his knuckles. He got up.

"Something wrong?"

"You know what," he said, all caution gone. The confession burned his mouth. Why not just hold her, hold her. But he couldn't, he couldn't. A double wanting, a double forbidding. Two of everything. Two eyes, two arms, two breasts. Two people. But only one longing.

"Maybe it would be better if you moved away," she said in a low voice.

"I make you that uncomfortable?"

"No, not that. I don't mind you here. You do good here. You have a good effect on Lou, more than you think. He learns things from you. He . . . well, he's more considerate of me when you're here. I would only ask you to go for your own sake."

Lou came in, and Fred went out. He couldn't stand it in there any longer, couldn't stand seeing them together, Lou's arm around her, the expression on her face. He walked around the house a couple of times to cool off. The kitchen door was open, and he couldn't resist stopping to hear what they said.

". . . needs someone."

"Pestering you?"

"Oh, no, he never does that."

"Time he got into Emily. You sure he ain't already?"

"Pretty sure."

"Well, he better find somebody. Like to blow up if he don't."

How right they were. Supper was a torment. As soon as it was over, he went out again, walked into town and down Elm to the harbor. His boat was in its berth with a dozen other little boats, a hatch of white minnows in black water. He hadn't used it all summer, not since that one trip to the island with Charlie and Lorraine. Why have it? For that matter, why have the island? It had brought him nothing but trouble. Though Charlie was convinced it would be a bonanza someday, he had to balance that off against the fact that it had nearly killed him. It had also been the instrument, through Charlie's relentless hospitality, of his entanglement with Lorraine. Was he going to have to fend her off again tomorrow night? It seemed exquisitely tactless of Charlie to ask him over after what he had been put through in the matter of Hugo and the motel. What was there to discuss about her that he didn't already know?

He walked along the waterfront. It was alive with strollers, the boutiques open, the parking lots jammed. The yacht club was also jammed, and a pounding beat of music overlaid with shrill conversation was coming from it, its lights a dazzle on the dark water.

On the town dock, more strollers. Two big white yachts were tied up to it, and people were staring at them, at yards and yards of mahogany and teak and brass and chrome, at gleaming wheels and binnacles and instrument panels that belonged in jet planes, at after-cockpits the size of verandas and full of chintz-covered wicker furniture. How changed from twenty-five years before, when Burton's dirty little fishing boat had tied up here.

As he stood there, three couples came strolling down to the larger of the two yachts. One madras jacket, two black yachting coats with metal buttons and braided sleeves. Three sets of pearly bare shoulders. Their clothes, their careless stroll, the pitch of their voices, all gave off an aura that recalled Bob Dixon and Walker Virdonette with his tall sexy women. What astonished him was their youth. Yachts like this were the perquisite of aging industrialists or Greek shipowners, not of people who were his age or younger.

When the young gods and goddesses reached the edge of the dock, a captain appeared as if by magic and handed them aboard. There was a deep purring as engines were started. Two crew members in dark jerseys sprang to the dock from bow and stern, undid mooring lines, hauled in fenders. A searchlight of blue-white power was turned on to pick up other boats anchored in the harbor, and a quietly throbbing whale slid from the dockside in a long slow curve and headed down the harbor to the open ocean, bound for Newport, Nantucket, Maine? One dizzying whiff of his old life.

He walked home to a restless night. Thoughts of Lou and Marge lying in bed together not eight feet away kept bolting into his head. He tried to banish them by conjuring up Lorraine, but she was so far below Marge that he failed. Jealousy of Lou, turning to tendrils of hatred, sprouted in him. He began to think of ways he might displace Lou. He would emphasize his gentlemanliness, his tact, his quietness, playing those off against Lou's oafishness. That didn't work, either. Lou was what he was, and she loved him. That being so, how could he stay there if he loved her?

Loved her? Lying in the dark, he faced up to that. He whispered it aloud: "I love her." He had never said those words before, except once when Fran had pried them out of him. He had never felt like this before. What else could it be, that total admiration, that desperate longing to be with her, to touch her, just to look at her? He would have to go. And yet he couldn't. Anywhere else he would be alone; the very word panicked him. Here he had a roof, company . . . her. She fed him, did his laundry, tolerated him—pitied him. He would settle for pity. He would stay.

331

37

HE WONDERED IF HE SHOULD TAKE ALONG A present, some sort of peace offering, to indicate to Lorraine that he held nothing against her and was willing to be a friend. A box of candy and a cake had been misinterpreted. Unable to think of anything else, he arrived empty-handed. Cheerful Charlie, looking anything but, met him at the door. Lorraine, thank goodness, was not to be seen.

"You don't drink," said Charlie, "but I'll have one." He poured himself a Scotch, set it down, picked it up, finally said, "Funny things happen in life."

"They do."

"I mean, you find you don't always know where you stand."

He waited, wondering if that meant peace with Hugo. Or was Hugo still in limbo—or even, perhaps, back in the picture?

"I mean, with other people, how far they will go with you, who your real friends are."

Maybe Hugo was back in the picture.

"You're my friend, Fred."

"I hope so."

"You once said I could call on you."

"You can. Anytime."

Charlie took a long shuddering breath, preparing for the dive into muddy water. "Lorraine . . . she wants to talk to you."

He should have seen it coming. "Not that, Charlie."

"You just said."

"I know, but there are some things you can't do."

"You said. I wouldn't ask, except . . . This is killing me."

"In that case, let's pretend we never had this conversation."

"I can't. I promised Lorraine I'd ask you. I'm asking you."

"Charlie, don't ask."

"Please." His voice was not his at all.

No longer his friend, either, but a desperate stranger speaking. "Where is she?" he asked, knocked hard by that desperation.

"Upstairs, in the room at the back of the hall."

How far could a friendship be stretched? And what would be the consequences if it was stretched too far? He took what might be his last look around Charlie's living room, at all the possessions. He caught a glimpse of the striving, the hope, that had gone into making this Charlie's home, much of it accomplished by Lorraine. He saw it all breaking. He saw Charlie receding, actually getting smaller and smaller as he looked at him. Charlie gone? So soon?

"We shouldn't be talking about this," he said.

"We are talking."

"I'm not sure I can do it."

"You can try."

Could he? Now that he had free access to her—permitted access, *urged* access—where was desire? What she had flaunted, tempted him with, what had started as hints, then grown to a timid but determined and finally explicit overture, had excited him, he could not deny it, even though he realized at the same time that he didn't like her. Nor could he deny that his excitement (along with his dislike) had continued to grow as he had watched her own heat rising. Her willingness to accept any available man, far from repelling him, was turning up the heat. She wanted a man just as he for so many years had wanted a woman, any decent obliging passionate woman. Forget about love. This was lust. He had ached with it long enough in himself to understand and excuse it in her. Right there lay the key to his desire for her. Lust speaks to lust. But with Charlie now coming back from the distant horizon to which he had receded a moment before, expanding to fill the room with an unspoken reproach even as he begged, lust went. He remembered instead that she bordered on being too fat. He remembered how meanly she ran down other people, that he didn't like her at all.

"Don't make it any tougher," said Charlie. "Just go."

He turned and went up the stairs. There, at the back of the hall, was a closed door. He went inside and shut it, picturing Charlie down below, listening to the click of the latch. She had pulled down the shades and drawn the curtains. But this was a long summer evening. There was still considerable light in the sky and far too much filtering into this room, where a greenish glow lit her up all too plainly, lying in one of a pair of twin beds. As before, she had drawn the covers up to her chin with both fists and was looking out over them with scared eyes. He stood by the door, unable to think what to say or do next, cold as a fish.

"Here," she said in a low voice. That one word told it all: over here where I am, in this bed, in me. He took off his clothes and crawled into bed beside her. She put an arm around him and gently nudged him toward her. The cold fish vanished. With an abruptness that astonished him, the sensation of her body stretched alongside his obliterated all hesitancy, all dislike, everything. As if reading his mind, she rolled over on her back in an unfolding gesture that was irresistible.

But the lovemaking went strangely, even allowing for the strangeness of the situation. Just as he had been, she now, apparently, was inhibited by the presence of the husband downstairs. She lay inert, her arms thrown backward, making no detectable response to his efforts. They were a sexual machine with two parts, a moving one and a stationary one, a piston and a cylinder, the piston playing its part but with no pressure building in the cylinder. What was wrong? Words like foreplay came and went, and with them the humbling knowledge that he really knew nothing about the sexual predilections of women. How could he? He had been meaningfully involved with only two in his entire life, and all too briefly and inconclusively with each. Forget the horrors of all those pickups in New York bars. He had been too drunk and too far gone in his own misery to have had the slightest awareness of them as women with needs of their own. Forget Alice the WAC. Again, he had been very drunk, as had she. He had no recollection of how they made love, only a semisober postcoital sense of disgust, which he had failed to conceal from her and for which he was ashamed later. Forget Julia, a sexual cipher. Remember only Fran and Violet. With them there had been an instant recognition of each as a vital wanting partner, therefore no problem of how to proceed. All had gone with a fiery rush. Time had been too short for thinking, feelings had flowed too fast. True, he had never been entirely sober with Fran, often far from it. Even so, he had been made keenly aware of her because her own feelings ran so obvious and so strong. True also that they had never fully consummated their passion; marriage was the price of that, and he had been unwilling to pay it. True again that his earlier experience with Violet had fallen short, that the sealing love act had, in the end, eluded him. As Violet herself might have said, with her shattering upper-class disdain for euphemism, a directness that obliterated vulgarity: "Lad, you have never properly fucked anyone." Now, in the act of doing just that, he was apparently failing. Where were the ardor, the stirrings, the utterances, the paramount shared need for bodies to get ever closer? How, indeed, could he entertain all these thoughts about other women while in the act of making love to this one? Did people, while so engaged, ever think of others? He simply did not know. But in remembering Fran and Violet, what came through was a profound sense of closing in, a shrinkage of the world down to just two, the obliteration of all else. The magic of those distant encounters lay in that total melting together at the expense of the rest of the universe, the mutual striving toward a common goal. No thought of how to get there, just instinct—and that all-consuming need for closeness.

These recollections of a nearly unbearable and forever lost sweetness were so powerful as to cause an interruption of the regular pulses of the piston.

Lorraine immediately whispered: "Don't stop," and he was yanked back to her room and to her body. The green gloom was settling into a more comforting dark, and he stole a glance at her. Her arms were still thrown back of her head in an attitude of careless abandon. Her eyes were shut, her mouth open. She was breathing through it in short breaths, which, as he listened, began to accelerate slightly.

It dawned on him that she was feeling something, that this passivity might be a kind of receptiveness, her way of concentrating on what was happening to her. If all but one of the strings of the body were slackened, if all its attention were focused on that taut one, might not the intensity of that focus become very strong? That seemed to be so. By tiny increments Lorraine began to respond. Her breath came faster. Her belly slowly swelled against his. It seemed to do that of its own accord, for the rest of her continued to lie still, as if under a command to stay so at all costs; moving would break some sort of spell. So, lying there, she proceeded to gather herself. It was not so much movement as an abandonment of lassitude, a tensing, the coiling of a spring. He became seized with a need to tighten that spring, to wind it tighter and tighter. This was becoming fiercely engrossing. He began to wonder how long he could hold off, when the spring suddenly let go, taking him with it.

Two women had invited him into their beds, and he had succeeded—at last—with the second. As he lay beside Lorraine, recovering his breath, his thoughts floating free for a moment, he could look at himself for what he was in this bed: a target of opportunity. But so had he been with Violet. Both, driven by need, had happened to select him.

In that sense both experiences were the same. Therefore, why did that early failure remain so sweet in his memory, while the present success was already beginning to turn sour? Was it time, the overlay of a romantic glow on that distant encounter, that made the difference? Even now he could scarcely believe that. He could still remember the ache when he realized that he would not meet Violet again, an ache that was reflected in her desolate expression the last time he had seen her face.

What, then, was the difference? He supposed any man or woman whose initial sexual encounter had held out the hope of flowering into something more, into a belief that a second encounter would be richer than the first, would have his or her own explanation for that belief. For him, the echo of Violet's attraction was her openness, the frank expression of her passion, her generosity in sharing it, her concern for him. That last in particular; was not reciprocity the key to true sexual loving as contrasted with mere coupling? Violet, in her letter, had mentioned recklessness. She had said that she could not love a man who was not reckless—or so he remembered it. And it came to him—released at last in this other bed—that what she meant was recklessness of the heart, a willingness to open it dangerously and give, rather than recklessness of behavior, although, God knew, her behavior had been reckless too. She had been a wholly uninhibited lover. What a contrast to the inert woman who lay beside him.

But was that comparison fair? What did he know about the mysteries of women's sexuality? Absolutely nothing. Did sheer athleticism confirm stronger feelings or greater commitment? How did he know that Lorraine's passivity did not conceal a more intense response than Violet's wilder behavior? Could not two dedicated lovers play out the slow inward-looking, concentrated buildup of a Lorraine and arrive at a distilled essence of great potency? Way out of his depth now, he fell back on emotional recklessness, which, he supposed, was the ability to give love. Certainly that, the parting with part of oneself for another, was at the core of it. Physicality meant nothing. It was merely a matter of style or taste. But to put the heart at risk—that was recklessness, Violet's kind of recklessness.

Lorraine whispered: "Thank you."

He wondered when it would be tactful to get out of her bed.

"But don't get any wrong ideas."

"About what?"

"About you and me."

"I don't have any ideas except for what we've just been doing."

"Well, you'd better not. Let's keep it that way."

That seemed about as good an exit line as he might hope for, and he was prepared to spring for his clothes, when she said: "It's Charlie I love, not you."

He thought: You choose a peculiar way to express it. He said: "I should hope so."

"It may sound silly, us being where we are, to say I love Charlie. But we wouldn't be where we are if Charlie could . . . well, what you just did."

"I only—"

"I need time. I guess you saw that."

He did. Her remark about Charlie made it all too clear that what she needed in bed was friction. Whatever love she had for Charlie was being expressed in other ways—that is, if she was speaking the truth.

"He doesn't give me time. He doesn't seem to understand."

"Maybe he—"

"I shouldn't say that. He understands all right. It's just that he can't. Now he doesn't. He's quit trying."

He said nothing, itching to get out of this bed.

"Used to be he could a little. Now he doesn't even try. I don't know which is worse. At first I thought that was; it would leave me so hot and bothered. But this year, nothing." That last came out in a smothered wail, overriding her previous whispers, and he wondered if Charlie could have heard it, could have heard anything. What an appalling conversation this was.

He said: "Maybe you don't need to be quite so—"

"I do need," she said hoarsely. "That's the whole point. You see how I am. Do you think I'd be here with you if I didn't? Do you think that for a minute? Because if you do . . . "

He got out of the bed and started to put on his clothes, his back to her, although by this time the room had gotten so dark that it wasn't necessary. But it seemed necessary because he was crawling with all sorts of shameful emotions by this time and already beginning to dread the encounter downstairs.

She said again: "So long as we understand each other."

"I think we do." Dislike had routed all desire, every shred of it.

Then she said: "I'll see you next week."

He buttoned his shirt. "That wasn't the deal."

"The deal was: Charlie wouldn't object if it was you. We didn't discuss how often."

"But he never—"

"We agreed on you. He trusts you. He knows you won't get any wrong ideas. I knew you'd be good for me. From New York and all, your experience, and the way I turn you on."

The experienced New York lover was tying his sneakers.

"So next week, okay?"

He couldn't answer. He closed the door and went downstairs.

First question: Do you stop for a chat, or do you sneak out? Surely not the latter; it would make a sleazy situation even sleazier. He entered the living room. Charlie was sprawled on the sofa. The small table next to him held a bottle and a glass. It was clear that he had had a second drink, probably a third.

"How was it?" said Charlie. "I mean, for Lorraine."

"Okay, I guess," thinking that this came pretty close to the old cliché: "Was it as good for you as it was for me?" Why should lovers, the perfect lovers of his imagination, have to ask such a question? They would know. Violet would have snorted at it. It struck him again how profoundly different his experience with Violet had been from the one just finished. Here Charlie's remark was appropriate, because no emotion had been exchanged, just heat. Was your heat as good as my heat? Yes, thank you.

"You were up there thirty-seven minutes," Charlie said belligerently. "What took you so long?"

"She's a slow starter."

"I didn't mean for any fancy stuff. I meant for you just to cool her off."

"She's cooled off."

"Thirty-seven minutes' worth?"

"That's what it took." He was standing behind a wing chair. "Charlie, I left as soon as I could. I didn't want to stay any longer. She didn't want me to. She doesn't even like me."

"How do you know that?"

"From things she said. She loves you; she told me that. I'm an embarrassment to her."

"Okay, Fred," he said thickly. "I don't know if this was a good idea or not. But thanks for trying."

"She wants me back," he said.

Charlie shot bolt upright. Apparently he hadn't thought beyond one encounter. "Wait a minute. I thought I could trust you. What kind of a prick are you?"

"Ask Lorraine," he said, his own feelings not up to taking abuse for what he still considered a favor done. "It was her idea, not mine. Get your ashes hauled, maybe you want them hauled again."

That remark made Charlie even madder. "Not by you, buddy."

"Up to you," he said. "I go only where I'm invited."

"Turn my wife into your lay?" Charlie slammed down his glass and headed for the stairs.

Walking back to Gott Street, his feelings in total turmoil, he scarcely noticed where he was going. Ordinarily he liked that walk on a summer night. The back streets of the town were narrow, with even narrower sidewalks, dark under the black trees except for an occasional street light that threw a theatrical glow on the picket fences, making them seem even whiter than they did during the day. Those streets were virtually deserted at night, in contrast to the restless din down by the waterfront. Many of the houses were crowded right up against the sidewalk, and as he went by he could almost feel himself inside the living rooms, some with their curtains drawn back to reveal people reading or talking—and that low drone, just a word or two, the only sound in that silent street, fell for a moment on his ear as he passed an open window.

It was those homely sounds and glimpses that made him long most painfully for Marge, for a loving sweet woman who would keep a neat cozy house like one of these for him, spend her days at pleasant domestic chores and her nights in his arms. How had he managed to conduct his life so poorly, to be as far removed from that dream as he was?

Now he had taken another wrong step and lost his best friend, to mistrust certainly and hatred perhaps. If he had had any sense at all, he would have realized that that would happen. The better solution would have been to advise Charlie to seek sex counseling or medical help. Didn't impotent old men with young wives resort to marital aids? There must be something that would work with Lorraine. Friction, he thought again, was what she needed. So let Charlie give her some, all she wanted.

Friction. It had heated him too, but with a coldness at the center that left him feeling profoundly sad and lonely as he walked. Was he fated to fail with all women? Fran had left him feeling worthless and bottomlessly ashamed of himself. Violet had left him feeling—feeling now, that is—that if he had been a little older, a little more experienced, a little more reckless (her word again), he might have prevailed over her dreadful husband. He could have tried harder, but he hadn't. And he remembered, as he turned into Gott Street, that he had not answered her letter.

38

SOMETHING WAS WRONG AS HE ENTERED THE kitchen. Marge was looking teary, and Lou was growling. "Bobby Black's been screwing up on our ditch contract."

"No," said Marge.

"You keep your big mouth out of this." When Lou was angry his voice was constricted, a prelude to shouting. He poked a heavy thumb on a blueprint that was lying on the table. "That, right there, is as far as he's got. Eight hundred feet. Two weeks, he goes eight hundred feet. How are we gonna— God damn it, he'll bust us."

"How far have you gone?" he asked.

"That's what I keep asking him," said Marge.

"And I keep telling her to keep her big mouth out of this," Lou roared. Under that menace she did begin to cry and went into the bedroom, closing the door.

"Putting the blame on. Keeps putting her goddamn nose in."

"Well, did you answer her question?"

"Huh?"

"How far have you dug?"

"Listen, Fred, I'm not gonna—"

This was one of those times to stare Lou down. He did that, saying nothing.

"Bad enough to have to wrastle with this—" Lou slammed a palm on the paper. "Don't have to have no—"

He got up and, under the pretense of examining the blueprint, said: "How much can you expect a shovel to dig in a week?"

"Five hundred feet at least. That's the very least."

"How long has Bobby been at it?"

"That's it. Two weeks already. Should have done more."

"How much more?"

"He didn't work Saturday at all."

"So he should have done another hundred feet?"

"At least. I told you, he's goofing off."

With his point made to somebody who seemed willing to listen, Lou became less explosive. So Fred risked: "I have another question. Are you going to punch me in the mouth if I ask it?"

"Depends on the question."

"It's the same one you wouldn't answer when Marge asked it. How much did you dig in those two weeks?"

"Nine hundred feet."

"So Bobby's a little slower than you. What's the big deal?"

"Because, you dumb turd, at the rate we're going we won't make it. Won't even come close. We'll be busted."

"That's Bobby's fault?"

"Well, he's so fucking slow. I mean, they begin laying pipe August twenty-first. There's five hundred bucks a day penalty if they're held up."

"Maybe they could start laying at the ends that are dug while you finish up in the middle."

"I already asked. I signed, Fred, I signed. The buggers would like to see me busted. They don't want me on that job."

"How long will it take to finish?"

"At the rate we're going? At least two weeks extra, give or take. That's seven thousand, eight thousand bucks I don't have. I'm down the pipe, Fred."

"Get another shovel."

"Costs money I ain't got. Couple of hundred a day."

"That's better than five hundred a day," he said. "We'll rent one."

"What with, Fred? Jesus, you got me in hock up to my neck at the bank already. Like to lose everything I got."

This was put-up-or-shut-up time. "Maybe we can raise a little on what I've got," he said. "We'll rent another shovel."

"Ain't none available. Abbey has them."

"Then we go to Abbey."

"Fred, as usual your brains are in your pants. Abbey would as soon give me a shovel as rent me one."

He continued to study the blueprint. Lou had marked with a red crayon the amount dug at each end. There was an ominously large gap between, and far too little time left to fill it. Lou had obviously made a major miscalculation somewhere. Recognizing that, he had tried to take it out on Bobby Black, then on Marge, and would probably try to do the same with him if he was not careful. He said as quietly as he could: "How did you estimate this job, Lou?"

"Same way as the last two. I undercut Abbey ten percent."

"You didn't make your own estimate?"

"Didn't have to. They done that for me."

"Too bad you didn't, because this time it looks as if Abbey goofed."

"Looks like it."

"So we eat our loss, get a shovel, cross our fingers—"

"Get a shovel? I just told you Abbey has the shovel and I won't go asking the fucker. Anyway, the money—"

"I think I can raise the money. If you won't go to Abbey, I will."

"You? They'll just laugh at you. The first thing they'll ask is what are you going to do with the shovel, and when you say it's for me and the ditch job, they'll bust out laughing. They'll know I blew it, and they'll sit back and wait. Somebody's got to finish that ditch, and it will be Abbey, on his terms. He ain't exactly dumb, you know."

"If he's not dumb, wouldn't he like to pick up some money on an idle shovel while he watches you go down the pipes?"

"Course he would."

"Then we should be able to rent one of his shovels."

"The money . . . the money . . . "

"I'll go to the bank."

"A useless trip, Fred. They own me already."

"I was thinking of raising some on my own. Make an investment in you. Maybe work my way up to junior partner someday."

"You would do that, Fred?"

"If you could stand a dumb turd like me."

"You know I don't mean them things."

"And another thing. Go tell Marge that you didn't mean what you said about her big mouth."

"She knows that, for Christ's sake." But he went.

He remembered the first visit to Hugo Westerveld's office, the time he had stuck his big muddy boots out on Hugo's clean green carpet, then a rough outsider. Now, partly by decree (he had been anointed by Charlie) and partly through complicity (because of the lies he had told on Hugo's behalf in Chief Booker's office), he was there as an old buddy—with an IOU in his pocket.

342

"I need some money and some help," he said.

"Just ask."

"Up to ten thousand dollars, maybe more. I can't be sure of the exact amount."

"What's in your savings account with us?" Hugo asked.

He didn't know. Astonishingly, for one to whom money had meant so much not so very long before, he had been too busy with other things to think about it recently. He knew that he had put in a little over thirty thousand when he opened the account, but he'd drawn down on it pretty heavily when he fixed up the house on Sheep Island. He had also made payments on his purchase agreement, bought a boat, and taken out a mortgage on the Cedar Street house. On the other hand, he had drawn out nothing lately, living on what Lou was paying him, and also getting interest on the balance in his account. He had no idea what he had left.

Hugo pressed a button and spoke into a squawk box on his desk. The answer came back quickly: seventeen thousand and change. "You'd be better off using than borrowing," said Hugo. "We would have to charge you more. You can build up your savings account again when the deal comes through. So what's the deal?"

"It's for Lou Mendoza again. He's losing money on a contract, and he might go under unless he gets some help."

"I'd keep out of that," said Hugo. "It's not a question of might go under. He *will* go under."

"How do you know that?" he asked.

Hugo gave it the full loan officer's treatment. He stared at the ceiling. He took a pair of glasses out of his desk drawer, studied them, and put them back in the drawer. "You're talking about the water-ditching job, right?" He tapped his teeth with a pencil, then said: "Your man's lost. Abbey set him up."

He remembered that Hugo and the current Abbey had married sisters.

"Yes," said Hugo, reading his face. "Joe Abbey. Your pal went to the well once too often," leaning forward and lowering his voice. Did Hugo have one blue-gray suit, he wondered, or three or four identical ones. And was the handkerchief in his breast pocket a real one or was it three white points sticking out crisply and transferable from one suit to another? "Joe's not stupid, you know," Hugo went on. "Underbid him once by ten percent—those things happen. Underbid him twice by exactly ten percent—he starts thinking. And he thinks about who in his organization might be slipping estimates to the competition.

And he comes up with a candidate, Antone Lopes, who is not only Portuguese but a pal of your pal and also helps work on estimates. So he backs Lopes against the wall and puts it to him: either cooperate or we'll break you. It's no contest. Lopes has a good job, he's in hock here for a house he's building, he's got another kid on the way, and he's getting close to being funded on a pension."

"You mean . . . "

"What I mean is that Lopes cracks. He agrees to feed your pal a phony figure, so low that it's sure to kill him. When it comes time to submit bids, Abbey goes in with two envelopes in his pocket. If Mendoza shows up to bid, Abbey submits the one with the phony low figure. If Mendoza doesn't show, he hands in the other envelope. That one has a real estimate in it, a hell of a lot higher than the phony one he cooked up for your pal."

Small-town bankers know a lot about their customers; they have to. Even so, it shocked him to realize that Hugo had been sitting there, watching Lou dig, knowing that he was digging his grave. It went beyond that. Hugo also knew that an old buddy was at risk—the new old buddy who had backed Lou's loan.

"So that's how it is," he said.

"He's a dead duck. Don't touch him."

"But I already have. I signed the note you hold on his house and all his equipment."

"You should never have done that."

"Easy for you to say now."

Hugo looked uncomfortable. If his three-point handkerchief had been real, he might have used it now to wipe his forehead. "I didn't know you then. You were just another customer. I would have advised you differently today."

"Well, you didn't," he said shortly. "Now it seems to me I have to protect that risk by taking this one."

"Don't do it," said Hugo. "You'll just lose more. That guy is dead."

"Not necessarily."

"He is. At five hundred a day penalty, he'll be wiped out forever. Serve him right, too. He shouldn't have tried to steal Abbey's estimates."

He conceded that that had been a mistake.

"And now he's paying for it. I say this to you as a friend, Fred: Stay out. There's no way you're going to bail him out of this one. You'll ruin yourself trying."

If Lou really sank, what would become of Marge? He quickly

pushed that thought aside and braced himself for the test, trying to find the right words. "Remember the motel—"

Hugo winced. Charge ahead anyway.

"That time. You said you owed me one."

"I do, Fred. I'm paying you. I'm advising you as a friend, not a banker. Don't do it."

"That's not paying," he said. "That's advice, and I'm grateful for it. But I want you to do something for me—in return for what I did for you."

Hugo waited.

"I want you to persuade Joe Abbey to rent us one of his shovels. While you're at it, make it both shovels. That's what I need the money for."

"I'm not sure I can do that," said Hugo, not looking at him.

Find an edge. Keep talking. "I thought you two were close."

Still Hugo said nothing. Fred hazarded: "You're not now—since your wife left?"

Hugo brushed that off. "Not that. He doesn't like Sylvia, never has. Sylvia's not the problem. It's Joe himself. I've known him a long time. I know how he feels about Lou Mendoza. He'd like to get rid of him. I just don't think I can go to him on that one."

He remembered what had broken him down when Charlie was begging him to go to bed with Lorraine. He repeated Charlie's line: "I'm asking you."

"Please don't."

He caught Hugo's eye and held it. No argument, just desperate need. Say more? Instinct told him not to, to let that naked plea hang in the room as heavily as Hugo's guilt and fear must have hung over him when Chief Booker burst into the motel room. Hugo obviously felt it too, for he struggled, finally said: "It's asking a lot."

"Two shovels," he said. "At their regular rates. You can make the point that Lou will probably go down anyway and Abbey might as well be picking up some money as he goes."

"A point," said Hugo.

"Also you're doing this for me. For a friend, not for Lou. Make that point too. Tell him you owe me one."

"He already knows that," said Hugo. "I told you, we're close— the reason I hesitated. I know that if I ask him, he'll do it. I just had to think hard about it."

He got up, grabbed Hugo's hand, and left before Hugo could change his mind. If Joe Abbey knew about Hugo and Lorraine, how many others in this town might, he thought as he walked to his truck, parked in one of Charlie's spaces. There was a sealed envelope on the front seat. He opened it and read: "Expect you a week from Monday, 8:30."

Apparently Lorraine had succeeded in changing Charlie's mind. But his? No, he didn't want to go back to that bed and face his friend again. The wrath and mistrust that had consumed Charlie as he had gone charging up the stairs was too painful to be endured a second time. Even though the memory of Lorraine thrust at him, he couldn't. He wouldn't, and stuffed Charlie's note into his pocket.

39

THE FAVOR HE HAD ASKED OF HUGO HAD BEEN done. On Monday, when he went out to the ditch, Abbey's two shovels were there, big green scoops busily chewing up dirt and spitting it to one side. They were already thirty feet apart, going in opposite directions, one toward Bobby Black, the other toward Lou.

He had sealed the deal the previous Friday, meeting Joe Abbey, a thin-mouthed man with a tanned face and hard blue eyes, in Hugo's office and giving him a check for five thousand dollars as the down payment without which Abbey refused to proceed.

"How do I know this is any good?" said Abbey, looking at the check. "It's not certified."

"It's good," said Hugo. "Or was five minutes ago. But we'll certify it for you if you want."

Abbey studied it again. "Ever run the mile?" he asked, looking up.

"Yes."

"Ever run against Cornell?"

"Twice," he said. "Once in my sophomore year and once in my senior year."

"Ever win?"

"Twice."

"Fred Fay," said Abbey, his blue eyes softening a bit. "I ran against you. Yeah—I remember you; we knew all about you."

"You were a runner?" said Hugo.

"At college."

"The Princeton Express," said Joe Abbey. "Was he a runner?" he said to Hugo. "Yes, he was. Won his races by getting so far ahead of everybody that they couldn't catch him. Boy, do I remember you and those huge leads of yours. Not much of a finisher, though."

347

"Very poor at the finish," he said. "No kick at all."

"We knew that. We figured to pull you out of your pace early. That's why they put me in. A rabbit. Just a sophomore. I was a quarter-miler, and I was supposed to draw you ahead of yourself. But you didn't bite. I don't suppose you remember that."

Now he did, a kid sprinting ahead in the first quarter mile. He had kept to his pace, and—Abbey was right—he hadn't bitten. He had let the kid run away, then reeled him in toward the end of the second quarter and not seen him again. That was the race he had won the weekend of his father's death.

Abbey put the check in his wallet. "No need to certify this," he said. "But you may be making a mistake here."

"Maybe."

"I mean, why get yourself mixed up with that guy? He's never going to get anywhere."

"Maybe not, but I owe him one."

They got up. Abbey stuck out his hand. He shook it, noticing that Abbey's hair was getting gray—although Abbey had to be two years younger than he was, only a sophomore when he was a senior.

"Ever run these days?" asked Abbey.

"No, I haven't run in years," remembering that the last time had been in Under Wixton. Good God, not since then?

"Me neither. Too old and fat. No wind."

He would have liked to stay and watch the gap in the trench widen, but he had a long list of jobs backed up for the big truck and was kept busy for the rest of the week. Wherever he went, though, there went with him the image of Lorraine waiting for him in her bed. He wouldn't go, he kept telling himself. There was something sick in being his friend's surrogate penis. He would have to tell Charlie that he wasn't going, but he kept putting it off.

In bed at night he would say to himself: Tomorrow, fumbling for the words he might use, at the same time flooded with a recollection of the tension in her body, of the power that was in him to tighten that spring. It was an angry power, power to dominate, to dictate. He had something he could give that woman, something she desperately wanted. He had the power to lift her out of herself, or to withhold and humiliate.

Why did his mind wander into those angry channels? Why wasn't the power to please a woman a good power, something to bestow, to be generous with, to share? Where was the sense of suddenly discovered strength, of the beauty in sharing, of the need for closeness, that he still remembered so vividly from his one encounter with Violet? None of that was there with Lorraine.

For all the heat, he had kept her at arm's length, although the power was there. If you are powerful, he thought, and if you have an enemy (an enemy?), isn't it natural to want to dominate, to hurt? An ugly thought, that. If he did go back to Lorraine—*if* he did—he would have to be careful not to abuse his power. Her situation was worse than his. It would be all too easy to humiliate her. He wouldn't risk that. He wouldn't go.

He tried instead to think of Violet, remembering again that he had not answered her letter. That was cruel in another way. He got out of bed and went into the living room for one of the yellow pads that were kept there. Lou was snoring in his chair. Now stimulated by the addition of Abbey's two men and by the hope that he might actually make the deadline, he was working until seven or eight o'clock every night and would get home completely exhausted, grab something from the refrigerator, and sometimes fall asleep while eating it. Marge was at the Blue Lobster. Fred found a ballpoint pen and got back into bed. He had taken Violet's letter out of his bureau drawer, wondering if Marge had ever noticed it while putting away his socks, realizing with an odd throb that he wouldn't mind if she did. A letter from another woman, discussing intimacies as explicitly as Violet's had done, might induce her to see him in another light. He propped the pad on his knee.

Dear Violet:

I apologize for being so slow to answer your letter. I will try to do it in the spirit in which you wrote to me, although you must understand that I am not the reckless person you are, and probably never will be.

You were right in some of your suppositions. I did what you expected of young Americans after the war. I got a good job in the advertising business and I married an heiress. But the marriage was a cold one and it didn't last. [No sense in going into Julia's lesbianism; that was Julia's business.] Things began to go wrong after I met another girl, a nicer one. I should have married her, but I couldn't. With your fine English sense of class distinctions, you will understand why when I tell you that she was a working-class girl, whereas I, through my marriage, had jumped up into what you would call county society.

I don't know if your experiences with Robert will help clarify what comes next, but the strains of my marriage, plus the strain of

349

my love affair, added to the strain of trying to hold down a job I couldn't handle. . . . I return to Robert. I don't know why he drank. Why he chased women. I don't know if you ever knew. But in trying to hold my life together, I began drinking heavily, and as a result everything fell apart. I lost my job, my wife, my girl, most of the money I had saved, and I washed up here.

"Here" is a small New England town, actually a summer resort but with a year-round population that supports itself mostly by hewing wood and drawing water for the summer people. I am now a member of the working class myself. I collected garbage when I first came here. I have now worked myself up to driving a larger truck. I no longer drink. I am healthy and work very hard. I don't know if you would find me sufficiently loosened up for your taste, but there has been some loosening. I have a couple of friends here, men I care about much more than the fashionable people I used to see in New York but no longer do. Those types make up the summer colony here, and we laborers never see them at all, except at the back door, so to speak, when we go around to empty what you would call their dustbins. That suits me fine, because I never fitted into that other world and am glad to be out of it. Here I am free to be myself. To that extent I have loosened up—or, to use your word, have become more reckless.

I have not remarried. In fact, there is no woman with whom I am intimately associated right now [how prim; how scathingly Violet would probably mock that statement when she read it, but it was the best he could manage]. There is a woman with whom I would like to be intimately associated, but she has another man and is not about to change. Since the three of us share a house, that is a problem.

I hope you are well. I can't believe what you say about your appearance. Even if it is true, I will continue to see you as you were in 1945, like no woman I have met before or since. [Now for the reckless shot, a surprising one for him to write but one that would surely hit home with her.] Nor can I believe that your fires are out. Fires like yours don't go out, they are merely banked. I wish I could be there to prove that to you.

Fred

P.S. I have been too busy lately to read Jane Austen, but I have spent a lot of time with her since you introduced us. I am grateful to you for that.

* * *

Not a truly reckless letter, all things considered, but far better than he would have been capable of in the past. And a tribute to Violet herself, he realized, as he finished it. She had drawn that last part out of him. He could never have imagined himself writing anything like that to another woman. But there never had been another woman to whom he might have sent such a letter—not one.

40

TWO DAYS LATER, EMILY ROLLED UP IN THE SMALL truck just as he was backing the large one into its place next to the shed. The tall weeds of August were rank back there. Somebody should cut them, but there wasn't time for such frills; everyone was working flat out. Marge stuck her head out the back door. "You both look so hot. Come in and have a glass of iced tea. I just made some fresh for Lou. I'll take it down to him at the ditch when I go to the Blue Lobster."

It was dreadfully hot. He felt grimy all over, and Emily was no vision of feminine daintiness. Her face was streaked and dusty. She went into the bathroom to freshen up.

"How are we doing?" Marge asked.

"I don't know," he said. "It's too soon to tell. All I can say is that Abbey's men are giving a fair day's work. If Lou can hold up at the rate he's going, maybe—"

"I mean, how are we doing with Emily?"

"Terrific. We couldn't get along without her."

"I mean, how are *you* doing with Emily?"

He blushed. "Nothing doing with Emily."

She studied him carefully before saying: "That surprises me. I could have sworn . . . That is, I was beginning to get the idea you were . . . with somebody." She took a long sip of iced tea. "A woman senses things, you know."

"In this case," he said hastily, "you sense wrong."

"In that case," she said, "I apologize." But when Emily came out of the bathroom, she subjected her to the kind of quizzical scrutiny that made it plain that she thought his denial had been too quick and too blunt. Okay, let her think that; better than giving her any reason to think about Lorraine.

Emily had wet her hair in front while washing, and a dark streak was plastered back to the knot at the rear, even tighter than usual. Again he was struck by her resemblance to Violet, except that Emily now looked a good deal healthier than Violet had. Her face was tanned from being out in the sun all day, and she had a new energy about her that tautened her whole body. Alongside her, Marge seemed like a sleek lazy cat.

"I'll leave you two to talk," said Marge. "I have to get this iced tea over to Lou." She dropped several ice cubes into a large-topped thermos jar and filled it with tea.

"You like her?" said Emily after the screen door slammed.

"Very much."

"Love her?"

The bluntness! The way these women poked and pried. "Not much point in that," he said. "She's with Lou." Then, to get on safer ground, he asked her how she felt about her job.

"Okay. Pretty okay. The trouble is I have no time to read or study."

He pointed out that she had had all the time in the world to do both in the library and had done nothing but mope and drink.

"Because that's such a dead place. There's nothing to read there."

"Nothing?"

"Nothing to interest me. Nothing but junk and old drudgy stuff. I wasn't allowed to buy books, you know. And when they decided to do something really important, they'd order one book by Grace Metalious or somebody like that." The recollection of the library and her suffocation there brought an angry frown. Her thin lips tightened.

"What do you read?" he asked.

"Modern stuff. Modern women writers. Virginia Woolf. The stuff I was reading when I got thrown out of Vassar."

She crashed some ice into her glass. "You should read modern writers. You might learn something."

"I think I'll stick with my regular stuff," he said.

"Like what?"

"Well . . . like Jane Austen. She's a woman writer."

"A woman with blinders. Nice girl uses feminine wiles to catch Mr. Right. Same mush every time."

"Not exactly the same."

"You know what I mean. Why does a girl have to use wiles? Why

353

does she have to be a second-class citizen? Why are men so gross, so stupid?"

"Is that what you get out of Jane Austen?"

"What do *you* get? Jane Austen doesn't even *know* how stupid her men are, and how nasty and tricky and spineless those women are." Off she went, shooting sparks again. Despite her healthy tan and vigor, she was the same tied-up infuriated girl as before. Was there any point in suggesting that Jane Austen's genius lay in playing up the stupidity and deviousness of her characters? He decided not. Lou came clumping in and went right to the sink for a glass of water.

"Didn't Marge bring you iced tea?" he asked.

"Must've missed her. I'm pooped. Too hot to work anymore."

Emily drained her glass, got up, and left.

"Getting in?" asked Lou, tossing his head in the direction of the departing Emily.

"No," he said hotly. "You ask me, Marge asks me. The answer is I'm not getting in and don't expect to."

"Too bad. She's one warm ticket, according to Davey."

Still fuming: "If she's such a warm ticket, why did Davey leave her?"

"Because she wanted romance. Today they got something called commitment. She wanted that. All Davey wanted was tail." He downed another glass of water. "I dug a hundred and ten feet today." He got out his red crayon and marked the progress. "Getting narrower. Might just make it."

They almost did. The deadline fell on a Friday, and by four o'clock that afternoon Lou had connected up with one of Abbey's men, who then departed, as did the other Abbey man. Lou moved in to replace him and began the last furious drive toward Bobby Black, who at five quit also. Lou was enraged. "We've got a hundred and fifty feet to go," he screamed at Bobby Black.

"Quitting time," said Bobby.

"God damn it—"

"Going fishing tonight. Tide's right."

"Fuck the tide. Fuck you." But Bobby was loading his shovel for departure and ignored him.

Lou whirled around. "Fred, you busy tonight? We'll work under lights. Use the truck headlights." They drove home, Lou slumped in the cab, obviously worn out. But after supper he was ready to go again. They drove back to the ditch. He watched Lou climb into the cab of the shovel and start it up. All alone now. One big mouthful of raw dirt after another. He wondered how Lou had stood it all these weeks, the vibration of the machine, the crashing and grinding. Most men wore earmuffs; Lou did not, which was one reason, he supposed, that Lou seemed to shout so loudly when he came home after a day on the shovel.

He went downtown and bought coffee, handed a cup to Lou, who kept on digging. It got dark. He turned on the truck lights and aimed them as well as he could into the ditch. As the evening settled down, the smell of raw earth grew stronger, an occasional spark flew up as the teeth of the hoe hit a rock. At ten it came up against a big boulder.

"Get the light down in here, God damn it."

He did his best, but without running the truck itself into the ditch he couldn't depress the lights enough for Lou to see what he was doing. Lou shut off the engine and climbed down, streaked with sweat.

"Only sixty feet to go, and that one fucking rock stops me."

"You can dig it up tomorrow," he said.

"We missed," on a whistle of exhausted breath.

On Saturday Lou went back to work, pried the rock up, and finished the ditch. On Monday it was inspected and approved, and a crew of strangers, who had previously set down large sections of blue plastic pipe along the side of the road, began lowering them into the ditch and fitting them together. Fred was on hand when the inspector gave his okay, and he asked for a receipt.

"No need for that," said the inspector.

But Lou's stories about town boards and their close relationship with Abbey, and his own growing perception of the way tight control of town affairs operated to the detriment of people like Lou, prodded him to say: "Just for our records, I'd like a release."

"We don't have any forms for that."

"We don't need a form, just something to show when we finished and that you approved the job," he said, aware of how increasingly easy it was becoming to stand up to others when he knew what had to be done, what he really wanted. "Here." He got out his job pad. "I'll write one myself." He wrote: "Town water ditch, completed August 21, inspected and approved August 23." "We finished this job on Saturday. That's one day late. I want to be sure the town knows that and doesn't stick us for another day."

"It's not my job to sign things like this," said the inspector, a short stout man, climbing out of the ditch.

He stood over the inspector, shoving his big red beard down into his face. "You inspected this job. It's okay?"

"It's okay."

"You didn't see anybody shoveling here today?"

"No."

"So sign this. All it says is what you just said." The inspector signed, got in his car, and drove away.

Lou had already gone. He was alone with the trench, in a way his trench, for it would not have been dug except for what he had done: the money, the extra shovels, persuading Hugo. He hadn't dug one bucketful of dirt himself, and yet, as he sighted along it until it disappeared around a bend in the road, it was his trench. His, in a way that the people whizzing by in cars, the men laying down the pipe, would never know or understand. He had done something himself. He had become more like Lou with this new capacity to face a tough problem and do whatever had to be done to solve it. He felt immensely proud, immensely strong, realizing that there were more ways than one of being a man. Lou couldn't have done what he had done. Lou had his strengths, he had his.

The feeling of elation persisted as he drove back to town. Walking into the post office, he felt very much at home. This was his town now. He was a part of it, he had made a contribution to it. He picked up his mail, nothing but junk and a couple of copies of *Time* magazine. He was standing in the street, sorting it out, when he noticed a young woman coming his way. She looked remarkably like Fran, and the resemblance shook him, reminding him of those terrible old days when he had wandered the streets of New York, seeing her everywhere he looked. This woman was about Fran's size. She was wearing white slacks and a blue-and-white-striped sailor's jersey. She was sauntering along, carrying a small paper shopping bag. Except for her hair, which seemed shorter and fluffier than he remembered, the resemblance to Fran was uncanny.

She came closer. By God, it *was* Fran.

He stood in the street, waiting for her. She walked up to him, glanced carelessly at the man staring so intently at her, and went right by.

Not Fran? It had to be, although this woman seemed more elegant, more casual and sophisticated, as she strolled. He had never seen Fran stroll. She had always been either part of the New York rush or else clinging to him.

"Fran?" he said.

She turned around, looked at him uncertainly.

"Fran?" he said again.

She came up to him. "Fred?" The back of her hand went to her mouth as she peered up into his face. "Is that you, Fred? Your beard. It covers you all up."

"It's me," he said.

"But you're so— What are you doing here?"

"I live here."

"Fred . . . ?" Such a look of confusion. Her hand had left her mouth and was clutching her paper bag to her chest. Meanwhile a rush of tenderness and old yearning came pouring in. The gift-shop image of her—huge eyes, shrinking mouth and chin, no body at all—vanished, and the real one clicked back into place. Fran herself, with one slightly crooked front tooth, but with shorter fluffier hair. "But . . . Your voice. I recognized it. But you . . . You live here all the time? What do you do?"

"I drive a truck."

The paper bag was still being crushed. She continued to examine him as if there were a strange and possibly dangerous animal lurking behind his beard. Apparently deciding there wasn't, she said primly: "You look well, Fred."

"So do you." She looked fantastic, standing there in the sunny street, one foot turned at almost a hundred and eighty degrees from the other; he remembered that. "What are *you* doing here?" he asked.

"I came on a boat. The Vogels brought me. You remember Ebby and Mindy. I came with them on a yacht. Ebby has a yacht now."

"Where are they?" Of all the people he hoped never to see again, Ebby and Mindy had to be near the top of the list.

"They're playing golf. I was doing some shopping. There are no needles and thread on the yacht. I was just going back there now."

He said: "Do you have to go straight back? I mean, maybe we could have a cup of coffee. It's been . . . "

"I would like that, Fred."

He steered her into The Nook. "Maybe you'd like a soda or a sundae."

"I would like iced tea. Too much ice cream makes me too fat."

"You're not fat, Fran." It burst out of him. "My God, you look absolutely gorgeous." She did, she did. That sweet face, come back to life. That air of propriety. So becoming. She still had it. She had always had it, except when—

She repeated: "You look well, Fred. But you look different. You look . . . wider."

"Maybe I am a little wider. I work out of doors a lot."

357

"You look healthy. That last time—"

"I *am* healthy. I don't drink anymore."

"At all?"

"Not at all."

She considered that, probably remembering, as he did, all his protestations of the past, and changed the subject. "To suddenly meet you in the street. It was so sudden. I never expected—I didn't think I would ever see you again."

"I wrote you a letter."

"I never got a letter."

"It came back. I sent it to the Advertising Council. I guess you'd left there."

"I did leave. What did your letter say?"

He tried to recall it. That letter, so carefully written, was now a blank. "It just said I was here. I was wondering how you were and what you were doing. I sort of hoped you'd answer. I didn't really expect you to, but . . . well, if you knew where I was, you might have."

She thought that one over too. He could see her sitting somewhere, reading the letter, trying to decide if he was worth another round of rejection, another wound, eventually crumpling it and throwing it away, for she now said: "I'm not sure. I was very unhappy after you. I thought my life was coming to an end." That cliché, so readily used in other contexts, so instantly disposable, now landed with the force of an avenging truth. His own grief, his shame, his loss—always his. He had never tried to imagine hers. But here it was, suddenly cracking him, delivered by a sorrowful face and brimming eyes.

"I loved you, Fred."

"Fran, I—"

"You never loved me. You were always trying to get away, to run home. It made me so tense. You never seemed to notice."

"I was—" What was he? He couldn't finish.

"That last time. I wanted to take care of you so that you would be grateful and love me. But you didn't."

That awful time.

"You just got drunk again."

He felt himself shriveling. He watched her take the spoon out of her iced tea, then the straw, and carefully line them up on the table, watched her wipe her eye.

"So that's over with. There's no point in crying over water that's over the dam. Mindy said for me to put you out of my life."

"You told Mindy about me?"

"Mindy is my closest friend. She said you were . . . not a good person."

"No good. Is that what she said?"

"Sort of, yes."

"What does she know about me? We only met once." Hot against Mindy but knowing she was right.

"From Ebby. Ebby thinks you are not a good person. I depend on Ebby. Ebby has been very good to me. Ebby is a good person."

To be weighed in the scales against Ebby and to have the scales fall so thunderously Ebby's way was excruciating—but, again, irrefutable.

Fran adjusted the spoon and the straw crossways to the table as she said: "Did you have anybody after me?"

"Nobody to speak of."

"Do you live alone now?"

"I live with a married couple. That is, they're not married, but they're a couple. I board there." A good safe word, board, and time for him to change the subject. "What does Ebby do for you?" he asked.

"Ebby does everything. Ebby and Mindy. They gave me my first chance to do a party." She went on to explain that her job at the Advertising Council had taught her enough about catering for Mindy to risk asking her to handle a cocktail party at her home. She had done so well that she was asked again, this time for a larger reception. Again a success. Friends of Mindy's had inquired about her, and she had been given other jobs. Soon she was so busy that she decided to quit the Advertising Council and become a full-time caterer.

"They saw how hard it was, doing things in other people's kitchens, running back and forth. Even Mindy's kitchen. Mindy has a beautiful kitchen, but it is too small for a hundred people. I would make some things at home, ahead. But Papa . . . And his kitchen was *so* small. Ebby said I should have a building, so he bought me one."

"You?"

"My corporation. Fran's Favorites. I am a corporation. Ebby incorporated me."

"You run a business, in your own building?"

"On Ninety-fourth Street. Ebby is so smart. His real estate people. They found it. He explained that uptown was much cheaper. And a kitchen. A professional kitchen that I designed myself. It cost fifty thousand dollars."

The kitchen, she explained, plus preparation space, occupied the entire second floor of a brownstone house. The first floor was for deliveries and storage and a shop. Fran lived on the third floor with a woman named Ginger Cracow. The fourth and fifth floors were occupied by eight young women who worked for Fran, either in the kitchen or as waitresses.

"Ginger finds them. Ginger is a dancer. Was a dancer. She knows all the young actresses and dancers who are trying to find work in New York and a place to live and a job. Ginger finds beautiful girls. Beautiful, with beautiful figures. I am so proud of my girls."

The girls, it seemed, had to shape up. No drinking, no drugs, no men in the workplace.

"There was marijuana at first. Ginger warned them. Two didn't listen to Ginger, and they had to go. Another time a man slept over, and that girl had to go. Now they know. Being a Fran's Favorite is getting to be known in New York, an advantage. It helps them find jobs. Annette Farnhorst, the rock and roll star, was a Fran's Favorite. A man at one of the parties where Annette was a waitress asked if she would like to try out as a singer. Look where Annette is now. She visited us last month and signed albums. We have twenty-five girls waiting to become Fran's Favorites and live with me. Some of the ones we have even refuse small parts, the little TV spots. They're afraid they will lose their place with me. A big job, a real part—that would be different. And some get married. When they do, we give them a beautiful wedding. Ginger does all that. She is my personnel director."

All this was coming at him with bewildering speed. Fran, running a business, hiring waitresses, owning a building? "Where did you meet Ginger?" he asked.

"Ginger was a waitress at the Advertising Council. Ginger was very reliable. She worked hard."

Still floundering: "Ebby gave you a building, and a kitchen?"

"Not gave. Bought. I am paying Ebby back."

"How much did the building cost?"

"The building cost eighty thousand dollars."

Eighty plus fifty? That would take her the rest of her life.

"No, Fred. I paid off twenty thousand the first year. This year I expect to pay back forty thousand."

"You can do that catering parties?" This was incredible.

"Except that I also have to pay for a truck. Ebby is so smart. He had his designers fix up one of his beer trucks with racks and shelves for our food—our cold food, our hot food. Boxes for our china and silverware. Now we can prepare a whole party right in our kitchen and deliver it in one truck."

This recital of her triumphs had Fran sitting straight up and breathing fast.

"Mindy was wonderful too," she said. "Mindy has all her clothes designed by Pauline Trigère, and she had Pauline Trigère design the uniforms for my girls. They are beautiful uniforms. Lavender, but just a bit darker than regular lavender. You know, to set off the white aprons better. And with pale-green trim. They make my beautiful girls look even more beautiful. And the guests sometimes try to date them."

"What do you do about that?"

She came back to earth. "That is hard, Fred, because most of the parties I cater have men from your background. I mean, men like you. Married. With social positions. Mindy says those men will flirt but they won't leave their wives. Don't take this personally, but a girl has to be more careful with her heart than I was. Mindy says the same thing."

"What do you know about Mindy's heart?" he asked.

"I know a great deal about Mindy's heart."

"Do you know that she was in love with another man when she met Ebby?"

"Yes."

"Do you know who he was?"

"Yes. He was your boss. And he was married—just like you. And he made Mindy very unhappy."

"Just like you."

"Yes, Fred. Just like me. But I have tried to get over you, and I am succeeding." She drew a long breath, folded the straw into little zigzags, and put it in her glass. "I think I should go back to the yacht now. They will be finished playing golf."

"Does Mindy play golf?"

"No. Mindy stays on the yacht. She is expecting another baby. Only Ebby and Corky play golf, with two friends here."

"Corky?"

"You remember Corky. He used to work for you. Now he works for Ebby."

"Corky Chalmers?"

"Corky is the eastern advertising director of Vogel Brewing. Corky is a wonderful person."

Corky Chalmers? "He never shed that awful name?"

"What name, Fred?"

"Corky. That's no name for a big-shot advertising director."

"Oh, no, Fred. Corky is known everywhere. His name is . . . well, in advertising, Corky is a famous name."

His head swimming, he reflected that Corky *was* bright, and perhaps a name wasn't all that important. Fran wiped her mouth on a paper napkin and prepared to get up. This meeting had gone careening by, catastrophically too.

"When are you leaving?" he asked.

"Tonight. We're going to Marblehead and then to Maine. Ebby takes people out in his yacht. Beer people."

"Is there any chance you may come back here?"

"We will come back. Sometime next week."

"Could you stand to see me again?" he asked desperately.

She gave it some thought. "I could do that. When we come back I could phone you."

"I have no phone," he said. "We could meet on the bench outside here. In front of the post office. I will be there every morning between ten and ten-thirty."

"Well, perhaps. You know, Fred, I should never have given you those first kisses. Father Ramirez was right."

"You're not kissing anybody now?"

"Just a few. Just a few with Corky."

"You kiss *Corky?*"

"I am engaged to Corky. When you are engaged, you can kiss."

41

WALKING BACK TO GOTT STREET, HE FELT NUMB and was not prepared to face the three of them—for Emily had stayed on. They all looked revoltingly cheerful.

"Where you been, Fred? Been waiting for you."

"Oh, just . . . "

Lou was in one of his expansive moods, a huge barrel of a man in an undershirt. "We ain't dead after all. Figure we should celebrate."

"Okay." Too weary even to pay attention.

"Out a few bucks. But thanks to you, we're still kicking. Time for a party. Fred, are you listening?"

He really wasn't.

"Putting that dirt back in that I took out, I'll make up some of what we lost. Take my time. One shovel. No deadline. Hey, boy!"

That was right; the ditch would have to be filled when the pipe was all in place.

"Figure to make it a reunion. Have another picnic. Like last time at your island. Just the four of us. Like before. I'll do bluefish."

"Maybe five?" said Emily.

"How's that?"

"I'd like to bring a friend."

"Figured Fred would be your friend," said Lou.

"This is a new friend. You don't know him."

"Of course," said Marge quickly. "Bring him."

"Where'd you run across him?" asked Lou.

"At the dump. He's a bird-watcher. Rare birds go to the dump."

"Sure do," said Lou.

*   *   *

Emily brought her friend, a slender dark neat man with a small neat beard and quick eyes. His name was Clifford Goodsell, and he had nothing to say for himself at all.

They went in the *Stinger*. Beers all round, jammed in a tub of crushed ice, except that there were some Cokes for Emily and for Clifford, who didn't drink beer. Emily didn't need beer. She was in soaring spirits. Her hair, instead of being tied tight with rubber bands, was held much more loosely by a large plastic barrette. There was more hair around her face now, and she looked remarkably less aggressive.

A deep fatigue flooded him. He drank a beer, felt nothing, opened another. Looking at the can, he noticed that it was Western Gold, the first he had tasted since that calamitous day of the sales kickoff, when he had made the mistake of putting it down on top of several shots of bourbon and promptly lost it all. He put the second beer aside. When they arrived at Sheep Island, he discovered that he didn't want to get out of the boat. But Lou shoved the tub of drinks at him. "Move your ass, buddy—we got work to do." He carried it ashore.

There followed the rituals of the fireplace and the fish. Emily and Clifford went off to gather firewood.

"Brung an extra plate and stuff for the new boyfriend, remembering you had only four."

"They're probably pretty dusty," said Marge. "I'll go up with you and help wipe them off."

He had forgotten the key to his house.

"God damn it, Fred. Last thing I said was the key."

"I guess we could break in."

"No need." Smugly: "I kept the dupe on my key chain. Just in case." He handed it over.

Going up to the house, through those familiar bushes, the path never quite straight but winding through them, they came to his door and to the driftwood bench alongside.

"What's the matter?" said Marge.

"I don't know. A little low."

"You shouldn't be low. This is a celebration. Don't think I don't know what you did. Don't think Lou doesn't know. He'll pay you back."

"Not the money."

"Look what you've done for Emily."

He said nothing.

"If it's me . . . "

364

"Not you." It could have been but no longer was. He sat down on the bench.

"I'll get the plates," she said, unlocking the door and going inside.

He sat looking at the water. Again, a perfect, golden, late-afternoon, late-summer day, a repeat of the one a year ago, but how different. Then there had been a sense of starting, the beginnings of reaching out, of closeness, of all those new sensations that had caught at him so hard. He had been aware of hope.

Marge brought out four large and four small plates. She went back for four cups, set them in the grass and sat down next to him. "I can't help it," she said. "I love Lou."

"Not you," he repeated.

"You look so sad. Is it coming back here? This is where we found you, right there, up against the house. You know, you never—"

"Never what?"

"You never really explained about that, why you—" She put a hand on his knee. "I don't know anything about you at all."

He felt that humiliating crumbling beginning to start in him. It always began with his chin. He raised his hand to steady it.

"So what's wrong?"

"I met a friend today," he said, and proceeded to explain what he could about Fran, discovering, as he talked, how much more deeply rooted she had been than he had ever realized and acknowledging that he had been incapable of even recognizing during his long and utterly selfish and, finally, bottomlessly shameful treatment of her what kind of person she was and how she spoke—had tried to speak—to some part of him that she sensed existed but that he had no experience of, was incapable of facing because he did not know it was there. All those daydreams about her, giving her that strange etherealized face with no body at all—clearly her body was too painful even to etherealize—were becoming wrenchingly plain. He had turned her into just a face, an unreal one. That way, the deeper feelings could be sodded over so securely that he would never know, never have to know, quite how he had been touched by her and what he had lost. Keep one part of yourself from the rest of yourself, whatever the cost.

That enormous revelation, foaming up in him, made it almost impossible for him to talk, because how could he explain such wide things, which, as they rose in him, grew wider. So wide that he gave up. "She's gone," he said. "She told me today that she's going to marry somebody else."

"She loved you?" said Marge.

"Oh, yes, I think so. She said she did."

"And you?"

"I just blew it. I'm finding that out now."

"Yoo hoo." A blast from the beach. "What's cooking up there?"

"You know how he is," said Marge. "We'd better get back."

The fish returned a little something, a memory on his tongue of that previous night. After supper they settled down again around the fire. Marge with her head in Lou's lap, as before, and, astonishingly, Emily, prickly Emily, crowded close to Cliff, with an arm around his shoulder. The fire had its mesmerizing effect as all gazed into it, even for him, the loner, the end man, sitting one space away from Cliff, with the empty beach beyond. He looked across at Lou and Marge, so comfortably nestled, wondering idly what their secret life together was like, wondering how long Marge would be content to be a live-in lover and not a wife, if Lou might tire of Marge and discard her, if he had any thoughts of marrying her, if he had ever suggested it—and remembered how Fran had begged him.

Cliff spoke for the first time. He had a measured thoughtful voice, or was it just the dream quality of the picnic fire?

"You lived out here last summer?"

"Yes, I did."

"Ever hear any birds at night?"

"Gulls. I heard gulls during the day."

"No squeaks or twitterings at night?"

He remembered that he had, those faint sounds somewhere in the dark sky, how he had actually gone outside to look but had seen nothing.

"I thought I did," he said. "But after a while they stopped. I thought it was just my imagination."

"That could be petrels," said Cliff. "You hear that, Emily? The reason you didn't hear them later was because they'd gone. They raise their young in burrows they make in the turf. When the young are able to fly, they leave and don't come back until the next year."

"Where do they go?" he asked.

"They go to sea. They live out there."

Emily dusted some sand from Cliff's back. "He's a scientist," she explained. "An expert on sea birds."

"If there are petrels here," said Cliff, "that would be very interesting, very rare. They aren't known this far south."

"You have to go all the way to Maine," said Emily. "To Canada."

Cliff, he learned, had done that and planned to do more of it. He had grants, several of them, from conservation organizations, from Harvard, from the state of Maine, from the Hinchfield Foundation, to study nesting-bird populations on sea islands. He asked if there would be any objection to his studying this island.

"Go ahead."

"How do you get back and forth?" asked Cliff.

"I have a dory. But it's a small one."

"He's been all up and down the coast in small boats," said Emily.

"I would want to stay a bit, make a thorough survey," said Cliff.

"In that case," he said, "use my house. But I must warn you, there's no mattress."

"We'd use sleeping bags," said Emily.

We? They all looked at her.

"His grant applications call for an assistant. He's asked me to be his assistant."

"Starting when?" said Lou.

"Right away."

Lou heaved himself up, giving poor Marge quite a jounce. "How about the little truck? You going to leave us shorthanded in the middle of summer? No notice?"

"He only asked me yesterday."

"Why does he need an assistant? In his sleeping bag I can see. But looking at birds?"

"Lou," said Marge.

"I know. My tongue. But"—he pointed a thick finger—"Emily, we need you on that truck. Fred, you got her. You tell her."

"I'm not sure I can," he said. "She's her own boss."

Emily was getting excited. She got to her feet and pointed a finger back at Lou. "I won't be pushed around by people like you."

Lou sat down again. "Don't mean it, don't," he mumbled. "I don't care what you do off the job. It's the job, the truck." Through this exchange Cliff had said nothing, just stared intently into the fire.

"Maybe we'd better start cleaning up," said Marge, and the second picnic ended.

He took his dishes back to his house, this time accompanied by Emily.

"You're not so bad," she said. "You're just too stiff."

"Not reckless enough?" Indeed, with great puffs of heat erupting wherever he looked, he felt the very nadir of recklessness.

"You never once even tried to lay a finger on me. I thought you'd try to collect a reward for what you did."

He put the dishes on the shelf.

"You could have. I could have liked you—maybe. Not at first. You were a total wimp. But you did get me out of the library. You did that for me. And into the truck. I could see that you were nice and that you took your work seriously."

As he stood in his almost black kitchen, listening to yet another woman—another woman attached to another man—tell him what a nice fellow he was, his already falling spirits took another plunge.

"But I'm glad you didn't. You'll really let us stay out here?"

"Just try to keep it clean." He ushered her out the door and into the summer sea night. He clicked the padlock.

"I'm not a champion for neatness. Of course you know that. But Cliff's a neatness freak."

"You'll have to fix the generator, or else haul water."

"Cliff can fix anything."

His turn. "You like him?"

"More."

"Are you sure there are any of those birds here?"

"I don't know. If there are, Cliff will find them. He'll look for burrows."

The return trip was quiet. Lou stood sullenly at the wheel. Marge, as always when there was nothing to say, said nothing. His new tenants sat in the stern, Emily with her arm about Cliff and her head on his shoulder. He sat by himself on the floor of the cockpit, his legs stretched out, his hands behind his head to soften the throb of the engine in the cockpit coaming, staring up at the stars, falling steadily deeper into loneliness. He was roused only when Lou said, "We'll get Tony Lopes."

That would be a disaster, he thought. Lopes was the man working for Abbey who had agreed to bankrupt Lou with a false bid.

"He can drive the little truck. He knows estimating."

"How can you trust him? He tried to—"

"I know. But I sort of brung that on him."

"Will he leave Abbey?"

"Ain't got the option. Abbey fired him. Fred, Tony Lopes and me are closer than he can ever get with Abbey. Sure I can trust him. And he needs the job, he really needs it."

They said good night to Emily and Cliff, who walked off down Harbor Road together. He wondered where Cliff was staying in that tattered mansion, whether the inside matched the outside, and what effect it would have on Cliff's ardor. He wondered if Emily's mother would object, as she did to everything else that Emily did. He squeezed himself into the truck beside Marge. This was the truck he had been driving himself now for several months and had learned to handle as easily as one of his own arms. Still, he was impressed by Lou's silky touch with the ponderous vehicle. Lou was simply a marvel with any kind of machine.

42

OR THE REST OF THE WEEK HE DROVE HIMSELF, trying to recapture the exhaustion that had put him into a stupor of sleep every night in the first months after his rescue. He failed. A real, and far more troubling, Fran now haunted him, and an insane jealousy of Corky Chalmers. He remembered Corky's mouth, a determined straight line, not a mouth for kissing. And Fran's: how could she fit her delicious lips against such a mouth?

Did they share a cabin on the yacht? He couldn't bear even to think of that. And yet he did, kept thinking of it, until it seemed to him that he would be unable to face her when she showed up again—if she did. If she was really engaged to Corky, why would she? But she had said she might. And he had promised to be there in case she did. He would have to go.

And what would he do then? Take her for another glass of iced tea at The Nook? Half an hour of agony and then walk her back to the yacht—and maybe run into Corky, or Ebby, or Mindy? He decided that the only place to take her was to his island. There they could spend several hours together. He could show her where he had lived during that hopeful and disastrous summer, even tell her a little about himself, for he was just beginning to realize that she hadn't asked, and he hadn't volunteered, anything about himself at all. She knew he was single, and sober; nothing else.

Sunday he spent getting the dory ready. He bailed it out, put in oars and oarlocks, tested the motor, put in a bailing can and an extra can of gasoline, and finally stowed two orange life preservers under the rear seat—all the things Charlie had taught him, which, forgotten, had led to disaster.

That night he told Lou that he would be taking off every morning for about half an hour the next week, that if he was needed he could be found on the bench in front of the post office.

"Watching the girls go by, huh? Taking my advice at last."

"Not exactly."

"Best place for it. But a whole week, Fred?"

"I'm not sure when she's coming. It's a particular girl—off a yacht." Then, viciously: "Why don't you get a telephone?" The slightest thing annoyed him now. The only emotion that seemed to stir in him was annoyance—that and apprehension. The two went together.

On Monday he was on the bench. He stayed until a quarter to eleven just to make sure. She didn't come.

That afternoon he went around to Joe Abbey's office. He had calculated that two of Abbey's shovels at two hundred dollars a day apiece for two weeks came to only four thousand dollars; Abbey owed him a thousand.

There was a group photo of the Cornell track team on the wall of Abbey's office.

"Beat your man in my junior year. Quarter mile, that was my proper distance. Name of Killian. Do you remember him?"

"No. I had graduated by that time."

"Didn't run my senior year. Had to leave college and come to work here." He explained that his great-uncle was ailing, that his brother had joined the army, and that he had got a deferment to run the company.

"Didn't run it. I worked as a laborer. Business was awful, had been ever since the bank failure. This town was dead. Uncle Chester couldn't meet a payroll, and I worked for nothing until we got an army contract for constructing the shore defense that's down by the lighthouse. Somebody in Washington figured the Germans were going to invade by submarine right here at Lincoln Harbor."

"You're kidding."

"I am not kidding. I guess they figured the Germans had some kind of a sub that could swim in twenty-five feet of water and turn around in its own length—or else back out of the harbor. Anyway, it saved our bacon. Things have been pretty good since."

"Was a man named Mendoza here then?"

"Worked for him. Only other employee we had until we began taking on people to do the army job. Mendoza was your pal's old man."

"What was he like?"

"Tough little guy. Hard worker. Uncle Chester loved him. Couldn't bear to let him go. Paid him out of his own pocket. When we got going again, Uncle Chester made him foreman."

This was not the omnipotent, entrenched, exploitative Abbey that Lou had described. He said: "So you know something about running a business on a shoestring."

"I know all about it, and I don't ever want to do it again. That's why I'd just as soon see your pal go away."

"Not room for two here?"

"Never room for two in a small town. Competition ruins the profitability. Now we have him in our hair all the time with his bids. I figured to kill him off for good with that phony estimate. I never expected you to come along and bail him out. Mistake number one. Mistake number two was to rent our shovels. Now you're out four thousand"—Abbey handed him the check—"and he's still in business."

That night Charlie was at the door again.

"Mister," growled Lou, "there's a knocker on that door. Use it."

"It's nearly nine o'clock," Charlie burst out. "Where were you?"

He had forgotten Lorraine!

"If I want you to come in, I'll tell you," said Lou, getting up. He ducked around Lou and pushed Charlie out the door and down the steps.

"Where were you?" Charlie repeated. "I said eight-thirty."

"I can't come."

"But she's waiting. You never said."

"I'm sorry. I should have." What a relief to know he wouldn't, wouldn't ever.

"Come on, there's still time."

He could picture a fuming Lorraine railing at him, but could think no further. "No. I did that once. You don't want me there again. You know that."

"But *she* does. This has been the worst week of my life. How can I . . . ?"

"Just tell her I refused. Anyway, she really wants you, not me. She needs you, not me. You should see a doctor."

With that he left Charlie and went inside. Lou was already in his pajamas. "That pal of yours should learn some manners," he said, and went to bed.

Twenty minutes later he heard another car pull up. He looked out and saw Lorraine opening its door. He ran outside to intercept her.

"Get in the back," she ordered.

"No, Lorraine. I told Charlie."

"Get in. You want me to start screaming?"

He got in. This woman was off her rocker. She started up the car and continued to the end of Gott Street and then on into a dirt road that petered out in a grove of scrub oak. He barely had time to wonder how she knew about this place and if she had ever used it before, when she climbed into the back seat with him.

"That was cruel. You said you would."

"No."

"Anyway, you want me." She felt for him and proved her point instantly. She fumbled at his belt buckle, tried to unzip him. "Come on, come on."

Booming with lust again, and thoroughly disgusted with himself for it, he slid out of his jeans. She tore at his shorts, a handsome heirloom pair from Sulka with buttons down the front. The buttons popped from them like seeds. He took them off. She rucked up her skirt—there was nothing under it—and planted herself on him. There was no slackness now, no waiting. She was frantic. "Come on," she said again. "You want— I know you want— Come on, come on." After that she said nothing. She craved friction. She got it. Gasping, again and again she got it. Cold and angry himself, he fed her. She didn't stop, wouldn't stop—couldn't stop. It became a contest. He gritted his teeth, determined to see her out, and after what seemed an eternity, he did.

"There," she said. "That's all I can—" She fell heavily against him, her chest heaving, as he continued to sit in the seat. But she made no effort to remove herself from him. He wondered if she might want to start up again.

But she didn't. She just slumped there—she had become her previous limp self—until she had recovered her breath. Then she swung her leg off him, pulled down her skirt, and sat next to him on the seat.

"Thank you."

"You're welcome." He tried to make it sound cold and formal.

"When you didn't come over tonight . . . I expected you. I was waiting, and I got all hot and bothered. Then Charlie came home without you. I just—"

"Took things into your own hands."

"That was really something. Thank you."

"You're welcome," he said again, trying to make it even colder.

She took no notice. "After last time, I didn't have any worries this time. I could really . . . you know, over and over. I knew you could, but I wasn't sure how much you would—so much. But I wasn't worried, because of the way you go for me. I mean, you did go, didn't you?"

"No."

"You *didn't?* You want to? We could—"

"I don't want to."

"But the way you go for me. The way you get. I mean, look at you."

He got into his jeans. The ripped underwear he would abandon.

"I don't think that's good for you. Why don't we . . . I mean, I could . . . Sort of your turn, do you know what I mean?"

"I know what you mean."

"So let's just—"

He removed her hand from his groin before she could change his mind and said: "Lorraine, I don't want to do this with you. I do it as a favor for Charlie."

"But the way I turn you on."

How was he going to stop this without getting ugly? "Yes," he said. "But I can't stand any more on account of Charlie."

"He lets you; he asks you."

"Only because he can't. After tomorrow I think you're going to see a change in Charlie. You won't be needing me."

"What if I do?"

"Then you'll have to persuade him to let somebody else haul your ashes."

"That's not a nice thing to say."

"That's not a nice thing we're doing."

"You know, you're not a very nice person." She got into the front seat.

"That makes two of us," he said. "Now will you drive me home?"

"I think you'd better walk."

It was a long walk back, the dirt road a faint streak in the starlight. As he trudged along in the sand, he had ample time to ponder this latest turn and to wonder if Lorraine would tell Charlie what had happened, and if she did, if it might not drive Charlie deeper into impotence, for once again she would have succeeded in satisfying herself where he had failed. Or she might decide not to tell, in the hope of preserving the thread of an ongoing understanding that she could summon up again. By the time he hit the pavement at the end of Gott Street, he had resolved that under no circumstance, *ever,* would he touch this woman again. He was humiliated by the ease with which he had capitulated tonight, having to face the realization that her threat of screaming was almost certainly fraudulent. Nobody, not even Lorraine, would do that. So how much of that overrapid capitulation was dictated by the threat, and how much by Lorraine herself? As he mulled that over, his humiliation deepened.

When he arrived home it was after midnight. Marge, back from the Blue Lobster, was sitting over a cup of tea in the kitchen. She said nothing when he walked in, but her face spoke several paragraphs.

"I was restless," he felt obliged to say. "I took a walk," and escaped into his bedroom. As he undressed, he was reminded that he had left his tattered shorts in Lorraine's car. He wondered if she would remember them and remove them, and if Marge, who washed them, would notice that his only remaining pair of special Egyptian cotton button-front Sulka shorts had vanished.

Fran didn't come on Tuesday.

She didn't come on Wednesday.

On Thursday she was sitting on the bench when he showed up at five minutes after ten. This time she had on a pale-pink button-down shirt, a lady's version of the classic Brooks Brothers model, blue linen slacks, and blue espadrilles with rope soles. She looked even better than she had a week before.

"Hello, Fred." She was holding a small handbag of blue wool with a teak frame and her initials on it: *FC* in white. She was totally up. How had she done it in so short a time?

"I wasn't sure you'd come," he said.

"I wasn't, either. But there's a dinner party tonight. At the Munsons'. And they're off playing golf again today. I mean, I knew that last week; I wasn't sure *I* would come back."

"I'm glad you did."

"I was hurting so much from you. I didn't want to be reminded of that."

"I—" How could he have? His crime grew and grew.

"Is this the right place for us to be talking?"

He grabbed for his flying wits, said that he would like to take her for a boat ride to see an island that he owned.

"You own an island?"

"Not exactly. I'm paying for it on the installment plan. I thought we might take a look at it, have a picnic."

"That will be nice, Fred. Did you bring food?"

The one thing he hadn't thought of.

"We'll make lunch right here." She pointed to a gourmet shop across the street. "Do you have a thermos?"

"There's one at home."

"Fill it with ice. I'll meet you here."

Relieved to have something to do, he ran to Charlie's parking space, drove the truck to Gott Street, filled Marge's large thermos with ice. Buoyancy had returned. He left a note on the kitchen table for Lou. "Have a date. See you later." He drove back, parked the truck. Fran was on the bench, this time with a sizable paper bag in her lap.

"I made sandwiches. But I forgot to ask for cups and forks."

"I have all those on the island."

He took the paper bag, and they walked together down to the marina. The tide was out, and he had to set the bag on the dock before lowering himself into the dory. Fran looked on in dismay.

"Are we going in that?"

"Yes."

"It's so small."

"It's safe."

"I don't know how to swim, Fred."

"It's perfectly safe. Here, give me your hand." She extended it nervously, gave a step into the air, and landed in his arms. The boat teetered, and she clung to him. Sweet Christ, what a moment! She let go of him and sat down in the bow seat, clutching the gunwale on each side of her. He handed her a life preserver and she put it on. She looked adorable with that lumpy orange object around her. It seemed to reassure her a little. She let go of the gunwale and watched him untie the painter, start the outboard, and move slowly and smoothly out of the marina. They had to pass the yacht club, to whose dock an enormous white vessel was tied.

"That's Ebby's yacht."

As they slid by, he read on its stern: *Minda, New York*. A woman in sunglasses and a large straw hat was staring at them from the after-cockpit. Fran waved to her and got a wave back.

"That was Mindy."

"Mindy knows you're here with me?"

"Not here in this boat with you. I didn't know that myself. I just told Mindy I had a date with you."

"What did she say?"

"She said I was very stupid to do anything with you. She also said an engaged girl didn't go out with another man and not tell her fiancé."

"You didn't tell Corky?"

"How could I tell Corky? It was hard enough to tell Mindy."

This was an illicit excursion!

"Mindy wants me to marry Corky. Ebby wants me to marry Corky. Corky wants me to marry Corky."

"Do you want to?"

"I think so. I'm working on it. Corky is a wonderful man. That's the Munsons', where we're going to dinner tonight." She pointed to a white house with a large veranda and an emerald lawn running down to the water and a long dock sticking out into the harbor. He knew one end of the Munson house well: that was where they kept their garbage cans.

"Mindy tried to persuade me. But I explained that I wanted to truly get over you. I wanted to be your friend and not leave it like that awful time before."

That awful time.

"That was not the way to end a relationship. It made me so unhappy." Holding carefully to the gunwale, she turned herself around on the seat so that she was facing forward. It was an absolutely still summer morning. The water flowed like oil past the slanted buoys. He ran along at half speed to stretch out this moment, as Fran sat with her head thrown back to catch on her neck as well as her face the slight breeze that the dory's motion made. Even when they reached the lighthouse and turned out to sea the surface was like glass, with a barely perceptible swell running. He was aware of it as the dory picked up a hair of speed sliding down the long invisible slopes, but he doubted if she was.

"That's the island," he said.

"It's so big."

"No. It's less than a mile long."

"It's so flat."

"It just looks flat because there are no trees on it."

"Did somebody cut them down?"

"I don't think there ever were any. It's too windy out here in winter for anything but little dwarf trees. And a lot of bushes." All those bushes that had tried to devour him when he went to get water from the pond.

They reached his cove and glided in to the beach. "You'll have to take off your shoes and roll up your pants," he said. "Or I can carry you in."

"I'll take off my shoes."

Once ashore, she dried her feet exactly as Marge and Emily had done that first time. Did all women have that behavior programmed in them? She selected a flat rock, sat down on it, crossed one leg over the other, and dusted off the drying sand, working carefully between her toes. He watched her intently.

"This is so attractive," she said, rolling down her slacks. "Is that your house? Did you live here?"

"One summer. Then I got sick and had to leave. I didn't go back because I got a job in town."

"You were sick here, Fred? All alone?"

"I got food poisoning, and I ran out of water."

"That must have been terrible. You were all by yourself? Why didn't you go to town?"

"I ran out of gas. I couldn't row. Some friends came and got me. They're the ones I live with now."

"Oh." She looked around. "This is so beautiful, so quiet. I'll tell you something. I was afraid to get in your little boat at first, but I like it better than Ebby's big one. Even though they do my laundry every night and the food is delicious, this is . . . It's so open here. It smells so good. Can I see your house?"

This time he had remembered the key. He let her in. She looked around dubiously, sniffing him out in his hidden den. "You need some furniture," she said. "Someone should fix this up for you." In the kitchen she said: "I don't see how you can cook here. Even Papa has a better kitchen." In the bedroom she said: "Where's your mattress?"

"I soiled it when I was sick," he said. "I had to get rid of it."

She went to the door and looked out, taking deep breaths of air. "But it's nice. It could be so nice. Why did you want to live here all by yourself? This would be a nice place if you had somebody."

"There wasn't anybody. After you, I—" Tell it? And if so, how much of what happened later? He was overcome by a need to be honest with her after all the dishonesty, but he couldn't resist putting in a small plug: "If I couldn't have you, I didn't want anybody." Anyway, it now had become true. She gave him an unfathomable look and went outside to sit on the driftwood bench. He joined her.

"You really did stop drinking." A statement this time, not a question.

"What became of 'jrinkingg'?" he asked.

"Oh, that. That was another thing that made me unhappy with you. You didn't like the way I talked. I wasn't in your class. You didn't hide that."

That was true also, horribly true.

"I took speech therapy. From the same person who cured Mindy of her Brooklyn accent. You know how Mindy talks now; it's so different from the way she used to. When she was trying to persuade me to go to the speech therapist, she went back to her old way, real Brooklyn-Jewish. That sold me."

How could he have done that?

"Of course, Mindy and I will never talk the same. We have different brains. Our sentences come out different. But I am improving the way the words come out."

"They come out just fine," he said.

"So I don't say 'jrinkingg' anymore."

"I don't care what you say. I just like to hear you say it."

"Back then you didn't."

"Back then I didn't know any better. I do now. Fran . . . " They were facing each other on the bench. This was a moment of great peril. He had crippled her once and could not bear to risk doing it again. At the same time, it seemed that if he didn't risk something now he would be forever crippled himself.

"I think we should eat lunch," she said.

"Fran . . . "

"Because if we should start . . . "

He reached for her. She turned her head away. The urge to grasp it and turn it back was overwhelming. Force her? He had tried it once; he could never do that again. He put his hand gently on her cheek. It turned of its own.

Wide open, defenseless. "Please, Fred. You know how we are."

He knew. He knew for a certainty.

"Once we kiss . . . "

The word shot him over the dam. Her too. She had said it, not he. She wanted him. He drew her to her feet, and she poured herself against him, pressing close, generating such a wave of tenderness and joy in him that he felt his chest might burst. Joy and tenderness . . . they made the desire inexpressibly keen. Tenderness; he would have to be gentle. He kissed her ever so gently and felt his mouth devoured by hers. Tenderness. He put his hands in her hair and drew her head back so that he could look at her face. Her eyes were as large as plates. He felt drowned in them.

"Oh, Fred . . . Fred." She wanted more kisses. He gave them, tried to be gentle. She ignored his gentleness. She was all fire.

"What are we doing?" he said.

"We are loving. Oh, Fred. Do you love me?"

"Yes."

"Three years . . . "

"I love you."

"Then kiss me more. You seem so timid."

"I don't want to hurt you. That other time . . . "

"That was that other time. I heard what you just said. I *made* you say it before."

"Not now."

"You didn't want to say it then."

"I didn't feel it then."

"I should never have done that. But I wanted you so much to love me. I was ashamed."

"Don't ever be ashamed."

They kissed again, dizzying themselves with their mouths and tongues.

"Is there a smooth place?" she said. "It's all prickly here."

"A smooth place?"

"My knees are melting from kissing. I want to lie down and hold you close."

He thought of the blanket he had wrapped himself in that cold night, huddling in front of the fire to write a letter. Maybe Marge and Lou had left it. He went in to look. It was folded neatly on the shelf. He spread it out in the sun, next to the bench, standing awkwardly by it. She immediately sat down in the middle of it and held out her arms. Blinded, he knelt over her. She put her arms around his neck, and they fell back together. There they kissed and kissed again, he making a series of ever more desperate pledges to himself to be gentle.

"I want to be close to you. There . . . " She pressed against him. "Closer." He tried to oblige and still remain gentle. It was supremely difficult.

"Oh, darling . . . " More kisses, accompanied by increasingly ardent pressing. "I think I should take off my slacks. Linen wrinkles so." She slid away from him, arched her back, and pulled them off, revealing a pair of white panties. "Why don't you take off your belt. The buckle's so big and hard. I want to be close to you."

He sat up and did so.

"Just the belt. We mustn't— You won't—"

"I won't." He wouldn't, he wouldn't, another vow. Anyway, their roles were being crazily reversed. She was the pacemaker.

"I just want to be close to you. That's all I want . . . all I want . . . all I ever want. Fred . . . "

He put his hand on her breast—oh, Christ, how unbelievably soft and sweet—then on her shirt button, but afraid to open it. She did it for him. She sat up and took her shirt off, then the small white bra underneath. The dazzle of her was stupefying. He kissed her breasts.

delivering to each a long but gently searching kiss, eliciting a tattoo of fingers on his back. He kissed her navel. He kissed the dampening spot in her panties, making her jump and squirm.

"I'll take those off too. I want to be . . . so close to you. You can kiss me." Again, she arched her hips, and skinned off her panties. "Now you can," she said. "If you . . . want." He did want. He wanted above everything to plunge his beard into that surprisingly thick, surprisingly black mass of pubic hair, to bury himself there, to live there. She took his head in both her hands and pressed it against herself. He kissed her with his tongue, and at each kiss her body leapt at him. "Oh," she said. "Oh my God . . . Oh darling. Oh please. Oh stop . . . I can't any . . . Here." She tugged hard at his head, drawing it up to her face, pulling him down on her. "Hold me. Just hold me. I'm . . . My God, darling, I'm . . . Here I am . . . Here. Hold me. Are you . . . ? I am . . . IamIamIam." With a loud cry, she nearly threw him off herself as she bucked against him, and finally let him go.

"Ohhh." She was panting hard. "Ohhh." She had run a long race. "Oh, darling, that was . . . It was . . . " She pulled him over on top of herself again and clung to him. "I came, darling. Oh, I did. I really did." Another deep spasm. "I still am . . . Oh my God, it isn't the same. I let go . . . I did . . . Because you love me. You do"—she gasped—"love me."

"Oh, yes." And not just for this. Not just for this unbelievable moment but for everything, for it all, for her unbelievably beautiful body, her unbelievably powerful response, her abandon—her love. That was it—he had an enormous love for this truly unbelievable woman.

"You don't have to ask me now," he said.

"Ohhh . . . "

"I love you."

"Ohhh . . . When you say that . . . I'm all dissolving inside. You don't know . . . I'm still . . . Just hold me and let me . . . There, darling, I can breathe a little. Did you . . . ?"

"Yes."

"When I . . . ?"

"Yes."

"How did you know?"

"You made it very plain."

"I suppose I did. I didn't know where I was. That was so strong. Do you *know* what that real orgasm was like?"

"I guess that's something I'll never know. But if it makes you happy . . . "

"It does, darling." And then she burst into a flood of tears. She lay against his chest, sobbing. He held her gently, recognizing the tearing wrenches that came on every breath, the kind that he had experienced a couple of times himself. And as he had done that day in the library with Emily, he let her cry herself out.

"I'm sorry." She recovered her shirt and wiped her eyes with it, then started to put it on.

"Don't do that. You look too beautiful." She did. Her pearly skin, her pert little breasts, her flat stomach with the hint of a crease and a curve in it, and that black forest of hair, with just the springiness in it to match the springiness and the curliness of his beard. The hair and the beard, the marvelous tangle.

"But it's so bright. I'm all naked. I have nothing on." Suddenly shy, she rolled over on her stomach.

"You're so beautiful," he repeated. He couldn't get over it. Radiant there in the bright sun, even to the damp little curls at the back of her neck.

He rolled her over. She tried to cover herself with her shirt. "It's all right for you. You're not all naked."

"I said I wouldn't. Remember?"

"I'm glad you didn't, because if you had I don't think I could have stopped you. Oh, Fred . . . " She began to cry again and buried her face in his shoulder. He stroked her back and her pretty rump, so round and smooth and white in the sun. Everything about her, everything . . . He felt ennobled. And the power came back to him, this time the power to be gentle, to protect, to give. He had given without forcing. She had wanted. She had taken. That exchange. All his life . . . He felt a prickle in his own eyes.

She noticed. "You've been hurting too?"

He nodded.

"That's why I cried. It hurt so. Three years. More than three years; four years. It hurt so. I thought my life would end." That cliché again, but it came out with such a quaver of earnestness that he was able to believe that she might well have felt like dying. She was all emotions, and such potent ones. "Mindy told me I had to get hold of myself. She really rescued me. She said you can't die over a man. She nearly did herself, she told me. She got hold of herself and married Ebby. Now please, Fred, let me put on my shirt. Where are my slacks?" They were on the edge of the blanket. In the hurricane of loving, she had not neglected to fold them neatly.

"All those things came off pretty fast," he said.

"Was I too bold, darling? Did I shock you?"

"No. It's just that you used to be so much more modest. Even in the dark. And now, right here—"

"I wanted to be close. I wanted to give you that present."

"It was—"

"Myself." She reached for her panties. Again that quick arch of hip, the mound of pubic hair sprouting skyward for an instant before it disappeared. She pulled up her slacks, then sat up to put on her bra. The way she bent her head down while she reached behind herself to fasten the hooks was devastatingly intimate. Such a frown of concentration and yet so graceful. Fran was a naturally graceful woman. All her movements . . . He remembered how she had handled her iced tea glass at The Nook, how her entire body was infused with grace when she danced at the awards party a century or two before.

"There." She got a small comb out of her blue wool bag and gave a vigorous fluffing to her hair, which, in the bright sun, had, he noticed for the first time, a faint coppery sheen.

"Your hair's not black."

"Not quite, darling."

"But down there—I mean your other hair—it's black."

She blushed. Self-consciousness was flooding back. "I don't tint there. Nobody tints there—that I know of. I go to Mindy's hairdresser now, and she tints me just a little. Do I look okay?"

"You look gorgeous."

"Shall we eat?" she said. "Aren't you hungry?"

With the return of her self-consciousness, he began to be aware of the extraordinary nature of this encounter, and it left some large questions.

"Before we eat . . . " He seated her on the driftwood bench and took her hands. "Did you plan this?" he asked.

"How could I? I didn't even know you lived here. When we met on the street I was startled. I was breathless. I didn't think we would ever meet again. You were out of my life. I was trying to put you out of my life. I was determined to do that."

"But you agreed to see me again."

"To get you out of my system. I still dream about you. I have those dreams of wanting you. Daydreams of kissing you. Mindy understands that. Mindy is a very passionate person. She knows how I felt about you, about wanting you. When I told her I had never given myself completely to you, she said that was good, that I could go and fall in love with somebody else. I'm doing that. I'm getting engaged to Corky. He is a wonderful person."

"So why did you see me again, take the risk?"

"Mindy asked me the same question. She asked what if I was attracted to you again. I said I didn't think I would be. I would have a nice talk with you. We would become friends. I would sort of . . . well, like, sign a letter. And you would be out of my life."

"The proper goodbye we never had."

"That's exactly it. But you were so different. You've changed. I don't mean looks. You do look entirely different. But inside you're different. You're nicer." She gave his hand a hard squeeze. "Now I will have to confess something to you. I wanted to be in love with you back then. I wanted you. I loved to be kissing and hugging you. Even when I knew all those bad things about you. I mean, I was half in love with you. I wanted to marry you because of who you were. Your social position. A rich man. And you were so glamorous. I let myself fall in love with you. And when we—when I had my first orgasm with you, I said to myself that I loved you. But even then I knew I didn't fully. I held back. And all those other times when we wanted each other so much. The physical side. I was holding back. I knew you didn't love me, and I was afraid to really let go. You know, you can do that. You can have an orgasm and it can run through you oh so strong. And at the same time you can realize that you are not truly letting go. Not giving. I did that because— Do I have to tell you all this?"

"Because of what?"

"Because of wanting you. Fred, you don't know how strong— What I feel when we kiss and hug. When I had those orgasms. Even holding back. When I was hoping you would marry me, when I was asking you. I knew somewhere that you wouldn't. Not having you was killing me enough. But if I had really let myself go . . . if I totally— I had enough sense to say to myself: If I do that, if I ever experience that, my whole heart, all of me, and he leaves, then I'll really die. So I never did, even though it may have seemed to you that I did."

Their hands were gripping so tight now that he wondered if he might not be hurting hers. He let go and stroked the back of one. He didn't have to remind himself to be gentle. He wanted to be gentle.

"So I said to myself I would say goodbye to you and go on with my life. You know, I have this business. It's very hard work. I would tell you about my business and say goodbye. But you were so different. Coming out here today, I felt . . . I had cheated you a little. You were not nice to me back then, but I knew that. I had been holding out on you, and you didn't know that. This may sound crazy, but I felt a little guilty about you. And when we came out here this morning, and it was so lovely and peaceful, and you were so nice . . . You are a nice man, you really are, and I realized that what Mindy had warned me about might happen. And when we began kissing and you said you loved me . . . And I could tell from the way you said it that it was the chruth." She caught herself. "I slipped, I'm so welling up. The *truth*. I could tell from the way you behaved all day long that you loved me. All I needed was for you to say it, and you did say it. Then I realized I wanted to give myself to you. I wanted to make a present of myself, all of me, this time, just once to let you know. And for myself too. And I did, totally. Anyway . . . Darling, I've been talking and talking. Aren't you hungry?"

He was, ravenously. She unpacked the paper bag. It had four sandwiches in it, a small cantaloupe, and two bottles of 7-Up.

"You said you had plates and glasses. So why don't you get them? And a knife for the cantaloupe."

They ate their lunch sitting on the bench, the sun full on their faces. She had gotten sliced tongue and lettuce, and some slices of small spicy Italian sausages, also on lettuce.

"Ice for the 7-Up." He remembered that she had made a punch of 7-Up, that sticky sweet stuff, for the awards party. He took a sip; it was sweet and sparkly. He bit into a sandwich. Another sip of 7-Up. It complemented the sandwich perfectly. How could food taste this good, and why had he ignored 7-Up for so long?

"Will you tell Mindy about this?" he said.

"I think not. Not right away anyway. Although Mindy would understand. Mindy is a very passionate person. She knows passion. Mindy recognizes that I'm a passionate person. She has already given me advice about you. Mindy does not want me to make the kind of mistake she made."

Mindy make mistakes? That cool, collected, self-created success?

"Her passion, her love. Mindy knows that passion can make her do the wrong thing. This is a secret, but I will tell it to you anyway. The baby that Mindy is carrying is not Ebby's baby."

That was a stunner. "Do you know who the father is?"

"Yes, I do. And you know him too. Mr. Wright. Mindy is passionately in love with Mr. Wright. She is very fond of Ebby and very grateful for all he's done for her—but she loves Mr. Wright."

Wright! That powerful, ugly little bulldog. How could he do that to Mindy? Did she know? Of course she did. Wright had persuaded her over the phone. He had been there, heard the whole thing.

"So when I announce my engagement to Corky and marry him, she wants to make sure that I am not in love with you."

"But you can't marry Corky now."

"I promised him already."

"Break the promise. You changed your mind. Women do that all the time."

"I don't think so."

"Stay here. Marry me." *Marry him?* Why not? It had not occurred to him until this moment that she might, after all she had been through with him. But after today? Today made things different. If he was different, so was she; she had admitted it herself just a few minutes before. He said again: "Marry me," aware as he said it of the irony; he was now begging her.

"No, Fred. I can't stay here. I have my business. I owe Ebby. You don't know what a big business it is becoming, how complicated it is. We have our own china now. Beautiful china. People at parties steal the demitasse saucers for souvenirs, for ashtrays. They put them in their pockets. They steal from their friends, because the hostess has to pay me for that stealing when we count the china after."

"You want to talk about china *now?*"

"We are discussing an exclusive with Tiffany."

"Listen to me. How can you talk about china?"

"Because I don't want to talk about us."

"But today . . . you wanted me to love you. Now I do. I want to marry you."

"Fred . . . "

"And I'm not the bastard I was when you were begging me. After today . . . ?"

"Today was my goodbye present to you. To give myself to you just once. I didn't do that before. I won't do that again. I should be getting back. What time is it?"

He looked at his watch. Only two-thirty? A universe had swung into view and then swung away in just a few hours.

"The golf will be over. I don't want to have to explain to Corky why I was gone so long."

"Fran, once again—"

"Why don't you put away the plates. We really should go."

Of all the trips he had made between the island and Lincoln Harbor, this was the one he would never forget. His life, his hope, was slipping away, and he could do nothing about it. Hennerkop had got it right: he would have to make some changes in himself before being able to recognize a good woman. Well, he must have changed, because he did recognize her, with stunning clarity. She was huddled against him as they went back in the dory. The afternoon breeze had come up, and with it a restless sea that made the dory slew and tip as it caught the quartering waves and rode down their fronts. Fran was terrified of the tipping and clung to him. He would have liked to put a reassuring, protective arm around her, but the numbness had returned. When they rounded the lighthouse point and came to the protected waters of the harbor, she crawled up to the front seat and, still suspicious of the dory, clung to its gunwales with both hands. The tide had turned, and the current was sweeping them in, shortening this icy journey. The step up to the dock was easy.

They held hands briefly. One last chance: "If you ever . . . Now you know where I am; you could write me. General delivery here. Lincoln Harbor."

"I will remember Lincoln Harbor."

"Then it's goodbye here," he said. "I don't want to meet those people."

"Goodbye, Fred."

He was tempted to say: "When you kiss Corky, think of me," but he didn't. That would have been too malicious. The last he saw of her was her back, pink shirt and blue linen slacks getting smaller as she walked. He watched her to the end of the street. There she turned into the yacht club and disappeared. He went up Elm, collected his mail without even looking at it, and walked home in such a daze that he forgot that his truck was parked behind Charlie's office. He threw the mail on his bed. Go back for the truck? Might as well; he had nothing else to do. Nothing at all now.

Later Lou came in and asked: "Your date show?"

"Yes."

"Gonna show again?"

"I don't think so. It didn't work out."

"Them yacht dames. She off that monster that was in today?"

"Yes."

"Watched two men drive up in a dinky little car. Your dame the one in a pink shirt?"

"Yes."

"Watched her run up and give one of them fellers a big hug. You better stick to local talent. . . . And then what do you think? They put out a crane and lifted that dinky little car right on deck. Chocks there for it, and a tarpaulin. That's the way to live."

She had climbed right into the lap of the world from which he had fallen.

Supper was minute steaks, a rare treat. He scarcely touched his.

Lou didn't notice, but Marge did, said nothing.

"Emily says she'll stay until Labor Day. We'll take on Tony Lopes then. He'll drive the little truck. For a while. I'm gonna get him a tractor so we can pull stumps. Lots of cutting going on when they clear them tracts for homes. We'll fell trees; Tony knows that business, knows the fellows doing it. I'll get him a wood splitter. We'll stack it here. We'll be in the wood business. You going to charge Emily and that fellow rent when they go out to your island?"

"I don't think I will. They won't be there long. They'll take care of it."

Then Lou noticed. "How come you're not eating your steak?"

"Not hungry."

"Mind if I do?"

"Go ahead."

"Waste not, want not." A big hairy arm reached across and speared his steak.

Later he walked down to the waterfront. He supposed he should clean the gear out of his dory, but he couldn't bring himself to do it, even though he knew things were being stolen from small boats like his. Ebby's yacht had been moved from the yacht club to the town wharf. He couldn't resist taking a look at it, noticing again the name *Minda* on the stern. Apparently Mindy had told Ebby something about her plain origins. He wondered if she had extended her confessional to include Mr. Wright, and how she was managing to conduct a love affair under Ebby's nose, then he remembered that Ebby traveled a lot on beer business.

Lights were on here and there in the *Minda*. He was drawn irresistibly closer and was able to observe the obligatory array of wicker furniture in the aftercockpit, see a dining saloon in the main cabin, with a table big enough to seat a dozen people. The staterooms had portholes, and each was curtained. Whichever was Corky's and which Fran's would remain their secret. There had to be two; his mind could not accept one—not after today.

Black as that picture was, he still couldn't tear himself away. He found a bench at the far end of the wharf. It was already ten o'clock. The din from the yacht club came racketing across the water. At eleven a car pulled onto the wharf and the four of them got out, Ebby towering over the others, half a head taller even than Mindy, who was a tall woman. Arm in arm, they strode aboard, followed by the much shorter couple. Fran had on a white evening dress and white slippers, and her arm was linked in Corky's. His last glimpse of her was of a white shape stepping aboard. She must have gone directly below, for she didn't join the others in the cockpit. From his bench he could just see the tops of three heads as they sat chatting while the crew cast off the *Minda*. Getting her swung out into the stream took some time because she was so large. Slowly the bow was edged farther and farther out, then with a deep purr she headed down the harbor, carrying sinners and sinned-against with her.

He walked home, so late now that the lights in the houses edging the street were all out, the people inside sleeping peacefully alone or in couples—but sleeping peacefully, he thought. When he got home he noticed the unsorted mail on his bed. Among the ads was a letter from England:

The Rectory
St. Barnabas Church
Under Wixton, near Hobbing
July 17, 1960

Dear Captain Fay:
  It is my sad duty to inform you that Violet Few-Strang has died. When she asked me to tea a week ago, she gave me the enclosed letter and asked me to send it on to you in case anything should happen to her. I took it, believing that her concern was for her health, because she had not been looking at all well for months. Two days later—or three: we cannot be sure because she lived alone in the Park House gate cottage—she took her life. May she rest in peace in the arms of Our Blessed Saviour.

Yours sincerely,
Enid (Mrs. Osbert) Appleton

Took her life? With a clattering heart, he opened the other envelope.

Dear Boy:
  Your letter arrived in the nick of time. Had it not, you can be sure you will never receive this one. But you did write, and I bless you for it, because it is the only nice thing that has happened to me in an increasingly desperate life. I have decided to chuck it. And when you get this you will know I have done.
  We are asked to ease ourselves along, and finally out, with the help of our memories. My good ones are so few (and none since you) that I find I cannot be supported by them. And you, dear Boy, were so short, the merest flicker, that any hope of being held up by that

one memory is a vain one. I tried it, and I had a couple of good nights thinking about you and what a lovely boy you were, and what a bloody fool I was not to continue with you. We had no life together with which I might console myself now. So, with nothing else to keep me, I shall go.

Desperate, I said, and desperate it has been. The people in the Park House, who had kept me going with the boarding of their horses and lessons for their children, proved to be flash. They went bankrupt and were sold out. I felt sorry for the children, who were just coming on to be good riders. The boy in particular. Twelve, he was, and had spirit.

The place was gobbled up by estate speculators. They have turned the Park House into flats. My garden is two tennis courts. Thirty villas are sprouting like mushrooms in the rest of the Park. They are all alike inside, duplicates or mirror images of each other, and the buyer can choose a fake Norman or fake Tudor or fake Georgian façade. Three styles fit all.

Next they took the stables, saying that my use did not run with the property but was a private contract with the previous owners and ended with the sale. I took them to court and lost. I am now without resources. I have been offered a position in the library at a salary that even a frugal person like myself could not get by on. Even so, I would take it, except that I cannot bring myself to enter the library now. It is being run by new people, who have taken out all the sets. They claimed that nobody read them and that the shelf space was needed. So they sold the lot up at auction in London—those beautiful books. And because many of them had the bookplates of the original titled owners, they were snapped up by people who wanted instant arms without the bother of going to the Herald. Also they were in such superb condition that they brought in enough to install central heating. Now the library is open four days a week and it has five thousand paperbacks, eighty of them by Barbara Cartland.

I sold my horse—I had nowhere to put him and no way of feeding him. I started a small garden to feed myself, but the effort of it all, with nothing, absolutely nothing to look forward to, got to be too much. I have no friends here any more save Enid Appleton, a widow herself now and going a bit dotty. I am myself considered certifiably dotty, a savage witch who lives by herself and rides the last remaining bicycle in the village. Everyone else races about in motors, and I have been nearly killed several times in the lanes. I wish to God I had been. So, dear Boy, don't waste time thinking that if you had written earlier you might have changed my mind. Not so. I am a fox brought to earth at the end of a long run, unable to run any more.

I realize this letter is an imposition on you. Without it you would never have known or perhaps not even wondered what happened to poor old Violet. So please consider this a last indulgence of myself, for you did write a sweet letter and it pleasures me to be speaking to you again and to be remembering the one glorious time we had together. It also gives me a chance to tell you how you warmed my heart when you said you would always remember me as I was then, which is how I would like to be remembered, my body full of passion and my heart full of love for you for having helped me release it.

Ever yours, Violet

Now he wept, for this woman dying alone in her cold stone house, then, and longer, for himself and Fran.

43

A T TIMES HE HATED HER. TRULY HATED HER FOR her stubbornness and stupidity. At those times her "gift" became nothing more than the opportunistic relief of an itch, something that an unexpected encounter had allowed her to indulge in. He should never have told her that he loved her. Then it wouldn't have happened. But—he couldn't dismiss it—he did love her. The hatred always washed away as that numbing truth reasserted itself.

At night, in his room, he would wonder if it wouldn't be better to throw away the copy of the letter he had written her, which lay in his top drawer along with his correspondence with Violet, all that was left now of the only two meaningful encounters of his life. He should throw it out, make a clean break, do what Fran herself had done on the advice of Mindy, get her out of his system and get on with his life.

But what kind of a life was there to get on with? He took out the letter and read it again. "Although it's more than two years since we last saw each other, I think of you often and wonder how you are getting along." The childish optimism of it now assailed him. How could he have hoped? He reread Violet's last letter, and choked over it.

Throw them all away? Then there would be nothing left at all. He was reminded of the day he had gone through his mother's things and found only a locket, no other clue to what she had been like, how she had felt, what she had done. Her drawer, her life, as far as anyone searching for evidence could tell, was empty. So would be his. He couldn't endure that thought, and put the letters back. Someone, sometime, picking over his things, should know that he had had feelings, had done something, tried something with someone.

But wasn't that unacceptably arrogant? Who would that examiner be? And would he or she pause even long enough to read these letters and wonder about what lay behind them? Did anybody besides himself remember the Rosie of the valentine he had found when he bought his bureau? He had not thought of Rosie since, and what good did it do Rosie to think of her now? Only when we have nothing else to cling to, he thought, do we cling to whatever slender threads identify us as living, as having lived.

Having lived! His future, the long future that had not yet happened, and about which, in the past, he had never had time to think, the present and the immediate future always being too difficult and frightening to think beyond, now collapsed in on him like an accordion. Suddenly it was there right in front of him. He realized that he had never contemplated his long future other than as a kind of easeful emptiness that he would live out on his island. He had been living on that fantasy as a substitute for real life, the kind of life that Hennerkop had told him he would have to acquaint himself with before he could begin really living himself.

Now he had been really living. He realized it, not because of the events of the last couple of years, but because of the new thoughts that were going through him, and the pain that accompanied them. For the first time in his life it occurred to him that he could end that pain whenever he felt like it. Another level of understanding hit him. That was what Violet had finally come to. She had looked ahead, clearly and boldly, and found nothing. You can do that only when you are capable of clear thought, not when fogged by anxiety.

So does reality require hurting? That should not be. Fran had hurt; now it was his turn. Maybe she was still hurting. If so, two hurts, two unnecessary ones. If she weren't so stubborn . . . Anger returned in another wave.

That was how it went. But it was mostly numbness, which he tried to deal with by hard work. Weekends he didn't let up. He applied himself to the house on Cedar Street and to the endless number of jobs to be done there to put it in shape. He started with the floors, finding iron layers of several colors of paint there, which he knew could occupy him for many weeks in a kind of dumb fury.

Meanwhile Emily and Cliff moved to the island. He took them down to the marina to show them his boat, and was impressed when Cliff refused to depart in it but insisted on bringing the outboard back to Gott Street, spreading a tarpaulin in the backyard and taking the whole thing apart, inspecting it, cleaning and oiling it, and putting it together again. Then back to the marina to help them load the supplies they had collected and to watch them spin down the harbor and out of sight. Everybody he knew was leaving, everybody but

Marge and Lou. And Marge had become a remote obstacle, while Lou . . . He couldn't make up his mind about Lou. Lou's coarseness had begun to grate on him more and more. He was going to have to settle accounts with this man, perhaps become his partner. Did he really want to do that? With his newfound ability to look into the future, he could see himself laboring as the junior partner in an enterprise that didn't really interest him, for ten, twenty, thirty years, until he was too old to work. Then what? Violet's solution? He would think more about that when he felt a little less numb, when a few more floorboards had been scraped.

Tony Lopes came aboard and drove the small truck until Lou supplied him with the tractor and log splitter he had promised. Under Tony's instruction, he learned how to use a chain saw, judging how a tree would fall, cutting it off about three feet from the ground so that Tony would have something to get a grip on with the tractor when it came time to pull out the stump. If the cut in the tree was made from the wrong side, it would lean on itself and lock the chain saw with its own weight, necessitating lost time while a rope was tied to the tree and pulled by the tractor so that the chain saw could be freed. He made this mistake a couple of times but soon learned to judge better. He became an expert with the saw and began spending most of his time in a woodlot being cleared, felling trees, cutting off the branches, sawing the bigger ones into two-foot lengths, then the trunks themselves into two-foot lengths, which Tony then split, crunching them in the log splitter, a gasoline-driven contrivance that they had trucked to the woodlot.

He liked Tony, a short stout quiet man who said little but worked steadily. They labored together all through the autumn, as a kind of peace began to filter into him. He learned to banish the whine of the chain saw by wearing earplugs. He would take them out at lunch while he and Tony sat on a log to eat their sandwiches, the smell of the fresh-cut wood all around them. Over time he learned something about Tony, but not much. Neither mentioned Tony's involvement in the matter of the ditch and his subsequent dismissal by Abbey, although Tony did say one day: "We keep going like this, we'll be right up with Abbey."

That seemed prophetic. Work was pouring in from all directions. Lou had several digging jobs lined up, and for trucking another man was taken on, Carlo Francona, a friend of Tony's. He began to sense the existence of an old-boy network among Portuguese, born more of necessity than of exclusivity, and perhaps tighter because of that. If so, it would explain Lou's assurance that he could trust Tony despite an initial betrayal. When the loyalties were not divided, when it was "them against us," there was no question of where the "us" would stand. Indeed, it could explain Tony's willingness to steal Abbey's estimates in the first place. A sense of "us" had enabled Lou to get to Tony.

As the trees were cut, trimmed, and split, the cordwood was dragged out to the edge of the lot, and a large pile began to grow, preparatory to its being stacked in Lou's backyard. Stumps and small branches were heaped in the center of the lot. They would be burned later in the winter, when the job was done.

Emily and Cliff came back from the island. They had found about a dozen of what Cliff thought were petrel burrows and believed that the island might hold many more. Cliff played it very cool, but Emily had found a new passion, in addition to the one she clearly held for Cliff, and was wildly excited.

"This is fantastic. You have no idea what this means for ornithology."

"Let's wait until spring," said Cliff, "and see if the birds actually come back. So far it's just burrows."

"Who else would be using them? You said yourself they looked fresh."

"Let's make sure."

They took him out to see the results of their work. They had cut trails through the brush. Here and there were small white stakes sticking out of the ground, each with a number on it, each marking a burrow. The sod on the tops of the burrows had been carefully cut away, a shingle inserted, and then the sod replaced. The burrows looked as they had before, but the tops could now be lifted off to see what was inside. In spite of his reservations, Cliff obviously thought petrels were nesting on the island, because he had made and painted a large supply of extra stakes, which stood in a neat pile next to the driftwood bench by the front door.

Emily looked magnificent. She had put on weight and was tanned and crackling with energy. On the way back in the dory, she announced that she was starting a new career as an ecologist and conservationist. He asked her how she would swing that and she explained that Cliff would be teaching a course at Tufts, that she would take the course free of charge as his assistant and add it to the credits she had already earned at Vassar. It was not necessary for her to explain that she would be living with Cliff and would be spared those expenses. She was clearly all out for him now and exulting in it. She had escaped from Lincoln Harbor for the second time.

"You have to learn to save things," she said. "These petrels, what a gift. It's as if God had spared them all these years for us to discover and protect. Think of it. Indians must have come to this island. Why didn't they stay? Why didn't their dogs dig out the petrels and kill them? Because there's no water here, just that little pond, and maybe it dried up a few times in the past. It's only a couple of feet deep now."

"All the little ponds here in the Northeast are slowly drying up," said Cliff. "All but the ones being fed by springs. The land itself is drying out. Your little pond is what's left from the ice sheet that was here ten thousand years ago. It won't last."

He remembered what Charlie had said to him at the time he bought the island. There was no reliable source of water there; nobody had ever succeeded in drilling a well. That was why it had been so ridiculously cheap.

"That pond will certainly last through my life," he said.

"Maybe yes, maybe no," said Cliff. "But the lack of other water has been a break for the petrels."

Emily and Cliff departed. He and Lou hauled the dory again. The weather gradually turned cold. He kept working at the woodlot, trucked several loads to Lou's yard, and was building up a second pile along the road that ran by the lot. He worked at a comfortable rhythm. The choices were simple: cut, trim, saw into lengths, haul out to the road. Some days it rained and he did truck jobs. But others, with the bright high stillness of late autumn all around him, he liked to be there, even though he was turning live wood into dead wood with each scream of his saw. All the leaves blew off the remaining trees. December came.

He decided it was time to clarify his position with Lou and broached the subject one evening.

"I been thinking about that too. You been good to me, Fred. I ain't forgot what you did on the ditch. Or what you said about us being partners. Supposing I took you off the payroll and cut you in for ten percent of the business."

He said that he thought that was a little small considering what Lou owed him and his other contributions in the way of bookkeeping, the consolidation of the equipment loan, and the fuel contract that he had promoted.

Lou countered by totting up the value of all his equipment.

He responded that with no salary, he would probably be no better off than he was now.

Lou had apparently prepared himself in advance for bargaining. He gave the matter some heavy thought and then suggested fifteen percent.

"I think twenty-five would be fairer."

"Okay," said Lou, and stuck out a massive hand. "Partners."

Fred then turned to a more delicate matter. Marge, he pointed out, had been working many afternoons on the accounts. Shouldn't she be a part of the business? That would enable her to quit her job as a bartender.

"I already asked her. She don't want to do it."

"She'd rather tend bar?"

"Makes good money there. Thinks it's too risky to throw in with me."

"But if you were together, really together . . . "

"Married? I asked her that too. Now don't get your hopes up, Freddie. She ain't holding back because of you. Our business simply ain't steady enough to give her that kind of courage."

"But it's getting better all the time."

"So maybe I ask her again."

He went to bed with the realization that Marge had been burned out of him by Fran. She still moved about the house with the same aura of smooth femaleness surrounding her, but now it was something to admire rather than agonize over.

"Don't think I like her working at the Blue Lobster," said Lou on another evening. "That's no place for a good woman."

He put it to Marge. She affirmed what Lou had said. "I have to look out for myself. He can't run a business. You and I both know that, although you've begun to get it organized. I have to wait and see if you can really do that."

It became another incentive in the quiet three-quarter life he was living; it and the long sessions alone in the woods—for Tony was hauling dirt for Lou now—and the weekends scraping floorboards. All that kept him comfortably numb. Walking down Elm, he would keep his eyes away from the window of Charlie's office. He couldn't bring himself to imagine what he might say to Lorraine should they meet, but that winter they did not.

January turned bitter cold. The ground froze, making it impossible to pull stumps. He was alone with his saw every day now, working with a heavy wool cap and mittens that made it hard to hold the saw. Once he slipped and fell in the snow that now lay on the ground, and the saw grazed his shoe. Another inch, and it would have cut off some of his toes. Alone in the woods, his foot spouting blood, unable to walk, would he have bled to death there among the stumps? Truly frightened, and determined to be more careful where he stepped, he discarded his mittens and went back to his regular work gloves, although he had to stop from time to time to revive his lifeless fingers by putting them inside his jeans and between his legs.

At those moments, with his saw silent, he was struck by the stillness of the winter woods. One morning it began to snow again, a faint silvery drift from a putty-colored sky, deadening all sound, putting a final layer of cotton silence between him and the rest of the world. He lugged armfuls of wood out to the roadside pile, and as the day wore on they became thinly dusted with white.

The snow stopped at nightfall. The next morning, the first thing he noticed was that the top of the woodpile had no snow on it. Someone had come along in the night and stolen some pieces. To make sure, at the end of the day he got out his pencil and marked an *X* on the butt ends of two or three of the top logs. The next day they were gone.

He had been using Emily's bicycle to get to and from the woodlot. That evening after supper he put on an extra sweater, his wool cap and mittens, and biked back. He rolled an unsplit log section to a position behind a bush next to the woodpile and sat down to wait. In no time the frozen log began to work its way up into him through his bottom, so he took off his mittens and sat on them. It was a still moonless night, but bright because of the snow on the ground, and now, with his bottom warm again, actually comfortable there, the stars as brilliant as glass. Where was Fran at this moment? Probably standing in somebody's house surrounded by a swirl of noisy nonsense and cigarette smoke, supervising her beautiful girls as they passed out food on her beautiful china. If somebody stole another dish, and she saw it, what would she do? Say nothing and report it to her hostess later? Would she identify the thief? That would be tricky—breaking up what passed in that world for friendship.

Would Lou ever steal from him, or he from Lou? He couldn't imagine a situation under which that might happen. Or Marge? Brokenhearted as he was, he couldn't help feeling that sitting alone on a log in the snow, with that assurance in him, was better than what Fran was doing. Better for him certainly. He tried to picture her sitting next to him, but couldn't. He remembered how frightened she had been in his dory. Here the night and the stillness and the cold would probably frighten her also. Her feet would freeze. Thinking of her that way, of the inappropriateness of trying to move her here, put her a little farther off, nudged her away from the numb raw center of himself. (How could things be numb and raw at the same time?) If he worked on that, he might be able eventually to push her out altogether.

A car came along the road and stopped. The lights were turned off. Somebody got out, opened the trunk, came over to the woodpile, and began to help himself.

He waited until the man had a full armload, then silently followed him back to the car. The man tumbled the wood in with surprisingly loud thumps in that very still night, then turned to see him looming. It was Davey, who let out a yelp of terror as he grabbed him by the front of his mackinaw and threw him into the trunk, where he landed on his back among the split wood, his legs sticking out. He had half a mind to slam the trunk lid on those legs, but he didn't. He stood with his hands on his hips, staring in at a paralyzed Davey.

"You again."

Davey said nothing. He had banged his head on a log, and he reached back to rub it.

"Why can't you do anything right? Is this your car?"

"Doris's," said Davey.

He reached in and hauled Davey out of the trunk. "How long have you been doing this?"

"First time," said Davey.

"I know that's a lie. We'll go back to Doris's and see how much you stole."

"None there," said Davey. "We burn it up."

"I don't believe you. Where do you live?"

"Mitchell Extension."

"All right, get in." He climbed in next to Davey, realizing after a minute that he had left his bicycle in the woodlot. "Turn around and go back," he said.

"What for?" Davey was still afraid of him, didn't want to go back to the woodpile.

He stuck his big red beard into Davey's face. "Turn around, I said."

Davey did.

"Now get out of the car. You'll find a bicycle back of that bush over there. Go get it." The numbness was melting away as the bully emerged. He ordered Davey to drive home, which turned out to be the trailer Marge had mentioned earlier. It was in a gravel parking lot, the only one there. He walked around it. There was no wood.

"Like I said."

"Inside."

Inside was warm and stuffy, a narrow jumbled room with an old-fashioned cast-iron potbellied stove in the middle. The stovepipe angled over to one of the windows, whose glass had been replaced by a sheet of cardboard to admit the pipe. There were half a dozen pieces of wood on the floor next to the stove.

"Almost all," said Davey, "we burned."

A short fresh-faced plump woman with curly blond hair came out of the bedroom. If this was Doris, she was nothing like what he had imagined. She reminded him of the cheerleaders at Whittington High, healthy bouncy schoolgirls.

"Hello," she said. "You here to party?"

"No," said Davey. "It's about the wood."

"Well, thank goodness. We're about to run out." She gave him a big warm smile.

"He come to take it," said Davey, "not bring it."

"Take it? But we just got the stove in."

Fred said to her: "Where do you think this wood comes from?"

"Crosstown somewhere. Davey, you said your brother—"

"He's been stealing it from his brother." He stooped to begin picking up the pieces.

"Davey . . ."

Davey said nothing.

"We'll freeze. Davey, stop him." But Davey did nothing, and she ran out of the room.

"Cut off the power," said Davey. "Got cold here. We been using the power outlet, but they cut it off when we didn't pay."

He dumped the wood back on the floor. "Why didn't you pay?"

"Couldn't. They let me off at the dump. Missed a few days here and there, wasn't feeling good. Then Doris was sick, like. And we got behind. I borrowed me this stove."

Davey had the resourcefulness of Lou but of a pitifully lower order. "What do you eat?" he asked.

"Oh, we eat. Doris is working again now. It's the cold that gets her. It's cold in there. No heat in there at all. She stays in bed in there."

"Works in bed too?"

"Yeah, but out here now. On this foldout sofa. I wait in there then. If we had the power, she could work in there like before."

This was pretty close to rock bottom.

"Not the best arrangement. Doris don't like it at all. Got the bed-room fixed up nice."

"Why don't you get a job?"

"Been looking. Right now I'm taking care of things around here until Doris catches up, like."

"You still drinking?"

"What do you mean, still? I drink a glass now and then, like any-body."

"Doris paying for it?"

"Well, when I get regular work again . . . "

He said: "Do you suppose you could stay sober long enough to drive a truck if I could persuade Lou to take you back?"

"I never drunk on the job."

"Then why did he fire you?"

"He shouldn't of. Like I said to you the first time, that's my job you took. And when I tried to explain that, you beat me up."

There was no point in reversing this rewrite of history. But it might be worth a try to get at him through Doris. "Would you ask her to come out?" he said. Davey called to her, and she reappeared, hugging herself. She had been crying—why was it that all the women he ever met seemed to cry?

"Don't worry about the wood," he said. "I'm going to leave it here. And there's some more in your car. What I want to know is, can you help Davey get a job?"

"He's been looking but can't find one."

"I guess you know why."

"Times are hard."

"I think if you stopped buying liquor for him he could hold a job."

"I don't do it that much," she said. "He just sips, like. He's never mean." She put a hand on Davey's shoulder. "Honey, maybe you should cut back some."

The great reformer of alcoholics spoke again: "If I paid Davey's salary to you and you paid for the electricity and stuff and didn't buy him any liquor . . . could you do that?"

"Course she could. You're talking like liquor is a problem with me."

He ignored that and said to Doris: "He'll ask you for it. He'll beg. He'll bully you. He'll do anything he can to turn you around. He'll beat you up."

"Honey, you wouldn't do that."

Davey shouted: "You're making out I'm a drunk."

"You are," he said. "Maybe you should join AA."

"Fuck AA. I take a drink now and then. I'll do that."

"So long as Doris pays, right? There's a word for that. It's pimp."

"I ain't no pimp."

He turned to Doris again. "Maybe you should put him out."

She said with destroying tenderness: "I wouldn't do that."

"He'll ruin you."

The cheerleader face darkened. "Ruin me?"

He persisted. "If you hide your money he'll find it. He'll sell your things, your car. He'll sell—" How was he going to put this. "He'll sell you and keep the money."

"Honey, you would never do that."

"I ain't no pimp," Davey repeated.

"The next time he asks you for money and you give it to him," he said, "he is."

"No," shouted Davey. "You get out of here."

He gave up. "All right. But you'll have to drive me home."

"I ain't driving you no place." Davey turned to Doris. "Anyway, we're about out of gas."

"I have a date tonight," said Doris. "Should be here now. We can get gas tomorrow."

He bicycled home and told the whole dreary story to Lou, asking how Davey had become a drunk.

"From baseball. It's that simple. Never wanted to do anything but play ball."

Davey had been a star ball player in Lincoln Harbor and captain of the school team in his senior year. His dream had been to play for the Boston Red Sox, and his hero was Carl Yastrzemski. For a while it had looked as if that dream might come true. He was drafted by the Red Sox right out of high school and sent down to play for Pautucket, a Red Sox farm team. His first time at bat as a professional ball player, he hit a home run and got his name in the minor league record book. He was a brilliant fielder, playing second base and shortstop with equal skill for two months into the Pautucket season. But the pitching in the league was a good deal better than anything he had experienced in high school. As soon as it was learned that he could not handle low outside curves, that was all he ever saw at the plate. At one point he went hitless forty-seven consecutive times at bat, another record for the book, and was dropped. Still a hero at home, he spent his evenings at the Blue Lobster, talking about the big leagues and letting admirers buy him drinks. During the day he drove the small truck for Lou, but he became increasingly erratic and ended up by pocketing money that should have gone to his brother.

"He's down and out," Fred said. "We have to do something for him."

"Dunno what that would be so long as he's drinking."

He suggested that Davey be taken on again as a truckdriver and his salary be withheld. "We could give it to Doris. She seemed like a nice girl."

"Doris is a whore. Become one right under our noses. Makes me sick to think of Marge being there when Doris begun."

"Even so, she seems honest."

"No such thing as an honest whore. Peddle your butt for money—Jesus, Fred, you surprise me."

Lou surprised *him* by being so puritanical. "So what do we do, let him steal wood for the rest of the winter?"

"If you want to give him some, go ahead. You can chalk it up against your earnings. You don't know that boy like I do. I've had three, four years of him, and I can't take any more."

He became a deliverer of wood to the trailer.

"This won't go on much longer," said Doris. "I'm saving money now. I'm limiting Davey to a pint a day. I'll get the electricity back pretty soon."

He asked where she put her money, concerned that Davey would get his hands on it.

"I put it in the bank. You know Hugo Westerveld?"

"Yes."

"Well, he's a client of mine. A once-a-weeker. He tells me what to do. And anytime you'd like to party, I wouldn't charge you on account of all this wood."

"That's kind of you."

"I mean, without the money we could have real fun. I always got a charge out of beards."

He thanked her again and left, thinking it a strange turn that Hugo, of all people, should be the one to precede him here, having failed by an eyelash earlier with Lorraine. But he had no intention of completing this new and awkward triangle. Granted that Doris was far superior to any of those dimly remembered gorgons of his drunken past, she was still peddling her butt, as Lou put it. That didn't go with her cheerleader demeanor at all. With that look and that sunny aura of schoolgirl innocence, she cut a sad figure when the truth about her was known, too sad for the role she was willing to play with him. And to be stuck with Davey—that was the worst of it.

The woodlot was finally done. The last tree was cut and the last stump added to the huge pile. They got permission from the town to burn the stumps. The boy scouts were recruited to monitor the blaze, and one night it was set afire. Flames shot into the sky for fifty feet, while the scouts hopped around it like goblins in the eerie light. He heard later that the fire could be seen from the other end of town.

Hugo was there to monitor the scouts. Fred said hello to him, but nothing more. He wondered if Doris had told Hugo about the wood delivery and that she was offering herself in return. He also wondered if Charlie had said anything to Hugo about Lorraine's involvement with him. So many secrets. So little on the surface, but a labyrinth just beneath.

The business was incorporated: Mendoza and Fay. For the second time in his life, he got possession of a stock certificate, two hundred fifty shares of a thousand issued. They put in a telephone. Marge took the calls during the day, when the others were out working. They also got an auditor and prepared to pay an income tax for the first time.

"You're killing me," Lou complained. "The overhead."

"We're starting fresh," he said. "A new corporation. No need to worry about what you did before. But you're going to have to file now because of the wages you're handing out."

"Shouldn't never have done it. I liked it better before."

"That's the price of success. You're getting too big to hide. Also, unless we keep good books and pay our taxes, how are we going to know how much money we're making?"

"Always knew before. Always enough."

He heard from Charlie again. "I want to see you." So he dropped in one afternoon, feeling extremely uncomfortable. But Charlie disposed of that in a couple of sentences. "I'm a happy man. Lorraine's a happy woman—at least I think she is. Only thing is, she's taken a strong dislike to you. Doesn't want to see you anymore."

"That's all right," he said. Actually better than all right.

"We can meet for lunch. Meanwhile, do you remember I said something about somebody being interested in buying your island? Did they ever get in touch with you?"

"No."

"They're back at me. Called again a couple of days ago. Miles of

Isles. Some kind of outfit that specializes in islands all up and down the coast. They'd like yours."

"Tell them to call me. I have a phone now." He wrote down the number and handed it to Charlie.

"I told them there was no water there. They said they knew that. They want to drill deep. They have their hands on a study that says there's a lot of water down there, five hundred, a thousand feet down. The only ones who tried it before never went more than a hundred feet. Solid clay all the way down."

"What should I do?" he asked. "You're the expert on these things. Why don't you act as my broker, my agent?"

"Happy to. But there's nothing to do until we hear from them."

They heard—quickly.

"They want to buy the island and then drill. I asked them how much. They said a hundred thousand."

"Shouldn't we grab that?"

"No." Charlie spun around in his chair, a complete circle. "You don't understand the nuances of this." He obviously liked the word, for he repeated it. "Nuances. If they're willing to pay a hundred thousand *before* they drill, that means really big money after they drill."

"Suppose they don't find water?"

"That's the risk. But if they do, the payoff will be so big that the risk is worth taking." He leaned across his desk. "I took the liberty of turning them down. If you think I did wrong, we can always go back and tell them we've changed our minds. But I wouldn't do that. Because if there is water, you've got a million-dollar island on your hands."

"A million dollars?" That seemed incredible.

"Yep. Maybe two. How do I know? The trick is to get them to drill before selling, and I think I managed that. I told them we would give them first refusal. If somebody else comes along with an offer, Miles of Isles can match it. That's a good deal for them because as soon as the word gets around that there is water, a lot of people will probably want in. Any offer you get, Miles of Isles can match."

"But suppose I don't want to sell. Then they've drilled a deep hole for nothing—even if they found water."

"I covered that too. I said you would dispose of the island within ten years. They said three. I'm holding out for ten. My reason: the boom's starting, and the longer you wait . . . Well, crazy things happen in real estate booms. You look back afterward and wonder what got into the heads of people, to pay the kind of prices they did. Anyway, this is all talk so far. Nobody's signed anything. All I need is the go-ahead from you."

"You'd go?"

"I would. Even though I lose a sure commission—that's eight thousand on a hundred-thousand sale. I figure to collect a lot more if there's water. I'm willing to take that gamble, and I think you should too."

44

SPRING CAME. HE HAD WORKED THROUGH THE WINter on his house, and now the downstairs floors were free of paint. They looked elegant after being sanded and waxed. The picket fence was whole again; he had taken a sample back to Gott Street, and under Lou's instruction had learned to use the table saw in the garage and made several new ones. He then installed them and painted the entire fence. He had some paint left over, so he used it on his dory, getting more of the same to finish the job. He and Lou launched it as before. This was done just in time for Cliff and Emily, who had returned from Tufts at the end of the spring term and were itching to get out to the island to see if any petrels had come back. They had obviously had a fine winter. He ached with envy. Cliff was his same contained competent observant self. Emily blazed with energy.

They were back in town two days later.

"The birds are here. They're laying. They're getting babies."

"Chicks," said Cliff.

"Whatever." Transported with excitement: "You ought to come out and see."

He did, a couple of days later, on a Sunday. Marge said that she would like to go too. Somewhat to his surprise, Lou made no objection. Whatever it was that had changed in Fred's behavior as a result of Marge's cauterization by Fran, Lou, with more sensitive antennae than he suspected, noticed it. He was no longer in love with Marge, and in some unwitting way, he showed it. Lou, with nothing now to be jealous of, elected to stay behind and work on his truck engines.

They went out after an early supper, in the long light of a May evening, the two women side by side in the bow, their faces, as they sat looking sternward, warmed by the setting sun to a refulgent glow that infused them with a surreal vitality and beauty: one serene, quiet, watchful, almost motherly now; the other full of fire and exuberance—neither his. How fine they looked, those contrasting glowing faces. How fond he was of both of them and yet how far away they were. What a contrast this trip was to that last plummeting one with Fran. It had been in the blaze of a summer afternoon, but for all that a dark passage.

It cheered him up to note how tidily the brambles had been cut back in the path leading up to his house. He was astonished at the domestic order within. The kitchen was like an advertisement from a homemaking magazine, with a bunch of onions hanging on the wall, a melon ripening on the windowsill, a washrag hung neatly over the edge of the sink. Folded towels were in the bathroom. He couldn't resist a glance into his bedroom and saw a tufted bedspread, procured from somewhere, on which two plump pillows lay. Two pairs of slippers were demurely peeping from under the bed. Again, he was savaged by envy and by the wasting feeling that his life had yet to produce anything like this.

Then out to the white stakes that had been planted here and there in the bushes. Cliff removed the sod-covered shingle that made the roof of one and lifted from the egg on which it was sitting a small soot-colored bird. It lay surprisingly quiet in Cliff's enclosing hand, its alert brown eye unwinking, a pair of delicate black legs with webbed feet dangling between Cliff's fingers. Emily fastened a thin aluminum band to the bird's leg, then entered the date, the number of the band, and the number of the burrow in a notebook as Cliff put the petrel back in its burrow and replaced the lid.

"Tonight the mate will come and relieve this one," said Cliff. "We'll wait for that. It's quite a show."

Other burrows were checked. The sun went down, and a dark tide of shadows began flooding up in the bushes, bringing with it the heavy salt smell of evening on this island. He had forgotten what a powerful scent that was, evocative now of his first weeks out here, when all had been fresh and hopeful, when he had stood in his doorway, looking out at the twinkling lights of the mainland, breathing that soft heavy salty air, laden with whatever the bushes and grasses gave up as the night settled down.

Cliff and Emily set up two poles and strung between them a net that resembled a volleyball net except that its mesh was of a gossamer-thin nylon. "A mist net," said Cliff. "The birds don't see it. They fly into it. We band them. As soon as it gets a little darker they'll start coming."

"Why do they only come at night?"

"Because of the gulls. Big gulls are tough on little petrels, especially the young ones when they leave the burrows for the first time. That's why they always leave at night."

"That's one of the great marvels of nature," broke in Emily. "Think about those babies living in the dark in the back of those burrows. They never come out. They just sit there getting bigger and bigger until they're even fatter than their parents. All they know is to eat. Then one night they don't eat; the parents have left. They don't eat the next night. They get hungrier and hungrier. Finally they crawl out to the entrance of their burrow. They stretch their wings for the first time. Think what it must be like to be one of those little petrels. He's never seen anything or been anywhere. He doesn't know how to feed himself. He doesn't know how to fly or swim. He has never seen the water, doesn't know what water is. But one night he takes off. He just launches himself into the darkness and flies out to sea—his first flight. He lands on the water—the first time. He learns how to feed himself. He travels all over the North Atlantic. Three or four years later, when he is sexually mature, he comes back. To this island where he was born."

"How does he do that?"

"Ask him. Nobody knows."

"Four years at sea," said Cliff. "Never sets foot on land. Sleeps, eats, lives out there."

"How do you know that?"

"By these bands," said Cliff. "Make a record of when they come and go. There's a fellow up in New Brunswick who's been banding petrels for years. He has one who's come back to the same burrow eighteen years in a row. He doesn't know how long the bird did that before he began studying it. He doesn't know how long it will continue. Nobody knows how long these birds live. All we know is that they live a lot longer than anyone thought. Could be thirty or forty years. Could be as long as you."

By this time the stars were out and only a narrow gleam of salmon creased the edge of the western sky. "Okay," said Cliff. "Now we catch a few birds." He turned on a portable tape recorder, and from it came a confused garble of chirps, twitters, whines, and croakings—the same strange sounds Fred had heard floating in the night air during his first months on the island, but much louder.

"I've got the volume up," said Cliff. "Lures them in." A moment later, a small dark body hit the net. Emily turned on the flashlight, and Cliff gently extracted a petrel from the nylon mesh. It already had a band on its leg, so he tossed it into the air. Moments later, another came in. This one needed a band.

"Why do you bother to do this?" he asked.

"Because there're a lot of burrows on this island and we've found only a few of them. So we band all the birds we can. Five years from now we may locate where this one nests. We'll have a record on him. Here, you try one. Be careful. It's not easy to untangle them."

That was an understatement. Under the spell of the night and these fluttering chittering little ghosts, his fingers grew fat and clumsy. The legs and wings of the bird were tangled in different strands of the net, its frail body too small and delicate for his gigantic poking. He was afraid of snapping one of those toothpick legs.

"Let me try," said Marge. With more skillful hands than his, she had the bird loose in a few seconds, and Emily clipped on a band. "This is beautiful," said Marge. "A miracle. Think of this going on here every night and nobody knowing about it."

"The miracle," said Cliff, "is that it goes on at all. If any dogs or cats or rats had gotten on this island, all the birds would be gone. This place is unique."

"I'll write a paper," said Emily. "My first scientific paper. My first act as a scientist." She handed the flashlight to Marge and gave Cliff an ecstatic hug. "This island. This place. It's so . . . it's just so *perfect.*"

Going home, the girls sat forward again, their faces in shadow this time. He sat slumped. His island was a miracle, a magic place, a perfect place for others but not for him. He felt profoundly depressed and had no words for Marge as he drove her home in the little truck. She, as usual when she had nothing to say, kept tactfully silent. She sat away from him in the far corner of the truck seat, as if to acknowledge that something had dropped out between them and would not be recovered.

Only when they arrived at Gott Street did she take his hand as they went up the kitchen steps. She gave it a small valedictory squeeze. "I hope you sleep well," was all she said.

He did not. He had to acknowledge that to be free of her was a relief. But the loss of Fran was piercing. Unable to sleep, he turned on his light and tried to read some of the verses in *Spoon River Anthology,* but they were so drenched with sorrow and loss and stunted lives and loneliness that he gave up. Looking through the dim square of his window, he could just make out the shape of the large truck parked outside. His life—a truck. It was better than drinking, but at this moment not much better.

45

HE WAS HAULING BRUSH NOW, TRUCKLOAD AFTER truckload from a new subdivision. In between he made the garbage run, Tony Lopes being engaged in other jobs. Marge had gradually worked herself into becoming the company dispatcher. At the end of every day she would have figured out the most efficient way to get the next day's jobs done, and he, Tony, and Carlo would get their assignments. He discovered that he could sit comfortably in a room with her now. What an enormous relief! At the same time, what a pang! He felt as if some vital force, the kick that made life interesting—and terrible—had washed out of him.

He got a call from Charlie, the first time in several years that a phone had rung for him. He went to Charlie's office.

"They want to drill. Fred, we may be onto something very big. They're thinking of putting a resort complex in there. They'll build a mole where that dinky breakwater of yours is. They'll dredge out the cove."

"If they find water."

"They want to take that chance. I asked them: how do we know they're serious. They wrote out a check for five thousand bucks. Hugo has it in the bank now. As soon as we sign, that check's ours. They guarantee to start drilling in a month. If they don't, we keep the money and tear up the contract. Here." Charlie handed him a document he had prepared. "We had a big argument about that business of selling in three years or ten years. They just wouldn't go for ten, so I worked out something different. No mention of a time at all. It says that if you *ever* sell, they get first refusal. Permanently. At a ten percent discount from any other offer. That's what nailed them.

"Ever? Why wouldn't I ever?"

411

"You might want to give the island to your kids or something."

His kids? What a hopelessly remote idea.

"Maybe to your wife. You have to think ahead. You don't know what you'll be doing a few years down the road." He paused. "You know, Fred—what you did for me. It turned out all right, I guess. But it might not have. I mean, suppose—"

"I told you, she loves you. She doesn't even like me."

"She doesn't. I have to confess that she can't stand you. I don't know what you did with her, and I don't want to ask. Although I was ready to kill you both when you came down the stairs that night and said she wanted you again."

"I'm not sure she really—"

"You're wrong. She was six-cylinder hell until I got medical help. I'm a little better now. I don't know what got into her. Maybe you do. I guess you know a lot of women. What makes them go crazy like that?"

Here was a golden chance to wrap this up. A clean exit. He grasped it gratefully. "Most women," he said sagely, aware, as he spoke, that he had learned this from Fran, "have a great reservoir of passion that they release when they are truly in love. If they can't release it they're in trouble. I think that was Lorraine's problem. She loved you, powerfully, and when you couldn't help her she got frantic. She lost her head." Then to nail it down: "If she hadn't felt so strongly about you, this probably wouldn't have happened."

Charlie drank that in, an expression of great comfort spreading across his round face. "Makes sense. Although I wouldn't know. Lorraine's the only woman I've ever been with. Even in school when everybody else—you know, guys like Hugo. He's been chasing girls since he was sixteen. That's why I got hit so hard when Lorraine fastened on him." The recollection knotted his face. "You probably wondered what happened after the motel night."

"I did, sort of."

"She locked herself in the spare room. Wouldn't talk to me. Silent treatment the next day after we got back from the chief's office. I said to her that we lived in the same house and couldn't go on like this. I said: 'Don't pick somebody like Hugo. If you have to have somebody, who would you pick?' She said you. That's how it happened. And you straightened her out."

"No, you did."

"I'm glad you didn't go back that second time."

"Me too." Clearly Charlie wasn't aware of the marathon session in the back seat of her car. With luck he never would be.

"Anyway, Fred, I know you think I've done some things for you. I just wanted you to know what you've done for me." An old-buddy pat, followed by an utterly un-old-buddylike embrace. There were tears in Charlie's eyes. Well . . . just keep away from Lorraine and hope for the best. Charlie was a friend, a true friend, and he had gotten him back.

"So we sign this?"

"If you say so. Who are these people?"

"I told you. Miles of Isles. That's a subsidiary of a big outfit in New York, Greenwillow Management." Charlie handed him another paper.

"What's this?"

"That's a permit to drill. They want to make sure you won't change your mind. They don't want to bring a rig out there and have you change your mind. Once you sign this, they drill."

A friend. His first, his best. And what a rotten woman he was married to. He supposed he should feel sorry for Charlie. But if she made him happy, what difference did it make? Illusions were what counted. He would just have to do what he could to keep Charlie's illusions intact. That would be easy. If Lorraine hated him—and there was every reason she should; he had humiliated her where it counted most with her, in her sexuality, that night in the car—he could avoid her. Even in this small town he could avoid her. He might never have to speak to her again.

He got into his truck. If Charlie loved her, that was what mattered. She was a good cook, a good housekeeper. That was a lot better than nothing.

The drillers responded with remarkable speed. Within days they arrived with a rig on a small flat-bottomed barge, and the following morning an enraged Emily was at his doorstep.

"Just what do you think you're doing?" she screamed. "They're destroying the place."

"Just drilling for water."

"We told them to get off. They wouldn't go. We threatened to get the police. They showed us a permit—signed by *you*."

"That's right."

She waved a fist in his face. "How can you do this? The petrels. They've even got a dog." He had never seen her so worked up. Bursting with health and energy, and now fury, she was like a volcano. He wondered how long the phlegmatic reflective deliberate Cliff could put up with a temperament as inflammable as this.

"Maybe I can do something about the dog," he said.

"Now."

On the way back to the island, she handled the dory. She drove it at full throttle, jerking the tiller about as she continued to scream at him. It was a windy day; the boat lurched violently, and both were soon drenched.

"Give it to me," he said, and told her to sit in the bow. He throttled down to three-quarter speed and began paying some attention to the waves.

"Go faster," she said. "Why don't you go faster."

"Not in this chop."

"What a bastard you are. You pretend to be a conservationist, and then you do this."

"A well, that's all. What's wrong with a well?"

"Because as soon as you get a well you'll sell the island to somebody and they'll ruin it. I know you. You're all alike. A bunch of greedy bastards." She then turned around and refused to speak again.

He steered the dory into the cove alongside a barge that was moored there, its deck loaded with sections of pipe. Emily jumped out and raced up to the house without speaking. He followed, noticing a drill rig that stood fifteen or twenty feet in the air and not more than fifty feet from the corner of his house. There was a stationary diesel engine throbbing alongside it, and the rig itself was working, *clang-thump, clang-thump,* steadily pounding its way into the heart of the island. Two men were attending to it.

"You have a dog here?" he said to one of them.

"How's that?"

"A dog," he yelled over the noise of the drilling. "Where is he?"

"Around someplace. Everyone worked up about my dog."

"Get him off of here."

The man looked him over. Then he reached into his back pocket and produced a wrinkled piece of paper, the permit. "Don't want trouble. We just dig our hole and leave. All you folks giving us a hard time."

"I signed that permit," he said.

"Well, then. You know our right to be here. That woman. She don't seem to understand that."

"This is a wildlife sanctuary. I didn't sign any permit for dogs here. I want yours off."

"Okay, I'll keep it in mind."

"I want him off now."

"Well, soon's he shows up—"

A coal of anger was brightening in him. He noticed a switch on the diesel engine, reached over, and pulled it. The chugging and pounding stopped, a blessed relief.

"Hey, you got no right—"

He was aware that Cliff and Emily had joined them.

"Mister, you got no right. I'm going to start this thing up again, and if you so much as touch it, I'm going to town and have the sheriff take you away."

"You start it up and I'll shut it off. Get that dog out of here."

"He's already dug up one burrow," said Cliff. "Number twelve burrow."

"Mister," said the man, "I don't think you understand. Me and Frank here"—he gestured to the other man, short but notably wide and carrying a large Stillson wrench—"we don't like to be interfered with in our rightful work. Now you just step back, and we'll get on with the job."

"Get the gun," he heard himself say to Cliff, "and shoot the dog."

"Hey. You can't—"

"I told you once to get him off of here. I want him gone before you start this drill again, before he does any more damage."

The man had now lost his own temper. "Mister, every time you touch this rig it's costing you money. So maybe I'll just sit down here while you think that over."

"Not me," he said. "I didn't hire you. And I don't want you to stop drilling. I just want your dog gone. So why don't you do that."

There was a moment of silent staring, then, "Get him," the man said to Frank, who pulled a whistle from his pocket and blew a shrill blast on it. Almost immediately a small terrier ran up.

"Thinks it's his lunchtime," the man said. "Don't do to go fooling with a dog's expectations. Don't feed him, and he might not come again."

"He won't be coming again," he said. "Take him down to your barge and tie him up. If he comes ashore again, Cliff will shoot him."

"By God—"

"And it will be self-defense. This looks like a dangerous animal. Likely to attack these two scientists."

On the way back, Emily said: "You know, you're not as wimpish as you seem. How did you know Cliff has a gun?"

"I didn't."

415

"And you called me a scientist."

"Isn't that what you want to be?"

"But to hear it out loud like that. Fred, what are you going to do when they find water?"

"They may not."

"But if they do?"

"I don't know. Maybe leave the place to my grandchildren."

"But who's paying for the drilling? Cliff says this is a big job. He says that the only way to get your money back is by development."

"Maybe."

"You would never develop this island, would you? Think of the birds."

"I don't know what I'll do. Right now I'm not going to do anything."

The garbage run had grown, and now, with all the summer people flooding back, it was going full blast. He had to get started at seven each morning if he was to be through by noon, hose out the truck, and get on to other jobs. His run began at the far end of Lighthouse Road, which was on the opposite side of the harbor. The opulent summer houses were strung out there, and as he picked up the cans he could look across the water at the older, squarer mansions of the town's past, the Cobb house at the end being the most prominent, and from that vantage point the finest, its shabbiness obliterated by distance.

Here on the lighthouse side it was all docks and lawns and wide verandas and striped awnings. The garbage cans were kept in wooden boxes with hinged slanted tops and latched doors on the fronts to keep raccoons from scattering garbage on the trimmed lawns and on the raked gravel drives. The Crenshaws had such a container. So did the Munsons next door. Their owners had designed their houses so that the kitchen-delivery-garbage ends faced each other, leaving the living rooms, the porches, and the master suites to look in the other directions. There was a low privet hedge between the two kitchens. One morning as he was picking up the Crenshaws' cans, he looked over the hedge and saw a woman in a terry-cloth bathrobe come out the back door of the Munson house and lift the lid of the garbage-can box. By the time he had driven around to the Munson side, she had lit a crumpled piece of paper and was holding it over one of the cans, letting it burn. He braked the truck and got out. She dropped the burning paper into the can. He recognized her instantly. Even at seven in the morning, with no makeup and wearing a bathrobe, she looked stunning.

"Hello, Mindy," he said.

She gave him a sharp look. "Do I know you?"

"We met once. When I introduced you to Ebby and you introduced me to Fran."

"Oh . . . You." She folded her arms, and her stare hardened. "Why don't you leave her alone?"

"I do."

"You don't. You ruined her life once. She got it straightened out. Then you come along and do it again."

"I don't," he said, bewildered.

"Yes you do. She was engaged to a fine man. She's broken it off."

Broken it off? Broken with Corky?

"It was right after she was here last summer. You ought to be ashamed of yourself."

"But—" His eye caught flames coming out of the garbage can. The paper she had dropped in had ignited others. He unlatched the door of the shed and dragged out the can. It was already hot to his hand. Oily smoke and larger flames rose from it. "Get some water," he said. "Get a pitcher."

Mindy ran into the house. He spotted a coiled garden hose near the kitchen door and turned on the spigot. When she got back he had already doused the fire. There was a smelly sodden black mass in the bottom of the can.

"That was stupid," said Mindy. "I meant to put it in the lid and let it burn out there."

He started to lift the can to dump its contents, but it was too hot to handle. "I'll have to wait until this cools off."

"I hope nobody comes," she said. "They'll wonder what I was doing out here."

"What were you doing?"

"Just . . . getting rid of something." She poured the contents of the pitcher she was carrying on the grass. "You're no good to her," she said. "Why don't you leave her alone?"

"I do," he protested. "I saw her only when you brought her here. I haven't seen her since. Haven't spoken to her."

"You're no good for her," she repeated. "I don't know what's worse, a drunken advertising man or a sober garbage collector. That's what you do, isn't it?"

"That's what I do."

"Stuck away up here. Can't you see how hopeless that is?"

"Hopeless?" he said, infuriated. "There's nothing to be hopeless about. If she wants to marry Corky, that's her business. If she doesn't, that's her business. I have nothing to do with it."

"She told me that you asked her to marry you."

"I did, but she turned me down."

"You shouldn't have done that."

"Listen," he said, so angry that he grabbed the can despite its heat and dumped it in the truck. "What's all this to you anyway? What are you doing up here? Where the hell's your yacht? Where the hell's your baby?"

"My children are here with me. We're visiting Cora Munson for a while, that's all." She started up the back steps, then came down again. "As for Fran, I don't want to see her ruined by you. She's my friend, my best friend. She was having a good life—finally a good life. She was going to marry a nice man. With a future. Not a—not a garbage man, like you." She was very angry herself now. "Why don't you just— You're the worst thing that could possibly happen to her."

He put the wet sooted can back in its box, then dumped the other one. Then he slammed the lids and bolted the doors. "She's left Corky?" he asked.

"I think it's temporary. I keep urging her to go back to him."

"Well, say hello to her when you see her."

"That's the last thing I'll ever do," said Mindy, going into the house.

46

HE DISCOVERED THAT HIS WHYTE SHOES WERE TOO small for him. Over the past couple of years, wearing only work boots, his feet apparently had spread. Also, his only socks were thick ones. He bought himself a pair of loafers and a pair of gray wool socks, packed his briefcase, which had somehow survived and found its way to Gott Street, with an extra shirt and a change of underwear.

"At least let me cut your hair before you go," said Marge.

He had told them of his plan. No longer entangled with her, he was able to confide in them both. Here were two people with whom he could discuss personal things. They were touchingly solicitous.

"And let her trim your beard," said Lou. "You'd be a good-looking fellow if you didn't wear that red mattress on your face."

It was pretty big, he had to admit, three inches long now and bushing out in all directions. Marge chopped away at it, then trimmed more and more carefully until it came down to a neat V under his chin. "Now you have to shave around your cheekbones," she said, so he got his razor, then remembered a toothbrush and toothpaste and prepared to throw them in the briefcase.

"Wait, you can't go like that." She went into the kitchen and got a plastic food envelope. "Use this." He was like a boy being sent off to school for the first time by a pair of clucking parents. Lou drove him to Newfield, where he boarded a bus to New York.

He located Fran's Favorites in the phone book, took the subway to Ninety-sixth Street and Lexington Avenue, and walked down a couple of blocks. He had no trouble finding it. There was a discreet lavender sign on the front door of a brownstone house, and a large lavender-colored van with a green border parked in front. He went up the steps and found himself in a small gourmet shop packed with cakes, jellies, cookies, spices, small jars of olives and truffles. He watched a customer pick out several items, produce three twenty-dollar bills, and receive only coins in change from one of Fran's beautiful girls.

"I'd like to speak to Miss Collins," he said.

"Do you have an appointment?"

"No."

"I'm sorry, Miss Collins doesn't receive people without an appointment."

"Then I'd like to give her a message. Tell her that Mr. Fay from Lincoln Harbor is here." He had worried all the way down in the bus that she might not want to see him and had debated phoning her first, but finally he'd decided that his best chance lay in a direct confrontation. Surely she wouldn't refuse if he had come all this way.

The beautiful girl phoned to somebody else, and another beautiful girl appeared a minute later, led him through a door and up a flight of stairs and into Fran's office. It was in the front of the building, with a large window facing the street. With her back to it, at a desk that Fenn R. Wilking would not have been ashamed of, sat Fran. She was wearing a gray wool suit and a pair of large horn-rimmed spectacles. She waited until the beautiful girl had closed the door, then jumped up.

"Fred, what are you doing here?"

"I was in town. I thought I'd drop in." He had trouble getting the words out.

"You look— You've shaved your beard." She came around the desk and held out her hand. He took it, shook it, didn't let go.

"You look well, Fred."

"You look terrific." Still he held her hand.

She made a small effort to withdraw it. He held on. "Let's not—"

Still he held on. He didn't know what else to do.

"Fred, you know how we—"

"Yes. How we." With those unlocking words, he drew her toward himself. Miraculously, she let him. They embraced. Oh, sweet Christ. Maybe there was a chance after all.

"Not here," she said breathlessly. "Lisa—"

"Lisa?"

"My secretary. She keeps coming in."

"Do you have a lock on the door?"

"Yes."

"Lock it."

"Oh, no." A shocked voice. "What would Lisa think?"

"The important thing," he said, still holding her, "is what do you think?"

"Me? I don't know what to think. You always come up so suddenly. You startle me. Please let me go. Lisa—" She was trying to withdraw her face to avoid his kiss but clinging to him with the rest of herself. "Fred . . . oh, Fred. Why did you come?"

"You didn't."

Her phone rang. She wrestled herself away to answer it. "Yes? But he's not due till four. . . . Oh, it is? Uh, I have a . . . I'll . . . Yes, I'll . . . Just give me a minute." She hung up. "I have to see him. I made an appointment. Go down to the shop and buy something. I'll call you back as soon as I can."

"I can't afford anything in your shop."

"Pretend to buy." She pressed a button on her desk and urged him toward the door. Lisa appeared. "Take Mr. Fay to the shop. I'll see Mr. Neefus."

Lisa did so, although she did give him a glance; his meeting with Fran had lasted about a minute, and Fran must have seemed breathless. He planted himself in front of a glass case full of small square iced cakes, pink and white and yellow ones, with chocolate designs scribbled on them. He studied them with great concentration. Two customers came in, and each parted with thirty or forty dollars before leaving.

"Try one," said the beautiful girl.

"Uh?"

"If you can't make up your mind. They're very good. They have mocha cream inside."

He pointed to a yellow one.

"You chose the best. They're made with grated lemon peel. Gives the mocha that tang."

He bit into it. It was indecently rich and delicious.

"I told you, didn't I? How many would you like?"

"How much are they?"

"A dollar apiece. Or ten dollars a dozen."

"Maybe I should try one of the pink ones."

At that point Lisa reappeared. "Miss Collins will see you now."

This time he went right to the point. "I came because Mindy told me you had broken off with Corky."

"You talked to Mindy?"

"She said you did that right after you left Lincoln Harbor."

"How did you talk to Mindy?"

"She was up there. I think she's there right now." He described the incident of the flaming garbage can.

"That was probably a letter she got from Mr. Wright. Mindy is in a terrible situation."

"Getting back to Corky—"

"Mindy is in a crisis with Ebby."

"If you're not going to marry Corky, how about marrying me?"

"They split. You don't know what a terrible situation this is. Ebby found out about Mr. Wright. What did you say?"

"I said something about marriage."

"Oh. Oh . . . that. Fred, I just don't . . . Things are in such a terrible mess here right now. I'm so worried about Mindy. And Ebby has been behaving terribly."

"How about Corky? How's he been behaving?"

"Corky has been behaving better than Ebby. But not well."

"Is that why you broke off with him?"

"No, Fred. Another reason."

"*Have* you broken off?"

"Yes. Mindy is correct in that statement about me and Corky."

"So what's all the big fuss about?"

"It's such a long complicated story. I just can't discuss it here. I'm so . . . I have another appointment at five o'clock. Where are you staying?"

"I'm not staying anywhere. I just got here."

"Maybe we could meet for dinner and talk. I could talk to you at dinner. I still have to make the waitress assignments for a party tonight. I have to do that now. You don't know where you're staying?"

"I could call Bob Dixon."

"Come back here at seven. I'll manage something." She pressed her buzzer again to summon Lisa. "Mr. Fay is taking me to dinner. Please make a reservation at the Caligula. Has Mrs. Buskirk come yet?"

Out on the street, he felt dizzy. She had seen him. More, she had seemed warm, actually more than warm. But it was hard to tell. She was whirling around so fast in the steam boiler of her business that there hadn't been any time to take reliable measurements.

He boarded a bus, rode down to Seventy-first Street, and rang the bell of Bob's house, calculating the exact balance of cordiality and reserve with which he would greet Fletcher. But Fletcher did not open the door; a maid did.

No, there was no Mr. Dixon living here.

No, she did not know where he had gone.

No, the owners were away and could not tell him.

Baffled, he walked over to Madison Avenue to consult the nearest telephone book. There was no Robert Dixon listed. Feeling somewhat jarred by the high pressure he had encountered in Fran's office, and now with his only remaining, reassuring contact gone in this city, which was calling up old insecurities wave on wave, he wondered what to do next, then thought of Walker Virdonette. Walker would know where Bob was. With relief, he located Walker in the phone book—office and home, he was glad to see—and rang the office, hoping that Walker would remember him. How could he not after all those evenings in Seventy-first Street? And the quail shooting in Georgia? And those tall sensational girls Walker liked to bring with him. Just the sound of Walker's cheerful voice coming over the phone gave him a lift. He explained that he was trying to locate Bob Dixon. "I was hoping to find a bed there, but there are new people in the house."

"That's right, he sold it. But if you're looking for a bed, I have one. In fact, I'm alone tonight. Want to have dinner?"

He explained that he already had a date but could drop in afterward.

"Good. I'm at 808 Park. Just a few blocks up from Bob's. See you later."

Now what?

With a couple of hours to kill, it occurred to him to make real a fantasy that had tickled him off and on for a year or more. As events had reminded him of Hennerkop, he had had several imaginary conversations with him, reminding him of the effort he had made to block the move to Lincoln Harbor. "See, it turned out well," he would say. "Look at me. I'm sober. I'm a respectable person." Lying in bed at night, it had been easy to conduct those conversations, but now, standing on a street corner in the same city with the man who was privy to the most humiliating and shameful parts of his life, who undoubtedly saw him as a worthless man who, in the end, had run away, could he face that dread authority?

He looked at his watch, remembering that Hennerkop's office was only half a dozen blocks away. Why not? Didn't he owe it to himself to show Hennerkop another side, a better side, of himself? And didn't he owe it to Hennerkop to thank him for whatever he had done to remake him? He went back to the phone booth.

"Yes?"

"This is Fred Fay."

"Yes?"

That careful, noncommittal, measured voice, that gray voice. In one syllable all the sessions came rushing back. He fought down an urge to hang up the phone. "You remember me?" he said.

"Yes."

"I'm in New York. I wondered if I might drop in."

"Yes."

"How about this afternoon? I'm free right now."

"Not this afternoon. I am sorry. But I can see you at ten tomorrow."

"Same place?"

"The same place."

Still with time to kill, he strolled up Madison Avenue, looking into the store windows. Never one to pay much attention to furniture or pictures or china—Julia had taken care of all that—he now found himself studying chairs and candlesticks and silver desk sets, feasting on the extraordinary bazaar that Madison Avenue was, as he for the first time began to imagine how this or that object might fit into his own house. He found it hard to do. Everything looked so rich and rare, and such a bewildering variety of styles were represented, that he again felt oppressed by the rush and opulence of this city, by the very crowding of wealth and choice that gushed out on him. Buy me, buy me. Preen yourself with me. Make a statement; let the world know what an appreciator of rarity and, even more important, what an afforder of rarity you are.

He did see one blue-and-white Chinese bowl that he instantly felt would look beautiful in his house. He went inside and asked the price.

"Six hundred dollars."

"Isn't that a crack there?"

"Yes, a very slight one. If it weren't for the crack, the price would be three thousand dollars."

He continued his walk, dawdling along. Even so, he got to Fran's house fifteen minutes early and found her in the shop, directing the arrangement of some of the merchandise. She was wearing a plain black dress and a string of pearls and looked ravishing as she scuttled about, getting a better display for tomorrow's pastries at the expense of the caviar.

"We have to sell these perishable things right away. So we have to give them a chance to advertise themselves. Like these croissants. Up on that shelf, nobody would see them. Down here, how could you resist them?" One of her beautiful girls followed her around, taking notes.

"We'll go to Caligula now. We'll talk. It's right around the corner." She slipped her arm in his, and he wondered if she remembered all those other times they had walked, dizzied by alcohol and desire, to his office—arm in arm then also, but bodies pressed close. If she did remember, she gave no sign of it but let her arm hang comfortably loose in his.

Caligula's was on Madison, a sumptuous small restaurant tucked away in the bottom floor of a brownstone. The proprietor greeted Fran effusively and led them to a banquette in the corner, handing out leather-bound menus two feet tall.

"I can't eat here," he said, looking at the prices.

"You can tonight," she said. "This is my treat. Anyway, I have an arrangement with them here. I come here so often and have sent them so many customers that they charge me twenty dollars, whatever I eat. Besides, I'm dieting to try and keep thin, and what they lose on you they'll make up on me. I think you should have the sweetbreads on toast. They're a specialty here. And so good. He gave me the recipe, and I use it often as a Fran's Favorite."

"I thought Fran's Favorites were your beautiful girls."

"No, Fred. A Fran's Favorite is something I serve. Those are the things I am known for as a caterer. Not a girl. I can't help it if people think of my girls as favorites. Anyway, every time somebody asks me about those delicious sweetbreads, I tell them that they come from the Caligula. We are good friends here, and when they have something else that seems special enough to be a Fran's Favorite, they give me that recipe too." Without even looking at the enormous menu, she signaled the waiter. "Mr. Fay will have the sweetbreads, and I'll have some veal with lemon. And a nice salad for two. And a glass of Sancerre for me." She glanced at him.

He shook his head. "Just water, please."

They were sitting side by side on the banquette. He would have preferred to be facing her so that he could talk directly at her, watch her expression as he spoke to see how she was responding. Now he had to sidle away a little and turn awkwardly to look at her, not the ideal setting for what he suspected would be the most important conversation of his life. Apparently she sensed his dilemma, for she backed away slightly herself and turned to face him. Her loveliness was stupefying, crooked tooth and all. So chic, so up now, so beautiful, so composed. His heart was wallowing in deep troughs, in such imminent danger of swamping that he plunged in recklessly, glimpsing that straight talk, fearsome as it might be, was the way to go.

"You never finished about Corky."

"Finished?"

"I asked you why you broke up with him. You never said."

"I am not in love with Corky. I will not marry Corky."

"Will you marry me?"

The waiter arrived with small slabs of pâté on beds of lettuce, and a plate of delicate melba toast. "Compliments of Monsieur Bourseau."

"He's always doing nice things like this," said Fran.

He shoved his pâté aside. "Will you?"

"Eat it, Fred. It's delicious."

"How can I eat it if you won't answer my question?"

"Fred . . . " Her face was pink. She picked at her pâté. "Fred, this is a poor time to ask that question."

"Why?"

"Because everything is in such a mess right now. You don't know what a mess everything has been since Ebby found out about Mindy and Mr. Wright."

"What's that got to do with us?"

"Everything. Ebby is very angry at me ever since . . . " Another attempt at her pâté and a nervous sip of the wine the waiter had brought. "Did you ever know that Mr. Wright had an apartment in New York? Not his home—that's up in Bedford Hills—but right here in New York."

He remembered, all right. He had been in the room when Mr. Wright set up Mindy with Ebby, promising her an evening in that apartment the following night.

"Ebby got suspicious of Mr. Wright. Up to this very moment right now I'm not sure why. Maybe it was because they were having Mr. Wright to dinner so often because of the advertising connection. Or maybe it was something he spotted between them that they couldn't hide. Or maybe . . . I sometimes wonder if Corky didn't know about this and say something to Ebby. Anyway, Ebby hired a detective to watch Mindy, and when she came home one evening he confronted her. He asked her what she was doing in Mr. Wright's apartment. She said she had just gone there for a drink after shopping. But it frightened her so that she refused to go back there again. And with no other place to go, she asked me if she could meet Mr. Wright at my place. You know, Mindy was passionately in love with Mr. Wright. How could I say no? So I said yes. And they did meet several times, when I had a party and they knew I would be home late. They always left the place so neat. You would never have known two people had been there."

She finished her pâté. He ate his, scarcely tasting it. "The trouble is Ebby found out about that also. I think Ginger told him. Ebby and Ginger have been very close lately. Actually they went on a trip together. To Dallas. Ebby has beer business there, and he took Ginger along because he says they should be thinking about opening up a Fran's Favorites there."

"A branch?" he asked.

"Actually I think Ebby and Ginger are lovers. Ginger was very cool to me when they got back. Ebby called me down to his office and said he didn't want Mindy going into my house anymore. I said that Mindy was my friend and that I wouldn't keep her out of my house. He said it was his house, because I had paid up only about thirty percent of what I owed him, and if I didn't he would put me out."

"Could he do that?"

"And the truck. I haven't paid for it."

"You could borrow the money."

"I don't think so. It's too much. I still owe fifty thousand on the house and fifteen thousand on the truck. That's sixty-five thousand dollars."

"Maybe I could raise it. I'll sell the island."

"And if they start bad-mouthing me, I'd lose business. In a way, they own me. Ebby is such a powerful person. And Ginger . . . I need her. Ginger looks after the girls, finds them for me, makes them behave and all. I can't do that—even if I had the time. I spend my day preparing parties. And in the evening I'm at them, seeing that everything is going right. I have to go to one tonight." She seemed on the verge of tears.

He said again: "I could raise the money."

"Ginger could wreck me just by having a few girls not show up or behave badly on a job. It's your name, your reputation. It's all you have. I'm a fad, you know. Fads don't last very long. I understand that. Rich people want me because other rich people do."

"But isn't your reputation based on the good parties you give?"

"That's part of it, of course. But not all. It's a risky business, because it depends on rich people. And you can't always depend on them."

"But Mindy would continue with you, wouldn't she?"

"That would depend on what happens to Mindy. I think Ebby wants a divorce. I know he wants a divorce. That's why he has that detective, to make sure Mindy doesn't get a big settlement and to make sure he keeps their children."

"Well," he said, "let her get a divorce and marry Mr. Wright."

She gave him a devastated look. "Men in your class don't marry the girls they love that aren't in their class. You should know that."

He did and had no answer.

"Things are too topsy-turvy now."

The sweetbreads came, bathed in a creamy sauce that was as good as Fran had promised. "The secret is a few drops of Pernod plus some other things."

In desperation, he said: "I asked you to marry me. I asked you twice. Why won't you answer?"

"Please, not now. It's too—" She actually was starting to cry.

"Are you saying no?"

"No, I am not saying no. I am just not saying yes. I can't answer you now. I am undergoing too much of a strain. You would understand if you knew what it was like to be poor."

"I've been poor. In fact, by your standards I'm poor right now."

"I mean *poor* poor. And the discrimination. You don't know how hard I've had to work to get out of that."

"Did you have to wear hand-me-down clothes?"

"All the time. From my sisters."

"Were you at the very bottom of your class in school, where everybody picked on you or looked down on you?"

"Oh, no, Fred. I was voted the second most popular and the third prettiest."

"I was never voted anything," he said bitterly. "And I think I know as much about poverty as you do." He subjected her to a long up-and-down gaze. "Just look at you, I mean, right now. I never even saw anybody who dressed like you until I was in college." His eye took in the restaurant. "And all this. You're paying for this meal because I can't afford to. So at least let me pay the tip. How much should I give?"

"Give eight dollars."

"In Lincoln Harbor, three of us could live for a couple of days on eight dollars. Just don't talk to me about being poor. As for prejudice, I'll give you that one. As I grew up, I got to the point where I was dishing it out, not getting it. But on a personal level, what do you know about being looked down on by everybody until you felt like nothing?"

"You felt that way, ever?"

"When you met me I was busy climbing just as hard as you are now. I just couldn't do it as well. That's why— Now listen to this. That was so hard, combined with everything else, that's why I drank." He grabbed her hand. She made a feeble attempt to pull it away.

"So marry me."

"You would come to New York?"

"No. I'll never be able to live here. Besides, I've got some responsibilities up there I can't run away from."

"So you see," she said, withdrawing her hand. "It's a problem, a thing to think about."

"You could become a caterer in Lincoln Harbor."

"I thought about that. When I was there. I asked Cora Munson if there were any caterers in Lincoln Harbor. She said no."

"There you are."

"I asked her why. She said there was no demand for caterers. People had picnics or servants."

"You could start a business. Be the first one there."

"No, Fred. Not now." She refused to say more. He had to be content—with what? A hope? A thin crack of hope? He walked her back to her brownstone. Was she holding herself a little closer to him? Or was it his imagination? At her doorstep: "Good night, Fred."

Again an engulfing desire to embrace her, but he could not bring himself to make the attempt.

"How about tomorrow? Can we have lunch?"

"I will be busy all day tomorrow."

"Will I see you again?"

"I don't know. I don't know."

"Can I write you?"

"You can write."

"Will you answer?"

"I will try."

"What is there to try about?"

"I don't know. Oh, Fred—" She ran up the steps and closed the door.

47

H E WALKED BACK TO PARK AVENUE, HIS MIND A confused dark sea, and started downtown. He had no notion of where he stood or how to proceed other than to send her a letter, no idea of what to put in it other than to reiterate his proposal. The thought of putting that down on paper curdled him. Spelled out, an awkward sentence or two—how could he expect her to accept, let alone respond? And if she didn't accept, what would there be left to say in a second letter? He arrived at 808 Park Avenue with the sickening feeling that, once again, he had blown it, had been too tentative, not masterful enough.

Walker greeted him holding a goblet the size of a balloon, swirling half an inch of amber liquid in the bottom. He led the way into a library with shelves running from floor to ceiling, many of them filled with identical green leather spines. There was a desk in the room, with a green-shaded light on it, a sofa, a couple of easy chairs, the ultimate up man's hideaway. Walker threw himself into a high-backed leather chair and put his feet up on the desk.

"Have a touch of this," Walker said, waving the big glass bubble.

"No, thanks."

"You're making a mistake. This is special old Armagnac. Nothing in the world like it."

"I don't drink."

"Too bad. I don't offer this to everybody. What brings you to New York? I haven't heard a peep out of you since you and Julia split up. That must be four or five years ago."

There rose in him the ghost of a feeling that this was where up men unbuttoned themselves, in a luxurious bachelor's haunt. Here two friends could exchange confidences, man to man, in a place never before entered by him, with an unspoken invitation to become a part of it. This feeling gave him the confidence to say: "I came down here to ask a girl to marry me."

"Well," said Walker, swirling his balloon and sniffing deeply. "Congratulations. Is it anybody I know?"

"I don't think so. Her name's Fran Collins."

Walker swirled his Armagnac; apparently the name meant nothing to him.

"She runs a catering service."

Another swirl. Then: "Hey, wait a minute. Is she a good-looking girl, you know, a smallish one in a black dress who runs parties?"

"That could be the one."

"Where did you meet her? She doesn't talk to people at parties. I mean, I tried it. She's all business."

He had a sudden glimpse of the role Fran had to play: attractive woman on public display all the time but oh so careful not to cross the line between business and coziness. "I met her before she became a caterer," he said.

"Oh," said Walker. "You want to *marry* her?"

It came out more easily than he had ever imagined it would: "I love her."

"Good in the hay?"

He flushed. If this was unbuttoned man talk, so be it. "Yes," he managed to say, realizing as he spoke that he didn't truly know. He had only divine intimations, dazzling glimpses.

"Sure you're not mixing love with sex?"

"Sure." That came out strong and clear.

"Easy to do, you know." Walker offered him a cigar, which was refused, and then lit one himself. "These are English-market Cubanas. Are you sure . . . ?"

"I don't smoke." Feeling a need for assertion after his rejection of all these manly vices, and such civilized ones when practiced in an environment like this, he was emboldened to ask: "Are you married?"

"Me? Oh, no."

"I thought maybe you and Irene George might . . . "

"Oh, no. Irene's not somebody to be married to. I don't mean to say that I'm not fond of Irene, that she isn't superlatively good at what she does best and what I like to do with her. But beyond that Irene has nothing to offer. She's interested in only two things, clothes and sex. As I say, she's a wizard at both, but I would never want to be married to her. She doesn't read, she doesn't play cards, she's not interested in politics or business or sports." Walker blew a cloud of smoke toward the ceiling and took another deep breath of brandy. "She's not someone you can love. She's someone you make love with, if you see the difference."

"I think so."

"And you really think you love your caterer? Why?"

To his astonishment, he discovered that he had never asked himself that question. Why did he? No need to ask it; it was just *there*. And was this any business of Walker's? Unbuttoned talk got out of hand too soon for comfort. He didn't answer.

"You don't know?"

"Of course I know," he said indignantly. "It's just hard to put into words." Then he let go as the torrent of her virtues fell on him. "She's honest. She's smart. She's got a lot of courage. She's overcome a lot of handicaps. I admire her for those things. I think she loves me. That's the important one." It was, it was. Bolder yet: "So who do you love if you don't love Irene?"

Walker thought that one over, inspecting the end of his cigar. "I guess I don't really love anybody in the way you're talking about. I like a lot of people. I like a lot of women. I—you know, if you want to put it in quotes, I do 'love' them, but I've never met anyone I'd like to marry. Irene would like to marry me. She smells a lot of money here, and she would know how to spend it."

He studied Walker, now a good deal heavier than he had been five years before, the ex–hockey player gone to fat. Walker had become a plump smooth man. His face was smooth, the skin tight and pink, his hair edging backward at both temples. He resembled a ripe plum, his maroon smoking jacket covering a comfortable paunch, which was just visible over the tips of a pair of black velvet pumps on the desk, each with Walker's initials braided on it in gold.

"Lot of divorces these days. Come from falling in love and then finding out you aren't. The sex thing. It's a great inspirer of sudden bursts of what people keep mistaking for love. What I love is all this." He waved his glass around the room. "I love my work. I love the life it lets me live. I love this"—a wave of the bubble—"and this"—a flourish of the cigar. "I guess you could say I love Irene; she's part of the package. But it's really my work I love."

A terrible truth hit him. "You could live without Irene?"

"Sure."

"Then you don't love her." Suddenly it was that simple, that awful.

"I guess not. I don't pretend I do, except when—you know—"

Feeling more and more unbuttoned and reckless: "Does Irene pretend?"

"You know, I never asked her. In those circumstances it's not exactly something you ask. In fact, it's not even the right question. She knows what she wants. I give it to her. That's it."

"You never really fell in love with anybody?"

"Oh, all the time. But it never lasts."

"Well, I guess that takes care of love," he said.

"It sure takes care of sex, puts it in proper perspective. After all, where do you find love after sex?"

Another insight. This was an astonishing conversation. "I would think that's where you should find it."

"No, pal. You're a romantic. After sex is where you lose it. Marry your caterer and you'll see."

If he only could. "So what does last?" he asked.

"My work," Walker repeated. "I love my work, and I'm very good at it. I specialize in residential properties on the East Side. Like this building. It's mine."

"You *own* it?"

"Well, not exactly. My company, Greenwillow, owns it. But I own a good hunk of Greenwillow, so it comes down to much the same thing."

"Greenwillow?" he echoed. "Do you go in for islands too?"

"A few. Just a sideline."

"Did you know you were drilling a well right now on an island that belongs to me?"

Walker sat up. "No, I had no idea of that. In Lincoln Harbor, right? I hope we do find water; it will be good for both of us. I'll make a note to check on it. Otherwise I might forget. These islands are little side bets on the boom that's sure to come in water properties along the coast."

"I signed a contract to sell it to you if I do sell."

"That's good. But I doubt if much will happen right away. Anyway, my real business is something that I don't understand why more people don't get into. It's ridiculously easy. It's a tax thing. You get together a group of people and buy a building. Then you write off big losses every year in depreciation and deduct those from your income tax. In a few years the building has no value on paper, although its real value has gone up—everything goes up because of inflation—and you sell it to somebody else, who will do the same thing with it. You pay the capital gains tax on your profit and buy another building. Pretty soon you're working three or four buildings at the same time.

Of course, this only pays if your income is up around five hundred thousand dollars." Walker looked at him over the top of his glass. "I guess you're not in that bracket yet, or I'd ask you into the next property we put together."

"My income," he said, "is about five thousand dollars a year."

"Come on. The last time I heard, you were knocking out big hits in the advertising business."

"I gave that up. I suppose you could say I drank it up. That's why I turned down the brandy you offered me."

"Funny," said Walker. "I always took you for the quiet type. You never got down in the mud when we were living it up on Seventy-first Street. Then you married Julia Fanshawe. I didn't know what to make of that."

He didn't know how to respond to that.

"I mean, Julia wasn't exactly a datable girl."

"Bob dated her. That's how I met her."

"Bob never dated her. Bob played *cards* with her. My God, did you really think . . . ? I mean, when did you . . . ?" Suddenly in too deep, Walker squashed his cigar in an ashtray. "I mean, you must have known that Bob didn't date. I thought you were a friend of Bob's."

"I was."

"Then you know he didn't like girls. I don't mean he went for men. I just mean he didn't go for girls. He never has."

A total stunner.

"Bob's interested in only one thing. He wants to be the best court-tennis player in the world. And he is—almost. You asked where he was. He's in England, playing the guy who thinks *he's* the best player in the world. The Englishman took him the first time around, but it was very close. You know those court-tennis courts, the funny shape they are, those funny angles. There apparently are some very slight differences in them. Not anything that you or I would notice. But if you've lived in one court day after day for years, the way Bob has, those little differences matter. They're the difference between winning and losing a close match. And the walls—they're not made of exactly the same stuff. Even the paint on the floor, so the balls bounce a little differently. Bob has a second match to play over there, and then they come back here for two at the Racquet Club. If Bob can stay close over there, he'll murder the guy over here. So he will be number one in the world. He might even win the second match over there. If he does, it will be a walkover here."

"What will he do then?"

"That's a good question. Maybe he'll begin to take more of an interest in women and a little less in his own body. Right now he's in training all the time. He doesn't seem to have any close friends anymore. I wouldn't see him at all, except that he lives two flights up from me."

"In this building?"

"I got him the apartment when I took over his real estate business."

He willed himself to keep his mouth shut and concentrate on the books in the shelves. Unbuttoning had two sides.

"Bob wasn't going anywhere. His family had some properties scattered around the city. But the old guy who was running the business wasn't going anywhere, either. I told Bob that I would give him an apartment here—*give* it to him—in exchange for his properties, and also give him half the income he was getting from them. If I didn't double that within five years, I'd return his stuff to him. He could keep the apartment. I put in that five-year clause because I didn't know how fast I could turn around some of the stuff he had— it was in parts of the city I was unfamiliar with. Anyway, he said yes and I went to work, and I did it in three years. Now Bob has more money flowing out of his ears than he knows what to do with. He pays no attention to it. As I say, he lives for himself, for his body, for the perfection of it. It's a kind of Greek thing. Remember those Athenians we studied at college, the ideal youth, the straining for perfection, the adoration of older men? All that. So when you ask me what he's going to do when he becomes world champion, I can't answer. My guess is that he'll defend his championship and go on defending it until some other young god comes along and takes it away from him. The tricky thing is, what will he do when that happens?"

"Doesn't he have other interests?" he asked.

"I don't know. I scarcely see him these days."

"But you said he lives right upstairs."

"We have different hours, different lives."

"At the Racquet Club?"

"Not there, either. I quit the Racquet Club. Nothing but young athletes and old drunks. My club is the Links now. It has members like me, people who know what they're doing."

The thought that his ideal could be as self-absorbed and as isolated as Walker made Bob out to be had such a stubborn angularity to it that he could scarcely fit it into his head. And yet there was a beauty to it that he could recognize in his memory of his college hero. Bob had a style, a distinction to him that, no matter how odd his goals might be, would still leave him standing high and bright. Anyone who sets out with an ideal and realizes it has achieved a glory of some kind and is entitled to rest on that achievement. He had his own goal now, although he had come to it very late and the prospect of realizing it was pretty dim at the moment. "So what's yours?" he asked Walker.

"My what?"

"Your goal in life. What are you aiming at?"

"My work. I'd like to take on something really big, like the Chrysler Building, or begin putting up skyscrapers myself. I haven't the capital to do it now. But maybe in another ten years I will. Meanwhile"—he waved his arm at the green book spines in his shelves—"there's my stamps."

His stamps?

"I'm trying to build the greatest collection of British-American stamps there is. Nobody's done that. You'll find a fellow who specializes in Newfoundland or Bermuda. But there's been nobody who's gone for the whole thing. Of course, there's the British royal family. They've been collecting stamps ever since George the Fifth. But most of those things went to him automatically, given to him by respectful colonies. He didn't really know stamps all that well. And I suspect the present queen knows even less. So I don't count them. All their stuff is locked up in a deep freeze, because they'll never sell it. I guess my practical goal would be to become the world's second-best collector of British America."

"But what is there besides Newfoundland?" he asked.

"*What is there?* There's Nova Scotia; there's Canada, there's Barbados, there's all those Caribbean islands. There are more than twenty countries I have to go after. The thing I have going for me is that I'm still pretty young. And I'm rich and getting richer. The men who have some of the most wonderful rarities are old. They'll die, and their heirs will auction off those beauties, and I'll have a shot at them. I'm already in a position where dealers in London and Switzerland and New Orleans know about me. They offer me things first." He swallowed the last remaining drops of his brandy and gave the bubble a flick with his finger, so that a clear bell-like sound echoed in the room. "Baccarat. Anyway, next to business I love stamps best."

He was reminded of a chilly evening in Under Wixton, when the Reverend Mr. Appleton had shown off his collection. "Are the Falkland Islands part of British America?" he asked.

"Yes. But they're very dull, unless you like pictures of penguins. Any slob could make a representative collection of the Falkland Islands. What they need is some history, some turbulence. Nothing ever happens there to change the stamps, to make them interesting or rare, to produce errors. Give me Newfoundland or British Guiana. There are things from the West Indies I'd give my right eye for. Want to see some of what I have?"

He looked at his watch. "I think I ought to be getting to bed."

"Okay, but just let me show you a couple of real nifties from British Guiana." Walker pulled a volume from the shelf and opened to some smudgy little squares in glassine envelopes pasted to the pages of the album, one or two to a page, like a fine painting hung on a museum wall with nothing near it to detract from its power. "Only four of this one known to exist in the world."

He stared at it. "You really like that better than Irene George?"

"Any day, Fred, any day. The world is full of Irenes."

He went to bed blessed—or cursed—with the knowledge that he was propelled by something that Walker lacked and in all likelihood never would possess. He took off his clothes to hang them in the closet and was made aware of a faint perfume coming from it. There was a nightgown, a flimsy silk one on a hanger. Irene's? Or the property of another lady, equally beautiful, equally tall, equally amorous—equally meaningless?

Hennerkop startled him; he looked so much smaller and wearier, so much grayer than he had remembered. His office was smaller.

"I never got in touch with you after— I mean, you probably wondered what happened to me."

"Yes," said Hennerkop.

"Well, it worked out better than you thought. I mean, I didn't just—you know—die up there. That is, I nearly did die, but—" How could it come out in such fragments? He felt acutely self-conscious facing this man who knew so much about him and now stared at him so intently.

"You went finally to the island you were talking about?"

"Yes. I lived there for six months. Then I got sick and had to move to the mainland. I've been living there ever since. I don't drink."

"That is good."

"I have some friends."

"That is better."

"I mean real friends. Not like— When I was with you, I didn't have any friends. None."

"I remember. You were very much alone. That is why I was concerned that you not leave here."

"But it worked out. I have friends I never would have made here.

I depend on them. They depend on me." Could he ever explain the long and tangled series of events that had brought him so close to Charlie and to Lou and Marge? He did his best. He even talked about Emily, but he decided to say nothing about Lorraine.

"You have done well."

"You thought I couldn't."

"Sometimes the patient is a better judge of what is good for him than is the therapist."

"But you got me started. I want to thank you for that."

"Nothing."

"No. A lot. I never did thank you."

"That you came at all is thank you. Patients do not ordinarily come to say thank you."

"They should."

"Perhaps, but they often do not. The relationship between the therapist and the patient is a difficult one. The patient wants to put behind him what has been a painful part of his life. He would prefer to forget it. He is anxious to go."

Hennerkop looked so small and sad as he said this that Fred quickly said: "They all go and they don't look back? You've put a lot of sweat into helping them, but they just run? Aren't you curious about what happens to them?"

"Always curious, but also fearful."

Fearful? Hennerkop?

"You touch a hard point. What is hard is the fear that you have not helped the patient. Too often you have not. You fear to face that failure. I believed you to have been one of my failures."

"Well, I'm not. I even learned the last lesson, the last thing you said to me."

"Yes?"

"You said I would have to— When I was talking to you about never meeting a decent woman, you said that I wouldn't recognize her because of the way I was. You pointed out that I had that chance and didn't recognize her. We were talking about Fran Collins, remember. And you were right. But I do recognize her now. I came down here to ask her to marry me."

Hennerkop's gaze was steady, still neutral.

"I asked her several times. She won't give me an answer."

"And how will you handle that?"

"I don't know yet. The last time I asked her was yesterday."

"I think you will handle it. You have handled some harder things."

At that moment he couldn't think of any.

"It is harder to come to terms with oneself, to accept oneself, than to accept a loss."

The old jargon beginning to creep back. "But I'll be alone again."

"Not as before. You have told me you have friends now. There are degrees of loneliness."

Slipping, slipping into those long-gone sessions, and with them a whiff of the old anger. "What do you know about loneliness anyway?"

"Much," said Hennerkop, his gaze unwavering. "I will say to you something I could not before. I was not entirely truthful to you in answering two questions you earlier asked. The first—Are you Jewish?—I avoided by sàying I was of Dutch descent. My reason: I did not think you would at that time accept a Jewish therapist. The truth: my father was Dutch, my mother was Jewish."

"No big deal," he said.

"No big deal now. But then . . . I think probably a big deal. Your second question—Are you an orphan?—I did not answer truthfully."

"I don't remember that one."

"My answer was no. Again, the truth would have presented difficulties better not introduced for us to stumble over. The truth was that my mother was imprisoned during the war and died of malnutrition. Many starved in Holland during the war. My father, learning of her death, shot himself."

This was so shocking that for a long moment he couldn't even look at Hennerkop, sitting so small and gray in his chair. When he did, he found Hennerkop's eye still boring steadily into his. "Do you have any brothers or sisters?" he asked.

"No."

"Where were you during the war?"

"I had already come to the United States, married, and started my practice."

"You told me once that you were divorced."

"Yes. My wife is with another man. So you can see I know something of loneliness. But like you, I have a few friends." A thin smile. "I manage, and so will you." The smile broadened slightly. "And your girl has not yet found another man?"

"She did, but she turned him down."

"So perhaps she will be with you. There is hope there."

48

ON THE BUS GOING HOME, HE HAD PLENTY OF time to think, several hours of encasement in what could have been a time capsule. The bus was well-sprung, and the seats were soft. There was almost no sense of motion. Rather, it was like being enclosed in some sort of large glassed-in projectile miraculously standing still, hung over the road while the landscape outside whizzed by, unrolling itself like an endless Chinese scroll. New Haven came and went, so did Hartford, as the bus bored its way relentlessly into remoter parts of Connecticut, sweeping in majestic curves around the flattened breasts of ancient hills.

I'm a fool, he thought, reviewing his conversation with Walker and the series of insights that had dropped into his head (or seemed to; maybe they had been hiding there unnoticed), insights that he felt sure other people had had for years but had been blocked out in him. Hennerkop . . . ah, Hennerkop. How right, how right. How could he have gone so long without noticing things that other people seemed to have learned to notice, probably in childhood, certainly as they grew up and encountered the world. How had he missed all that? How had he been so blinded by admiration and envy of Bob not to notice that for all his surface charm and friendliness, he was a lonely man? That is, if Bob *was* one—for he had no assurance that Walker was right. Walker himself had shown an unexpectedly shallow attitude toward the one thing that he, Fred, valued above everything else: intimacy. And intimacy, on the scale he was now thinking about and had so desperately sought for so long, had to be with a loving woman. With him, before, the only road to intimacy, the only one he could think of, had been sex—it was the only way he knew of risking closeness with another. But if there was only sex, then flight, as he knew so well, was the inevitable follow-up. Therefore there had to be more: companionship, admiration, tenderness—love. Now he understood that. In fact, he had tried to express it to Walker the night before, though he could no longer remember exactly what he had said. What he had *meant*—and now when he thought about it it was so simple— what he had meant was that through sex the sudden intimacy, the self-exposure, was so great—and, if it was to have any meaning at all beyond self-gratification, so risky—that it forced on one the need to confront those risks, to see for oneself how one truly felt. In other words, sex was a sort of testing ground, a door that could be opened to deeper feelings. Then, if those deeper feelings appeared, one could say that one was in love. From then on, sex was simply a way of expressing that love.

All very neat. Just the thing for a course on ethics and social behavior in high school, which would be totally ignored by the students, who were in such a boil about their newly discovered sexual ardor that they could scarcely think of anything else. Sex was *the goal.*

His own social development had been so stunted that he was clearly still at the high school level when he had his first encounters with Fran. Now he knew more. He wanted to share the rest of his life with her, but to his dismay, he suspected he never would. She was on another track, and the longer she stayed on it, the more hopeless his case would be. Hennerkop had given him a small ray of hope. Sitting in the bus, he tried to brighten that, but without much success. His loss, compared to Hennerkop's, made him squirm, it was so shallow.

He had phoned to say what bus he would be on, and he was still turning over in his mind how he would break the news of his failure to whoever met him when he arrived in Newfield. He hoped it would be Marge; for some reason it would be easier to talk to her than to Lou. And it was she who waited in the small truck.

"Well?" she said, sliding over so that he could drive.

"I don't know. She didn't say no, but she won't say yes." He went on to describe the problems involving Mindy, Ebby, and now Ginger. "She's trying to hang on to her business. It's making a pile of money. For a young girl brought up poor, it must seem like a miracle to her. I even wonder if I have the right to keep pestering her. I have so little to offer."

"You have yourself," said Marge. "If she loves you, that's all you need. If she doesn't, well . . . But until you make sure, I wouldn't give up."

Somewhat buoyed by that, he asked: "How are things here?"

"Not good. You can't have your room back."

"But we aren't—"

"It isn't you. It's Doris. She's in your room. Davey beat her up. She had nowhere else to go."

"Davey?" He might have known.

"Lou doesn't want her living with us. He wants to put her out. But where will she go?"

He had never seen her so distressed. "Why would Davey do that? He was totally dependent on her."

"That's the reason. They had an argument. She refused to give him any more money for liquor." Marge put her face in her hands. "It's terrible. You should see her."

He drove on, wondering if anything he had said to Doris might have precipitated that. If so, his own ineptitude again.

Marge said: "Davey had stopped even looking for work. That's when she told him she wasn't going to give him anything until he found a job."

"Did he try?"

"No. He just beat her. She looks terrible. She can't go out looking the way she does. And Lou says he won't have her any longer. I'm scared he might throw her out while I'm getting you."

But Lou hadn't. Instead, he was sitting in the kitchen, looking menacing. "Fred, you got a hitchhiker in your bed. Expect Marge told you. Time you went in and threw her out."

"Maybe she's not in shape to be thrown out," he said, as mildly as he could.

"That's right," said Marge.

Lou whirled on her. "I don't want a whore in this house."

"She's not. Not really," said Marge.

"Fuck for money, you're a whore," Lou shouted.

"Be quiet. She'll hear you."

"Hope she does. Save me telling it to her face."

Fred got up, blasted by the terrible tension in the room, and looked out into the hall to see if his bedroom door was shut. It was. He then closed the kitchen door and sat down again. Marge was at the table. As he watched her, he saw her stiffen. Her back straightened and she got a good grip on her arms, which were folded on the tabletop. "What's your definition of a whore?" she asked.

"I just gave it to you."

"She gets something back for what she gives with her body?"

"What I said."

"I have the feeling that Hugo Westerveld's paying her trailer fees."

"Not surprised. Never could stand the bastard."

"Would that make her a whore?"

"I just told you. You lay on your back and spread your legs—I don't care if you get paid your rent or a bushel of potatoes or a fifty-dollar bill. It's the same thing."

Marge got to her feet. "Then you have two whores in this house." She walked out of the room.

Lou's face, as he stared at the shut door, was a study in rage being gradually overcome by bafflement. There was a long silence. Fred sat and waited, said nothing. Lou avoided his eye, finally muttered: "She knows better than that."

"Of course she does. Maybe she's trying to tell you something about Doris."

"She ain't no Doris, for Christ's sake."

"Of course not. She's just asking you not to be so hard on Doris."

"I want to marry her. I told you that."

"That's the difference. That makes two of us. Why don't you tell Marge that Doris can stay for a bit. I'll take a look at her."

He knocked on the closed door of his bedroom. There was no answer. He opened the door slowly and looked in. Doris was in his bed, propped up slightly by a couple of pillows. She looked truly dreadful. One entire side of her face was a deep purplish black, swollen enormously to give a squat pumpkin dimension to her naturally rather square face. The eye on that side was tight shut under lip-sized lids. The other side of her face was a rainbow of red, yellow, and purple, the eye there a slit. That slitted eye—where had the cheerleader look gone?—gave her a mean crafty look. She squinted out of it without saying anything.

"I just thought I'd look in to see how you were."

She continued to squint. A teary squint.

"I hope it's nothing I said."

"No."

"How did you get here?"

"Hugo. I had a date with him. He found me on the floor."

"Was Davey there?"

"No, he left. He took my car. Hugo thought I was dead." She had difficulty talking. He noticed a large scabbed crack in her upper lip. "He picked me up. I was all bloody."

He had a momentary glimpse of a raging Davey, consumed by anger, desperation, frustration, fear, all of it exploding in him.

"I fell down. He came down and kept hitting me. He broke my finger." She took a hand from under the covers and showed him a

443

splinted forefinger. "I was covering my face. He took my hand and bent back the finger. That hurt. The next thing I remember was Hugo."

He tried to keep a neutral expression as he stared at that grotesque face—and apparently failed.

"Do I look that bad?"

"Worse." Might as well give her the dark side and then be able to tell her the next day that she was improving.

"I heard what he said out there."

"Forget it. We're not going to throw you out."

"I didn't want to come here."

"All right."

"There was no other place. When Hugo said I couldn't go to his house, I had to stay here."

"How about the hospital?"

"Not the hospital. They'd ask questions. Anyway, Marge was a nurse. She fixed me up." She was gripping the covers just as Lorraine had done, her one splinted finger sticking out like a miniature semaphore.

"Can I get you anything?"

"Some more water. I drank the other."

He went to the bathroom and refilled her glass, then returned to the kitchen. Something had passed between Lou and Marge. Lou looked rather swollen himself, but the swelling was contained. Marge was at the stove, cooking something.

"You seen her. Looks pretty god-awful, don't she?" Lou said.

"Yes."

"She should be in the hospital. Except that she don't want to go there. A lot of questions. Press charges against Davey."

"Where is Davey?"

"Dunno; probably left town. Should have." He turned to Marge. "You making enough for four?"

"I'm making oatmeal, something that she can get down. She can't chew very well."

"*Oatmeal*. That does it. I'll eat out. Leave her to you two."

When they were alone, Marge said: "I can cook you something else."

"No; I like oatmeal."

"Then I'll just fix up this tray for her."

"When did all this happen?" he asked.

"The night before last. Hugo brought her about nine o'clock. She wasn't so swollen then, but she was all bloody. Her nose was bleeding, and her lip. Lou thought she'd been in an automobile accident. I wasn't here. He came and got me at the Blue Lobster."

"Can she walk?"

"Oh, yes. She walked in here. But she's had a terrible shock. She doesn't want anybody to see her. She needs to be in bed for a few days. She cries all the time. Hugo came around. She won't see him. I think this has got to her. She's beginning to think about what she's been doing. Brought face-to-face with it, see how she's been drifting."

"Will Lou keep her?"

"Yes. Until she looks respectable. Where are you planning to sleep?"

"I could sleep at my house, except that I have no bed."

"You want to go to your friends?" She avoided his eye as she said that. Clearly something about Lorraine had leaked out. Everything in this town seemed eventually to do that.

He quickly said: "Not there," quickly enough, he thought later, to confirm any suspicion she might have.

"Then you'd better go to Hugo's. That's the least he can do."

Which was where he went—for five nights, never asking any questions about Doris, never given any opening conversational gambit by Hugo. He made a point of coming in late and going directly to bed. In the mornings, of course, he was up and gone before Hugo was out of bed. He had his breakfasts in Gott Street and gradually became accustomed to Doris's face at the kitchen table. Its slow transformation toward normal had a horrible fascination. All the blood in her bruises was gradually moving downward under the force of gravity. Her jaw and neck were now the darkest parts of her, and she was able to open the puffed eye a little.

During the day, when Lou was working, he imagined that Marge and Doris were having long conversations. She appeared for supper every night, but as soon as she was finished, she went to her room. Lou never spoke to her. Only: "She could at least stick around to do the dishes."

"She does them after breakfast and lunch," said Marge. "She also cleans. She's a big help."

"Huh."

"She wants a job. She says she will take anything as soon as she looks presentable."

"Let her try for dumpmaster, now that Davey's gone."

"No. She would see nothing but men there. She doesn't want to have anything to do with men right now."

"That's a switch. Give her time for her black eye to be fixed, then watch which way she jumps."

All this with all doors shut.

On the sixth night, Hugo was waiting up for him. "I saw Doris today. Finally."

"She's looking a lot better."

"I want to get her out of that house. She's not happy there. I figured you might let her stay in your house."

"There's no furniture."

"Supposing I buy some."

"Okay."

"I'd pay you rent."

"No need for that. Let the bed and whatever else you get stay. That would more than take care of the rent."

"I also want to get her a job in the laundromat. Less likely to run into men she knows there."

"She'll run into their wives. From what I've learned about this town, they'll give her a hard time."

"I talked to her about that. All the hurdles, the bad talk. She wants to stay here."

"You have anything to do with that?"

"Well, yes—sort of. She's a nice girl. Just got off on the wrong foot, you might say."

"She got a right one?"

Hugo reddened. They were standing in the hall of Hugo's house, an extremely feminine, not to say prissy, house. The hand of the absent wife was visible everywhere, from the rose-patterned runner that carpeted the stairs to the collection of small china figures that cluttered the piano in the living room. "Yes," Hugo said. "She's a nice girl, very friendly. She likes company. She was just a little too frisky when she first came here. Then, when she couldn't get a job, and her boyfriends began— She needed money. She needed a man. Not a lot of men, just one."

"Like you?"

"Well, yes—sort of."

"How are you going to handle that?"

"I don't know yet. I'll see how things go." Then he repeated: "She's a nice girl; a loving woman, you might say."

"That's what everybody says."

446

Hugo flushed deeper. "Don't underrate that."

He had spoken too quickly. "I don't. I only mean that it will be rough here."

"I know that. I'll have to work on it."

Doris moved into his house. Hugo had furnished one room: a bed, a small carpet, a bureau, and a chair. One standing lamp.

"This is cute."

"You'll be needing some kitchen things."

"Just a hot plate and some china." Her appearance was improving rapidly. With dark glasses and a heavy application of pancake makeup, she looked almost normal. But she seemed apprehensive, and when he moved to leave he found her blocking the door. "It's just that . . . "

"Nothing to sit on downstairs?"

"It's just that I don't want to go out. Marketing and like that."

"If you expect to stay here, you'll have to get over that."

"I know. But suppose I meet. . . .?"

"You will meet. You'll say you've retired. You have, haven't you?"

"Oh, yes. I wasn't too comfortable with . . . I wanted to be with one man. Like everybody else."

He recalled the moment when she had spoken so caressingly about Davey. Her need must have been enormous. She was like a sponge, ready to soak up anything that came her way, unlucky to have soaked so badly. . . . She was still standing between him and the door.

"Anything the matter?"

"Could you bring groceries?" So timid, almost beseeching.

"If you make me a list. How about reading? You want some magazines?"

"I'm not much for reading. I could watch television."

"How about the one in your trailer?"

"I don't know anything about my things in the trailer. Hugo said he would get them. My clothes, like, and also a TV."

"You like Hugo?"

"Oh, yes."

"He like you?"

"I hope so."

49

EMILY DROPPED BY. SHE WAS WEARING INORDI-
nately tight jeans and a man's blue work shirt. Her hair was
pulled back tight again. Now deeply tanned, she was a strikingly
handsome woman, albeit a formidable one. "I guess you heard they
struck water."

"No, I didn't."

"At six hundred feet. They told Cliff that they were willing to go
to a thousand, but they didn't have to."

Water.

"Lots of it. More than you'll ever need. They capped the pipe and
left. So what are you going to do now? People are going to be after
you to sell. Cliff knows about those things. He's been involved in saving a couple. He says your island is now worth a million dollars."

His first thought was that he could settle the debt on Fran's house
and her truck, leave her in control of her business. His second was
that he didn't want to do that; better to shake her free of them. His
third was that his second thought was a rotten selfish one.

Emily said: "You're going to get offers. What are you going to
do?"

The first thing he was going to do was talk to Charlie. He wondered if Charlie had got the news yet.

"Yep," Charlie confirmed. "Came yesterday. An offer of four hundred thou. I told you, didn't I?"

Holy mackerel. Four hundred thousand—on an investment of
thirty.

"That was from Greenwillow. We'll turn it down, of course."

"But—"

"That's just for starters. I'll put out that the island's for sale. Give the water story. Get some competition."

He said: "I know the owner of Greenwillow. He's a friend of mine."

"All the better. He won't try to skin you."

Four hundred thousand? The offer seemed astronomical. What would he do with it all? First he would pay off the mortgage on his house and all the installments due on the island. Then what? His mind flew to Fran again. If he cleared up her debt to Ebby, she would be free of the danger of losing her business. But if she did that, she would be even more closely knitted into her career in New York. Again he weighed the alternative of letting her struggle, and maybe fail, and then maybe come to Lincoln Harbor—and again he forced himself to push that out of his mind. But it kept returning. On one bright summer day after another, as he wheeled the little truck around on the garbage run, he drew pictures of Fran—not Doris—presiding in that small house, making it into a proper home. He would build an extension on the back, put in a real kitchen. She could run a catering business from there. Not approaching the scale of her activity in New York, an extraordinary achievement the more he thought about it, but a modest enterprise in keeping with the scale of everything else in Lincoln Harbor, just enough to keep her busy and happy.

He met Mindy again. She was sitting on the Munsons' back doorstep, apparently waiting for him.

"You went to New York."

He unlatched the trash box and pulled out a can.

"I thought I told you to keep away from her."

He dumped the can in the truck.

"Listen to me. She told me all about your visit. She's very upset."

The second can.

"You see what you do. Why don't you say something?"

"Nothing to say."

"You can at least hold still and listen to me. What do you hope to do with her?"

"I hope to marry her."

"Well," said Mindy in a hard voice. "That will mean giving up a great career and coming up here. She says you won't live in New York. How can you expect her to live here?"

"Other people do."

"Not by choice."

449

"I chose."

She brushed that off with a disdainful gesture.

"You're here," he went on. "You're here with people who are here. They chose."

"That's summers. That doesn't count. I'm talking about all the time."

"So am I."

"You'll just bring her grief. Trevor says you're a total loss, a weak man, an alcoholic."

"Whoever Trevor is." As he spoke, he remembered.

"Trevor Wright. You used to work for him. Didn't Fran ever tell you about me and Trevor?"

He was so angry that he said: "She didn't have to tell me about you and Trevor. I was there when Trevor fixed you up with Ebby." The words came in short bursts. "That first time. When I met Fran. You introduced us. Is that what's bugging you? A guilty conscience?"

"Don't be ridiculous."

"All she ever told me," he ground out, "was that you're still shacked up with Trevor and that Ebby is divorcing you because of that."

"Actually I'm divorcing Ebby. I have grounds too." She stood up. He put away the second can and latched the door with unsteady fingers. The heat of this conversation roared in him. Afraid of what he might say next, he looked away from her, over the top of the garbage bin to the water beyond, specked with the white wafers of yachts. The tide was flooding, all the buoys pointing inward, the intense deep blue of the water reflecting an even deeper blue of an infinite sky. The instant glimpse took away some of his wrath.

"This is a better place to live than New York," he said thickly.

"Maybe for you."

"For anybody."

"For drunks like you—who wash up here because they can't function in a real place."

"This is a real place."

"It's a backwater. Look at you—hauling garbage."

"Look at you," he said. "If you've got such a great life in New York, what are you doing here?"

"I'm leaving. This is just temporary."

He took another look at the harbor—for stability, for confirmation—at the cluster of buildings at the head of it, at the two church spires poking up into that sapphire sky. All that had happened to him

450

here was encapsulated in one quick glance. It caught him by the throat, made it hard for him to speak. "Look," he said, spreading an arm. Then, with great emotion: "If Trevor were living here, where would you be?"

"Trevor would never live here."

"But if he did? Wouldn't you like it—here with him?"

That shook her. "You don't know anything about me and Trevor."

"I know enough." He lowered the container lid. "If you had him here, you'd be better off than you are not having him in New York."

"That's totally off the point," she said agitatedly. "It's the people, not the place."

"I agree," he said. "So why not here?"

"Because—" Then it erupted from her. "It's not the place. It's you. You treated her abominably."

"Not anymore."

"You didn't even write her."

The first flash of Fran herself. He pounced on it. "She said that?"

"Just in passing." Then she turned and went into the house. He got into his truck and spent the rest of his run wondering if he hadn't made another terrible blunder. What was the sense in fighting with the woman who was Fran's best friend? But he would write. Mindy had given him that sliver of hope.

He sent her a letter, a single sentence:

"I ask you for the third time, I won't ask again."

Things began moving faster and faster. Charlie informed him that two others were interested in the island and that the bid was now $520,000. "Don't forget," said Charlie, "that your friend at Greenwillow gets it for ten percent less."

"That's right."

"And that I get another eight percent. You'll still wind up with about four hundred thou."

"Wonderful."

"But we don't sell. These things take time before you get the feeling that you've reached the limit. We're not there yet."

Doris moved back into the trailer. "Maybe she'll settle down now," said Marge.

"With other men again?"

"Maybe not. She's crazy about Hugo."

"Is Hugo crazy about her?"

"She thinks so. He says he is."

"Men have said that before."

"I know."

"So what does he do? Visit the trailer once a week? I don't think he can keep doing that. Not in this town."

"Maybe. But don't count on it. Life is loosening up, even here. I noticed it myself in little things."

"Like what?"

"Like your friend Lorraine. When I was marketing yesterday she noticed me. Gave me a little smile."

"Do you think she'd ever smile at Doris?"

Marge turned from the sink. "Don't be mean."

"I'm not." He wasn't; he felt endlessly sorry for Doris. "I'm just wondering how long Hugo will want to go back to that trailer. My guess is not very long. What'll she do then?"

She wiped her hands. "Start fresh somewhere else, I suppose. Like you. You did." She folded the dishcloth on the edge of the sink. "The trouble with Doris is that she's not very good at anything else. It's too bad the world's the way it is. I mean, why shouldn't you get paid for what you're good at and what you like to do?" She turned to face him. "Does that shock you?"

"You're beginning to sound like Emily," he said.

"I'm beginning to think like Emily. There should be a place for Doris. I mean a respectable place. If you have something people are willing to pay for, why shouldn't you sell it? Why is that any different from painting pictures? You're just selling another part of yourself. Or writing poetry? Is your body any less precious than your mind?"

She continued to amaze him. "Would you do that?" he asked.

"No; I'm not in that business. Besides, I love Lou."

"But if you didn't? You say she loves Hugo. Does that mean she should stop hustling?"

"I can't answer that," she said.

"Will she stop?"

"Probably not. Not the way the world is. The way men are."

Emily returned, insisting that he go out to the island. On Sunday he did.

"We have forty-seven active burrows," said Cliff, "and we've banded twenty-four other birds, whose burrows we haven't found yet. Of course, two of them may be mated and using the same burrow.

But still, this is an important place. There's a lot of work to be done here yet."

"Look at this." Emily handed him a magazine. "It came this week. We worked on it over the winter."

He read the title of the article: "A New Island Population of *Oceanodroma leucorhoa leucorhoa,* by Clifford Goodsell, Ph.D., and Emily Cobb Watson." He looked at the cover. It was a square-backed thick magazine called *The Auk.* "What's this?" he said.

"It's *the* ornithological publication. We'll write other articles. We're just getting started."

"We've surveyed less than half the island," said Cliff. "I'm not sure you understand the significance of what's here. This is a large population of a species unknown to breed this far south."

He looked at the article again, saw the name Sheep Island, saw Lincoln Harbor. "What's *Oceano*-something?"

"Our bird. Our petrel. Leach's petrel," sang out Emily. "We're *published.* We're in *print.* Have you any idea what this means? We'll finish the first fast survey this summer, write another paper next winter, do a more careful job the following year."

Cliff said: "This is ornithologically significant. With your permission, I'd like to come back here summers for ten, maybe twenty years. Maybe longer. There are probably more than two hundred burrows here."

"Our site. We developed it." Emily's voice was full of an old Cobb power. "We'll get other scientists to come here. When they read this they'll be clamoring to come. We can put up tents right over there."

He said nothing about the half million that had been offered him.

One evening the phone rang.

"For you," said Marge.

"Fred?"

He gripped the phone. "Yes."

"How are you, Fred?"

He could scarcely speak. "Okay."

"I want to talk to you. I think we should talk."

"Okay."

"Not on the telephone. I mean . . . together. Could you come to New York? Or maybe I could come up there. I have Saturday and Sunday free."

With a strong sense that here would be better than there, he said: "We're pretty busy here. Could you come up?"

"I could come up."

"Wait." He got the bus schedule, told her what bus to take. "Get off at Newfield. I'll meet you there."

"How will I know Newfield? The last time I came was on a yacht."

"The driver will tell you. Sit up in the front and tell him you want to get off at Newfield. It's simple."

"I never rode on one of those. Where do I start from? Maybe I should fly. Is there an airport at Newfield?"

"Nearby, yes. But there's no direct service."

"I would ask a man. He buys all his bread from me. He borrows planes and flies them weekends."

"That would be hideously expensive."

"No, Fred. He would enjoy doing it. We're friends."

When he had hung up: "That her?" said Lou.

He nodded.

"We'll tidy up a little," said Marge.

He was early at the airport and waited for more than half an hour before the small plane drifted in. He walked over and watched the pilot step out on the wing, then instruct Fran where to step, then reach in and retrieve a small blue suitcase. What a relief to see that suitcase. He shook her politely by the hand, constrained by the presence of the other man. She introduced them, thanked the pilot for the ride, and together they watched the plane take off. He picked up her suitcase. "You'll stay?"

"Tonight. Ren will come back tomorrow."

"Pretty generous of him."

"Renfrew Byles. A nice person. He has to put in flying hours. He's glad for the company."

"What do you talk about?"

"Oh, we don't talk much. It's too noisy. But it's such a good way to get here. You just sit, and there you are."

"What does Renfrew do?" He was itching with jealousy and uncertainty.

"He's a jewelry designer. He has designed some beautiful things for Mindy. That's how I met him. And his wife, Lilla. She gets many things at my shop. Lilla is a very nice person."

By this time they were in the truck and were headed home.

"You said you wanted to talk."

"Yes, Fred. But not here. In a quiet place."

"There's my house."

"I was thinking of your island."

A jagged shaft of desire cracked him. "There's a problem with the island," he said. "I have two friends living there, and they have my boat."

"Oh." A hint of disappointment?

"Maybe I could get Lou to take us out. He's the man I live with. Lou and Marge. You should meet them."

"I would like to meet your friends."

So they rode, she apparently composed, he in a whirl of hope and dread, underlain by a nagging picture of Lou at his worst, in an undershirt and using foul language.

"If you're spending the night, you'll be sleeping there."

"That would be nice, Fred."

When they got to Gott Street, both were in the backyard, and Lou was in an undershirt.

"This is Fran Collins."

"Colinari," she corrected him.

"Pleased to meet you," said Lou.

"Likewise," said Marge. Both were watching her intently.

"Just in time for lunch," said Lou. "Marge here was picking a couple of dandelion leaves to give the salad some bang. You like fish stew Portuguese style?"

"I love it Sicilian style," said Fran.

"What's the difference?"

"I don't know, but I'd like to try it your way."

They trooped into the kitchen. It was immaculate. The stew was ready. Marge ladled out large helpings into soup bowls.

"This is like Sicilian style," said Fran after a couple of mouthfuls. "Only it's richer, more—you know—oniony. Except it's not onions."

"That would be the leeks. Do you use leeks?"

"No, but I put in a red pepper, cut small."

"Hey, you sound like a cook," said Lou. "If you're Sicilian, you make linguini?"

"Yes. Do you like it with white clam sauce?"

"Only way to go. Red kills the taste of the clams some. How about we have it for supper, hey, Marge?"

"I don't think we should ask a guest to do the cooking."

"I'd like to do it. I love cooking."

"That's her business," he said. "She's a professional cook."

That was all he did say during that meal. Fran obviously felt at home with these people. They seemed enchanted with her. A plus sign?

Lou agreed to take them out to the island in the *Stinger* and did so, running up to full throttle as he rounded the last harbor buoy in a sweeping, tipping curve, showing off as he slammed his boat into the waves, roaring in on the beach and throttling down at the last moment.

"Want to take off your shoes?"

A guarded look. "Can you carry me in?" Another plus? It was shattering to be doing this, hoarding every straw.

"I'll be going," said Lou. "You can get your pals to take you back. Be sure to come in time to make supper."

Emily and Cliff appeared, alerted by the arrival of the *Stinger*. He introduced them. "Don't want to interrupt your work. Just showing the island to a friend."

"Got eight more burrows," said Cliff. "Gets better as we work toward the other end."

"Will one of you take us back in an hour or so?"

"Just yell," said Emily. "I have to go to the supermarket anyway." She and Cliff disappeared down one of the trails they had cut in the bushes. Alone at last—a veritable soap opera line. He sat her down on the driftwood bench, where it had all started the last time. He took her hand.

"I'm here to talk, Fred, not to make love."

"So we'll talk."

"With those other people here . . . "

"I agree; we should talk."

"I mean, I wanted to be somewhere quiet so that I could explain things. It's very complicated."

He waited.

"What I said about Ebby and Ginger is right. They want to push me out."

"Can they do that? Why don't you just keep paying? The way you've been doing."

"I would, except I'm not getting enough money. Business is off. Suddenly Ginger can't find girls. I had to cancel some parties. Also the one I could count on, the big Western Gold party they give every quarter for the sales reps. Ebby isn't giving me that. I'm dropping back on the payments. I'm a month behind."

"We can take care of that."

"I talked to a lawyer. Mindy has a lawyer now, for her divorce. He asked to see the contract. I told him there was no contract. We had a verbal agreement. I trusted Ebby. He said that in that case Ebby owned the business and could put me out tomorrow."

An overpowering rush: let them push her out. "We'll pay them off."

"I talked to Ginger. Ginger said a very mean thing. She said: 'Ebby wants you out of the business, so why don't you go?'"

"So?"

"After all I did for her? To say that? I don't want to be in business with Ginger anymore. I *would* go, except I have thirty thousand dollars invested there. The lawyer says I won't get any of it if I leave. I'd have to buy the whole business and sell it back to them."

"We'll do that."

"I can't. I couldn't run that business by myself."

"So leave it." It was amazing how his sudden wealth could make him a spendthrift of hers.

A visible effort to pull herself together. "I can't do that, don't you see? If I lose everything I'd be back where I was before."

"So you start over again. Start here, with me."

A searching look from her. "You mean that?"

"Of course I mean it. Didn't you listen to me? Didn't you read my letter?"

"But you were asking somebody different, a successful person."

"I was asking *you*."

"I'd be back where I was when you didn't want me."

A vast rush of relief. If that was all . . . "I want you." Only then did she permit him to embrace her.

They went looking for Emily and Cliff. He felt light-headed, drunk with joy. Never had the island smelled so fragrant, looked so beautiful.

"Do you think we should ask them for supper?" whispered Fran.

"Why not? Make it a party. We could make an announcement."

"Oh, Fred." She clung to him. "This is such a place. Only magic happens here."

Four returned in the dory, a heavy load that left little freeboard. Cliff motored carefully at half speed, facing into a dazzling late-afternoon sun, big and fat, slowly turning orange as it fell into the thicker air near the horizon. The wind was dying; the sea was flat. Nobody spoke. There was just the purr of the motor and a comforting low chuckle of water as the dory pushed along. A journey into a dream, he thought, by far the best he had ever made.

In the kitchen, six people crowded, riding a high wave of hilarity. Lou was shucking clams, eating one for every three he set aside for the pot.

Fran took over, asking Marge for this and that. Soon steaming plates of linguini were on the table.

"You call yourself a cook?" said Lou. "I call you a chef. I think Portuguese and Sicilians are pretty much alike." He raised his glass to Fran with a big grin. "Ain't you the one off of the yacht?"

She lowered her glance. "Yes."

"What's it like on one of them things?"

"It's very comfortable, but I like it better here." Then she said something that wrenched his heart entirely. "I only wish my papa was here. He would like this."

"Well, get him," shouted Lou. "Can he drive a truck?"

That was Fred's opening. "Maybe he will come. Fran may stay, because she's getting married."

"To you, Fred?" It came in a roar that nearly shook the house. "The bearded boy wonder?" He had just time to catch a glimpse of Marge's delighted face before Lou was on him with a crunching one-handed bear hug. With the other hand he held out his glass to Fran. "You picked a good one. But how did you land him? He's as shy as a lobster that just shed his shell. You must have found him under a rock someplace."

"I didn't have to land him," said Fran. "He landed me."

"Well, whichever," with a joyous bellow. "Look at us. Three couples. Happy couples. And none married. Shows the way the world's going."

"I expect to get married," said Fran.

"Me too," from Emily. "Sometime in the not too distant future."

All eyes turned to Marge, who flushed scarlet. "Me too," she finally whispered. "Sometime."

During cleanup, the phone rang. It was Charlie. "I think we've hit the top. One guy's dropped out. The other went to five-forty. I think you should take it."

"Okay."

"I'll call the people in New York tomorrow. Tell them to send along a check."

"Who was that?" asked Lou.

"Charlie Barker. I've sold the island." He had to say it sometime.

"What!" screamed Emily.

"Good," said Lou.

Emily stood over him. "You bastard. You utter bastard! I knew it all along—"

Lou got in front of her. "Let's not have that kind of talk in here."

Emily ignored him. "You're just a puking little bastard. Think of the work we've done. You think that's nothing? You think we can just go away?"

Lou took her by the shoulder. "I said not to talk like that here. If you want to talk like that, go outside."

"Come on," said Cliff to Emily. Then to him: "We've got to talk. Call your man back and tell him to wait."

"Wait?"

"Just don't make that phone call tomorrow until you and I have had a chance to talk. There are other ways of looking at this."

"He won't listen!" screamed Emily. "The rotten little bastard!"

Cliff maneuvered her out the door. He followed. Cliff said to Emily in a quiet voice: "Go back to the boat." Amazingly, she went.

"Now," said Cliff. "I want to make sure you understand what you're doing. Emily gets excited. She thinks of it as something that directly affects her. I want to talk about the birds. This is a much more important thing than you think. These birds have been coming to nest on this island for five or ten thousand years. Once, they did it all along the coast, wherever there was a suitable habitat for them— where predators couldn't get at them."

"Do they nest anywhere else?" he asked.

"Oh, yes. Up north, in places where they're not disturbed, they're common."

"So there's no danger of them going extinct?"

"That's not the point. The point is that here, along the New England coast, they're gone. In one place after another, the biggest predator of all, man, has exterminated them. Not deliberately but just by being there with his cats, his rats, and his dogs. I said to you before that this find is extraordinary. It's unique. It would be an act you could never forgive yourself for if you sold your island to that developer. I talked to the men who were digging the well. They say the plan is to put in a resort complex there. That will exterminate the birds immediately. Can you let that happen?"

"I'm not sure I have a choice. The money's too important to me right now."

"If it's just a question of money—"

"Not just for me but for my girl, for Fran. They've got her over a barrel in New York."

"How much money are we talking about here?"

"Five hundred thousand. More."

"Maybe a conservation organization like the Nature Conservancy could be persuaded to buy it. They probably wouldn't be able to meet the full sum. But you could write off the difference on your tax return. In the end it would be almost as good as getting the entire sum. You'd have to pay a big tax on that."

Now he remembered the terms of the deal Charlie had cut. "I'm afraid I can't do that. If I sell, I have to sell to Greenwillow. I had to agree to that to get a well dug."

"Then you should give the island away."

"Give it?"

"Zero tax then. You could write off big earnings for several years."

"But I don't have big earnings. I have hardly any earnings at all."

"Then we should create some earnings for you. How would you like to be the permanent warden of Sheep Island for . . . well, maybe twenty thousand a year?"

"That's possible?"

"Let me work on it. I helped do something like that with the Eugene Moxby Marsh and Pond Refuge. Saved some bitterns, some rails and other things. That wasn't half as important as this thing. If that worked, this one should. Just make that phone call. I'll wait out here."

He went back inside, and under the eyes of the three sitting there, he phoned Charlie. "Hold up on calling Greenwillow. I have to give it some more thought."

"Ain't selling?" said Lou.

"Not just yet."

"Sell your island?" said Fran. "You'd even think of it?"

"Not just yet."

"You shouldn't sell it at all. That beautiful place."

How could he explain in front of the others? He went out and told Cliff.

"Okay. Now come on out and treat yourself to one more night of netting. We're coming to the end of the season. The chicks are about grown and ready to fly."

"My girl. I can't leave her. She just got here."

"Bring her along."

He went back inside.

"Go," said Marge. "It's something you'll never forget. Take these sneakers."

Again the dory was loaded deep. Emily sat alone in the bow and refused to speak to him. He and Fran sat on the center thwart, holding hands. Small wisps of fog floated wetly across their faces as they slid down the harbor. When they rounded the lighthouse point, the bright beam of the light caught the fog patches like wash hanging on a line as it revolved slowly above their heads. The sea was rippled black glass pricked with stars, the air heavy with salt; he could taste it on his lips. "I like this," whispered Fran.

When they reached the island, Emily sprang out and held a hand for Fran. "You come," she said. "I don't want him. He couldn't care less about what we're doing."

Fran looked at him.

"Go ahead," he said.

He waited until the others had gone up the path, gave them another five minutes to set up the mist net, then followed. Up the winding way through the fragrant bushes. It was very dark; he went from memory more than sight. Beyond his house he could see the beams of flashlights twitching here and there. He followed them, heard the chitterings of the tape recorder, came closer, watched all the lights go off, leaving everything but the deep sky pot black. Birds were moving. He could hear them talking in the air. Abruptly the flashlights went on again; something had hit the net. He went closer, stepped into the circle of light.

"Get out of here," snarled Emily, waving her notebook at him.

"Pay attention," said Cliff. "I have another bird."

He watched from the edge of the circle as Fran was introduced to the delicate task of extracting a petrel from the net. She did it deftly.

He stood at a respectful distance, on the verge of trespassing into the flashlit zone of activity. Emily continued to ignore him. Fran said: "This is—this is just—they're all around us, under our feet. I put my ear to the ground and heard them cooing."

Cliff said: "We're getting mostly repeats now. We're going to have to move to the other side of the pond and set up there. We'll do that next summer."

"If there's anything here to do next summer," said Emily.

When they were finished and rolling up the net, Fran hugged him. "I held one in my hand. A little bird."

That night Fran slept in Gott Street and he went to his house, sliding into the bed that Hugo had bought for Doris. Whatever her failings, she was a conscientious cleaner. There was no sign that she had ever occupied the room. He was back in Gott Street for his regular early breakfast. Lou said: "The girls are still sleeping. You know Marge, how she is. Your girl seems the same."

"She often works late nights too."

"What's her line exactly?"

"She's a caterer. She prepares parties for rich people."

"Well, she's a lulu. Lucky you landed her." Then, leaning across the table: "You heard what Marge said last night?"

"I did."

"I asked her later did she mean it, and she said yes. That if I can hang on to you and make a real business out of this, she'd marry me. I asked her what kind of a business she thought we had now. She said barely floating. I told her we were making more money than ever before. She said it was because of you and that if I didn't want to lose you I'd better raise your share to thirty percent."

"Well, that's—"

Lou stuck out his huge hand.

"I'm not sure you need to—"

"Now don't go all soft, Freddie. This is a tough world. And don't forget I'm still the senior partner."

50

HE GAVE IT AWAY. AFTER VISITS BY TWO MEN FROM the Nature Conservancy and long speeches about petrels by Cliff, punctuated by shrill exhortations from Emily, the men went away. A few days later came the news that the conservancy would accept the gift and install him as permanent warden at a salary of twenty-one thousand dollars a year.

"That's for life. I asked for twenty-five, but they just don't have it. Anyway, it's a super deal," said Cliff. "Three ways super."

"How three ways?"

"You got a well dug for nothing. You got a lifetime pension. Most important, you established a sanctuary for the birds."

"And shafted two people."

"One I can see, your friend from Greenwillow." He had told Cliff of a phone conversation with Walker Virdonette in which he had asked for release from their contract. He had pleaded the case for the birds and been turned down. He had offered to reimburse Walker for the cost of the well. "No way," Walker said. "A deal's a deal." After that conversation he felt free of Walker.

"So who's the other?" asked Cliff.

"Charlie Barker. He's out about forty thousand as his commission. I feel terrible about that."

He took Fran to see the house they would live in. Empty of furniture, it looked tiny.

"This is not a good kitchen. I would need a better kitchen."

"I was planning to make this into a pantry and build a new kitchen in back. To your specifications. You can develop a catering business there."

"This is a pretty floor. Did you fix that?"

"Yes."

"We could put a sofa in front of this fireplace. And do we really need a dining room? Let's make this into a library. We'll make the old kitchen into a little dining room."

Dizzying prospects. Inspired homemaking thoughts. He would do anything she wanted. "We would have to go at this bit by bit, you know. We'll have very little money."

"Yes, darling."

For the last time, to make rock-bottom sure: "You're throwing away a great deal coming here."

"You threw away more. For the birds. I'm glad you did. We could put another sofa in here. A foldaway bed. Mindy could visit. I would love Mindy to see this."

"I doubt if Mindy would want to come here. She doesn't like me."

"Mindy will come if I ask. If I love you, Mindy will like you."

Upstairs. "Why, there's a bed and a bureau here—and a chair."

He sat on the former and pulled her toward him. With a tidal wave of gratitude cascading through him, and now unable to speak at all, he buried his face in her breast.

She held him close, her fingers in his hair. "Darling, you know how we get . . . "

He nodded.

"Somebody will come."

He shook his head.

"But they might. We wouldn't want to be . . . "

With a monstrous effort, he pulled his face away and looked up at her. "I locked the door," he croaked.

Some time later, she said: "I think white curtains would look nice in here. You know, frilly white country curtains."

"Yes." Riding on a trackless sea of peace.

"And a hooked rug right here by the bed."

"Yes."

"If you can do the floors up here the way you did downstairs, one hooked rug would be nice. Not too big a one. An oval one."

"Yes, baby."

"You never called me baby before."

"You never looked so young and innocent and pink before."

"All right. I'll call you baby."

"Baby."

"Baby."

Utterly ridiculous. He caught a glimpse of what it might have been like to be a happy four-year-old. "What are you going to say to Father Ramirez now?"

"When I am married I will go to Father Ramirez and confess everything. I will tell Father Ramirez that I will never have a reason to sin again."

"Ever?"

"I don't mean little sins. There's no problem in confessing little sins like lies. I mean a big sin like this one."

"You call this a sin?"

"I did once, darling, when you didn't love me. Now that you do . . . When two people love, it's not a sin. It's just a beautiful way of saying I love you."

"Okay, tell me that you love me."

"Oh, Fred . . . "

"But before you do, I have a question for you. Why did you correct me when I was introducing you to Marge and Lou and say your name was Colinari?"

"I wanted to be myself. Like you. You turned yourself into yourself. I wanted to do the same. That was the moment I truly gave myself to you."

"Not now?"

"No, baby. This is just expressing that gift."

80 12/01

4/54

PLAZA